THE IMPORTANCE OF BEING SEVEN

Praise for the internationally bestselling
44 Scotland Street novels

"[McCall Smith] is a pro, and he delivers sharp observation, gentle satire . . . as well as the expected romantic complications. . . . [Readers will] relish McCall Smith's depiction of this place . . . and enjoy his tolerant, good-humored company." —*The New York Times Book Review*

"Alexander McCall Smith . . . proves himself a wry but gentle chronicler of humanity and its foibles."
—*The Miami Herald*

"McCall Smith's plots offer wit, charm and intrigue in equal doses." —*Richmond Times-Dispatch*

"Just about perfect. . . . Contains a healthy helping of McCall Smith's patented charm." —*St. Louis Post-Dispatch*

"McCall Smith shows an Austen-like sensitivity to the interactions of daily life. . . . [His] prose is smooth, easy and fluid." —*The Gazette*

"Entertaining and witty. . . . A sly send-up of society in Edinburgh." —*Orlando Sentinel*

"McCall Smith, a fine writer, paints his hometown of Edinburgh as indelibly as he captures the sunniness of Africa. We can almost feel the mists as we tread the cobblestones."
—*The Dallas Morning News*

Alexander McCall Smith

## THE IMPORTANCE OF BEING SEVEN

Alexander McCall Smith is the author of the international phenomenon The No. 1 Ladies' Detective Agency series, the Isabel Dalhousie series, the Portuguese Irregular Verbs series, the 44 Scotland Street series, and the Corduroy Mansions series. He is professor emeritus of medical law at the University of Edinburgh in Scotland and has served on many national and international organizations concerned with bioethics.

www.alexandermccallsmith.com

# ALEXANDER
## McCALL SMITH

# THE IMPORTANCE OF BEING SEVEN

*A 44 Scotland Street Novel*

*Illustrations by* IAIN McINTOSH

VINTAGE CANADA

VINTAGE CANADA EDITION, 2012

Copyright © 2012 Alexander McCall Smith
Illustrations copyright © 2012 Iain McIntosh

Published in Canada by Vintage Canada, a division of Random House of Canada
Limited, Toronto, in 2012, and simultaneously in the United States of America
by Anchor Books, a division of Random House, Inc., New York. Distributed by
Random House of Canada Limited.

Vintage Canada with colophon is a registered trademark.

www.randomhouse.ca

This is a work of fiction. Names, characters, places, and incidents
either are the product of the author's imagination or are used fictitiously. Any
resemblance to actual persons, living or dead, events, or
locales is entirely coincidental.

This book is excerpted from a series that originally
appeared in *The Scotsman* newspaper.

Library and Archives Canada Cataloguing in Publication

McCall Smith, Alexander, 1948–
The importance of being seven : the new 44 Scotland Street novel /
Alexander McCall Smith.

(44 Scotland Street ; 6)
Issued also in electronic format.

ISBN 978-0-307-39962-5

I. Title. II. Series: McCall Smith, Alexander, 1948– . 44 Scotland Street ; 6.

PR6063.C326I47 2012          823'.914          C2012-900493-6

Author illustration © Iain McIntosh
Cover illustration by Iain McIntosh

Printed and bound in the United States of America

2  4  6  8  9  7  5  3  1

This book is for
James Naughtie

# Preface

I started writing the *44 Scotland Street* series without any idea that it would turn into something of a saga. Now here we are six volumes later, returning to the world of that motley collection of people who live in the Edinburgh New Town and whose lives I have recorded in daily episodes in the *Scotsman* newspaper. I am very pleased to be back amongst these characters, and do not intend this to be my last visit to them. Domenica Macdonald, Angus Lordie, and all the others have somehow become part of my world, just as I believe they have become part of the world of quite a number of readers in many countries. That, incidentally, gives me the greatest possible pleasure – the knowledge that we are all linked by our friendship with a group of fictional people. What a pleasant club of which to be a member!

I am often asked at events whether I have a favourite fictional character. I find that a difficult question to answer, but it is certainly the case that Bertie, the six-year-old boy in these novels, is somebody for whom I have particular affection. It will not have escaped the attention of readers that Bertie started as a five-year-old five volumes ago and has not really progressed very far. In fact, Bertie is still awaiting his seventh birthday, although it does not actually happen in this book. Why has time stood still for Bertie? The main reason for this, I think, is that Bertie at six is absolutely perfect, and I have no wish for him to grow up. He is at that wonderful stage where he understands the world, but not quite; when his mother is still in complete control of his life; when he has yet to learn how to lie and dissemble, or indeed to be cruel, in the way in which adults seem to find so easy. His world is an attractive one – a sort of Eden – from which we know we are excluded by the loss of our own innocence.

I have lost count of the number of times I have met people on my book tours who say to me that Bertie is a special character for them. This happens throughout the world. Earlier this year I was in India, at the Jaipur Literary Festival, and I met numerous Bertie fans there. The same was true in Australia, Singapore, Dubai and Hong Kong – places that I went to after my Indian trip. The question I was asked most frequently in each of these places was the same: when will things get better for Bertie? And in each of these places there was a great groundswell of support for this poor little boy, egging him on, wishing him freedom from the regime of improvement planned for him by his mother, Irene, and siding with him against the dreadful Olive and the appalling Tofu. I wish I could have said that things were soon to change, but, alas, that would have been untruthful. Bertie's situation is as difficult as ever; his is a hearth from which freedom seems for ever excluded. And that, alas, is true for so many of us. How many of us are really free of our past, of the things we have to do that we do not want to do, of the furniture of our life that is never really in quite the right place? Perhaps that is why Bertie is so popular. He reminds us of a yearning that many of us instinctively recognise within ourselves: the yearning to be seven – *really* seven.

I have dedicated this book to one of our greatest broadcasters, James Naughtie. James is a central pillar of the national conversation that we have with each other in Britain. I can imagine him engaging with any of the characters in this book – interviewing Angus Lordie, perhaps, on some artistic project, talking to Domenica Macdonald about her latest anthropological essay, or simply chatting to Big Lou about Arbroath and her years in Aberdeen. But he could also talk to Bertie, I think, and Bertie would be comforted by the conversation. James would make Bertie *feel* seven, even if he is still six, and that, I think, is a great art. Thank you, James, for everything you have done for me, for the cause of rational debate, and for the millions of people to whom you have brought enlightenment, amusement, and comfort.

Alexander McCall Smith
Edinburgh, 2010

# THE IMPORTANCE OF BEING SEVEN

## 1. *Nothing but Tenderness*

If there was one thing about marriage that surprised Matthew, it was just how quickly he became accustomed to it. There is always the danger that a single person becomes so used to the bachelor or spinster routine that a sudden change in circumstances proves difficult to accommodate. Or so the folk wisdom goes. There is a similar piece of folk wisdom that claims that parents, on launching the last of their children, feel the loss acutely, rapidly declining into the empty-nest syndrome. Both these beliefs are largely false. Married couples – or those choosing to live together as bidies-in (and there is no more appropriate term to express that notion than this couthy Scots expression) – both adjust remarkably quickly to the sharing of bed and board. Indeed, after a few days, in many cases, a previous life is more or less entirely forgotten, and each person believes that he and she, or he and he, or she and she, have lived together for a very long time. In this way Daphnis and Chloë, or Romeo and Juliet, can only too quickly become Darby and Joan, Mr. and Mrs. Bennet, or any other famous domestic couple.

As for the received view about the so-called empty-nest syndrome, like many syndromes, it barely exists. In most cases, parents do feel a slight pang on the leaving of home by their children, but this pang tends to occur before the offspring go, and it is largely a dread of the syndrome itself rather than concern over the actual departure. In this way it is similar to many of the moral panics that afflict an imaginative society from time to time: the fear of what might happen in the future is almost always worse than the future that eventually arrives. So when the child finally goes off to university, or takes a gap year, or moves out to live with coevals, the parents might find themselves feeling strange for a day or two, but often find themselves exhilarated by their new freedom. Very soon it feels entirely normal to have the house to yourself, such is the rapidity with which most people can adjust to new circumstances. And of course if the child has been reluctant to leave home and has remained there until his late twenties, or even beyond, how much more grateful is the parent for this change. Empty-nest syndrome, then, might be redefined altogether, to refer to the feeling of anticipation and longing which affects those whose nest is not emptying quickly enough.

For Matthew and his wife, Elspeth Harmony, the adjustment to married life was both rapid and thoroughly pleasant. Neither had the slightest doubt that the right choice had been made – not only in respect of deciding to get married at all, but also in their choice of partner. Matthew loved Elspeth Harmony – he loved her to the extent that everything that was associated with her, her possessions, her sayings, her friends and connections, were all endowed with a quality of specialness that attached to nothing else. The mug from which she drank her morning coffee was special because her lips had touched it; the tortoiseshell comb that she kept on top of the dressing table was special because it had belonged to Elspeth's grandmother rather than to any other grandmother; the shopping list that she wrote out to take with her to Valvona & Crolla was special because it was in her handwriting. His affection for her was total, and touching.

For her part, Elspeth could not believe the sheer good fortune that had brought them together. She had always wanted to get married, from her university days onwards, but as the years passed – and she was only twenty-eight at the time of Matthew's proposal – she had become increasingly concerned that nobody would ask her. There had been one or two boyfriends, but they had not been serious, and her intuitive understanding of this had meant that the relationships had been brief. She saw no point, really, in persisting with a man who would not be with her in a year or two's time. Why invest emotional energy in something that was not expected to last? In her view that led to disappointment and loss, and this could be avoided by simply not taking up with the man in the first place.

Then Matthew came into her life, and everything changed. It was at such a difficult time, too, very close to that traumatic incident when she had succumbed to her irritation over Olive's mistreatment of Bertie – Olive had used her junior nurse's kit to diagnose Bertie as suffering from leprosy – and had pinched Olive's ear quite hard, something she had wanted to do for some time but which she had refrained from doing because to do so would be contrary to every principle of education and child care she had been taught. The fact that Olive richly deserved this pinch, and indeed might benefit from such a sharp reminder of moral cause and effect, was not a mitigating factor, and she had been obliged to resign from her position at the school. Matthew had been there to save her from the consequences of all this. While other boyfriends might have expressed regret over what she had done, and questioned its wisdom, Matthew sided with her completely and unequivocally, making it clear that he believed that the act of pinching Olive's ear was a blow for pedagogic sanity.

"There are many children who would be improved by such a pinch," he observed.

Elspeth thought about this. In normal circumstances she would follow the party line and say that one should never raise a hand to a child or indeed pinch any of its extremities, but mulling over Matthew's pronouncement she came to the conclusion that she could think of quite a number of children who would benefit from a short, sharp pinch. Tofu, in particular, might be improved by a small amount of judiciously administered physical violence, even if only to stop him spitting at the other children. Perhaps if teachers spat at him he would get the message, but modern educational theory definitely frowned on teachers who spat at their pupils. That was the world in which we lived.

And now all that was behind her. Matthew had rescued her from professional ignominy and given her a new purpose in life. He had showered her with love, and she felt nothing but tenderness for this kind and gentle man, who had given her his name, his home, his fortune, and himself.

## 2. *A Very Considerate Husband*

For Matthew's part, the nicest thing about marriage was the opportunity that it presented to do something for another person. By nature he was a generous man, but had been inhibited in the practice of this generosity because of emotional insecurity. When he had been with Pat, in that curious on-off relationship, he had wanted to do things for her but had felt unable to do very much because of fears that she would reject what he did. With Elspeth it was completely different. He felt quite confident in giving her presents, because she received them with such evident pleasure. And anything he did – from dealing with the washing-up in the kitchen to buying her an Art Nouveau gold bracelet at a Lyon & Turnbull auction – had been received by Elspeth with both grace and gratitude.

Inspired by this, Matthew took every opportunity he could to do things for her.

"Please let me" was one of the most common phrases to be heard in their household. And "No, you've done enough, it really is my turn" had become one of the most common responses.

The whole process started at the beginning of each day when Matthew got out of bed and went through to the kitchen to put on the kettle for a morning cup of tea. Elspeth loved drinking tea in bed, as many people do, and he would take her a piping hot cup of Earl Grey/Assam mixture before turning on the bedside lamp and opening the shutters.

From the comfort of the matrimonial bed, Elspeth would look up at her husband in his tartan dressing gown and smile. She knew that he would now go into the bathroom, shower, dress, and then make breakfast for the two of them. By the time that she emerged, the breakfast table in the kitchen would be laid, the muesli jar would be in position, and a pan of water would be boiling on the Aga, ready for a free-range egg. The Aga, a rich red, had been a wedding present from Matthew's father, along with a matching Aga fridge and freezer.

"Couples with an Aga stay together," her new father-in-law had observed, jokingly, she thought. But he was serious.

"How do people know that?" she asked.

"They just do. It's the attitude that does it. A person who buys an Aga is going to be . . . how should one put it, solid. They want a solid and reliable cooker because they are solid and reliable themselves." He paused. "Do you get flashy types buying Agas? How many flashy types do you know who have an Aga?"

She thought for a moment. Did she know any flashy types? Did she know anybody who had an Aga? Her own parents might have liked one but could not have afforded it, she thought. Agas were expensive, and even an Aga fridge cost about £5,000 or, if one chose the option with the built-in freezer compartment, £7,000. So none of her colleagues had an Aga, and indeed neither did any of her friends, or even acquaintances.

"Do you know anybody who has an Aga?" she had asked Matthew after that conversation with his father.

"Hundreds," said Matthew. "Why?"

Elspeth frowned. "Do you really know hundreds of people who have one?"

Matthew nodded. "Yes. I thought they were pretty common. They're very nice things, you know. They make for a lovely warm place. You can put your wet washing on the rail, socks, underpants, the works. They get dry in no time."

Elspeth looked thoughtful. Matthew's comment – made so innocently – spoke to the very different circumstances in which they had been brought up. Elspeth's father, Jim Harmony, had been a good provider, but had never been able to provide an Aga. She had been brought up in circles where people had modest means; where the overseas holiday was a treat rather than an expectation; where money was tight, as it is for the overwhelming majority of people. Now she found herself married to a man who had a considerable amount of money, and was used to moving in circles where that was the norm. Not that Matthew was any sort of snob – quite the opposite, in fact, as he seemed completely indifferent to wealth or position in others. That was an endearing quality, and she could not have been happy with a man who thought the value of others was determined by their means. But Matthew's world was certainly different.

So it was upon an Aga that Elspeth's breakfast egg was cooked. And once again, Matthew took great pains to make sure that he did everything he could to please her. When she had told him that she was quite happy to have her boiled egg "as it comes," he had insisted on having a trial boiling of four eggs for different periods and then asking her to state a preference. She had chosen an egg in which the white was solid, rather than hard, and in which the yolk had at least some motility. Thereafter every egg he boiled her was done for that exact length of time; and every bath, which he ran for her while she ate her perfectly timed egg, was brought to just the right temperature. That temperature had been ascertained by the running of a trial bath in which she had lain while Matthew had gradually brought the temperature up, stirring the water with a large wooden spoon from the kitchen to ensure even distribution of the heat.

After her bath, he would bring her a large towel that he would have specially heated on the towel rail.

"It really is very kind of you," Elspeth said. "But I think I can manage. Why don't you go for a run in Queen Street Gardens?"

The suggestion had been intended to be a helpful one – Matthew liked going for a run in the mornings – but he had taken this badly.

"But I want to be here to help you," he said. "Don't you like what I do for you?"

She had reached out to embrace him, dropping the towel. Matthew shivered with delight. "Of course I do, my darling," she whispered. "Of course I do. You do whatever you like."

She realised how fortunate she was. Many women had husbands who were not in the least attentive – husbands who never ran their wives' baths, nor made their breakfast, nor sent roses to the flat during the day, as Matthew often did. She was so lucky, but of course one needed a bit of space in a marriage, and she knew that sooner or later she would have to talk to Matthew about that. The problem, though, was that people often misunderstood a mention of space, and interpreted it as a suggestion to go away.

## 3. *At Big Lou's*

Elspeth need not have worried; of course Matthew understood all about space within a marriage and it was for this reason that he had not suggested that Elspeth help in the gallery. It would be better, he thought, for each of them to have a separate career: "I've seen too many couples come unstuck because they were working together," he said to Angus Lordie. He made this remark without really thinking, and even as he said it he realised that he could not think of a single marriage in which that had happened. On the contrary – all the marriages of that sort that he had seen were rather successful.

"Or perhaps not," he added lamely.

Angus had nodded wisely at Matthew's original observation, and had not really heard the retraction. He knew very little about this as he had never been sufficiently stuck to become unstuck. It was a mystery to him how anybody lived with anybody else let alone worked with them too, and he could imagine nothing worse than having another person in his studio, painting her own paintings while he worked on his. He found that painting required complete silence – an artistic stillness – and the muse, fickle as she was at the best of times, would surely retreat in a huff if she had to contend with two painters in the same studio.

"So I'm not going to ask Elspeth to help me in the gallery," Matthew went on. "I couldn't bear it if we disagreed."

"That girl you had," said Angus. "Pat Macgregor. Did you disagree with her at all?"

Matthew looked over Angus Lordie's shoulder. They were sitting in Big Lou's coffee house during this conversation and he was watching Big Lou wiping the stainless-steel counter with her cloth, or cloot, as she called it. Had he seen eye to eye with Pat on matters artistic? He thought that he had, but then that was before he knew very much about anything, and he had probably not been in a position to challenge her views. It would be different now; Matthew had opinions, and some knowledge of art to back them up. He watched Big Lou at work. She was a handsome woman, in a big-boned, rather rural sort of way (Big Lou, of course, came from Arbroath, a part of Scotland noted for its handsome people). Now, as she polished away at the counter, a seemingly Sisyphean task, he saw her as she might appear in a painting by Bonnard, or possibly Vuillard.

Those artists were exponents of intimism, in which small domestic scenes were captured and placed at the heart of a painting: interiors showing a woman sewing, or arranging flowers; a girl picking up a soup spoon at a table; a woman lying in the bath. Bonnard would have loved Big Lou, and had he been there would have depicted her in the act of polishing, her head down, intent on her task. And he would have caught the sun that filtered in through the window – the cold, Edinburgh sun, so unlike the light that he found in the south of France – and the colour of her dress, and the faded apron that she had tied carelessly about her waist. Bonnard would have captured all that and in so doing would have portrayed Big Lou in all her essential Arbroathheit.

"No," Matthew said to Angus Lordie. "Pat and I did not disagree. Not then. It might be different now."

"You'll find somebody else to help you," said Angus. "There must be plenty of people looking for a job like that. You'd probably not even have to pay them."

Matthew looked doubtful. "I couldn't take advantage of somebody," he said. "I know people do it, but . . ."

"You're right," said Angus. "They do it all the time. They call it the internship system. Interns are usually unpaid labour."

"A grand name for an old system," said Matthew. "It used to be called slavery."

Angus laughed. "Slaves were never volunteers. Interns are."

"I still disagree with it," said Matthew. "I would always pay."

Angus thought for a moment. "How about Domenica? How about asking her whether she'd like to help?"

Matthew did not warm to this suggestion. "I know you like

Domenica," he said, "but do you really think she'd be easy to work with?"

"No, I suppose not," mused Angus.

Matthew looked at him quizzically. "Could you work with her?"

"The occasion has never arisen," said Angus. "But I imagine that I could. On the other hand, I think that she would have to be the boss. I don't think she would play second fiddle."

"No," said Matthew. He looked at Angus with interest, and continued, "Angus, don't you think that you and Domenica are . . . are an event waiting to happen?"

Angus looked at him in astonishment. "You mean . . ."

"Yes," said Matthew. "Listen, I can tell you about marriage – it's great, it really is. You feel somehow so complete. Yes, that's the word for it – complete. It's like having two moieties united."

"'Moieties'?"

"A moiety is a portion or a part. A half."

"I see." Angus wondered whether one might call one's spouse one's "better moiety." That sounded better than "better half," which was an expression he did not like at all. It reminded him of golf clubs. Not that there was anything wrong with golf clubs – it was just that sometimes one heard things in the bar of a golf club that sounded as if they belonged there. Not that I've ever been in a golf club, he thought. "So you are happy being married?" Angus asked.

"Yes. Blissfully." Matthew reached out and touched Angus on the forearm. "Why don't you give it a try, Angus? You'd love it."

"She'd never look at me," he said. "Not in that way."

Matthew shook his head vigorously. "Of course she would! You're a handsome man, Angus. You're talented, witty. She would hardly be able to believe her luck."

Angus raised his head. Big Lou had sniggered at the counter. He had heard it.

"So what's funny about that?" he called over to her.

"Nothing," said Big Lou quickly. "It's just that you men need to think twice before you assume that we women are grateful for your company. It's not always like that, I can tell you."

"Don't listen to her," whispered Matthew. But Angus was listening.

## 4. Auden and Burns, and Bertie

Irene Pollock stood at the window of her flat at 44 Scotland Street and thought about identity. She had recently walked past a sign outside a church that read: *Consider your Life; Think of who you are*. Irene had little time for churches, which she regarded as hotbeds of reaction – if reaction can have hotbeds – but she found this message curiously affecting. Yes, perhaps it was something that we all should do from time to time – examine our lives. And now, back in her flat, with Bertie at school and little Ulysses halfway through his morning sleep, her thoughts focused on who she was.

I am, first and foremost, she thought, Irene Pollock, a person to whom the first name Irene had been given, who had then married a man called Stuart Pollock. That made her Irene Pollock, although she had always had her reservations about women adopting their husbands' surnames. That was changing, of course, and more women were retaining their maiden names, but it would be a little bit complicated now to do that because Bertie was Bertie Pollock and Ulysses was Ulysses Pollock. She had her reservations, too, about the term "maiden name." What a ridiculous notion that one was a maiden of all things before one got married. It would be far better, she felt, to use the term "woman's name," or possibly "birth name," rather than "maiden name." Or possibly "authentic name"; that had a good ring to it. You would have your authentic name, and then you would have your "second-ary name," another good term.

She knew of the old Scottish habit of calling women by their maiden names – or authentic names – first, and then writing "or" and giving their married, or secondary, name. This was the way legal documents had always been worded. So she was Irene Burgess or Pollock, which was better than being Irene Pollock née Burgess, because this form put the authentic name after the secondary name, which gave the wrong message. That implied that the state of being married – the state of being a Pollock – was more important than the state of being a person with an authentic identity – that of a Burgess. And then there was always the problem of people being unable to spell, which would mean that she might be described as Irene Pollock, nay Burgess. Of course, that at least had the merit of suggesting that Pollock was the less important identity, the "nay" negating its pretensions.

Had she retained her authentic name, of course, there would have been a question of what Bertie and Ulysses were called. Bertie's full name was Bertie Wystan Pollock, but in a more egalitarian, less patriarchal society, he could as easily be called Bertie Wystan Burgess. Bertie Burgess, however, was rather too alliterative, and she had been determined not to burden her children with awkward or

embarrassing names. What was that girl at school called? She cast her mind back to the roll call at the Mary Erskine School for Girls: Lorna Anderson, present, Nicola Ross, present, Mhairi Smellie, present . . . Poor Mhairi Smellie. Her first name, a Scots Gaelic name, was pronounced "vary," which sounded close to "very." The name Smellie was common enough in Scotland, but to be called something which sounded like "very smelly" was a singular misfortune, and indicative, surely, of a lack of parental foresight.

The "Wystan" in Bertie's name was, of course, after Wystan Hugh Auden, or W. H. Auden, as he was usually known. Irene admired Auden's work and liked the name. Bertie did not. She had introduced him to Auden, of course, concentrating on the more accessible poems, but Bertie had not responded as warmly as she might have wished. She had read him "If I Could Tell You," and he had listened intently, but then he had shown by his questions that he had clearly missed the point.

"Why does Mr. Auden," he asked, "say that all the brooks and soldiers will run away, Mummy? How can brooks run away if they haven't got legs?"

"Auden used something called personalisation, Bertie," Irene explained. "He makes inanimate things talk, or have attitudes. It's very clever."

Bertie thought about this. "And then he says that perhaps the roses really want to grow. How can roses want to do anything, Mummy? They haven't got brains, have they?"

"Mr. Auden is very clever," said Irene patiently. "He makes us think about the world by making the world think. That's frightfully clever, Bertie."

Bertie looked thoughtful. "We learned some poems at school," he said. "There was one about some daffodils. It was when Miss Harmony was still there. She told us to close our eyes while she read it and try to think of daffodils. And then she taught us some Burns."

Irene was silent for a moment. "Burns is a folk poet, Bertie. He really isn't very deep."

"She read us a poem about two dogs," Bertie went on. "There was this very grand dog, you see, and this other dog . . ."

Irene looked pained. "I know all about that one, Bertie. It's very sentimental, you know. A lot of Burns is."

Bertie remembered something that his friend Tofu had said. "Tofu asked Miss Harmony whether she could read something from another of Mr. Burns's books. He said that there was a book called *The Merry Muses of Caledonia* and the poems were very rude. Miss Harmony said no and went very red."

Irene glared at Bertie. "That boy, Tofu, is . . ." She did not complete her sentence. She disapproved of Tofu and would have preferred it if Bertie had chosen some other friend: Olive, for example, to whom she had given every encouragement, and whose mother was a member of her Melanie Klein Reading Group. But Bertie seemed to have set his face against Olive, and even went so far as to say that he hated her. Children were always saying such things, of course, and then deciding the next moment that the hated person is their best friend.

If Bertie disliked Olive, he also did not particularly like Tofu, who was always getting him into trouble. Bertie was a kind boy, though, and he felt that he could not really abandon the other boy, particularly since Tofu had lost his mother, a prominent vegan, who had unfortunately died of starvation. Bertie felt that Tofu needed him, and was loyal, in spite of the other boy's selfish and sometimes alarming behaviour. Bertie, for instance, did not approve of Tofu's spitting at people, but when he had raised the subject with him, Tofu's response had been to laugh, and then to spit at him. So the subject was dropped and not taken up again.

## 5. Pre-Natal Classroom – for Babies

Irene's process of self-examination – her stocktaking – now proceeded from names to relationships. She had married Stuart Pollock because he was the first man who had ever paid any attention to her. She liked him, and was so moved by his crestfallen look after she had initially turned him down that she subsequently relented and agreed. Bertie had arrived a few years later, when Irene was just about to embark on a master's course in social theory at the University of Edinburgh. The pregnancy had not been an easy one – Bertie had been unusually active in utero, kicking with some force, "as if he wanted to get away from me," as Irene put it to her doctor.

"Oh?" said the doctor. "I'm sure he's not doing that!" And then he had paused, and asked Irene whether she was doing anything that might be making the baby uncomfortable. "You aren't drinking too much, are you?"

"Certainly not," said Irene. "I know the risks."

"When does this tend to occur?" asked the doctor.

Irene thought for a moment. "It happens most frequently in the late afternoon."

The doctor looked thoughtful. He had learned his diagnostic skills at the feet of a particularly acerbic professor of medicine, but one who was much admired by his students for his deductive ability. In this respect he was a later version, perhaps, of the great Dr. Joseph Bell, a surgeon at the Royal Infirmary who had taught Conan Doyle, and from whom no secrets could be hidden, either by patients or by students. Now he remembered what this professor had told him about asking what the patient was doing when, or immediately before, the symptoms first manifested themselves.

"What do you tend to do in the late afternoons?" he asked. "Rest? Read? Do the housework?"

Irene gave him a withering look. "In our house, housework is shared. Stuart does his share. More than his share much of the time."

The doctor looked abashed. "Of course. Quite right. But could you tell me what you tend to be doing when this kicking starts?"

Irene waved a hand in the air. "This and that. I'm usually in the flat then. And I take the opportunity to play Bertie some music."

The doctor, who had been staring at his notes, looked up sharply. "Bertie?"

Irene smiled, and pointed to her stomach.

"You play the baby music?"

Irene nodded. "Yes. I take it that you've read about the benefits of in utero musical training?" She waited for an answer, but the doctor said nothing. "Well," she resumed, "there is plenty of evidence that the unborn child can hear music and will react accordingly."

The doctor stared at Irene wide-eyed. "So Bertie, if I may call him that, may not be kicking – he may be conducting?"

Irene pursed her mouth. This was not a subject for humour – particularly heavy-handed medical humour. "There's a very interesting book," she continued. "It's called *Your Own Pre-Natal Classroom* and it has a great deal about how the foetus reacts and how the baby can be given a head start. The man who wrote that book said that he witnessed a thirty-three-week foetus synchronise its breathing with the beat of Beethoven's Fifth Symphony. Can you believe that?"

The doctor wanted to say no, but did not.

"Yes," said Irene. "Quite astonishing. But perfectly credible, if you begin to think about it. So I have introduced an educational hour for Bertie each afternoon. We listen to music together and then I play him a tape of a reading of Dante's *Divine Comedy*. In Italian."

The doctor picked up a pencil and played with it. "I wonder if Bertie appreciates this. You don't think that perhaps he's a little young . . ."

"No," said Irene. "I do not."

The doctor was silent. He was remembering something else that his professor had told him about how patients often themselves provide the answer to the questions they raise. Irene had told him exactly why Bertie kicked so much; he objected, as any unborn child might be expected to do, to this early in utero education. If there were school refusers – children who objected to being sent to school – then why should there not be unborn babies who objected to attempts at pre-natal education? But even as he reached this conclusion, the doctor thought it highly unlikely that Irene could be persuaded to leave Bertie alone to enjoy his last few months in the womb without a programme.

"You don't think that he might be . . ." the doctor began, but stopped. "I don't know," he said. "Just a thought."

Irene had now reached her own conclusions. "I'm rather coming round to the view that this child is very keen to get started," she mused. "Yes, that's probably it. He wants to get on with it. He must have a natural curiosity about the world."

"Very possibly," said the doctor. "Let's wait and see. Some babies kick, and some babies don't. Perhaps we shouldn't read too much into the situation."

Bertie continued to kick, but then he arrived and proved to be a very good-natured baby. He seldom cried, even if he had a slightly puzzled expression from an early age, his eyes following his mother around the room as if he were in some way wary of her. Irene was thrilled with him; every day was a new challenge in which Bertie could be taught something new – the Italian word for something, or the composer of the opera he was being played, or the name, and Köchel number, of the piece of Mozart to which they were listening.

And then, a short while after Bertie's sixth birthday, Irene's second son arrived. Ulysses was not planned; in some respects, in fact, he was extremely unplanned, but once his existence was established, Irene put a brave face on it.

"Did we mean to get pregnant?" asked Stuart, mildly. "I thought that . . ."

"These things happen," said Irene briskly.

"But . . ."

Irene cut him short. "There is one thing we must never do, Stuart," she warned. "And that is to do so much as breathe a word that this child is unwanted. It is so easy to communicate that to a child inadvertently, even if one actually says nothing – one has to be really, really careful. *Capisce?*"

"*Si,*" said Stuart. "*Pero . . .*"

"*Allora,*" said Irene. "Enough. *Silenzio.*"

## 6. *The Ways of Ulysses*

It was Bertie who first noticed that Ulysses bore a striking resemblance to Dr. Hugo Fairbairn, the noted child psychotherapist and author of *Shattered to Pieces: Ego Dissolution in a Three-Year-Old Tyrant*. Initially he had not been able to make much of Ulysses's face, and could detect no similarities to anybody, such was the formlessness – fluidity, even – of his brother's physiognomy. This impression was shared by Tofu. A few days after he had paid a visit to the Pollock flat in Scotland Street and seen Ulysses for the first time, Bertie's friend had passed him a note in the classroom, saying: *Your little brother is really ugly, Bertie, don't you think? You know what his face reminds me of? A bottom!* Bertie had torn the note up and pointedly ignored Tofu for the rest of the lesson. But at the end of the class, Tofu had approached him and asked, "Did you read my note, Bertie? Did you?"

"It was very rude," said Bertie. "You should never say that anybody else looks like a bottom. It's rude."

"Even if he does?" asked Tofu.

Bertie thought about this. He was an extremely truthful boy – indeed, the only truthful boy in his class, as all the rest of the children (as Bertie could not help but notice) appeared to lie whenever it suited them to do so. Tofu, of course, lied about most things, more or less as a matter of course, and Olive, although more circumspect, always twisted the facts to suit her, while vigorously claiming to be an occupant of the moral high ground. The occupation of that high ground was useful in disputes – as Olive well knew – as it enabled her to invoke threats of divine intervention should anybody thwart her.

Olive was always warning others of the consequences of disagreeing with her version of events. Bertie, for example, who was said by Olive to have promised to marry her once they both turned twenty, was warned severely as to the fate that lay ahead of him should he renege on this alleged promise.

"It's not just that you won't be able to look at yourself in the mirror," said Olive. "It's not just that, Bertie. You'll also be struck by lightning."

Bertie was silent for a moment. "I'm not calling you a liar," he said mildly. "Sometimes people misunderstand what they hear. Sometimes they hear things that nobody actually said. That doesn't make them liars."

Olive fixed him with an intense stare. "Oh yes? And sometimes they hear things exactly as the other person said them. So when somebody says, 'I promise to marry you when I'm twenty,' they hear that and they remember it. What about that, Bertie?"

"I really don't think I ever said that, Olive," protested Bertie.

"Well, you did," said Olive. "You said it and I wrote it down on a piece of paper. Then you signed it."

Bertie was shocked at this claim, which was outrageous even by Olive's standards. "I didn't, Olive! And, anyway, where's the paper? Show it to me."

Olive was ready for this. "You're not going to trick me that easily, Bertie Pollock. If I gave you the paper, you'd tear it up. I've seen that sort of thing happen before." She paused, and then uttered a final warning. "And if you carry on lying like this, you know, your pants are going to go on fire. I'm warning you, Bertie!"

It seemed to Bertie that truth for people such as Tofu and Olive was an entirely flexible concept, and that what determined truth for such people was the vigour with which a proposition was asserted, even in the face of all the evidence. He, of course, knew differently, but he was still unsure as to whether there were circumstances in which one should refrain from revealing a truth because of the effect that this might have on others. Some observations, it appeared, were just too hurtful or troublesome to make, even if they were completely true. It was hurtful of Tofu to be so rude about Ulysses, and it was evidently very troublesome that Ulysses bore such a close resemblance to Dr. Fairbairn.

Certainly when Bertie had first mentioned this to his mother, he had been surprised by her reaction. There had been silence at first – as if Irene had somehow been put into a state of shock by Bertie's remark – and this had been followed by a strained retort to the effect that one did not comment on any resemblances that babies had to anybody.

"Just don't do it, Bertie," warned his mother. "Mummies, in particular, don't like that sort of remark."

"But I thought that a mummy might be interested to know that her baby looks like one of her friends," said Bertie. "There's not much you can say about babies, but you can say that."

Irene's voice now rose slightly. "No, Bertie. We can't say that sort of thing. Rest assured – Mummy knows. You don't tell a mummy that a baby looks like another . . . another daddy. You don't. Did you hear me? You don't! So let's not have anymore of this. *Capisce?*"

Bertie had left the matter at that. He was still sure that Ulysses looked extraordinarily like the psychotherapist – they had exactly the same, rather unusual shape of ear, and there was something in the eyes, too, which strongly suggested this. He pointed this out to Dr. Fairbairn himself during one of his sessions, but the psychotherapist had said nothing, and had then gone off to Aberdeen, to a chair. Bertie could not understand why Dr. Fairbairn should find it necessary to go to Aberdeen for the sake of a chair, of all things. But the ways of adults were strange, and the ways of Dr. Fairbairn were particularly so.

And now there was an additional thing for his mother to worry about. Ulysses, who was not an easy baby and was given to girning, had started to be sick whenever Irene picked him up to feed him. Indeed, more or less every time Irene picked him up, he brought up over her shoulder. It was very trying for everybody – for Irene, for Stuart, and for Bertie himself, who did not like the smell.

"We'll have to move out of the house if Ulysses carries on being so smelly," he said to his mother. "We'll have to go and live in a hotel."

Bertie yearned to live in a hotel, or possibly a club. He had read that there were people who lived permanently in hotels and clubs, which seemed to him to be an impossibly wonderful exist-ence. If only a boy could live there, all by himself, in his own room, away from his mother; if only.

## 7. *Anthropological Issues*

The flat immediately above the Pollocks' flat in Scotland Street belonged to Domenica Macdonald, briefly Varghese and now Macdonald again. Varghese had been the name of her Indian husband, a man who showed patient, dogged devotion to Domenica, but had been accidentally electrocuted in his small private electricity generating station in Kerala. Widowhood, though, had suited Domenica, and she had returned to Scotland with some gratitude, ready to pursue her interests as a private scholar. This role – that of the private scholar – was one that very few people still claimed, although there had been a time when it was a fairly common one for people in whom both means and scholarly interest happily coincided.

The contribution of private scholars to knowledge was, of course, immense. In the past, virtually all scholars were private: Galileo was, as was Hume, and Darwin too. They could be: science then was on a scale that did not preclude private experiments in one's kitchen and did not require a particle accelerator several miles long. Philosophy and anthropology – and a whole lot else besides – could be pursued without the assistance of public grants, forms, and the approval of research-ethics committees.

The description of private scholar was one that Domenica had resurrected for herself and that enabled her to feel that she was doing something useful after she had left her small academic position in the department of anthropology at the University of Edinburgh. She had enjoyed that post, but it had been funded by grants that had eventually dried up. Anthropology was vaguely exotic, and spoke little of the everyday social reality with which the bureaucrats felt the social sciences should concern themselves. So while investigations into familial structures amongst the Nuer might be all very interesting – though not necessarily for the Nuer themselves, to whom all this was just the way they did things – in the eyes of those who dispensed academic largesse it was not quite as compelling as a study of job centre accessibility in Airdrie. The Nuer and the residents of Airdrie are indeed quite different – both groups have considerable merits, and rich traditions – but for Domenica the Nuer had the slight edge in terms of anthropological interest.

This was a result of the lure of the distant and the different – she knew that very well. And she knew, too, that the days of anthropological condescension from the West towards everybody else were over, and rightly so, a matter that she had discussed with Angus Lordie on more than one occasion.

"Do they send anthropologists to Scotland?" Angus once asked.

"Of course they do," replied Domenica. "The notion that it's we who study them is quite abandoned now. We are all the object of anthropological interest – potentially. All of us. Even you and that malodorous dog of yours, although strictly speaking he's nothing to do with anthropos."

Angus ignored the gibe at Cyril but thought about Domenica's broader point. "So would you get anthropologists going to, say, Saltcoats?" He paused, and then added, "Not that I'm suggesting that there's anything wrong with Saltcoats. It's a great place, of course."

Domenica nodded. "I knew an American anthropologist who went to do field work in Glasgow," she said.

There was something about the tone with which she said this that interested Angus. Had something untoward occurred? "How did he get on?" he asked.

Domenica looked out of the window. They were having tea in her kitchen in Scotland Street and she was staring at the view of the chimney pots on the other side of the road. We did not need these chimney pots anymore, now that we no longer used our fires, but how bare, she thought, would rooftops seem without them.

"How did he get on?" She repeated Angus's question. "Not too badly, to begin with."

"And then?"

"Well, there was an incident. He was head-butted."

Angus felt a momentary shame; a shame for Scotland. There was so much we had to be ashamed of: too much drinking, too much aggressive swearing, too much head-butting . . . And what did people do about it? Nothing, he thought. Because it was unfashionable, uncool, to protest the values of civilisation, those discarded, despised notions that actually made life in society less like Hobbes's nightmare.

"I'm very sorry to hear that," he said.

Domenica nodded. "He was a very agreeable man," she said. "He came from Chicago, I seem to recall, and he had that typical Midwestern politeness about him. He wrote to me for a few years after his return to the United States, always referring to what he described as his very happy memories of Scotland. He never talked about the head-butting."

"They are very considerate people, Americans, like that," said Angus.

They were both silent, as there was nothing more to be said. Did anybody actually apologise, Angus asked himself.

For her part, although she recognised the merits of work in one's own back yard, Domenica continued to be attracted by radically different societies and by not-too-prosaic projects. Her last piece of research, which she had then written up in several well-received scholarly articles, had taken place in the Malacca Straits. She had gone there to investigate the domestic life of contemporary pirates, and she still remembered with affection the welcome that the pirate households gave her. Some of the pirate women still wrote to her occasionally, giving her news of their families; and she always responded, sending books to the children and the annual *Scotsman* calendar to the pirates themselves.

But after that there had been nothing, and she wondered whether it would be more truthful to describe herself as a some-time private scholar. She liked the word "sometime," which people still used occasionally to refer to a previous position or status. There remained a few scholars – institutionalised, not private ones – who described themselves on the title pages of their books as sometime Fellow of this or that Oxbridge college. There was nothing wrong with that – if you once were something, then it was understandable to remind people of the fact, if it was relevant. But one should not cling too doggedly to these scraps of past dignity, as was being done, Domenica feared, by a friend of hers whose hall cupboard she had once inadvertently opened, thinking that it was the bathroom. And had seen, hanging on a rail, an old coat belonging to her friend, with, pinned to its lapel, a familiar old badge bearing the legend *Captain of Hockey*. She had wanted to laugh at the discovery, but had stopped herself. The thought occurred that this was all that her friend had; this was the summit of her achievement, and that life for her thereafter had been a matter of disappointment. Small things may be important to us; to be a sometime anything is sometimes something.

## 8. Domenica Has Coffee with Dilly

As a private scholar, of course, Domenica's only motivating factor was the intrinsic interest of her subject. In her position there were no considerations of promotion and the financial advantage it brought; there were no chairs to be won, no colleagues from whom to receive plaudits – her only gain was the satisfaction of finding something out, of shining a light upon some obscure passage in the human tapestry. That was reward enough, of course, and Domenica needed none other – but it did mean that if she wanted to do fieldwork, she had to do it entirely off her own bat. And that was not always easy.

She spoke to her friend Dilly Emslie about this, meeting her for coffee in the Patisserie Florentin in North West Circus Place. It was Dilly who had encouraged her to go to the Malacca Straits and had enthusiastically supported her project there. Now she looked again to her friend for guidance: should she start another piece of research, or should she hang up her . . . whatever it was that anthropologists hung up – their mosquito nets, perhaps? – and lead the life of a sometime private scholar?

"You have to do something," said Dilly. "Sitting about is not an option for somebody like you, Domenica."

For a brief moment Domenica imagined what it would be like to be banned from sitting about. One might sink gratefully into a comfortable chair at the end of a demanding day, only to be urged up out of the chair and back onto one's feet. No sitting about, please. Surely there came a point at which one was entitled to a bit of sitting about?

"I suppose so," she said. "They do say, do they not, that one should keep one's brain active."

"Of course," said Dilly. "And it would be such a waste if you stopped writing. I love your papers. That piece on the domestic economy of pirate households was very good indeed."

Domenica accepted the compliment gravely. "I was rather pleased with the way it worked out."

"Of course you were," said Dilly. "Now what?"

Domenica reached for her cup of coffee and took a sip. "The difficulty with anthropology is the going away side of it. I'm not the sort of anthropologist who can work on museum collections. I have to get out into the field. And that takes a lot of planning."

"But surely you don't have to go far," said Dilly. "What about that work you were talking about on Watsonians in Edinburgh? Weren't you planning to do something on Watsonian social networks?"

Domenica nodded. "I was. But I thought it might be a bit too dangerous. And I discovered that there's somebody working on that at the moment. Somebody from St. Andrews is already in the field."

Dilly wondered what the implications of being in that particular field would be. For a moment she pictured the field at Myreside, where Watsonians played rugby. Would it be dangerous for a researcher to position himself on the edge of that field? Would the Watsonians suddenly object to the presence of an anthropologist?

"Of course, it's complex research," went on Domenica. "It involves looking at a whole set of social practices and assumptions. How does one become a Watsonian? What are the enforcement mechanisms for the values they espouse? How are social practices and expectations passed on? There's an awful lot there."

As she reeled off these questions, their answers occurred to Domenica. There was little mystery in the way in which one became a Watsonian: one was enrolled at Watson's and taken there as a small child. But the interesting thing, of course, was the uniform, and the function it performed. This set one aside from other children, who belonged to different clans and social subsets: there was a badge, and this badge displayed the tribal totem of the Watsonians, a picture of a boat. That was very important, as Watsonians recognised the display of this boat as conferring membership of the group. Indeed, above Watsonian headquarters, a long, low, classical building on Colinton Road, an ironwork boat dominated a prominent weather vane, thus signalling to any passing alumnus that this was a place of succour for Watsonians.

As for Watsonian enforcement mechanisms, Domenica realised that there was a great deal of work to be done there. The main mechanism of this type, she thought, was the look. There were various sorts of looks in Edinburgh, the best known and most widely used being the general Edinburgh look, which was best described as slightly discouraging. It did not involve a narrowing of the eyes; rather it entailed keeping the eyes quite open, but sending forth a sort of steely air of disapproval mixed with feigned surprise at what was being surveyed – surprise, really, that the other person actually existed. This was quite a difficult thing to do, in fact, and not easily mastered by incomers. Years of practice were required, although this Edinburgh look was best passed down from generation to generation if it were to be practised at its highest level.

The Watsonian look was not quite like this general Edinburgh look; it was not so disapproving, or discouraging. It said something quite different: its message, in essence, was This is how things are, and how they are meant to be, aren't they nice, don't you agree? That was quite a complicated message, with layers of social meaning, and would in itself require a major research project to be fully analysed. And that is something that Domenica felt she simply could not face. No, there might have been a time when she could take on fieldwork among the Watsonians, but not now. Especially since she was a Watsonian herself.

Her coffee with Dilly was enjoyable, though, as it always was. Dilly did not press her, but gently encouraged her to consider various possibilities. Voluntary work? There were plenty of good causes in Edinburgh. The Art Fund? The National Trust for Scotland? The Cockburn Association, that brave band of conservationists who fought such heroic and important battles against insensitive plans for the city? All of these would appreciate support, and Domenica was certainly willing to provide it, but she felt a certain restlessness that she feared voluntary work would not address.

"Italy," she said to Dilly, as she drained the last coffee from her cup.

"Italy?"

Domenica nodded. For centuries Italy had provided balm for the troubled spirit. Even a small dose of Italy – a week or so – helped. And, as she contemplated this, she remembered that she had been invited to Italy by her neighbour Antonia, who had been offered the loan of a villa in the Sienese hills. At the time, she had not paid much attention to the invitation, which had been a vague one, but now it seemed to her to be the perfect solution to her disquiet. And one never knew what minor research project might suggest itself as one sipped cappuccino in a piazza café. Peer group relationships among visitors to Italian art cities? A Room with a View! One might even get such accommodation; one never knew.

## 9. *The Grosseto Road*

It seemed to be a perfect plan. A couple of weeks in Italy – perhaps even a month – would be just the tonic that Domenica required. What could be better, she asked herself, than slipping into the routine of the Italian villa life in summer? A leisurely, late breakfast on the patio would be followed by a walk into the nearby village. There she would drink a lingering cup of coffee in the piazza, followed by the purchase of a few necessities for lunch: olives, prosciutto, a lump of pecorino, crisp rolls. Then back to the villa for a late morning read of the paper or some slow-moving summer novel, followed by lunch itself, and then a siesta through the heat of the early afternoon. By which time she would be ready for another walk, breathing in deeply the country air, with its tang of white dust and lavender and complex spices; oh, bliss, and bliss again.

Antonia had not given many details of the villa when she issued the invitation. All she said was that it belonged to a distant cousin of hers, a woman who lived in London and had inherited it from her mother, a noted art historian of the 1950s who had known Berenson, she said, and Pope-Hennessy, and "all the others". At this, Antonia had waved a hand airily, as if to encompass a host of art historians, milling about vaguely, attributing here and there, passing on vaguely scandalous stories about one another over agreeable lunches in the hills above Florence.

The villa, she said, was called the Villa Oregano, and was half-way between Montalcino and Sant'Angelo in Colle, on the Grosseto Road. Antonia spoke as if Domenica should know the Grosseto Road, as one might be expected to know Lothian Road, or Princes Street, perhaps. This was a habit she had which mildly irritated Domenica. She would suddenly mention one of her obscure, undoubtedly nonexistent Scottish saints, as if Domenica should be as familiar with him as she was with rather more historical figures of Scottish history, such as James VI or John Maclean.

"The Grosseto Road?"

Antonia nodded. "Yes. You know how it runs from Montalcino down to Grosseto?"

"Actually, I don't," said Domenica. "I've been to Tuscany once or twice, but only to the obvious places. Pisa. Florence."

"Ah, Firenze," said Antonia.

Domenica stared at her. It was the height of pretension, she felt, to use a foreign name when there was an established English one. Not only was it pretentious, it was absurd, even if people insisted – ridiculously – on calling Peking Beijing. Did those same people refer to Roma or Köln when talking about Rome or Cologne? They did not.

"Tell me about the Grosseto Road," Domenica said. "Has it got fine views?"

She knew immediately that Antonia had never seen the Grosseto Road – her hesitation, slight though it was, was enough to make that quite obvious. She decided to press her advantage; Antonia must be helped to abandon her habits of affected intellectual superiority.

"Does it give you good views of the marble quarries?" Domenica asked. She had no idea if there were marble quarries in the area, but then neither, she felt, did Antonia.

"Sometimes," said Antonia lightly. She spoke as if marble quarries were not the sort of thing she would deign to notice.

Domenica insisted. "Of course Cardinal del Monte had a house down there, didn't he? And Berenson's villa, I Tatti, was near there, or a bit closer to Florence, I think." She paused. Antonia was looking uneasy. She decided to go in for the kill. "I Tatti is such a wonderful name for a house. It's named after the nearby potato fields, I believe."

"Yes," muttered Antonia. She was not sure – did I Tatti have anything to do with tatties?

Domenica looked at her friend through narrowed eyes. With any luck, that would be enough to stop too much further posturing about Italy. And Antonia was being kind to her, she reminded herself; no matter what flaws Antonia had – and they were legion – she had been kind enough to make this generous offer and it must be appreciated.

But then Antonia delivered her bombshell. "I've asked Angus, of course. And I think he's going to come."

Domenica could not conceal her surprise. "Angus Lordie?"

Antonia nodded. "I was telling him about it the other day. He was walking that ridiculous dog of his in Drummond Place Gardens. I mentioned I had been offered a villa in Italy and he started going on about how he had gone to Italy on a travelling scholarship when he finished at the art college. He said that he'd love to go back and do some painting. So I asked him."

"I see," said Domenica.

"And he was very keen on the idea," went on Antonia.

Domenica was thinking quickly. Why had Antonia asked Angus to go to Italy? Only one explanation suggested itself: she was making a play for him. That was the only possible reason, and it infuriated Domenica just to think of it. Antonia was a notorious man-hunter – utterly incorrigible. Of course she frightened off any half-decent man, and ended up with people like that Polish builder whose only English word had been "brick." That had been a most unfortunate affair, but Antonia, true to form, had simply dumped the builder, as an expert bricklayer will toss aside an imperfect brick. No, I should not pursue brick analogies, she told herself, but it was a bit like that.

Domenica said nothing for a few moments. Angus was a free agent – he could go to Italy or not, as he wished. But unattached men were few and far between, and if Angus belonged to anybody, then he belonged to her, and not to the grasping Antonia. This meant that she could not possibly miss this trip; she would have to go and do everything within her power to stop Antonia from ensnaring poor Angus.

Then a further thought occurred. What about Cyril?

"And his dog?" she asked Antonia. Angus would never be able to leave his dog behind; they were far too dependent on one another for that.

"One of these new pet passports," replied Antonia. "Angus has obtained one for him. Photograph. Usual occupation. Name and address of next-of-kin. The lot."

## 10. *The Return of Pat Macgregor*

Pat Macgregor, Matthew's former assistant at the Something Special Gallery, former admirer of Bruce Anderson, surveyor and echt narcissist (now reformed, apparently), former classmate of the curiously named and somewhat hypnotic boy known as Wolf, former . . . There were so many respects in which Pat, even though only twenty-one, was a former something, but to list them all would give the impression that her best years were behind her and that she was now somewhat washed up, which was far from being the case. In fact, as she strode purposefully across Middle Meadow Walk, on her way back to her flat in Warrender Park Terrace, she would have appeared to any passerby to be anything but finished. Indeed, such a passerby would have thought that this person was not a student at all – given the usually leisurely gait of students walking across the Meadows – but a person with a sense of wanting to get somewhere, even if that somewhere was only Warrender Park Terrace.

It was Friday afternoon, and Pat had been in the university library on George Square. It was late May, and the university examinations were all well out of the way, as were lectures and tutorials. Pat had worked hard throughout the year – she was extremely conscientious, even if some of the others in her tutorial group were less so, or were conscientious enough, but only in a very-last-moment way. In fact, towards the end of the semester, as examinations loomed, she had met classmates whom she had not seen for the entire year. Suddenly they appeared at lectures, looking slightly confused and worried, desperate to make up for a year of neglected studies. One of them, a young man with long blond hair and Raphaelesque features, to whom Pat found her gaze returning after he took the seat next to her in the lecture theatre, had even revealed that he had come to the wrong lecture altogether. He was a student of English literature who had attended so infrequently that he was unaware of where he was meant to be.

"This is Art History," Pat whispered to him.

The young man turned to her and fixed her with a gaze that was a mixture of regret and resignation. "I've had a rather busy year," he said.

She wondered what his busy year had consisted of, and then decided. That could keep one busy, she supposed. "You could always repeat," Pat reassured him. "Plenty of people do."

"I don't have the time," he said. "Tempus fugit, et cetera, et cetera. I must try and pass. It's not difficult to scrape a few ideas together, you know."

Pat was not sure about that. She thought it was quite difficult, at least it was for her. She was getting reasonable marks – somewhere around a good upper second – and would end up, in two years' time, with a respectable degree at about that level. It was always possible – just – that she might even get a first; one or two of her essays had been rated that highly by Dr. Fantouse, in particular, who said that he "liked her insights."

That compliment had puzzled her. On occasion she had felt that something she had written was mildly original, but "insight" was a strong word and suggested so much more. Mere students, surely, did not have insights. They had ideas, scraped together perhaps, but those ideas were usually no more than a mish-mash of what they picked up through reading the books and articles of those who really did have insights, scholars at the Courtauld, for example, or people like Duncan Macmillan, who wrote such entertaining and forceful art criticism in the paper. Professor Macmillan no doubt woke up each morning with his head full of insights, whereas she woke up in the morning with her head full of . . . well, she would have to say that it was not really full of anything at all first thing in the morning: thoughts of breakfast, perhaps, or thoughts of who would get to the bathroom first and take all the hot water before the others got up. So if any insights were to come her way, they would have to take their place in the queue of other concerns, most of which were really rather mundane and hardly insightful at all.

As she walked along Middle Meadow Walk, she was, in fact, reflecting on the difficulty she was experiencing in marshalling insights for her honours dissertation. She had agonised over the choice of subject before coming up with what might prove to be a fertile source of insights, or might not. The idea had come to her when she was standing in front of Sir David Wilkie's painting *The Letter of Introduction* in the National Gallery of Scotland. She knew the painting well, of course, having been first shown it when she was twelve, and had been taken round the Gallery on the Mound on a wet Saturday afternoon. Her father, who had been showing her round, had pointed out Wilkie's painting and she had looked at it solemnly, a few drops of rain still making their way off her hair and coursing slowly down her cheeks. They had been caught in a shower and her hair had got thoroughly wet.

"That," said Dr. Macgregor, "is a very emotionally charged painting. Do you know what 'emotionally charged' means?"

She had looked up at the painting. A young man stood awkwardly by the side of an older, seated man. The older man was holding a letter that had been given to him and was looking up from it. His gaze was not directed at his visitor, but went somewhere off to the side, in annoyance and suspicion.

"He doesn't like him," she observed. "That man sitting down isn't pleased that the other man has come to see him."

"Exactly," said Dr. Macgregor. "And we know that from his eyes, don't we? And look at his dog. Even his dog is suspicious. You can more or less hear him sniffing."

She had no idea then, of course, that she would return nine years later and, standing in front of the same painting, have an idea for a dissertation. "Space and Emotion in Painting" would be the title, and the subject would be exactly that: how a painter can reveal the emotion that space evokes. The visitor intrudes on the space – and the life – of the other man in the Wilkie painting; cold hostility leaps from the canvas. In other paintings, the slight attenuation of space underlines the emotion of a parting. There would be so much to explore, and perhaps an insight might come along. Surely it was not too much to hope for just one insight; even if only a small one.

## *11. Pat's Flat*

Pat had lived for the last year or so in a student flat on the top floor of a Warrender Park tenement. Her room overlooked the Meadows, and for this reason was the most sought-after bedroom in the flat. But it was not just the view that made it so attractive; it was the shape, which was perfectly circular, determined by the fact that the room nestled below one of the conical roof-towers gracing that eccentric piece of skyline. To live in a circular room, Pat felt, made one rather more interesting; after all, few of us knew people who lived in circular rooms, and there could be little doubt that the room in which one lived defined one in the eyes of others – to an extent.

The small community in which Pat lived – the four students who shared the flat in Warrender Park Terrace – had every bit as much a pecking order as any group of people will inevitably have. It was not a formally constituted pecking order – only a society with a fixed order of precedence will have such a thing formally laid out, and in no society will the official order of precedence represent the real order. So while Scotland has an order of precedence, it is never enforced and people may walk through doors in front of others who really should be allowed to go through the

door before them. That, of course, is how things should be; who would wish to live in a society in which the order of walking through doors was something that anybody cared about? The important thing is that traffic through doors should flow freely, and that there should not be awkward moments when people hesitate, politely ushering another before them, who demurs, and invites the other to go before. Such a situation can result in small knots of people building up in front of a door, with very little through traffic.

The answer, of course, is a system based on common courtesy and consideration, mixed with a measure of sheer practicality. In general, women should be invited to precede men, not because this in any way endorses chivalric notions that many may now find awkward or even condescending, but because it provides a totally arbitrary rule that at least minimises the chances of congestion. It may be viewed, then, in the same light as the rule that states one should drive on the left of the road rather than the right. There is no real reason for that: countries in which people drive on the right are in no way different from those where people drive on the left, or, if they are – and they may be – then that is for historical reasons quite unconnected with driving on the left or the right. So the fact that historically women have been invited to go through doors before men provides a basis for a contemporary rule that this should continue to be done.

Unless, of course, the man reaches the door first; in which case he should go through naturally, rather than wait until the woman catches up with him. An exception to this simple, practical rule would be where the person reaching the door first wants to show particular consideration to the other; in such a case the first person should yield to the second person, ushering him or her in with an appropriate gesture. This makes the second person feel better about himself or herself, in that he or she has been shown by the first person to be somebody the first person particularly respects. For this reason, it is a good general rule to allow everybody to go through the door before you. People who do this are usually much appreciated for their manners, but may not get very far in life, owing, perhaps, to the number of doors through which they do not ever pass.

People with obvious infirmities should be allowed to pass through a door before those who are hale; under no circumstances should they be pushed if they take a longer time than usual to pass through the door. Very aged people, those approaching a hundred years of age, should also be allowed through first on the simple, compassionate grounds that there will not be many doors left for them to pass through.

Such rules, of course, have no currency in student flats, such as that occupied by Pat, even if there be a pecking order. This order – in that flat at least – was based on a combination of who was there first and who was prepared to shoulder the administrative burdens of living in the flat. On both counts, Pat trumped the others. She had been the one to find the flat and sign the lease; she was the one who paid the electricity bills; she was the one who tidied the fridge and apologised to neighbours for the noise after a rowdy party. In return, her right to occupy the circular bedroom and enjoy its superior view was unquestioned.

None of the other occupants of the flat knew one another before they started to share, which was not surprising, as they had very little in common. But random groups of people with little common ground may work very well – and this was the case here. So Pat found herself getting on very well with Anton, a Dutch student of economics; with Tommy, a young man from Dundee who was studying electronic engineering; and with Lizzie, a medical student from Inverness. And they all got on equally well with one another, making for a very contented community.

"I really like living here," Lizzie once remarked to Pat as they sat together in the kitchen waiting for the kettle to boil. "I hated my last place. I really did."

"I like it too," said Pat. "The guys are fine, aren't they?"

Lizzie hesitated. Then she said: "Yes, the guys are fine. Most of the time. I like them. Yes . . ."

Pat had picked up the hesitation. "But?"

"Anton," said Lizzie, lowering her voice. "Have you noticed something?"

Pat thought for a moment. What had she noticed about Anton? There was nothing unusual about him, was there? He had quite a pleasant face – he was rather good-looking, in fact; he spent a lot of time in the library; he watched European football on a small television set he had in his room. That was about everything, as far as she could make out.

"I think he's hiding something," said Lizzie.

"Hiding something? In the flat?"

"No, I don't mean that. Hiding something about himself."

Pat shrugged. Most of us had something that we hid about ourselves. Her father had told her that. "Everybody," he said. "Everybody has a secret, my dear. Even if only one."

## 12. *The Green Hotel*

If Pat's life was serene, it was possibly because she was currently unaffected by what one of her teachers at Watson's had once described as boy trouble. Boy trouble for girls started at about the age of fifteen, which was roughly the time that the male equivalent, girl trouble, began for boys. It lasted usually for about six years, when it transformed itself into man trouble, for many women a much more serious and more intractable problem.

Pat had experienced her fair share of man trouble in the past. First there had been Bruce, the narcissistic surveyor with whom she had shared a flat in Scotland Street. He had at first infuriated her, and then she had found herself being strangely drawn to him. Fortunately she had wrenched herself free – just in time – as some moths manage to escape the candle flame at the very last moment. Then there had been Matthew, for whom she had felt considerable fondness, but with whom she felt ultimately there was just insufficient chemistry to make it work. Poor Matthew, with his distressed-oatmeal sweater and his Macgregor tartan boxer shorts. She still thought that those were a bit of a cheek, given that Matthew had nothing to do with the Clan Macgregor; but she had bitten her tongue on that, as Matthew seemed to have so little in his life, and one should not begrudge somebody like that a bit of colour, even if only in their boxer shorts.

Matthew had gone off to get married, which had pleased Pat. She wanted him to be happy, and she thought that Elspeth Harmony was ideal for him. She could sort out the distressed-oatmeal issue; she could try to make the flat in India Street a little bit more exciting. There was a lot for her to do. But the important thing for Pat was that Matthew was happy. She had seen him once or twice in town, and he had invited her to drop in on the gallery some day. She had not done that yet, but would do so, she thought, when she was next down in that part of the town. She also wanted to see Big Lou, of course, whom she liked a great deal, and Angus Lordie; and Domenica Macdonald, who had been so kind and supportive to her when she lived next door in Scotland Street. Yes, she would go back at some point and see all these people again.

After Matthew there had been a year without a boyfriend, which had suited her. Then she had met a fellow student at a party and had rather absentmindedly accepted his invitation to go out for a meal and see a film the following Saturday. He was called Andrew, and he came from Ayrshire, where his parents ran a hotel, the Green Hotel. "It's not green," he explained. "It's a reference to a golf green. In case you're wondering."

The comment was made in a flat, literal tone; Andrew spoke with the air of one who had explained things many times.

"I wasn't, actually," said Pat.

"Well, some people do," Andrew explained. "You'd be astonished at how many people are surprised to find that our hotel isn't painted green. They say things like, 'We were looking for a green building, not a white one.' You really would be astonished."

Pat was not sure what to say.

"And then there are people," Andrew continued, "who think that we're called the Green Hotel because we're green in the sense of being environmentally friendly. But we're not."

Pat made a face of mock disapproval, making Andrew laugh. "Oh, don't get the wrong idea. We're very conscious of environmental issues. We recycle like mad. Glass. Paper. Everything. It's just that our name is nothing to do with that."

Having accepted Andrew's invitation to dinner, she began to wish that she had not. She toyed with the idea of calling it off, and already had an excuse lined up when he called her on the phone to confirm the arrangement. They could go to the Dominion Cinema, he said, and there was a Nepalese restaurant almost opposite, on Morningside Road. "I'm really looking forward to it," he said. "I love Nepalese food. I love Indian food too, of course. And Thai." He paused, before adding, "And Chinese."

She did not have the heart to cancel. "Tell him you can't go out because you have to wash your hair," counselled Lizzie. "It's such an outrageous excuse that even the dimmest boy gets the message. Or you can give an even stronger message by saying that you can't go out because your friend has to wash her hair."

"I can't do that," said Pat. "I couldn't keep a straight face. And he's sweet enough, I suppose, in a funny sort of way . . ."

"Sweet? Be careful, Pat. Lots of boys are sweet. Sweet but boring."

Pat sighed. "I know, I know. But if you say that you'll go out with somebody you can't just . . ."

Lizzie cut her short. "Can't suddenly remember that you have to wash your hair? Of course you can. You have to, Pat. Otherwise you just make it worse. It's far more difficult to get out of something after you've got further in. So don't go there in the first place."

Pat knew that what Lizzie said was true, but she could not bring herself to phone Andrew and tell him a blatant lie. So when the

time came she went off with him to the Dominion Cinema and went for a Nepalese meal afterwards. Andrew talked a lot about Ayrshire and about the things that had happened in his parents' hotel. One of the guests had flooded a bathroom once and another had caused a small fire by trying to iron something on top of the bed.

"People do really stupid things," he said. "You wouldn't believe it, Pat. They can be really stupid."

Pat agreed.

"And then there was another guest who left his dog in the room. We went in and found the dog sleeping on a chair."

"Did you get the dog back?"

"No. The problem was that this guy had given a false name and address. He had dumped the dog on us. Can you believe that?"

The conversation continued in this vein until the end of the meal.

"I must get back," said Pat, looking at her watch. "I have to . . ." She paused, and then it came to her. "I have to wash my hair."

"You've got really nice hair," said Andrew. "Can I come and wash it for you?"

## 13. *On the 23 Bus*

Now that Ulysses had arrived, the well-ordered routine that Irene Pollock had in place for Bertie, and that had worked so well, was subjected to the occasional moment of strain. Getting Bertie to the Steiner School in the mornings had once been a simple matter but now became considerably more complicated. In the past, Irene would dress Bertie, comb his hair, and place him at the table in front of a bowl of Bircher muesli. Then, ten minutes later, taking him by the hand, she would lead him off to the 23 bus, on which they both travelled over to the other side of town. The muesli was prepared in advance, to a special recipe that she felt gave Bertie exactly the right nutritional start to the day.

Bertie did not mind his muesli too much, but occasionally asked if it would be possible to have something different. "Not every day, Mummy, I promise. But just now and then. Maybe sausages. Hiawatha says that he has sausages for breakfast three days a week. He brought one in to show me."

"He brought a sausage in to school?" asked Irene.

"Yes," said Bertie. "It was really nice. Tofu took it off him and ate it, but he let me look at it first and smell it."

Irene did not approve. "How perfectly disgusting, Bertie! Do you realise what goes into sausages? And what on earth is Tofu doing eating a sausage? Does his father know?"

"Tofu says that his daddy is getting weaker every day," said Bertie. "He's a vegan, you know."

Irene gave a snort of disagreement. "That's absolute nonsense, Bertie. Complete nonsense. Tofu's daddy is a picture of health. I saw him last week at the school gate. He was radiant."

"Is that the same as radioactive?" asked Bertie. "Tofu said that one of his daddy's friends has become radioactive from eating mushrooms brought to Scotland from Eastern Europe." He looked suspiciously at his muesli – this conversation was occurring over breakfast. He had not seen any mushrooms in his muesli, but his mother often put strange things in it and he could not be sure that these did not include the occasional mushroom.

"Oh, really, Bertie! What nonsense people speak in the playground. I do wish that you wouldn't play quite so much with Tofu. He really has some very odd ideas."

Bertie took a spoonful of muesli. He also wished that he did not have to play so much with Tofu, but what were the alternatives? Olive? She was even worse, and Hiawatha was unpredictable and somewhat moody, and there was the problem of his socks. What Bertie needed was a good friend, somebody who thought the same way as he did, and who was neither selfish, like Tofu, nor bossy, like Olive. But it seemed that there was nobody like that, and so he had to make do with what he had.

The disruption to the morning routine had been brought about by Ulysses, and by Irene's need to get Ulysses ready to accompany them on the bus to school. This was not an impossible task, of course, but it was a time-consuming one, as was any chore associated with a one-year-old baby. And now matters were complicated even further by the fact that Ulysses was developing a rather worrying pattern of behaviour that manifested itself with particular vigour in the early mornings.

The behaviour in question had first been noticed by Irene a few weeks earlier, when Ulysses had started to scream on being picked up out of his cot in the morning. As she bent down over the cot, Ulysses had opened his eyes, focused on his mother's face, and then uttered a startling cry of distress. At first she had taken this for hunger, and had hurried to give him his small yellow feeding cup of milk. This worked, but only for a few minutes, as Ulysses had soon rejected his cup, looked at his mother again, and then been sick all over her blouse.

Irene knew that babies could feel out of sorts, and she did not think much more of the problem, even when he was later copiously sick over her shoulder as they travelled up the Mound on the 23 bus.

"His little stomach is a bit upset this morning," she explained to Bertie. "And don't look so embarrassed, Bertie. Nobody on this bus is going to bat an eyelid because a little baby like Ulysses brings up a few drops of milk! They're probably remembering how they used to be sick themselves when they were younger!"

Bertie glanced at his fellow passengers. A teenage girl sitting opposite them, bound for Heriot's School, was looking at Ulysses with evident disgust. When he was sick a second time, on this occasion somewhat more copiously, the girl got up and moved to a seat farther down the bus. Bertie, glowing with embarrassment, stared fixedly at the floor. If only his mother would stop talking to him, he thought, then the other passengers might think that she and Ulysses had nothing to do with him.

"Here, Bertie," said Irene. "Take Ulysses for a moment while I attend to my blouse. There's a good boy."

"But what if he's sick all over me?" Bertie protested. "I've got to go to school. I can't go if I've got sick all over my shirt."

"He won't be sick again, Bertie," Irene said reassuringly. "His little stomach is quite empty now."

Bertie took Ulysses gingerly and propped him up on his lap. The baby, recognising that he had been transferred from Irene to his brother, beamed with pleasure.

"He seems quite happy now," said Irene. "Hold him carefully, Bertie, in case the driver has to put the brakes on suddenly. We don't want little Ulysses flying out of the window – like Hermes."

While Bertie held his brother, Irene wiped at her blouse with a baby-wipe. "They have such delicate little tummies," she explained to Bertie. "So any odd organism can make them bring things up. It's perfectly normal."

"Maybe he doesn't like milk," said Bertie. "Maybe you should give him something else."

"Of course he likes milk," retorted Irene. "You've seen him guzzling away on that yellow cup of his. He loves it."

She finished her cleaning and gestured for Bertie to hand Ulysses back to her. The baby was handed back unprotesting, but when he saw his mother's face again, he immediately started to wail and was promptly sick again, this time over the back of the seat.

"Oh dear," said Irene. "We're really feeling out of sorts this morning, aren't we?"

Bertie was silent. He had noticed something: it seemed to him that what prompted Ulysses to bring up was the sight of his mother's face. Poor Mummy, thought Bertie; she loves little Ulysses so much and already he's sick of her.

## 14. *Regurgitation Issues*

If this distressing vomiting by Ulysses had lasted for no more than a day or two, then Irene would probably have continued to treat the matter as no more than a passing bug of the sort that children pick up so easily. Irene was not one to bother doctors – therapists were a different matter – partly because she felt that they often knew little more than she did, and sometimes rather less. However, after it had persisted for three days, she thought it wise to consult her doctor, a mild-mannered man who ran a small practice round the corner from Scotland Street. The doctor took Ulysses's temperature and gave him a general examination, during which Ulysses behaved impeccably.

"This young man seems to be doing perfectly well," he said. "But you say that he seems distressed on occasion and then brings his food up?"

"Yes," said Irene. "He cries and then regurgitates."

The doctor looked down at Ulysses. "These stomach issues can be problematic. They can resolve, of course, but sometimes it's necessary to have further investigation." He looked thoughtfully at Irene. "I think that we should perhaps watch the situation for a little while before we do anything more." He turned his attention back to Ulysses, who smiled back at him. "He seems a contented wee chap."

"Most of the time he is," said Irene. "It's just when I pick him up. That's when it tends to happen."

"It's possibly just reflux," the doctor mused. "I wonder whether

the movement has anything to do with it? I've not seen this before."
He tickled Ulysses under the chin, and the child burst into a
delighted chuckle. "He doesn't seem to be dehydrated, so he's
obviously keeping something down."

Irene nodded. She was looking over the doctor's shoulder at
the books on the shelf behind him. Shelves gave so much away
about a person. Melanie Klein? Nothing as far as she could see,
but then perhaps one should not expect too much of somebody
who had to spend most of his time dealing with colds and rashes
and things like that.

"Shall we just watch over the next few days?" said the doctor.
"We may need to get the paediatric gastroenterologists at the Sick
Kids to take a look at him. But not just yet, I think."

The consultation clearly at an end, Irene reached forward to
pick up Ulysses. As she did so, Ulysess, who had continued to
gurgle contentedly, puckered his face in rage and brought up over
the front of his mother. The doctor was momentarily taken aback,
and it was a few moments before he produced a wad of moist
wipes to help Irene clean up.

"There!" said Irene. "You see."

The doctor nodded. He was watching Ulysses, who was glaring
at Irene, his small features contorted with emotion. Although until
now he had refrained from reaching a diagnosis, he now felt sure.

"It's as if he's overexcited," said Irene.

"I've been thinking," said the doctor. "Sometimes these things
are nothing to do with the stomach. Sometimes they are more on
the mental side." He chose his words carefully; not everyone was
comfortable with the term psychiatric.

"Psychiatric?" asked Irene abruptly.

The doctor raised an eyebrow. "Yes, possibly. I'm not suggesting that you yourself are doing anything wrong. But sometimes
the relationship between mother and baby gets a bit – how shall
we put it? – complicated."

He watched Irene carefully, but he need not have worried.

"Well, we do have our other child in therapy," said Irene. "It won't be hard to arrange."

"I could give you a referral," said the doctor. "There may be a bit of a waiting list, you know. Infant psychiatry services are in heavy demand, and . . ."

Irene stopped him. "I am sure that Dr. St. Clair will see Ulysses," she said. "He's seeing Bertie at present."

The doctor nodded. "Very well," he said. "And how is Bertie doing?"

"There are oedipal issues to be resolved," said Irene. "We're working on that."

The doctor bit his lip. "Sometimes, of course, it's best to let these things get sorted out by themselves. Most boys turn out all right if you leave them . . ."

He faltered. Irene was glaring at him. "That's hardly what one expected of a medical person," she said icily. "I thought that benign neglect was no longer encouraged."

The doctor made an effort to defend himself. "That's in relation to somatic illness," he said mildly. "Of course one shouldn't ignore worrying symptoms. But there's always a common-sense limitation to intervention. Iatrogenic illness . . ."

"I am not concerned with iatrogenic illness," Irene said, accentuating the iatrogenic; she, at least, was aware of what that meant, and she would not be condescended to by a mere GP. "My concern is with the psychological issues. Somehow I feel that a laissez-faire attitude in the face of developing psychopathology is hardly appropriate."

"But do your boys really have symptoms of psychopathology?" asked the doctor. "Bertie seems to me a very easy little boy – a bit intense, hot-housed, perhaps, but . . ."

He did not finish. Irene had fixed him with a gimlet eye. "Hot-housed, you say? May I ask exactly what you mean by that?"

The doctor clenched his fist in a gesture of nervousness. He thought quickly. "Oh, I merely thought that perhaps you had your central heating a bit high. He looked a little bit pallid, that's all. Children shouldn't be too hot."

Irene continued to glare at him. "I see."

The doctor sighed. "Well, let's see how he does over the next few days." He looked at his notes. "I see from the hospital records that Ulysses is not the same blood group as Bertie, who's O, I notice, as are you and Stuart. Whereas little Ulysses here is . . ." He stopped. His voice had become quieter – barely a whisper.

Irene sat quite still. Her glare had been replaced by a look of anxiety; the look of a creature caught in the headlights of an approaching car.

"Whereas Ulysses," the doctor continued, "is AB."

For a few moments there was complete silence in the surgery. Even Ulysses, who had been niggling, stopped doing so. He, like Irene, was watching the doctor.

"Strange," said the doctor. He was enjoying himself. He disliked patients who knew more medicine than he did – or purported to – and this woman was a bad example of that. She was impossible – really she was – and his heart went out to those two little boys of hers.

Irene cleared her throat. "Well, these things happen, don't they?"

The doctor raised an eyebrow. "Do they?"

"Yes," said Irene as firmly as she could. And yet there was a wavering in her voice. "Mistakes are made in the laboratory. Every day."

"And elsewhere," said the doctor quietly. "Every . . ." He wanted to say night, but decided that it was unprofessional.

## 15. Edinburgh People

Like St. Augustine of Hippo, who had exchanged a life of casual venality for one of monastic virtue and moral self-examination, Bruce Anderson had undergone a significant change. Bruce was no saint yet – or at least not one in the same class as St. Augustine; nor was he contemplating writing any Confessions to rival the saint's. But he was certainly a better man than he used to be, if the progressively marked absence in his life of any of the great vices was to be taken as the measure of improvement.

Bruce's abiding vice – at least until his apparent reform – had been vanity. He was undoubtedly extremely handsome – so good-looking, in fact, that female heads regularly turned when he entered the room or walked along the street. The reason for the turning of heads was obvious enough: any woman seeing Bruce felt an immediate, puzzling, and sometimes frankly alarming desire to stroke him. Few acted on this, even if on occasion one or two more temporarily disinhibited women got close to doing so, reaching out before being brought to their senses and controlling themselves. Had they carried through with their impulse, Bruce would not have minded; in fact, he regarded such attentions as no more than his due. "I suppose I'm just destined to give women pleasure," he had once remarked to a male friend while they had been sitting over a drink in the Canny Man's. "See her," he went on, nodding in the direction of a woman sitting on the opposite side of the room. "I reckon she fancies me." The friend had glanced across the room and saw, with dismay, that the young woman in question was throwing Bruce a look of only lightly disguised longing. Notice me, the look said.

The friend had gritted his teeth, and at that moment had decided that he hated Bruce. And yet they would remain friends, in the way in which people do with those whom they find themselves allocated by chance. Everybody has friends they dislike; people they have slipped into relationships with, people they would not have chosen had they been more cautious, more circumspect.

But that was the old Bruce; the Bruce before the moment of insight in Leith changed him so profoundly. Now he could look back on his old life, at its various stages, and it seemed to him that he was looking at the history of another person altogether.

Bruce had lived in Scotland Street, then in London, then back in Edinburgh, although not in Scotland Street. On his return he had moved in first with Julia, to whom he had been engaged for a short time, and then he had gone to live in Leith with George McNair, the freelance photographer and advocate of moral renewal. George had both photographed and renewed Bruce, who had then taken up with Lizzie Todd, daughter of Raeburn Todd, the well-known Edinburgh surveyor and Watsonian-Rotarian. This had led to another engagement, announced in *The Scotsman* in that time-honoured and rather embarrassing fashion as being a cause of pleasure to both families. Often both families are not delighted; indeed not even pleased. In this case, though, both families were happy enough with the engagement, but not quite in equal measure. Bruce's parents were immensely relieved that their son was re-engaged, and heartily approved of Lizzie. By contrast, Raeburn Todd, although prepared to forgive Bruce his previous indiscretions, was secretly disappointed that his daughter had not set her sights somewhat higher. But he did not show that, although he was careful to avoid giving Bruce – or Lizzie – the impression that a partnership in the firm was in the offing.

The thought had occurred to him – more than once – that Bruce might have asked Lizzie to marry him for reasons other than love and affection. The Todds were not conspicuously wealthy, but they were comfortably off, and their firm had done reasonably well. If Bruce became a partner, then he would probably make about three times what he could expect to make as an employee, a fact of which he was surely fully aware. And there was also the question of the legacy left Lizzie by her maternal grandmother, which consisted of a portfolio of shares and, more significantly, a flat in Morningside. Put together, this all amounted to a fairly attractive package for a young man who, as far as Todd could tell, had no assets whatsoever.

He had raised the matter with Lizzie as delicately as he could. "Bruce is very fond of you, isn't he?"

"Of course he is. He asked me to marry him, didn't he?"

Todd nodded. "Of course he did. And any young man in his right mind would be fond of you. It's just that . . ."

"Just that what?" Lizzie asked sharply.

"It's just that people in our position sometimes have to be a little cautious as to motives. That's all I'm saying."

Lizzie glared at him. Her father had always been utterly transparent to her, and she knew exactly what he meant. "People in our position?" she snapped. "What exactly is our position? Are we grand, or what?"

Todd laughed – nervously. "Of course we're not grand. We're perfectly ordinary Edinburgh people." If Edinburgh people can be perfectly ordinary, he thought. "But I have achieved a certain – how shall I put it? – achieved a certain amount and we live in the Braids and there's the firm . . ." He trailed off. Lizzie's glare had become more intense and he was feeling distinctly uncomfortable.

"Are you saying that Bruce is after my money – such as it is? Is that what you're saying?"

Todd waved a hand airily; the very thought. "Of course not. I'd never say that."

"Then what are you saying?"

Todd swallowed. His daughter had always been direct, and he should have known better than to be so oblique. "What I'm saying is this: sometimes people – and I'm not saying that Bruce is one of those – calculate what marriage will bring them in terms of a job and a house and so on. Bruce works for me – I'm his boss. You're the boss's daughter. Now it doesn't take much imagination to see that a young man in his position might – and I say might – be thinking of what he could get out of marrying you. I just raise the possibility, that's all."

Lizzie stared at her father. Her angry expression was now more baleful than anything else.

"But Bruce isn't like that," she said. "He just isn't. You've completely misjudged him." She paused; she was on the point of tears. "You don't even begin to understand, do you?"

## *16. For Love or Money*

Ideas planted in the mind may be rejected, pooh-poohed, and then unexpectedly and insidiously return to disturb our equanimity. Lizzie had rejected out of hand her father's barely veiled suggestion that Bruce may be a fortune hunter. Her father knew nothing about it, that was clear; Bruce had asked her to marry him because he loved her, and she had accepted his proposal for the same reason. It may be that people married for money in the past – Jane Austen had something to say about that – but who did that nowadays? Surely nobody.

And yet her father's words continued to haunt her, and she decided to raise the subject with her friend Diane, whom she met every Friday in a coffee bar near Holy Corner. Diane could spare the time for long coffee breaks – she was a freelance interior decorator with a largely empty diary, a diary that had potential, certainly, but not a potential that was being achieved. No matter; Diane was convinced that the big commission, the one that would change her life, would come in, and she would feature in *Scottish Home* or *House Beautiful*.

If Diane had time on her hands, so did Lizzie. Since graduating from Strathclyde, she had held down a number of temporary jobs, but nothing permanent. Again this did not matter unduly; if the worst came to the worst – and she was confident it would not – she could always work for a maternal uncle who ran a small chain of restaurants and had promised her work if she ever needed it. For the time being, though, there were plenty of jobs to be applied for and interviews to attend.

On this particular morning, Lizzie asked her friend if she thought that it was possible that people still married for what she described as "other reasons." Diane was not sure what she meant, and looked puzzled. "Other reasons? You mean because they're forced to? Or in a fit of absentmindedness?"

No, that was not it. "For . . . well, I suppose you'd say for money. For somebody's money."

Diane shrugged. "I don't think so," she said. "They used to do that sort of thing back in . . . back in prehistoric times – the 1960s and so on."

"So you think it doesn't happen today?"

Diane thought for a moment. "Maybe now and then. I suppose that money comes into the picture with arranged marriages, but otherwise . . . no, I don't think so."

"So when you see a man of seventy marrying somebody of twenty, it's nothing to do with the fact that he's rich?"

Diane laughed. "No. Of course that's all to do with money. What I meant is that when there's nothing like that in the picture then people these days marry because they like the person." She paused. "Why do you ask? Has anybody said anything?"

Lizzie hesitated. She was loyal to her father, but she nonetheless felt that she needed to discuss this with somebody, and Diane was as close a friend as she had.

"My dad said something," she confided. "He tried to be tactful about it but I could tell what he meant. He asked me whether I

thought Bruce had asked me to marry him because of my money."
Watching the effect of her remarks on her friend, she quickly
added, "Not that I've got any."

Diane smiled. "You must have. You must have something.
There's your flat. You own that outright, don't you?"

"It was my grandmother's," said Lizzie apologetically. "She left
it to me. So I didn't have to pay anything for it."

"But it's worth quite a bit, isn't it? A three-bedroom flat in
Morningside . . ."

"Only two proper-size bedrooms," interjected Lizzie. "The third
one's really a boxroom."

Diane ignored the objection. "Three hundred thousand pounds,
at least," she said, a note of wistfulness in her voice. "Three
hundred and fifty thousand, maybe. Even in this market."

Lizzie looked out of the window again. "Look," she said. "The
sun."

But Diane was not to be so easily distracted. "And you inherited
a whole bunch of shares, didn't you? You told me that a long time
ago. What are they worth now?"

"Not all that much," muttered Lizzie.

"How much?"

Lizzie did not feel that Diane had the right to know the value
of her portfolio of shares that McInroy & Wood had so prudently
nurtured for her. But having started this discussion, she could
hardly drop it now, and so she mumbled a figure.

"What?" asked Diane. "How much?"

"Four hundred," said Lizzie, looking away.

"Four hundred pounds?"

"Thousand."

"A thousand pounds?"

Lizzie was now virtually inaudible. "No, four hundred thousand."

Diane sighed. "So that's three-quarters of a million altogether.
You realise that, I suppose? You're almost a millionaire."

Lizzie turned to her friend. "Please keep your voice down," she said. "I don't want people thinking . . ."

"So no wonder your father asked that question," said Diane. "I'd ask it too."

Lizzie was silent for a while. It was one thing for her father to think such thoughts; it was quite another thing for her close friend to harbour similar doubts.

"Does Bruce know?" Diane suddenly asked. "Did you tell him?"

"He knows that I've got my own flat," answered Lizzie. "Obviously he knows that."

"Does he know that you own it outright?" asked Diane.

Lizzie thought for a moment. She remembered talking to Bruce about it once, but she did not think that they discussed mortgages. And as for the shares, she was sure that she had never mentioned . . . She stopped herself. He had said something once about a share tip that he had received and had told her that she should get her financial adviser to arrange for the purchase of some of the shares in question. "That is, if you have a financial adviser," he said casually. "Do you?"

And she had answered, equally casually, "Yes, I do." And had proceeded to mention McInroy & Wood.

Diane had been watching her. "He knows something, doesn't he?"

Lizzie nodded. Suddenly she felt miserable, as if she had uncovered some unpleasant secret. And now she tried to tell herself that Diane was as little justified as her father in entertaining these doubts. They both had suspicious, uncharitable minds. They both had no reason to think that Bruce, of all people, would stoop so low.

"But I don't think there's the remotest chance that he's after my money," she said. "He just isn't."

Diane raised an eyebrow. "Prove it," she said. "Prove it to yourself."

"How?" asked Lizzie.

Diane replied immediately. "A love test." She was clearly serious, even if she smiled as she spoke.

Lizzie was on the point of laughing. This was ridiculous. One did not have love tests in real life; they were the stuff of fiction – and unlikely fiction at that.

And yet fanciful fiction could reflect real life just as vividly as its more prosaic equivalent; she had read that somewhere, in a novel perhaps.

## 17. The News from Arbroath

In a quite different coffee bar, on the other side of town, Big Lou was preparing to receive her morning regulars – Matthew, Angus Lordie, and Angus Lordie's dog, Cyril. Angus was generally unreliable, she thought, and might drop in any time between ten and ten-thirty, whereas Matthew was punctual to a degree. If the citizens of Königsberg had been able to set their watches by the sight of Immanuel Kant taking his morning walk, then the citizens of Edinburgh, or at least those who lived in Dundas Street, could do likewise with Matthew. He left his gallery on the other side of the road at exactly ten o'clock, and began his descent of Big Lou's stairs precisely three minutes later. Marriage had not changed his habits in this respect at least, thought Big Lou – which was reassuring; she liked Matthew and, although she would never say it, she would not want him to change.

Now it was exactly 10:03, and from her position behind her counter, where she was polishing the surfaces with a cloth, Big Lou could see Matthew's legs at the top of her stairs; soon the rest of him would heave into sight, and she would be able to see whether he was still wearing that distressed-oatmeal sweater of his. That was one thing his new wife could do for him, thought Big Lou; the distressed-oatmeal sweater could go.

Matthew, in fact, was not wearing the distressed-oatmeal sweater, which had already fallen foul of Elspeth Harmony's reorganisation of his wardrobe. In its place he had a light grey linen jacket that Elspeth had found for him somewhere on George Street. It was not ordinary linen, in that it had none of the vices that make linen such a contrary fabric; this was easily ironed linen that did not crumple excessively and did not look like Auden's face, with all its lines and crevasses.

Complementing the jacket was a pair of black jeans – a garment that Elspeth had found in a drawer in Matthew's (now their) room and of which she had expressed approval. Matthew had donned the jeans gingerly, as he had no idea where they came from. If they were in his flat, and in his drawer, then they must belong to him, but he had no recollection of either ever buying them, or even wearing them. They fitted, though, and even if he found a receipt in a pocket, indecipherably signed with a signature other than his own, the fact that they were his exact size was a prima facie indication of his ownership of them.

"You look good in those," said Elspeth appreciatively. "They sort of hug your thighs. There. Look. Isn't that nice?"

Matthew blushed, but at the same time he felt a strong sense of satisfaction that Elspeth appeared to find him attractive. Nobody had ever paid him that sort of compliment before, and he had assumed that this was because nobody thought of him in that way. He was just good old Matthew, as he always had been, even back in his teenage years. He had been the boy that people liked having about them, but not with them. Nobody had ever said to him that anything looked good on him; nobody.

"So you like them?" he said, smoothing down the side of the jeans with his open palms.

Elspeth nodded. "I like you," she said. "That's what I like."

He blushed again, but felt grateful, too, for what she bestowed on him, this gift of love, that had been so unexpected.

He was not thinking of her, though, as he began his cautious journey down Big Lou's steps; he was thinking, rather, of what these steps had seen. He had heard from Big Lou, who had in turn learned it from people who knew the coffee bar in the days when it was still a second-hand bookshop, that it was down these very steps that the poet Hugh MacDiarmid had stumbled one day; stumbled, but recovered his footing and made it to the bottom alive and in a position to write more poetry – whereas poor Lard O'Connor, that well-known Glasgow informal businessman, had failed to recover and had toppled, as a great Norwegian pine might in its native forest fall to the axe. Matthew remembered the sense of sudden loss as the ambulance men shook their heads; and he remembered how they had asked him whether Lard was his friend and he had hesitated – just momentarily, and shamefully, before he had replied that he was.

That was some time ago – last summer – and he had almost forgotten about Lard O'Connor, although presumably there were people in Glasgow who remembered him – his victims, certainly, Matthew thought grimly; those people with scars and scowls, like the mourners at Lard's funeral in that soft West of Scotland rain.

Now, as Matthew entered the coffee bar, Big Lou looked up from her task of polishing the counter and moved over to her coffee machine.

"The usual?" she asked over her shoulder. She required no reply; Matthew always had the usual, and even if he had wanted something different, there was very little choice in Big Lou's coffee bar, with or without milk being the only options.

Matthew picked up a newspaper from the table near the door; a ten-day-old copy of the Dundee *Courier*, the paper that kept Big Lou informed about events at home. The articles and photographs in these stale papers, posted down to Lou from Arbroath, were annotated by an ancient relative with little observations and reminders. "Remember him? The loon with glasses?" Or, "He tells terrible lies. He always has." Or, "No surprise: he had it coming to him after what he did to Maggie's tractor."

The events of small-town Scotland, seemingly so local and irrelevant in the greater scheme of things, were in fact ciphers for the life of all humanity. These marginalia, penned in a crabbit hand, had an irrefutable profundity to them: so many people did indeed tell terrible lies, always had – and always will. So many people, in all sorts of places, have it coming to them, and fuel the schadenfreude of the rest of us, who are secretly relieved that it is they, rather than we, to whom what was coming came.

Matthew glanced at the newspaper in his hand. Big Lou's relative had underlined a sentence in an article and written beside it, in blue ink: *I kent his faither!*

He looked at the subject of the article: *Local man comes second in national competition*. He smiled, and was seen by Big Lou as she poured her coffee grounds.

"Something amusing you?" asked Big Lou. She was sensitive about urban condescension in all its forms.

"No," said Matthew. As he spoke, he imagined the unseen hand of an Arbroath body inscribing shaky letters in the air beside him: *liar*.

## 18. *Ten Years with the Pygmies*

Barely had Big Lou served Matthew with his coffee when Angus Lordie and Cyril arrived. They had walked in a leisurely way from Drummond Place, stopping here and there for Cyril to investigate some intriguing scent either on the ground or in the air. His nose told him that a lot had been happening in Abercromby Place, where a farmer, having driven in from Kelso earlier that morning to consult his lawyer, had walked from his parked Land Rover – a cornucopia of scents for a dog – along the north side of the street, leaving Cyril a trace of sheep, fried bacon (the farmer's breakfast), cattle dip, and old copies of *The Scottish Farmer*. The farmer, attired in the suit that he kept for visits to Edinburgh, might have imagined that he smelled of good-quality Borders tweed, topped up with the sandalwood aftershave lotion that his daughter had given him for his birthday the previous week; but to Cyril, who picked those up too – although he had difficulty with the sandalwood – the story was far more complex than that. For him a smell was a biography: it told the story of what some-body did, and thus of who they were. Angus was a painter and, in Cyril's nose, he was redolent of paint, varnish, the dust that accumulated in his studio, carpet, whisky, and, occasionally, kippers; a motley collection of scents, but to Cyril it was the smell of God, as powerful an invocation of sanctity as incense is in Rome.

Other interesting things had happened in Abercromby Place that morning. Two police horses had been ridden down the road, quite recently, and Cyril looked up, half expecting to see them still there. But that was the problem with scents; they faded, they were overlaid by other, more recent clues, as a palimpsest will be built up of added layers; they became part of the background noise, like static on short-wave radio. Every so often a station comes through loud and clear, and then fades away in a noise that sounds like rain, or sausages frying, or wire wool being scratched across a surface.

Just outside the Open Eye Gallery, Cyril picked up the scent of a cat. This made him stop, stubbornly sitting down on the pavement in an indication to Angus that this was a matter that required to be investigated and could not be cut short by a sharp tug on the collar. Angus understood: he knew that Cyril had no choice but to attend to these scents; it was part of what he was;

it was his duty as a dog. And it would only take a minute or two of sniffing around the pavement and the steps of the gallery to deal with the evidence.

Cyril applied his nose to the stone. The scent of cat was strong – frustratingly so – which meant that he had probably only just missed it. And the annoying thing about cats, or one of the annoying things – there were so many – was that they would often watch one from a place of safety while one looked for them. This cat, whom Cyril recognised from his scent, was a particularly irritating creature. Large, smug, green-eyed, he positively invited dogs to pursue him. But, of course, none would ever succeed in bringing him to justice. Cyril knew that; with an aching wistfulness he knew that he would never come as close to this particular cat as he wished.

He dreamed about it, and Angus would smile at the sight of Cyril's legs twitching in his sleep as the dream of pursuit and capture unfolded. Dogs regularly dream of such things but, of course, have no concept of dreams and so cannot distinguish between what happened in the dream and what happens in real life. So if a dog dreams that he has caught a rabbit, or a cat, or has found a particularly tasty morsel to eat, then that, from the dog's point of view, is what happened. In Cyril's case, he had caught whole legions of cats, because that is what had happened in his dreams; he had taught them a thing or two, filling his mouth with their fur and then spitting it out in triumph, exacting sweet revenge for all the insults that cats had heaped upon the canine world, going back such a long time. That had all happened, as far as Cyril was concerned, because he remembered it.

When they arrived at Big Lou's, Matthew had finished his first cup of coffee and was waiting for Big Lou to serve his second. Angus Lordie greeted Matthew with a nod while he enquired after Big Lou's health.

"Can't complain," said Big Lou. She said the same thing every day – can't complain – and it was true. It was not in her nature to complain; she simply could not. Not once had she complained during the years when she had looked after her aged uncle, or when she worked as a care assistant in the Granite Nursing Home in Aberdeen. She came from a place where people did not complain, where it was understood – quite correctly – that moaning and groaning only made things worse. There was no word for self-pity in the language of the north-east of Scotland – the nearest being a word which is defined in the Scots dictionaries as being "a term used to express self-reproach on paying too much for something."

Angus Lordie noticed that there was a book lying open behind the counter. Big Lou was a voracious reader and, having bought the remaining stock of the bookshop that had previously occupied the coffee shop premises, she was slowly working her way through every volume. She had started with philosophy, with Hume, whom she had read with pleasure and a feeling of growing agreement. From there she had moved on to topography (*The Glens of Aberdeenshire*) and social history (Iain Thornber's edition of *Morvern: A Highland Parish*) and now, it appeared, had arrived at memoirs. *Ten Years with the Pygmies of Ruanda-Urundi*, he read, upside down.

"Interesting," said Angus. "Pygmies?"

Big Lou glanced at the book as she finished preparing Matthew's coffee. "Aye," she said. "Pygmies."

## 19. The Question of Cosmetic Surgery

"Are we allowed to call them pygmies these days?" asked Angus. "Or are they something else? Forest people?"

Big Lou glared at him. "If they're called forest people now," she said, "it must be for a good reason."

"Political correctness," said Angus. "That's the reason."

Big Lou made a dismissive sound. Attacks on political correctness, in her view, were often made by those who had never suffered insult or known what it was like to be at the bottom of the heap. Not that she approved of the wilder excesses of the movement – the Stalinist prohibitions on simple human expression and feelings – but she applauded the increased sensitivity that had grown around the vulnerabilities of others. She was pleased that people were no longer left out because they were different; or made to think the less of themselves because of what they were. She fixed Angus with a stare. "Maybe they had good reason not to want to be called pygmies," she said. "You've never had to worry about that sort of thing, have you? You don't know what it's like to be called something belittling."

"But they are little," said Angus, looking to Matthew for support. "You don't belittle the little by calling them little. What should we call them? Big?"

Big Lou shot Matthew a discouraging glance. "They're not little in their own eyes. Not as far as they're concerned."

"Does it matter?" asked Matthew. "Does it really matter whether you're short, like a pyg . . . like a forest person, or whether you're tall? Does it matter?"

"No," said Big Lou. "It doesn't." She passed Angus his cup of coffee and looked at him challengingly.

"Actually, Lou," said Angus, taking the coffee over to Matthew's table. "Actually it matters quite a lot to some people. We had a very short man in the Scottish Arts Club once, and it made him very unhappy. If he had been granted one wish – one wish – I know what it would have been. To be taller. Poor chap. He used to paint pictures of very tall people. All his figurative studies were of tall people."

"How sad," said Matthew.

"Yes, it was," said Angus. "It must be very sad to have to go through life wanting to be something that you can't be. To be gay when you want to be straight, for instance. That can't be easy."

Matthew frowned. "Except that most people who are gay are actually quite comfortable with their identity. These days, at least." He paused. "Do you think there are straight people who would prefer to be gay? Do you think it works that way round?"

Angus thought for a moment. "I've not heard of it. There's no pressure to be gay, you see. The reason why gay people sometimes want to be straight is because they've been put under such strong pressure to be straight. It's oppression, really; it's very cruel. So they find themselves wishing that they were what society wants them to be. How many lives have been ruined by that."

"It's like tall people not wanting to be short," said Matthew.

Big Lou looked at him. "I'm quite tall," she said. "I wouldn't mind being a wee bit shorter sometimes."

Matthew looked apologetic. "I wasn't thinking of you, Lou," he said. "You're . . . the right size, I think."

"This wee chap," Angus cut in. "The one in the Scottish Arts Club – he had a pair of elevator shoes. We could tell. They had very large heels."

They were silent for a moment.

"People should be allowed to do what they want with themselves," pronounced Big Lou. "It's none of our business. If somebody wants to wear elevator shoes, it's up to him."

Angus smiled. "And cosmetic surgery, Lou? What about that? All that nipping and tucking and tightening of the skin round the eyes. Don't you think that's grotesque?"

Big Lou reached for her cloth and began to polish the counter top. There was a certain frenzy in her movements. "If they want it," she said, "then it's up to them. You've never had to worry about your nose, or your chin, or whatever. But what if you had?"

Angus rolled his eyes. "I can't believe I'm hearing this from you, Lou. These women with their cosmetic surgery . . ."

"And men," interjected Big Lou. "Men go in for it too. I saw a film, about men who were anxious about . . ."

"Yes, yes," said Angus hurriedly. "That may be so. But you see the results on the women. Those awful tightened faces that end up looking like Japanese Noh masks. All the character taken out of the face. Just this tight skin. It's ghastly."

"And such a waste of medical resources," said Matthew. "You get all those doctors doing good things – missionary doctors and so on, the flying doctor service – and then you get these greedy surgeons fiddling about with people's double chins for large payments. Operating for money – pure and simple."

Angus took a sip of his coffee. "You could have a flying cosmetic surgeon," he mused. "He could get in his plane and fly off to deal with remote cases of dissatisfaction with the shape of a nose or something. You could get that."

"Don't be ridiculous," said Big Lou.

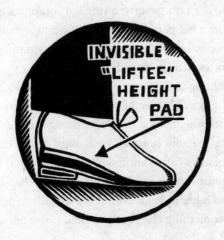

"Where's your sense of humour?" Angus asked. "I was just speculating."

Big Lou said nothing. She had put down her cloth and sat down on her chair behind the counter, picking up her book as she did so.

"She's offended," whispered Matthew. "You've offended her, Angus."

"I can't see why she's so touchy," protested Angus. Big Lou appeared to be far more sensitive than usual and it seemed that he could say nothing without incurring her disapproval.

"Perhaps she's contemplating cosmetic surgery," said Matthew.

He had spoken in a low voice, not one he would have thought that Big Lou would hear, but she looked up sharply and gave Matthew a look that made him wonder – absurd thought – whether he had alighted, unintentionally perhaps, on the truth.

## 20. *The Aphrodite of Dundas Street*

Some time later, Angus Lordie and Matthew went their separate ways, leaving Big Lou to serve a small group of visitors who had wandered down her perilous steps. These newcomers had caught a whiff on the street of the coffee brewing within and had been drawn down towards it, as by Sirens.

Angus, although reluctant to leave, returned to his studio in Drummond Place. He would have willingly stayed at Big Lou's the whole morning, talking to whomsoever would engage him in conversation, verbally sparring with Big Lou or discussing the world and its ways with Matthew. But he knew that he could not put off his return to his studio indefinitely; he had a painting to finish, he had a life to lead, even if it was a life of loneliness and longing for something else that he could never quite define, and would probably not recognise if he ever found it. For his part, Matthew crossed the road to his gallery. In the past he had stuck up a Back Soon notice on the front door when he went off for his coffee break, but recently he had decided that this was unprofessional and had engaged an assistant to help him in the gallery for several hours each morning and to cover for him when he went out for his regular coffee session. This young woman, Kirsty, was a student, as had been Pat, his last employee, but there the similarity ended. Whereas Pat had been a relatively quiet girl, an observer, Matthew thought, rather than a participant, Kirsty was gregarious and enthusiastic, perhaps even a bit opinionated at times. But she was forgiven that – not only by Matthew, but by everyone – on the quite simple grounds of her extreme physical beauty. And the beautiful are forgiven; no matter how egregious their shortcomings, they are forgiven.

Matthew had noticed this when he was still a schoolboy. There had been a boy in his class, Hector McFarlane, who had been blessed with a countenance and smile so appealing that even the sternest heart would melt on being exposed to this double-barrelled charm offensive. This youth, whose boisterous boyish misdeeds were legion, got away with them all because none of the teachers could bring themselves to punish one who looked so like a Florentine painter's image of innocence in the garden. And this had continued, Matthew believed, throughout Hector's career. Women forgave him everything, and men too, although none realised that they were doing it. Lookism, thought Matthew in retrospect. Like ageism and sexism, lookism was everywhere, resulting in the good-looking getting the best jobs, winning all the plaudits, being let off the most parking tickets by soft-hearted traffic wardens; being generally favoured.

And Matthew himself had been guilty of this in his choosing of Kirsty for the position of his assistant. Kirsty had seen the advertisement early and had been the first to telephone to arrange an interview. Matthew had invited her down to the gallery and had asked no more than three questions when he offered her the post.

"You're just the person I've been looking for," he announced. "If you want the job, it's yours."

Kirsty had been slightly surprised and had asked him if he wanted to hear about the experience she had had in helping out in a Glasgow gallery owned by friends of her parents.

"Yes, of course I'd like to hear about that," said Matthew politely. "I was going to ask you. Do tell me."

He half listened as she told him of the exhibitions she had helped to organise, but his heart was not in it and when she had finished he merely nodded and said, "That's all fine. When do you want to start?"

Angus had seen Kirsty when he had walked past the gallery on the day that she started work. He had paused, pretending to look at a painting propped up on an easel in the window, but had been secretly staring at the glamorous new assistant sitting in the desk on the other side of the room. Later he reported to Big Lou what he had seen. "Matthew has a new little helper in the gallery," he said. "I take it you've seen her."

"I have not," said Big Lou. "Have you?"

Angus rolled his eyes. "Very pretty."

Big Lou gave him a scathing look.

"I don't know where he finds these girls," Angus went on. "That girl Pat was attractive enough, but this one, my goodness me!"

"Matthew's a married man," said Big Lou. "I'm sure that how this girl looks is neither here nor there."

Angus corrected himself. "Of course, of course. It's just that . . . well, she's very . . . how shall I put it?"

Big Lou shook her head. "Matthew isn't like that, Angus. He's not like you."

Angus showed his indignation. "Like me? Of course I appreciate beauty – I'm an artist, as you may have observed, Lou. What artist isn't sensitive to beauty – in all its forms?"

"Aye, well, that may be so," said Big Lou. "But I've got better things to do than to listen to your blethering."

But Angus had sown the seed in his own mind, even if not in Big Lou's. He wondered whether Elspeth Harmony had met the new assistant yet, and what she would think about her. Would any wife be happy to think that her husband was working in close proximity to a girl like that? We are weak creatures, thought Angus. We are very weak, and what woman does not sense that, no matter how constant her husband appears to be; what woman does not fear that deep weakness in the make-up of every man? It may be no more than a niggling doubt – a twinge of insecurity – but it is there.

Back in his studio, on the day of that first encounter with Kirsty – through the glass – Angus found his thoughts returning to the young woman. He closed his eyes, re-creating the vision he had been vouchsafed: Kirsty, with her back turned towards him at first, her long hair over her shoulders, half turning to reach for something at the side of her desk, thus affording him a view of her profile; such perfection of proportion and attitude, like a gazelle glimpsed in the half-cover of grass, a pert gazelle, nervous, ready to bolt if it sensed an observer.

Iris Murdoch once revealed that the idea for an entire novel had come to her following upon the sight of a boy on a road, caught in the headlights of a car. Why should not an entire painting – a *Judgement of Paris* – come to the eye of an artist who looks through a window? Yes, a *Judgement of Paris*, with Matthew's assistant as Aphrodite herself, resolute, calm, and, as in Jan Bruegel's treatment of the subject, disrobed. Would she agree, he wondered.

## 21. *Impressionists and Postimpressionists*

It had been an uneventful morning for Kirsty. She had hoped that somebody would come into the gallery, would buy the most expensive painting on display, and then pay in cash. When Matthew came back, she would then inform him of the sale, modestly of course. But that was not the way the morning worked out. In fact, from the time that Matthew had gone off for coffee and left her in charge, hardly anybody had so much as lingered outside the window, let alone come in to buy a painting. At one point a tall man in an overcoat had almost entered, but had then glanced at his watch, looked up at the sky, and moved hurriedly away, as if he had just then reminded himself of an appointment, and of rain.

Kirsty sighed. She had taken the part-time job in the gallery because she felt that it was so much more interesting than the usual sort of job offered to students. Most people in her year – or at least most of those who did part-time work – were employed in bars or cafés. They might have considered it interesting to be a barista, but she did not. They were hard-worked and had no time to chat – she had heard that from a friend who worked an early shift at a coffee bar on South Clerk Street. Bars were no better, indeed were worse; there one had to contend with the flirting of middle-aged men. What made them think that somebody like her would find them even remotely attractive? It defied belief – it really did.

No, working in a gallery would be infinitely more exciting and a much more glamorous thing to report to others. "Actually, I have a job in an art gallery," she said to one of her friends. And her friend, who occasionally worked as a waitress in a lowly Italian restaurant on Lothian Road, looked suitably impressed.

"You must meet some interesting people there," said the friend wistfully. There was nobody of any interest to be encountered on Lothian Road, she had decided.

"Of course you do," said Kirsty airily. It was a lie, but most lies can be airily tossed off. Or perhaps it was not so much a lie as a statement that was not yet true in the strictest sense, but that was teleologically so. There were probably interesting people to meet, but she had not yet encountered any of them. So far, she had met only a few rather fusty clients of the gallery – rich people with nothing better to do than to buy paintings; and none of these were young men, who were the desired class of person with whom Kirsty wished to rub shoulders.

There was Matthew, of course, but he hardly counted as interesting. First of all, he was married, and only recently so, and then even if he had been available he was so . . . She struggled to find the right word to describe Matthew – so domestic? Or beige? Beige was a good word, and its application to Matthew was particularly appropriate because of the colour of the sweater that he wore. Kirsty had complimented him on it – another lie – and Matthew had explained about distressed oatmeal and how that was the colour that he had read was being taken very seriously by menswear designers. And then there were those crushed-strawberry cords of his . . .

Matthew warmed to the theme. "Denim's finished," he said. "Very yesterday."

Kirsty smiled. It was very yesterday to use the expression very yesterday, but poor Matthew could hardly be expected to know that. And denim was not finished. Everybody wore it. All the guys, as she put it; all of them; and they look so cute in denim, she thought, and out of it too, now that she came to think of it. Wicked, she whispered to herself. Wicked!

"Oh well," she said. "It's all about what makes you feel comfortable. That's what clothes are for, aren't they? To be comfortable in."

Matthew agreed, but he doubted very much that this was Kirsty's own philosophy of dress. One only had to look at her shoes, with their narrow, pointed toes, to see that if she believed in comfort this did not extend to her feet; nor, it had to be admitted, to her midriff, which was exposed to the elements and must have been cold, even in the summer weather, when the wind came from the wrong direction, which in Edinburgh was from the north, the south, the east, or the west. And that was not the end of her stomach's suffering; her jeans were extremely tight and one could see how they pinched the skin when she sat down. They were very affectionate, of course, hugging the contours of her hips and elsewhere – as Matthew politely put it.

He wondered whether she had put on weight and had been unable to buy a new wardrobe to cope with increased girth. Many students were extremely hard-up and presumably had to economise on clothing, but Matthew sensed that Kirsty's garb reflected fashion rather than financial considerations. That was not an entirely bad thing. It was better, in general, from the gallery's point of view to have a fashionable assistant rather than one who was a frump.

When Matthew returned to the gallery that morning, he found her sitting at his desk paging through a catalogue from one of the London auction houses.

"Enjoy your coffee?" she asked, looking up from the catalogue.

"Same as usual," said Matthew. "And what happened in my absence? Sell anything?" He knew what the answer was, and waited for her to reply. Kirsty, however, merely gestured to the cover of the catalogue.

"You seen this?"

Matthew glanced over her shoulder. He wished that she would not sit in his chair so often, but he had lacked the courage to confront her about it. He would just have to try to get into the chair before she could sit in it, and then he could guard it for the rest of the day.

"Impressionist and Postimpressionist," said Kirsty. "And not as expensive as you imagine."

"But expensive enough," said Matthew cautiously.

Kirsty looked up at him and smiled. "To make money you have to spend money," she said.

Matthew said nothing. The catalogue was open at a Vuillard picture of a woman sitting on a sofa.

"That's a lovely painting," Matthew said. "So peaceful. I love Vuillard."

Kirsty seemed pleased with this response. "We could buy it, you know. It's coming up next week in London. We could buy it and then resell it here."

Matthew frowned. "I don't go in for those really expensive paintings," he said.

Kirsty smiled again. "That could change, you know. Come on, Matthew, let's get things going round here."

Matthew looked at the estimate: eighty to one hundred thousand pounds. He felt flushed, as if he had been given some sort of challenge; or it could have been the effect of Kirsty's jeans. They are so tight, he thought.

For reasons which he could not quite understand, Bertie had been allowed by his mother to remain a member of the First Morningside Cub Scout Pack. His original assumption had been that his father, who had supported his membership, would be defeated by his mother, who was vigorously opposed to what she described as a "junior paramilitary organisation of dubious pedigree." His father was usually defeated – on everything – but on this issue his view had somehow prevailed, with the result that Bertie was allowed to continue his Friday night trips to the Episcopal Church Hall at Holy Corner. There the pack met under the encouraging but watchful eye of Rosemary Gold, cub mistress and Akela.

There were numerous grounds upon which Irene objected to the cub scouts, but at the root of her position was a strong antipathy towards the founder of the movement, Robert Baden-Powell. "What a ridiculous man," she said, when she found Bertie reading an account of the original scout's life. "Look at his stupid shorts. One has to be deeply suspicious of a man who feels the need to dress up like that. How absurd."

Bertie studied the picture of Baden-Powell in his Chief Scout uniform. He thought that the uniform looked rather nice; in fact, Bertie rather liked uniforms and unusual outfits of any sort and would have loved to have had one himself. Uniforms were frowned upon at the Steiner School that he attended, but Bertie would have willingly worn one, particularly if it was anything like the Watson's uniform, with its plum-coloured blazer. And then there was the uniform worn by the pupils of Daniel Stewart's, who sported bright-red socks; or the kilts worn by boys at some of the other schools. Bertie would have liked to have worn a kilt, even if he were to be denied everything else, but again he discovered that his mother did not approve.

"Kilts are reactionary," said Irene. "I don't expect you to understand completely, as I do know that there are lots of people who wear them. But you must never assume that something is right just because lots of people do it. You do understand that, don't you, Bertie?"

Bertie pursed his lips. "But some very important people wear kilts, Mummy," he protested. "Look at the First Minister. He wears a kilt. I saw a picture of him in *The Scotsman*. I saw it with my own eyes."

"One would hardly see with any other eyes," said Irene drily. "And as for *The Scotsman*, that newspaper is rather inclined to encourage that sort of thing, if you ask me."

Bertie looked puzzled. "What sort of thing, Mummy?"

"Oh, all this business of kilts and the like," said Irene. "It's sentimental nonsense. If you go to the real heart of Scotland, Bertie, to the factories where people make things, then you don't see kilts, I assure you."

Bertie was intrigued. He was conscious of the fact that he was Scottish, but he was not quite sure what that meant. Did it merely mean that he had been born in Scotland – did that make you Scottish? Or was it something else? And as for these factories, they sounded intriguing, but where were they? "Where are these factories, Mummy? Have you ever been to them?"

Irene did not answer for a moment. "They're in Glasgow, Bertie. But that's neither here nor there. The point is that dressing up in kilts hardly solves the problems of the day, does it? Anybody can put on a kilt, but that changes nothing, does it?"

Bertie wanted to say, maybe they feel better in a kilt, but something in his mother's expression told him that this would not be helpful. He would wear a kilt when he was eighteen, he decided. His mother would not be able to stop him then, and anyway, he would be living in Glasgow by then. He would move to Glasgow on the day after his eighteenth birthday. He would stay in Edinburgh on the actual birthday, to lull his mother into a false sense of security, but on the very next day he would move to Glasgow. He would learn how to speak Glaswegian – he would buy a book to help him do that – and he would only come back to Edinburgh once a year, or once every other year perhaps. That all lay ahead.

Uniforms were anathema to Irene, but her objections to the cub scouts went deeper than that. These had not been expressed to Bertie – other than in a rather vague, disapproving way – but had been articulated very clearly to Stuart.

"Your insistence that Bertie should be allowed to continue with this scouting nonsense is really very unhelpful," she had said to her husband. "You know my feelings on the matter, and yet you went and told him that it was all right. Well, it's not all right, Stuart. It really isn't."

Stuart looked out of the window. The matter had been raised in the kitchen, where he and Irene were sitting with a glass of wine while they waited for a pot of potatoes to boil. Bertie was in his room, practising his saxophone.

"But he loves it," said Stuart. "You've seen his face when he gets ready on Fridays. He obviously has a whale of a time."

Stuart continued to gaze out of the window. In the evening sky above the city, the sun had touched a bank of high cumulus with reddish-gold; behind that, the thin white line of a jet's vapour trail, heading west, high over Scotland. Stuart imagined the people in the jet, in their tube of metal, hurtling through the attenuated air at thirty thousand feet. He imagined the pilots, sitting in front of their glowing instruments, thinking the thoughts that pilots think. What a fine career it must be; one would see one's wife so infrequently – three days out of seven, perhaps. Or if one were on long-haul duty, perhaps even a whole week might go past before one saw her. That was if one was a man, he corrected himself quickly. There were women pilots, of course, and they would see their husbands – or their partners, Stuart again corrected himself – equally infrequently. Indeed, if two pilots married, or entered into a civil partnership – Stuart corrected himself yet again – then they might never see one another at all. It would all be a question of rotas and their adjustment; and surely the airlines would be sympathetic to a request to arrange duties in such a way that one never had to see one's wife. Surely they would understand . . .

"Stuart? Are you with me here? Or are you in one of your dissociative states?"

Stuart shook his head. "I'm listening," he said.

"I was saying that it's a matter of real regret that you interfered over this scouting issue."

Stuart frowned. "Interfered?"

"Yes."

He looked at her. When I'm fifty, he thought, I'm going to go and live in Glasgow. By myself. On my fiftieth birthday. On the very day.

## 23. *The Insouciance of Tofu*

That Friday evening, Bertie was ready for cub scouts at least half an hour before he was due to travel up to Holy Corner on the 23 bus. They were going to play games that evening; Akela had promised that, and Bertie was excited. He would have liked to play games more often, perhaps even at home, but it seemed that there was little time for such things, what with yoga sessions in Stockbridge, his psychotherapy with Dr. St. Clair, Italian conversazione with his mother, and his saxophone lessons with Mr. Morrison. He had asked his mother whether he could give up at least some of these things, but she had been unwilling.

"But you love all the things that Mummy plans for you, Bertie!" she replied. "All of them. You have such fun, and you'll thank me,

Bertie, when you're a big boy. You'll thank Mummy for making . . . helping you to do all these things."

Bertie did not think that he would, but his natural politeness prevented him from saying it. He also knew that there was no point in arguing. His mother was so sure of everything; other people's parents, Bertie had noticed, seemed to be less certain about things. Hiawatha, for example, had told him that his parents could make their minds up about nothing, and were even uncertain as to whether or not to get up in the morning. "Sometimes my mother lies in bed all day," he said. "You wouldn't believe it, Bertie, but it's true. She doesn't get up. She lies there all day, drinking cups of tea and smoking. Not ordinary tobacco. Some health stuff she likes."

Bertie thought for a moment. He was glad that he was not Hiawatha – who had other problems – but he wondered if his own mother could be persuaded to stay in bed longer. If she did, then he could perhaps go outside and see if there were any boys to play with in Drummond Square Gardens. He had seen a group of boys there once, throwing sticks at each other, and had longed to join them. But his mother had forbidden him, and he had only been able to look on wistfully.

If Bertie had his way, the first thing he would have got rid of was yoga. The class that he attended, Yoga for Tots, had, to begin with, an insulting name. Bertie was not the oldest member of this class – there were one or two children coming up to their eighth birthday – but he still felt that it was inappropriate for him to be attending something that professed itself to be for tots.

"I fully understand, Bertie," said his mother. "I've spoken to Mrs. Naidu about the name, but she says that it's not intended to be insulting. The purpose of calling it Yoga for Tots is to demonstrate that you're never too young to begin yoga. She said that we are all children, anyway, in the eyes of Krishna. And I can see what she means, can't you?"

"No," said Bertie. He had heard Mrs. Naidu refer to Krishna

from time to time, but he had never found out exactly who he was. Now, when he asked his mother, she was uncharacteristically vague. "Krishna's a concept, Bertie. Not a real person. Religious people often give names to feelings they have about things. Mummy, as you know, rather sides with Professor Dawkins on these things. But there we are. I'm sure that Mrs. Naidu knows in her own head what she's talking about."

Bertie had left the matter at that; perhaps Professor Dawkins was a concept too, and Melanie Klein as well. He decided to try a different tack. "Anyway, Mummy, I think that some people in the class are too young. What about that little boy who got himself all tied up in a knot and nobody knew how to untie him? He was only three, wasn't he?"

"That was an unfortunate incident," said Irene. "But it was exceptional."

"Is he dead, do you think?" asked Bertie.

Irene laughed. "Oh, Bertie, don't be ridiculous. Of course he's not dead. He would have been perfectly all right. He just got a bit stuck. We can all get a bit stuck now and then."

And it was the same with psychotherapy. Bertie had suggested to his mother that he might give up his weekly psychotherapy session with Dr. St. Clair. "It would save a lot of money," he pointed out. "And just think, Mummy, we could go to Valvona & Crolla and spend it. Or you could spend it all yourself – I wouldn't mind."

Irene laughed. "But that's not the point, Bertie. It's not the money – it's the benefit that you're getting from seeing nice Dr. St. Clair. He's helping you a lot, you know. He's helping to make sure that you make the right decisions. He's helping you to under-stand things – to grow up without neuroses. That's what that's all about, Bertie." She paused. "And you're a lucky little boy to have this opportunity. There are quite a few young people who could do with the help of somebody like Dr. St. Clair but who aren't getting it."

"Such as?" asked Bertie.

"Well, Tofu, for one. There's a young man who needs a bit of help to control his aggressive urges."

Bertie had to agree; not that he could say it. He did not think, though, that Dr. St. Clair would be a match for Tofu, who was robustly defiant of any authority, the one quality of his that Bertie secretly admired, of course. If Bertie had been Tofu, then his mother would not be able to push him around quite so much, he thought. Tofu would never agree to go to yoga and would resolutely refuse to play the saxophone or to speak Italian. The saxophone he derided by making a vulgar noise by putting the back of his hand to his mouth and blowing loudly.

"That's what you sound like on the saxophone, Bertie," he crowed. "Recognise the sound?" And when the subject of Italian had come up, "Macaroni" was what he said, adding, "Spaghetti! Hah!"

Bertie had tried to put hah! at the end of his sentences, as Tofu did, but he found that it did not sound quite the same in his mouth; there was none of the insouciance that Tofu managed so easily and with such apparently effortless insolence. It did not do to say "Yes, Mummy, hah!" – the hah lost all its effect, somehow.

Tofu was a member of Bertie's cub scout pack too, as was his archenemy, Olive. And that was difficult. Indeed, Tofu had already spoken to Bertie about that evening's meeting.

"There's going to be trouble, Bertie," he said. "I can feel it coming." Then he added, "Hah!"

## 24. Some Sophisticated Colours

They were marshalled in their sixes – the red six, the violet six, the ochre six, and so on. Not many cub scout packs had an ochre six or even a violet six – at least not many outside Edinburgh;

most packs went in for primary colours for their six names, but this was Edinburgh, after all, and Morningside too, and more sophisticated colours were permissible. Bertie was in the red six, along with Tofu,' Olive, and Ranald Braveheart Macpherson, a small boy with spindly legs, who stood in awe of Tofu and, to a slightly lesser extent, of Olive.

"We're going to have a lot of fun this evening," said Rosemary Gold, clapping her hands to get everybody's attention. "And we have two new members. Yes, two!"

She turned to a boy and a girl standing awkwardly beside her. "This is Fergus," she said, pointing to the boy. "And this is Chloë. Fergus will be in the ochre six, and Chloë will be in the reds. Isn't that nice now?"

Tofu, standing beside Bertie, let out a groan, followed by a mumbled comment.

"Did you say something, Tofu?" asked Mrs. Gold. "Did I hear you say welcome? That's what I heard, I'm sure."

Olive raised her hand. "He didn't, Akela," she said. "He made a noise like this. Then he said: 'Not another girl!' That's what he said."

Tofu glowered at Olive before turning to face the cub mistress. His face, like his flat denial, was filled with the innocence of the falsely accused. "I didn't say anything," he protested. "Did I, Bertie?"

Olive looked at Bertie. "You tell her, Bertie," she whispered. "And don't lie. You know what happens if you lie. Your pants go on fire."

Bertie swallowed hard. Unlike Olive, who enjoyed denouncing wrongdoing, he did not like to inform. But nor did he like to lie. It was not that he feared the consequences threatened by Olive – that was an empty threat, as Bertie had heard Tofu lie regularly and had never seen him engulfed in flames below the belt. When he had pointed this out to Olive, though, she had dismissed his objection with the observation that Tofu wore special flame-proof pants – that was well known. "They call them fibbers' trousers," she said knowledgeably. "They're more expensive, but they stop your pants going on fire when you lie. Tofu's father buys them on the internet because he knows that Tofu can't wear ordinary pants because of all the fibs he tells. I'm surprised you didn't know that, Bertie – he's meant to be your friend."

"We don't need to involve Bertie in this, Tofu," said Rosemary Gold. "All I have to say is this – Chloë is very welcome, and we're all thrilled to have her in the pack, aren't we, Tofu?"

Tofu looked down at the floor. "Yes, Akela."

"He's crossing his fingers," shouted Olive. "I saw him, Akela! He crossed his fingers when he said that. That means he doesn't mean what he says."

Rosemary Gold chose, quite wisely, to ignore this. For his part, Bertie tried to be helpful. "She can stand next to me, Akela," he offered.

"Well, isn't that nice?" said Mrs. Gold, pushing Chloë towards her new six. "You'll be very happy in the reds, Chloë. Bertie, at least, is a very kind boy."

The new recruits now integrated, it was time for the evening's business to begin in earnest. "Does anybody know what this is?" said Rosemary Gold, holding up a round metal object.

"A compass," called out Bertie.

Mrs. Gold nodded. "Indeed it is. And what does a compass do? Does anybody know?"

Bertie, of course, knew, but did not wish to claim all the limelight. So he was silent.

"It tells us something, doesn't it?" prompted Rosemary Gold. "What does it tell us, boys and girls?"

Bertie looked about him, and realised that he would have to speak. "It depends on what sort of compass it is," he ventured. "A magnetic compass tells us where north and south are."

"Exactly," said Rosemary Gold. "And I don't think there are any other sorts, are there, Bertie?"

"There's a moral compass," said Bertie. "I haven't seen one ever, but I've read about it in the newspaper. The Prime Minister says he's got one."

Rosemary Gold suppressed a smile. "Well now, Bertie," she said. "I believe you're right. But we've never really seen a picture of the Prime Minister's moral compass, have we?" She paused. "Perhaps it's in Kirkcaldy. And I'm not sure if he's the only one who's got one. Maybe we've all got a moral compass tucked away inside us, you know." She looked at Tofu as she spoke – she could not help it; that was where her gaze went. "But enough of that, boys and girls! Let's get on with our exciting little compass game. It's called North by North-East."

The rules of the game were carefully explained. Everyone was to have a turn at holding the compass and then looking in a particular direction. They were then to identify one object that lay along that bearing. Then the compass was passed to another, a bearing would be called out, and the children had to rush in the direction of whatever object had been associated with that direction. The object would be touched, and the one who touched it first would have the opportunity to hold the compass when the next set of objects was identified.

It was a thrilling game, played with exuberance. At the end of the session, when minor wounds had been dressed and Rosemary Gold had adjudicated on Olive's complaint that Tofu had pulled her hair and spat at her in the rush to touch a chair at the end of the hall, the compass was put away and the children were all given a sealed envelope to take back to their parents.

"This is a very important letter," explained Rosemary Gold. "It's about an exciting thing that we're planning for you and that I think you're going to enjoy very much indeed! But we won't talk about it just yet, as it's often better to keep some things until nearer the time. It's a bit like saving the best bit of cake until later."

The envelopes were handed out to the children and the meeting came to an end with the singing of a cub scout song, "Always share the campfire with the ones who are behind you." Bertie glanced at his envelope as he sang. There was a label stuck on it which said, *To the parent or guardian.* Bertie looked up at the ceiling. It did not say which parent the letter was to be given to, which meant, he felt, that he had a choice. It would be safer, perhaps, to give it to his father, as he was more likely to say yes to whatever proposal the letter contained. But it would be even safer, he thought, to read the letter before he passed it on at all. There was nothing on the envelope to say that one could not open it before passing it on to the parent or guardian, and Bertie had once read somewhere that what was not forbidden was permissible. You can do what you like unless you can't, he thought. It was the sort of thing that a moral compass would say, perhaps.

## 25. *100 Things for a Boy to Do: Part 1*

Bertie was collected at the end of the cub scout meeting by his father and together they travelled back to Dundas Street on the top deck of the bus.

"Another exciting evening, Bertie?" asked Stuart.

Bertie nodded.

Stuart smiled encouragingly at his son. "And did anything happen?"

This was the question that Bertie had been dreading. The usual answer of most children to such a question from a parent is that nothing happened – the lives of children, by self-report, are barren and empty, quite devoid of incident. Nothing happens, nobody says anything, and indeed nobody is present at any function they attend. By the same rule of infantile omertà, nothing is learned at school, where the resolute silence of the classroom is never punctuated by any observation on anything. By contrast, the telephone conversations of children – among themselves – reveal lives crowded with incident, with high drama and intrigue, with passions and plots.

Bertie was not like this. He usually gave a reasonably full account of what happened, censoring only those lurid details that he thought would be an undue shock to parental ears, particularly those of his mother. Thus he had never told his mother about Tofu's habit of spitting at others, nor of the small-scale numbers racket that his friend ran in the playground at school. Bertie felt outrage over that, because he knew that it was essentially criminal: Tofu more or less bullied everybody to put part of their pocket money into a pool, the winner taking the entire proceeds. All the participants had to pick a number between one and fifteen – there were fifteen members of Bertie's class – and then Tofu would announce which number won that week. The problem, though, was that it was Tofu who picked the winning number, and he only revealed it after everybody had chosen their number.

"You should write the winning number on a piece of paper before we choose," Pansy had suggested. "That would be much fairer."

Tofu smiled. "Not possible," he said.

"And you've won three out of the last six times," pointed out Hiawatha.

"I'm really lucky," said Tofu.

Bertie had said nothing about this to his parents, who would not have understood it, nor possibly even believed it. But now, faced with this direct question from his father as to what happened, he vacillated as to whether to mention the letter at this stage. He had decided that he would read it first, and, if necessary, lose it if its contents were in any way likely to threaten his continued membership in the cub scouts. It could be a letter about some new activity of which his mother disapproved, and that might mean the end of his cub scout career; one could never tell with her.

He decided that the best thing to do in relation to his father's question was to pretend not to have heard it. But Stuart persisted. "I said, did anything happen, Bertie? Anything interesting?"

Bertie told his father about the compass game, but resolutely omitted to say anything about the letter. He felt it in his pocket, as bulky and as obvious as any incriminating object tends to be, and when they got back to Scotland Street he rushed into his room. Taking the letter from his pocket, he held it up against the light of his reading lamp. Through the thin paper of the envelope he saw a folded piece of paper, but that was all; he could make out that there was something printed or written on the paper, but he could not decipher what it was.

Bertie put the envelope down and closed the door of his room. If he had had a lock, he would have locked it, but his requests for a lock had been turned down by his mother.

"A lock, Bertie?" she said. "Whatever would you want a lock for?"

Bertie thought quickly. It was no use telling her that it was to lock her out; that would not have gone down well. "Security," he said quickly. "If a burglar climbed down the chimney, then he wouldn't be able to steal my things."

Irene raised an eyebrow. "Oh, I see. But it would be all right for him to steal my things, would it? Or Daddy's? Or even little Ulysses's things?" She paused. "But not yours. What sort of attitude is that, Bertie?"

Bertie could see that he was being misconstrued – again. "But I didn't mean that, Mummy!" he protested. "You and Daddy have a lock on your door, so you could stop him taking your things."

Irene gave Bertie a hug. He felt himself being enveloped; it was like drowning, he thought. "You shouldn't want to lock Mummy out," she said. "Boys should have no secrets from their mummies, Bertie! A boy's best friend is his mummy – not only when he's a boy, like you, but for the rest of his life too."

Bertie looked dismayed. Could this possibly be true? If it were, the future certainly looked bleak.

"Of course, you can have other friends," conceded Irene. "Olive, for example. She's a nice little girl, isn't she? And you appear to be very friendly with her, don't you?"

"No," said Bertie. "I hate her, Mummy."

"No, you don't," said Irene quickly. "Don't talk such nonsense, Bertie, even as a joke. How can you hate Olive? She's lively and engaging. She's fun. No, you don't hate her, Bertie."

Bertie wanted to say: how do you know, Mummy? But he could not say that. In fact, he could say nothing, because anything he said would be immediately refuted by his mother, and it was no good arguing with her. She was like the weather – always there; and to resist her was like trying to resist the weather itself. There was just no point.

Now, trying to make out what was in this letter from Akela, he remembered something that he had read in that book he had borrowed from the library, *100 Things for a Boy to Do: Part 1*. There had been a feature in that book called "Tips for Spies," and it purported to be written by somebody called the Grand Spymaster, First Class.

"If you need to read an intercepted letter," the article ran, "don't slit the envelope open – the recipient will be very suspicious. Rather, wait until the letter is passed on to you to forward to another person. Then, making sure that you are not seen by the first person, you should gently steam open the flap. The contents photographed, the letter can then be re-sealed, and the information passed on to headquarters."

Gently steam open the flap. Well, Bertie had no steam in the room, but he did have his breath, which was, he believed, warm and moist.

### 26. *100 Things for a Boy to Do: Part 2*

Bertie drew in his breath, held it for as long as he could – to warm it up – and then exhaled across the flap of the envelope. He was surprised at how much air his lungs contained and at how long it took him to expel it. His surprise, though, was matched by his disappointment when he discovered that the flap seemed as obstinately stuck down at the end of this exercise as it had been at the beginning. He drew in another breath, held it, and then breathed out again, this time placing his lips so close to the paper that they were virtually touching it. Once again, although the envelope felt slightly moist at the end of the exercise, it still remained firmly sealed.

Bertie tried to remember the pages from *100 Things for a Boy to Do: Part 1*. The "Tips for Spies" section had featured a line drawing of a spy opening a letter, and he now tried to remember exactly what the illustration had shown. There had been a kettle – he remembered that clearly enough – and there had been a cloud of steam. But he could not remember where the letter had been placed and exactly how the flap had been opened. Was it necessary to use a knife? Bertie ached for a Swiss Army penknife, but his mother had forbidden him to have one, and so he would have to find a knife in the kitchen. Well, there were plenty of knives there, even if none of them was as useful, or as exciting, as a Swiss Army knife.

Bertie had noticed that there seemed to be some sort of campaign about boys not being allowed to have pocket knives. Mr. Baden-Powell had suggested that every boy should be equipped with a pocket knife, and had said as much in the old copy of *Scouting for Boys* that Bertie had managed to obtain and had hidden under his mattress. But now he had read in the newspaper that the government itself was saying that scouts should not be allowed to carry knives. This was upsetting for a number of reasons. Not only did it mean that scouts would be unable to do the sorts of things that they needed to do – whittle sticks, take stones out of horses' hooves, or cut pieces of string to the desired length – but it also was a sign that the government was beginning to side with his mother.

Bertie had always believed that the government, if it were to hear of his difficulties, would side with him – after all, he had read that there was something called the Human Rights Act which he had always hoped might refer, even if only indirectly, to the position of boys whose mothers were . . . well, whose mothers had never heard of the European Convention on Human Rights. But now it seemed that the government had come round to his mother's position, which made the world rather less comfortable from his perspective. Freedom – that tiny square of blue sky – could only be glimpsed with difficulty in Bertie's world; now it seemed at once smaller, more clouded, and more distant.

Bertie decided that he would have no alternative but to use the kettle to steam open the letter. Poking his head out of the door to check that there was no sign of his parents, he crept along the corridor that led to the kitchen. When he saw that his mother was not there, he quickly put on the kettle and waited for the water to boil. This happened quickly, and there was soon an obliging cloud of steam issuing from the spout. It was into this that Bertie inserted the letter, and he watched with pleasure as the flap wilted and opened – exactly as had been predicted in *100 Things for a Boy to Do: Part 1*.

Back in his room, Bertie extracted Akela's letter from the damp envelope and sat down on his bed to read it.

Dear Parent or Guardian,

It is at this stage in the summer term that we begin to think of plans for the holidays. Here at the First Morningside Cub Scout Pack we have been putting our heads together to think of what we can do for the boys and girls during the summer break. I had planned to see whether we could manage a three-day camp at Bonaly some time in August, but unfortunately that just does not look possible for one reason or another. However, I am happy to report that a cancellation has opened up a weekend slot in three weeks' time and I have taken the plunge and booked the facilities for that weekend. We shall therefore be offering everybody in the pack a two-night camp (Friday evening to Sunday afternoon) at Bonaly. We shall spend the night under canvas, and all catering will be done on open fires (weather permitting!)

Bertie read this with a growing sense of excitement. He had never been camping before and the prospect of spending the night under canvas was profoundly thrilling. And their food would be cooked over fires, which they might be allowed to make themselves by rubbing sticks together, as Mr. Baden-Powell had demonstrated in *Scouting for Boys*. He could almost smell the sausages already – and the marshmallows that they could put on sticks and toast on those same open fires. With racing pulse he read on.

As you can imagine, with so many children at the camp we shall require adult helpers. It is for this reason that I am writing to ask you (1) whether you wish your child to attend the camp, and (2) whether you are prepared to come along yourself as a helper for the weekend. If you can see your way to doing that, I am sure that you will have a good time, and I hasten to point out that adult helpers will not be required to sleep under canvas but will be accommodated in the very pleasant bunkhouse rooms which the Association maintains at the Bonaly site.

Bertie let the letter drop to the floor. His hands were shaking. He closed his eyes, in sorrow, in resignation. His mother would want to come as a helper – of course she would.

## 27. *Forgery Exposed*

When Bertie returned to the kitchen in response to his mother's call that supper was ready, he was holding the newly re-sealed envelope in trembling hands. Noticing, with relief, that his father was in the room, already seated at the table, he approached him shyly and handed over the letter.

"It says this is for my parent or guardian," he muttered. "I think that's you, isn't it, Daddy?"

Irene looked up sharply. "And me, Bertie," she said. "In fact, when a letter is addressed to the parent or guardian, it usually means that it's for the mummy. Just for future reference."

Stuart threw her a glance. "Not always," he said, mildly. "Sometimes, perhaps, but not always."

Irene, who had been stirring a pot of soup, put down her spoon and crossed the room to her husband's side. Reaching out, she took the still-unopened letter from his hands. Stuart raised an eyebrow, but did nothing.

Bertie watched, his heart sinking. "I don't think it's important," he said quickly. "Maybe Daddy can read it later." It was all he could say; he knew that there was little point, though, in trying to forfend what now seemed inevitable.

Irene picked up a table knife and slit open the envelope. "Now let's see what this is all about," she said.

Bertie sat down at the table. He put his hands about his head, but watched his mother between his fingers. Her expression, he noted, was changing, from one of mild irritation to one of puzzlement. He closed his eyes; he could not bear to see his efforts at forgery so publicly uncovered.

Bertie had changed the terms of the letter. Using the treasured fountain pen that had been sent to him by a distant relative on his last birthday (his sixth), he had carefully changed the text of Akela's letter by the insertion of a certain number of negatives and by making a number of other subtle changes.

The effect was not perfect – he would have been the first to admit that – but he had hoped that in the dim conditions of the kitchen he might get away with it. The letter, therefore, now read: "As you can imagine, with so many children at the camp we shall not require adult helpers. It is for this reason that I am writing to ask you (1) whether you wish your child to attend the camp, and (2) whether you are prepared to come along yourself as a helper stay at home for the weekend. If you can see your way to doing that, I am sure that you will have a good time, and I hasten to point out that adult helpers will not be required to sleep under canvas but will not be accommodated in the very unpleasant bunkhouse rooms which the Association maintains at the Bonaly site."

Irene read the letter, and then re-read it. She smiled. "A charming letter from that Akela woman," she said. "Do read it, Stuart."

Stuart took the piece of paper from his wife and perused it quickly. He looked at Bertie, who was still hiding his head in his hands, and then he gave Irene an imploring look.

"Bertie," said Irene. "This is a very interesting letter from Akela. Why did you change it, darling? Don't you want to go to cub scout camp?"

Bertie did not move. From behind his clasped hands came a little voice. "I do want to go."

"Well that's perfectly all right," said Irene. "Mummy may not be wildly keen on the cub scouts but I understand that you want to go off with your friends. With Olive and the others."

"Not her," said Bertie. But he spoke too quietly and neither parent heard him.

"Of course it will be fun for you," Irene went on. "But all this business about not wanting the mummies and daddies to be helpers – that's not what Akela really said, is it?"

Bertie said nothing.

"And it would be fun for the mummies too, wouldn't it?" she continued. "I can't remember when I last went camping. Can you, Stuart?"

Stuart shook his head. He had given Irene a warning glance, but she appeared not to have noticed.

"We'll have such fun," said Irene brightly. "I think I've got a sleeping bag somewhere in that cupboard in the spare room. And we'll probably find one for you too."

Bertie took his hands away from his face. Rising to his feet, he rushed out of the room and down the corridor, back to his room.

"Funny little thing," said Irene to Stuart. "What can possibly have got into his mind?"

Stuart looked up at the ceiling. "He doesn't want you to go," he said evenly. "Bertie doesn't want you to go as a helper. I think he wants to get away from . . . from us for a day or two."

Irene looked surprised. "Surely not."

"No, I think he does."

"Well, I disagree. All boys sometimes feel the occasional tinge of embarrassment over their parents, but they get over it. And Melanie Klein . . ."

"I don't see what she's got to do with this," said Stuart.

"But, Stuart, can't you see? What we're witnessing here is a token rejection of parental involvement by a child who really needs his parents to support him but fears that they will not answer his call. He therefore feels anxiety and needs to test the depth of parental commitment by appearing not to want parental involvement. Can't you see that?"

Stuart shook his head. "No."

"Well, I assure you – that's what's going on. And as far as I'm concerned, I would see myself as failing little Bertie if I did not go to Bonaly as a helper."

Stuart bit his lip. "Irene, sometimes I wonder . . ."

Irene glared at him, and Stuart got up from the table. "Where are you going?"

He pointed to Bertie's door at the end of the corridor. "To have a word with my son."

He knocked on the door but did not wait for a reply. Going in, he found the little boy stretched out on his bed, his head buried in the pillow.

"Cheer up, old chap," Stuart whispered. "And don't be too cross with Mummy. She's just trying to help – she really is. And she loves you very much, you know. You do know that, don't you?"

Bertie sniffed. "Yes," he said. "I know."

"Let me tell you something," said Stuart, sitting down next to Bertie on the bed. "I'm going to take you fishing in the Pentlands. Just you and me. Would you like that?"

"When?" asked Bertie.

"Next weekend," said Stuart. "We'll go on Saturday. But one little word of advice. Don't tell Mummy we're going to catch fish. I think we'll tell her we're going to look at them. Understand?"

Bertie understood perfectly.


## 28. *A Game of Bridge*

Bruce Anderson enjoyed going to the gym. For years he had belonged to a health club in Fountainbridge; now he had "traded up," as he put it, to a gym in the Sheraton Hotel in Lothian Road where, in addition to working out on the various exercise machines, he could swim in the pool and use the various saunas and Turkish baths on offer.

Bruce liked Turkish baths; he liked sitting on the tiled benches, unclad apart from a pair of swimming trunks and a towel wrapped around his waist. He liked to flex the muscles that he had just put through their paces in the gym below, feeling the satisfactory ripple of tendon and muscle under his gently perspiring skin. He liked it when others in the Turkish bath, although mostly strangers, watched this display from the corner of their eye; the women in frank admiration, the men in barely concealed envy. He felt like saying to some of the men, "You could have a body like mine, you know, if you only spent more time on the rowing machine." But one could not say that; in fact, there was a strict etiquette about not talking in such circumstances; one sweated away in silence.

Bruce preferred to go to the gym by himself, and would usually call in for an hour or so each evening after he had finished work in the offices of Macaulay Holmes Richardson Black or, as Bruce called the firm, Mac and Co. After that, he would go to pick up Lizzie from her parents' home in the Braids and take her out for a meal somewhere, or they would go to a restaurant or bar. Then they would go back to Bruce's shared flat for coffee and to listen to music. That was what they did.

Recently, however, the routine had been disturbed by a new feature of their lives that Lizzie had insisted on introducing. She had joined a bridge class attended by her friend Diane, and had suggested that Bruce should join her. He had viewed the invitation with suspicion.

"Where is it?" he asked.

"It's in a room in the university," she said. "Buccleuch Place. They rent it out cheaply as a sort of community service."

Bruce was silent. Community service? Cheap university rooms? This was not, as he put it, "part of the plan."

"Bridge," he said doubtfully.

"Yes, bridge. Have you ever played it?"

Bruce shook his head. "My parents used to play," he said. "In Crieff." There was a lot of bridge played in Crieff, he thought. He drew some air in through his teeth – a habit that Lizzie had begun to notice in him; she would have to say something, she thought; but not just yet.

Bruce looked at her quizzically. "Excuse my saying this," he said, "but isn't bridge a bit old?"

Lizzie knew exactly what he meant, but would not show it. "It was invented in the nineteenth century," she said. "Lots of the rules are twentieth century, though. So, no, I wouldn't call it old. Chess is an old game. Did you mean chess?"

Bruce laughed politely. "No, I don't think you get my meaning. I meant that the people who play the game tend to be . . . well, they tend to be pretty old, don't they?"

Again Lizzie answered brightly. "Old? Not in our class. Everyone's under thirty-five, as far as I can make out. One or two are eighteen or nineteen. Students. You don't think eighteen's old, do you?"

Bruce shrugged. "When you see it on television, they've all got one foot in the grave," he said. "Seriously old. But it doesn't matter. Old people need to do something, I suppose. Keeps them off the streets."

Bruce laughed, but Lizzie did not join him. "Would you like to learn?" she said. "I'd like you to, you know. You need a bridge partner, you see, and since we're going to get married and everything, I thought it might be nice if we could go to bridge together."

Bruce looked thoughtful. "What's the big attraction?" he asked at last.

"Intellectual," said Lizzie. "It involves memory and strategy and so on. And there is so much to learn – you could spend a lifetime learning bridge."

Bruce shrugged. "If you're so keen, I could give it a try."

They had gone to their first class together that week. The instructor, a Dundonian with a central parting and horn-rimmed spectacles, had welcomed Bruce warmly and had pressed Ron Klinger's *Bridge Guide* into his hand. "This is the Bible," he said. "Think of Mr. Klinger as Moses and this guide as the Ten Commandments." He put on a deep, stentorian voice. "Thou shalt not open with less than twelve points," he intoned. "Thou shalt not communicate with thy partner other than by bidding."

Bruce stared at him blankly, and the instructor laughed nervously. "It's a useful book," he said lamely.

Lizzie dug Bruce in the ribs. "Bruce is really looking forward to learning, Arthur," she said. "Aren't you, Bruce?"

They went to their table, where Lizzie introduced the other players. "This is Carol and this . . ." she hesitated very slightly, "this is Diane."

Bruce greeted the two young women. He had never seen Carol, as far as he knew; Diane, for some reason, seemed slightly familiar. Edinburgh was not a large place, of course, and one ran into people here and there.

Diane looked at Bruce and smiled warmly. "Lizzie says that she thinks you'll be really good," she said. "She said you were good at figures."

"Yes," said Bruce. "I appreciate figures."

He raised an eyebrow suggestively, and Diane looked away. Carol did not notice. Lizzie was busy shuffling the cards.

"Right," said Diane. "This is the way it works. We play four hands to begin with. Then Arthur gives us a talk on some convention or some tactic. That takes about half an hour. Then we play a whole rubber. Then we go to the pub."

"Fine," said Bruce. "Lizzie has explained the basic rules of bidding. I'll pick up the rest as we go along."

The cards were dealt and the bidding began. Bruce opened

with an impossibly high bid, which led to a sharp telling-off from Carol. The bidding resumed and eventually Carol played to Diane's dummy. Bruce watched the cards go out and tried to remember them. For her part, Lizzie played carefully and confidently and Carol and Diane were two tricks down.

"So," said Bruce. "My first game, and we've won!"

"It's not that simple, Bruce," said Diane. She was watching him closely, and now and then exchanged a glance with Lizzie. Bruce was unaware of this. He could think of many better ways to spend an evening. Yet he had noticed that Diane's gaze was upon him rather more than necessary. Fancies me, he thought. It was what he would always have thought in such circumstances, even if, since he had turned over a new leaf, he had thought it less often. But now it was coming back, as an ancient habit will return, persistently, perversely, as a weed with a long root will come up from below no matter what is done on the surface.

## 29. Underneath the Lamplight

It was a ten-minute walk from the bridge class in Buccleuch Place to Sandy Bell's bar in Forrest Road. It was not a large group that made its way there – six in all: Bruce and Lizzie were joined by Diane and Carol, their partners at the bridge table, and then there was another couple, Alex and Frances. Alex was a Glaswegian, and, unusually for one from that gregarious and entertaining city, almost completely silent; Frances made up for this, though, with a high-pitched, penetrating laugh. Bruce noticed that her eyes stayed on him as they were introduced. Hello! he said to himself. So Frances isn't entirely satisfied with Alex! Diane noticed this too; she saw the smile play about Bruce's lips. She looked at Lizzie, but Lizzie was talking to Carol and had not noticed.

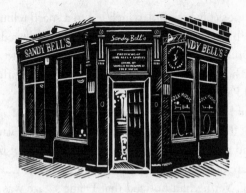

They walked through George Square. Lizzie was still engaged in the conversation with Carol that she had started as they left the bridge class and so Bruce moved to Diane's side.

"I think we've met before," he said. It was a gambit he used even when he had not met somebody, but on this occasion it was more than that. He was sure that he had seen her somewhere before.

She smiled at him. "I don't think so. I would have . . ." She did not finish what she was saying.

Bruce laughed. "You would have remembered me? Is that what you were going to say?"

Diane bit her lip. "Well, maybe. I remember faces."

"Especially some?" asked Bruce.

"Meaning?"

He shrugged. "Nothing," he said. "One remembers some people and not others."

"Maybe. But I don't think we've met. I really don't. I've heard about you, of course. When you and Lizzie got engaged. I was working down in London then and that's why we didn't meet."

"I see," said Bruce. "London. I worked there for a while. I got a bit bored and came home. Give me Edinburgh any day. London – everything's stale and used up. Even the air has been breathed twenty times before by somebody else. All sorts of people."

"But you could say that about the air anywhere, surely," she said. "Aren't all the world's molecules mixed up? I remember reading somewhere that there are fragments of Julius Caesar in every bit of dust."

"Julius Caesar?"

"Yes. We breathe in tiny bits of him – and everybody else – when we fill our lungs."

Bruce laughed. "He gets about."

Diane was silent for a moment. They were walking rather faster than the others, and she looked back towards them. "Poor Lizzie," she said. "I was worried that she wouldn't be able to concentrate this evening."

Bruce frowned. "Why? Something's wrong?"

Diane looked over her shoulder again. "I'm not sure whether I should be telling you this. Lizzie said that she didn't want you to know about it – she doesn't want you to worry."

Bruce raised an eyebrow. "Doesn't want me to worry? Worry about what?"

Diane hesitated, as if uncertain whether or not to continue. Then she said, "You won't tell her I told you? Promise?"

Bruce nodded. "Yes. I promise." He paused. "Is there something wrong with her?"

Diane shook her head. "No, there's nothing wrong with her. She's not ill. It's just that . . ."

"Go on," Bruce encouraged her.

"It's just that Lizzie has had a really horrid bit of news. She knows that it's not the end of the world, but it's still pretty hard to take."

"Her job?" prompted Bruce.

"No. But yes, it's to do with money. Yes. She used to have quite a bit, you know. But her father's had a bit of a financial disaster.

Something to do with insurance – he signed up as a name, whatever that means."

"I know what that means," said Bruce. So Todd was a name. Disaster.

"Anyway, her dad's lost a serious amount of money," Diane continued. "Big time. Lizzie said that she had to give everything back to him – she had some money, and a flat from her grandmother. But if she didn't hand it over to her dad, then he stood to lose their house. The lot. She felt she had no choice."

Bruce listened in silence. They were now passing the university union and a group of students had spilled out onto the square outside. Nineteen, thought Bruce inconsequentially. To be nineteen again, instead of twenty-something and getting this bad, bad news.

"Better to know," he muttered.

Diane heard. "Better to know? Better for you to know?"

Bruce did not reply. He seemed deep in thought.

"At least she's still got you," said Diane. "And that's what counts, isn't it?"

Bruce said nothing to this. He looked up at the sky, which was overcast and was reflecting the light of the streetlamps. He was conscious of Diane's eyes upon him, but he was unconcerned. It was no business of hers how he reacted to the news of Lizzie's misfortune. And what did she expect? That he should break into tears?

Diane knew, of course. She could tell from his expression how Bruce had reacted to this story. He was thinking; of course he was thinking. He would be wondering how he could get rid of Lizzie – poor Lizzie – because that was the reason why he had become engaged to her in the first place. Money. Now she had flushed him out, and that meant that Lizzie had been saved.

Bruce suddenly turned and looked at Diane. "I'm really sorry to hear that," he said. "I was . . ."

Diane waited. She noticed the effect of the streetlight on Bruce's profile. She caught her breath. Cupid's dart. She began to panic. Don't be ridiculous. And yet it was like a pain, an excruciating pain. I've fallen for him, she thought. No, impossible. She allowed herself to look again. How could she ignore this? How could she be indifferent to this . . . she struggled to find the word. Then it came to her: vision. He was a vision, and she was smitten.

Bruce smiled at her and bent down to whisper to her. "I know what you're thinking."

She shook her head. Impossible. Stupid, stupid girl.

"Don't fight it," whispered Bruce. "What's the point?"

"I don't know what you're talking about," she stuttered.

"Never fight it," said Bruce. "I don't."

## 30. *Trust and Revelation*

That Saturday morning, Angus Lordie called on Domenica Macdonald. It was not unusual for him to visit his friend in Scotland Street on a Saturday, although Domenica had made a point of warning him that he could not always expect to find her in. "I can't sit here waiting for you, Angus," she said. "It would be just too pathetic a spectacle. I am not one of those spinsters who waits in her flat for a man to call. Be warned."

"Of course not," said Angus hurriedly. "I know just how busy your Saturdays are. What with . . ." He tried to recall what it was that Domenica liked to do on a Saturday; was it something to do with the Farmers' Market? Or did she go to see somebody, some old trout (as he referred to her) who lived down in Stockbridge and was something to do with the Labour Party? Angus had a habit – a most annoying one, Domenica thought – of calling any woman over forty an old trout. He had not dared do this with Big Lou, of course, who was thirty-eight, or thereabout – nobody quite knew, and it was well known that people from Arbroath often looked younger than they really were. And even if he had not trouted her, she had taken him to task for this, although he had defended himself vigorously.

"You call women 'hen,' Lou. You're one to talk."

"Nothing wrong with that," said Big Lou. "It's a term of endearment."

"As is 'trout,'" said Angus.

They had left it at that.

Even if Domenica had been intending to go to the Farmers' Market or visit a woman in Stockbridge to discuss Labour Party matters, she would not be doing this on that particular Saturday as she had a very good reason to have a word with Angus. Ever since she had heard that he was included in the planned Italian trip, she had been anxious to discuss the matter with him. What she wanted to find out was the circumstances in which the invitation had been extended, and what Angus thought about it. Did he know, she wondered, that she was coming too? If he did not, then she might wait to see if he mentioned the trip; a failure to do so would indicate that Angus was hoping to slip away to Italy with Antonia without letting her know about it. That would be an unequivocally disloyal thing to do and their friendship, she feared, would surely run aground on such dishonest and duplicitous rocks. Angus was not a dishonourable man, but he was a man, after all, and men were unquestionably weak. Jezebels like Antonia – or would-be Jezebels, perhaps – would know how to exploit a man's weakness, how to turn his head by inviting him to a villa in Italy.

By the time that Angus arrived in Scotland Street that morning, Domenica had worked herself up into a considerable lather at the thought of Antonia's tactics. Angus, though, appeared breezy.

"So," he said. "Here I am. Cyril, you'll be pleased to hear, has chosen to remain on your landing, tied – ignominiously, for such an intelligent creature – to a railing. Uninvited, be it noted, in spite of having had a bath only two or three weeks ago."

Domenica tried to smile. "I'm sure that he doesn't mind too much. And I'm sure that Antonia will pay him some attention if he feels left out. She is, after all, quite willing to include him in things."

It was the first of a number of attempts to flush out some mention of the Italian trip; Cyril was included in that, as Antonia herself had revealed.

Angus appeared to ignore the remark. "He'll be all right. He knows that I'm in here and that I can't go anywhere without walking past him. Dogs are always worried that their owners will leave them."

"To go on holiday, for example," said Domenica quickly.

Angus nodded. "Maybe."

Domenica led the way into the kitchen. "Would you ever take Cyril on holiday with you?" she asked. It was an innocent question, posed casually.

"He'd like it," said Angus. "Dogs love to be involved."

"And of course now they have these pet passports, don't they?" said Domenica. "There used to be such a fuss about rabies and quarantine. Now they can have their injections and go off with their owners. France, Germany, Italy . . . The world is a dog's oyster nowadays, or bone perhaps."

Standing in the kitchen, Angus looked out of the window over the rooftops on the other side of Scotland Street. "Are you looking forward to Italy?" he asked suddenly.

For a moment Domenica said nothing. Angus turned round and smiled at her. She noticed his eyes; they were so clear, the colour one imagines to be that of the eyes of those born in high, northern places. He was smiling – wryly. "You're very transparent, you know," he said. "All this business of taking Cyril on holiday and so on. Utterly transparent!"

"I don't know what you're talking about."

"Come on, Domenica! Italy. Antonia. We both know what you're driving at. So let me set your mind at rest: yes, she asked me. And my first reaction, naturally, was that I wouldn't dream of going off with her. Not after that business of the blue Spode teacup. It would be an appallingly disloyal act. So I said no, and then she said that I could bring Cyril. I still said no, but then I thought: what if I say I shall only go if you ask Domenica? So that's what I said."

Domenica thought: you wonderful, loveable man. And there I was thinking ill of you, and all the time you were on my side.

"What did she say?"

"She looked a bit put out, but then she came round."

Domenica looked down at the floor. She felt ashamed. "I'm sorry," she said. "I thought that you and she might be . . ." She broke off.

"Us?" exclaimed Angus. "She and I? Oh, really, Domenica!"

"She's such a man-eater, you see. That Pole. That other man. That twenty-year-old, barely out of short trousers."

"Tsk, tsk!"

"*Exactement.*"

They sat down at the kitchen table. The air had been cleared; suspicions of treachery had been dispelled, and now it was time to do some concrete planning.

"We must take plenty of factor forty," said Domenica.

Angus agreed. "At the very least! Do you know that the noses of dogs can get sunburned?" He thought for a moment. "And factor forty makes a tremendous thinner for oil paints, Domenica. Did you know that?"

## 31. Pregnancy Plans

That same Saturday morning, Elspeth Harmony was still in bed at 9:30 a.m. when Matthew left for the gallery. She was not feeling well, but had not told him so, as she did not want him to make a fuss. Pregnancy, she thought, should not be something that people made such a fuss about.

"You don't need to get up," he said brightly, when he came in to kiss her goodbye before going to the gallery. "Spend the day in bed if you want. I'm sure rest is good for you."

She smiled wanly. Perhaps she should have told him that today was the day she was due to have her three-month scan at the hospital, but if she had done that, again he would have made such a song and dance about it. It was far better to get things like that over and done with, rather than to have anxious husbands getting in the way.

She knew, of course, that this was not the way most people thought. The current view was that men should be almost as involved in the pregnancy as women, going to classes with their wives or partners, discussing childbirth options, doing exercises together. She did not hold with this at all; she had no objection to the idea that Matthew would be with her at the delivery – that was perfectly reasonable – but she did not necessarily want him interfering in everything that went before that. Morning sickness was unpleasant, but did it really have to be shared with one's husband? And as for medical examinations, those, it seemed to her, should be something between the doctor and the patient, and not to be participated in by others.

She had known for six weeks now that she was pregnant. Matthew had known for almost as long, and had, as she had feared, moved rapidly from euphoria to neurosis over the whole thing. To begin with, he had tried to get her to stop drinking either tea or coffee in case the foetus was adversely affected by caffeine. Then he had removed all the shampoo from the flat after he had read somewhere that hair products contained chemicals that were dangerous for pregnant women.

"Listen, Matthew," she had eventually said. "I know that you're excited about this baby, but you really must let me go through this pregnancy on my terms. Obviously I'm going to be careful, but you can't wrap me in cotton wool – not for the next six months!"

He looked hurt. "I wasn't trying to wrap you in cotton wool. I was simply trying to . . ."

She reached out and took his hand. "Of course. Of course. You spoil me, my darling – you really do. But I'm quite robust, you know!"

"I just want our baby to be . . . to be . . ."

"Of course. And he will be. Or she. He'll be strong and healthy, just like his daddy."

Matthew grinned. He liked to be called Daddy; and it would almost definitely be the baby's first word. Mummy would be the second one, following shortly after that. Of course Edinburgh babies were sometimes surprisingly sophisticated. He had read recently of an Edinburgh baby whose first word had been olive. That was very advanced. Glasgow babies were advanced too. He had heard of one whose first word was bevvy. Referring to milk, of course.

Matthew was already beginning to think of the baby's future. "We must plan," he said. "We've got six months to get it right."

She had laughed at this. "Oh, surely not, Matthew. You don't need to have everything in place by the time the baby arrives. We've got years and years to sort things out."

Matthew had become quite animated. "Not so! Not so! Babies creep up on you – or crawl perhaps. Then suddenly you discover that there are all sorts of decisions you should have made much earlier. Believe me, Elspeth, you have to plan these things."

She had looked at him in astonishment. Was this the sort of father that Matthew was about to become? "So what are you thinking of, then?" she asked. "Give me an example."

Matthew shrugged. "There's so much. Disposable or non-disposable nappies. Feeding . . ." He trailed off. "Well, I know you're going to laugh at this, but I was thinking of putting his name down for Muirfield. If he's a boy, that is."

Elspeth gasped. "For that golf club? Oh really, Matthew! You must be joking."

Matthew laughed. "Actually, I was. But there are some things we need to decide."

"All in good time," said Elspeth. "And anyway, we don't know whether he's a boy or a girl. There's no point in doing anything until we know that."

This exchange had been followed by a discussion as to whether it was better to know or not to know. Elspeth, being practical, felt that it might be useful to be told whether it was a boy or a girl, but Matthew thought it would be better not to know. Elspeth understood; the point that he was making was about the mystery of the whole process. It seemed to her astonishing that new life could be created in this way – it was such an astonishing miracle: all those cells, millions and millions of them, falling into place after a moment of contact between two people. It was a miracle of the most profound nature. And yet, miracle or not, there were ordinary questions that needed to be resolved. The colour of the nursery was one.

Clothing was another. On that subject, Matthew had already commented.

"If you look at portraits of children in Dutch seventeenth-century art," he said, "you'll see that boys wore skirts until they were six or seven. That made things simpler."

"But our child, Matthew, is going to be a twenty-first-century Scottish child."

"Of course he is. I didn't mean that we should dress him in skirts. Although that would put him in touch with his inner girl, I suppose."

They both laughed. "What will we call him?" Matthew went on. "If he's a boy? I've always liked the name Dunstaffnage, you know. It's a place near Oban. But it could also be a boy."

"No," said Elspeth. "It never helps to be named after a geographical feature." Some of the Steiner parents might be reminded of that, she thought. Waterfall's mother, for example. Or Tarn's father. "Let's choose something simple. Children with simple names are never embarrassed about them. How about Jamie?"

Matthew looked doubtful. "Jamie's fine," he said. "But if he's called Jamie he's going to end up being a particular sort, if you know what I mean. He'll play rugby, he'll go to New Town bars after the international matches. Being called Jamie signs you up to an awful lot of Scottish upper-middle-class stuff."

Elspeth thought that their child, whatever and whoever he was, was signed up to that already, just by being their child. We're all signed up, she thought. Matthew for what he is, for what his father signed him up for; me for . . . for motherhood. And that lasts forever. Forever. For the rest of your life, you're a mother, whatever happens.

## 32. Dramatic, Life-Enhancing News

Matthew phoned Elspeth shortly after he arrived for work in the gallery. "Are you sure you're all right?" he asked. "You mustn't overdo things, you know. Not in your condition."

She sighed, and looked at her watch. He had only been out of the house for twenty minutes; surely he must think her capable of looking after herself for that length of time. But then she thought how fortunate she was to have a husband who cared, even if he cared rather too much. Dear Matthew; solicitousness was a good quality, in general, particularly in a world where selfishness was so common.

She felt a bit too queasy to have much breakfast, but forced herself to eat a couple of oatcakes and drink a cup of black coffee. So far she had experienced no cravings of the sort that she knew might come in pregnancy, although when she had been in the supermarket a few days earlier she had found herself looking with sudden and unexpected longing at a tempting punnet of strawberries. As pregnancy cravings went, strawberries were innocuous enough; she had read of people gnawing coal, of all things, or wanting to sprinkle powdered ginger on everything.

After the oatcakes and coffee she walked up India Street and along Heriot Row, to catch a taxi on the corner of Dundas Street. Her destination was the Infirmary, where her scan was due to take place at half past ten that morning. The thought of seeing her baby, whom she now imagined as a tiny flutter of life within her, was strangely exciting. She was not sure whether to look, given that they had decided not to know what sex the baby was, but surely a little glimpse would give nothing away – not at this stage of development.

That would be a very significant moment – the first sight of the child who would dominate her life day in, day out for the next how many years – eighteen? What would she say? What could anyone say in such circumstances? She would cry, she suspected – she would cry from sheer joy.

At the hospital, a large complex of buildings on the outskirts of the city, she was directed to a waiting area. A sympathetic nurse took her details and gave her a form to sign, and she was then offered a seat. There were magazines and newspapers; she looked at the front page of a paper, but could not concentrate.

Her consultant appeared and called out her name. She had seen him once already, when she had first learned she was pregnant, and she had taken an immediate liking to him. He was a man in his late fifties, with a quiet, reassuring voice. He had heavy, black-rimmed glasses that seemed to add to the impression he gave of being in complete control of what was happening to her.

A nurse came to her side and watched as the consultant spread the gel on the probe. "It might feel a little bit cold," the nurse said. "But only for a moment."

Elspeth tried to smile, but she was nervous. So much more of this lay ahead, she thought; so many indignities; indignity and pain and surrender to the pokings and proddings of nurses and doctors. She looked up at the ceiling, at the harsh light shining down upon her. That is what her baby would see when it came into the world – harsh light and strange faces peering down at him or her. And sounds too; how strange to be taken from a world of gurgles and thumping – the world of fluids and heartbeat – out into the cacophony of a hospital. No wonder there were people who wished it had never happened; perhaps they remembered, after all, those first few minutes and regretted them.

The consultant moved the probe. "I'm just going to take a wee look at baby now," he said. "We'll get a picture in a moment, if you want to look at the screen."

She felt the smooth surface of the instrument against her skin. She closed her eyes.

The consultant said something to the nurse, and an adjustment was made to the machine.

"There we are," said the consultant. "And . . ."

He stopped. She waited for him to continue, but he did not. She felt the probe glide over her stomach. It had warmed up now from contact with the skin and all she felt was a very slight pressure. Within her, as if reacting to the intrusion upon his privacy, the baby moved.

"I'm just going to move this a little bit," said the consultant. "Nothing to worry about – oh . . ."

"Is everything all right?" Elspeth asked. The conversation between the consultant and the nurse had unsettled her. What was there to see? An abnormality?

The consultant cleared his throat. "Well, I do have a bit of news for you. There's more than one baby, Elspeth. There are . . . two, I do believe. Oh . . . Is that another? Three. You're expecting triplets."

Elspeth gave a little cry. "Twins?"

The nurse reached out to take her hand. "No, triplets. Three babies."

Elspeth closed her eyes. She could not think of what to say, and so simply sighed.

"It's a bit of a shock, I should imagine," said the consultant. "But you're young and healthy. Fortunately."

"Three," said Elspeth, her voice sounding small and distant.

"A ready-made family," said the consultant. "So there we are."

Elspeth began to cry. She was not sure why, but it was what she felt she had to do. "I'm sorry," she sobbed. "I know I should be grateful, but it's just that we were thinking of one baby, and now there are three, and I really don't know how I'm going to cope . . ."

The consultant switched off the machine. "Well, I understand all that," he said. "But, you know, I suspect that you'll rise to the occasion. People usually do, and are often very grateful for triplets at the end of the day."

Elspeth took the tissue that the nurse offered her and blew her nose. "Maybe . . ."

"That's the spirit," said the consultant. He now became businesslike. "I'll need to see you a bit more often than would otherwise have been the case. So we'll set up an appointment for a month's time and see how things are going."

Elspeth got down off the couch. Suddenly she felt very heavy. Three babies. Not one; three. Three names to be chosen, or, if they had two names each, six names altogether.

"I've changed my mind about not knowing," she said to the consultant. "I'd like to know now. Are they girls or . . ."

"Boys," he said, smiling. "You're having three boys."

## 33. *The Implications of Boys*

The nurse was hesitant to allow Elspeth Harmony to leave in a state of shock. "You can stay here for a couple of hours," she said. "Get your breath back, so to speak. Or get your hus . . . I mean, a friend . . ." She stopped herself; years of official hectoring that staff should not make assumptions about marital status had had its effect. You should not mention husbands, the advice ran. Many women don't have them.

In her emotionally charged state, Elspeth was in no mood for such scruples. "I've got a husband," she blurted out. "Some people still have them, you know."

The nurse looked apologetic. "Of course."

Having assured the nurse she was capable of getting home, Elspeth left the hospital and caught a taxi that had just discharged its passengers at the hospital door. She sat back in her seat and watched the city go past: the Dalkeith Road with its acres of flats; the Commonwealth Pool; Arthur's Seat off to the east like a great crouching lion. Three, she thought. Three boys. Three boys.

Suddenly she felt overcome by weariness. I am tired, she thought, and I've hardly even started. How shall I feel when the boys are back home and crying at night? What if they wake up at different times – which is perfectly possible, indeed inevitable? Or will their hours of wakefulness be coordinated by some strange synchronicity, that odd biological phenomenon that made people want to march in step, or feel hungry at the same time? There was certainly something in synchronicity, even if one declined to explore its more exotic edges – those unsettling instances where events happen in such a way as to suggest a causal link. Jung talked of that, of course, and wrote about discussing a scarab with a patient, turning round, and seeing a scarab at the window . . .

No, this was not the time to think about such matters. This was the time to think about what she would say to Matthew. Good news, Matthew, it's triplets! Or something less Pollyanna-ish. Matthew, we have a tiny bit of a challenge ahead of us . . . Three of them, to be precise.

She wondered whether the shock might be mitigated by the news that the triplets were boys. She had suspected that Matthew had been secretly hoping for a boy – there had been those references to rugby and to the possibility of acquiring the baby a debenture seat at Murrayfield, strong clues by any standards, but there had also been the use of the male pronoun, another clue, perhaps. But even if Matthew was hoping for a son, one could not, by extension, assume that he was contemplating three. Three, as Oscar Wilde might have remarked, sounds rather like carelessness.

For her part, Elspeth had been hoping for a daughter. One daughter, to start with, and then perhaps another, with a son somewhere along the way as well. Girls were undoubtedly easier than boys . . . The conventional wisdom was certainly that girls

were less physically demanding than boys, as they played happily
with their dolls and dolls' houses, re-enacting domestic events in
apparently complete contentment, for hours, whereas boys seemed
to have an endless appetite for physical activity. Matthew, she
remembered, had a friend with three boys, each an unremitting
dynamo of activity. "Such nice boys," he said, "but when they were
small I saw his moustache droop further and further from sheer
exhaustion. It's picked up again, though, now that the boys are
older and less physically rumbustious."

She stopped. It was so easy to be caught up with stereotypes.
Were girls really easier, or was that just the way we thought of
them? She did a mental roll-call of the children she had taught at
the Steiner School – Bertie, Hiawatha, Pansy, Tofu, Olive . . .
Olive gave her pause for thought. What a manipulative little piece
of work she had been, with her constant playing off of one classmate against another. And poor Bertie, who only wanted to be
left in peace, being ruthlessly hounded by Olive at every turn. It
really was too much. Bertie, of course, being the boy that he was,
tolerated it, but for Elspeth Harmony it had eventually proved
insupportable and she had pinched Olive sharply on the ear,
thereby bringing her career as a teacher to a premature end.

That, of course, was utterly unfair, and, as the taxi turned the
corner at East Preston Street and began to trundle down South Clerk
Street, she smarted at the memory. Teachers put up with constant,
unremitting provocation and were expected to have the patience of
saints. Well, they were human, and if every so often their human
tempers showed then the self-same parents who had produced such
ill-behaved offspring would launch a tirade of self-righteous com-
plaints. What were teachers to do? Well, she had resigned – admittedly
before she was pushed – and many others were thinking of doing
exactly the same thing. Which meant the schools would become
worse, with not very well-trained teachers taking over from those
with more experience. Thus the culture spiralled downwards . . .

No, girls could be manipulative and every bit as trying as boys. Girls kept arguments going and loved using psychological warfare to achieve their aims; boys might be pugilistic at times, but they did not bear grudges to the same extent as girls. So three girls, while not as physically demanding as three boys, could be even more psychologically exhausting. She sighed, and, as the taxi reached Surgeons' Hall, began to cry.

The taxi driver looked in his mirror. He was a driver of the old school – part social worker, part psychologist, witness and confidant to a thousand secrets.

"You all right?"

"Yes."

Having picked her up at the Infirmary, he knew.

"Are you going to live?" It was a risky question; the answer might well have been no.

"Yes, I'm going to live."

"So it's not that bad, is it, hen?"

He looked again in the mirror and winked. He was right. Of course it was not that bad.

"No," she said. "It's not. It's just that . . . just that I'm going to have triplets."

He was silent for a moment. "Oh, michty!" he said. "I was wrong. It *is* bad!"

## 34. Carnoustie Shortbread

Elspeth decided that rather than going home to the flat she would go straight to the gallery and break the news to Matthew there. The taxi driver had been kind, as most Edinburgh taxi drivers were, and her tears had stopped by the time they reached Queen Street. As a result of this, when Elspeth spotted Big Lou's

café coming up on the right, she asked the driver to stop and let her off there. Several hours had passed now since her modest breakfast, and she thought that she might have a large, creamy cup of latte accompanied by a piece of Big Lou's shortbread. That shortbread, which Big Lou made according to the recipe of her aunt from Carnoustie, was renowned for its calorific punch and its contribution, small but significant, to heart disease in the east of Scotland. But Elspeth said to herself, as she contemplated the shortbread ahead of her, I'm eating for two. No, three; no, four . . .

The taxi paid off, Elspeth made her way down the steps to Big Lou's basement. The rail, she noticed, was as rickety as ever; Matthew had said something, she recalled, about Hugh MacDiarmid, the poet, having stumbled while descending these steps many years before, and it was here too, she remembered, that Lard O'Connor (RIP), Matthew's Glasgow friend, had fallen. She steadied herself, the rail moving slightly as she took hold of it. She felt heavy again – much heavier than she had felt before she had been told of the triplets. That was psychological, of course; she could hardly have put on much weight over the last couple of hours. And yet, she would weigh more, surely, than most other pregnant women, because they only had one baby to carry about whereas she had four . . . no, it was three, wasn't it?

What if they had made a mistake? What if a fourth boy was hiding in there, having been missed by the scan? She had read in a magazine of people only finding out about twins in the delivery room, but she assumed that this was before ultrasound. It must be impossible nowadays to miss twins, or triplets, with all that sophisticated equipment. And yet mistakes were made in all branches of medicine, because sophisticated equipment had to be operated by mere humans, and mere humans, as everybody knew, were humanly fallible.

No, there would be no surprise fifth, no, fourth, boy. There were few surprises in life today; no babies found in handbags (handbags!) at railway stations; no unexpected triplets; and few, if any, successfully concealed pregnancies. In the past, she thought, children must have been like rain; they were not planned – they simply occurred; no longer, at least in western Europe, where birth rates were plummeting. The same magazine article that had discussed unexpected twins had also commented on the decline in the number of Russians through their declining birth rate. Soon, they said, there would be none left at all, and Russia would return to being a land of vast, frozen forests. Could the same thing happen in Scotland? Don't look at me, she thought; I'm doing my best to prevent that – not that I intended to.

There was nobody in Big Lou's, apart from Big Lou, of course, who was cleaning the steam spout of her coffee machine.

"These things get awfully dirty," Big Lou said as she saw Elspeth come in. "They build up a crust of white if you aren't careful. We used to call that sort of thing the coo's breeks."

Elspeth eyed the shortbread that Big Lou had laid out on a display plate. "Has Matthew been in?"

"Aye," said Big Lou. "In and out. Him and Angus, and that dug, of course." She glanced at Elspeth. "You all right?"

Elspeth moved over to the counter. She looked at the shortbread again. "I really need a piece of that shortbread, Lou. I'm . . ."

She swayed slightly, reaching out to steady herself by holding on to the counter.

Big Lou reacted quickly. Dropping the cloth she had been using to clean the coffee machine, she moved round the counter to Elspeth's side. Then, putting an arm round her, she led her to a chair.

"You sit down, hen," Big Lou said. "You need something to eat. And a glass of water?"

Elspeth nodded weakly. "Sorry. I just felt a bit weak there. I'm fine now."

Big Lou gave her two pieces of shortbread, with a glass of milk for good measure. "Did you eat your breakfast?" she asked. "Folk forget about breakfast. You need it."

Elspeth nodded. "I had oatcakes. And coffee."

Big Lou shook her head. "Not enough. Remember that you're eating for two. Matthew told me, by the way, and I was very pleased for you. That's good news."

"Four," said Elspeth. "I'm eating for four. I've just been told."

Big Lou sat down. "Four? Four bairns?"

"No, three. Four including myself."

"Oh . . ."

"Yes."

For a few moments, Big Lou said nothing. She was remembering a woman in Arbroath. "There was a girl at home," she said. "Prinny Mackenzie. I was at school with her. She had a brother called Billy, I think, who fell into the Tay once on a school expedition and travelled a mile downstream before he was fished out – unharmed. Anyway, this girl had triplets. Three boys."

Elspeth looked at Big Lou weakly. "That's what I'm having. Three boys."

"Very nice," said Big Lou. "Keep you busy, of course."

"I think so."

"Mind you," Big Lou went on. "I'll tell you one thing about Prinny Mackenzie. She was the happiest girl you ever saw. After the triplets and all. Happy as they come. And the wee boys were real bonny. Everybody loved them. One was called Billy, after his uncle, and another was . . . Tom, I think. I forget the name of the third. No, he was called Mike, after his dad. Such a nice man."

Elspeth tackled the shortbread; Big Lou had given her generous slices. "They were all happy?"

"Yes," said Big Lou. "Very." She paused. "And that's the important thing, isn't it?"

Elspeth looked at her. "Happiness?"

"Yes. If you've got your health, and you're happy, what else is there?"

Elspeth thought about this. Was life quite that simple? Surely not, but then she looked at Big Lou, who was smiling, and who had taken her hand in a gesture of comfort and friendliness. She felt the roughness of Big Lou's hand; work, all that work, had taken its toll. How vulnerable was a human hand, she thought, and how precious. With her free hand she took the last fragment of shortbread and ate it.

## 35. *Édouard Vuillard and the Interior Vision*

Matthew was surprised to see Elspeth. He looked up from his desk and saw her standing at the front door of the gallery, about to enter. She seemed to be hesitating, and it was a moment before she saw him looking at her from within. He rose to his feet and went to open the door for her.

"I was worried you'd be busy," she said.

He leaned forward and kissed her on the cheek. "Never too

busy to see you, my darling." He gestured at the empty gallery behind him. "And anyway, we're not exactly run off our feet today." He smiled ruefully. "Or any day, come to think of it."

He ushered her to the seat beside his desk. As she sat down, she glanced at the large volume lying open before him. "Vuillard?"

Matthew pushed the book towards her. "Yes. Édouard Vuillard. Postimpressionist. This is the catalogue raisonné – it has everything he did in it."

"I've seen some of his paintings," she said. "Women arranging flowers. Sewing. That sort of thing."

"Exactly," said Matthew. "They're very peaceful. Take a look at this one."

The book was open at a picture of a woman watering a clump of indoor hyacinths. Elspeth read out the title. "*Madame Vuillard with Hyacinths.*" She looked enquiringly at Matthew. "His wife?"

Matthew shook his head. "No, his mother. Read what they say about it. It's his mother in her flat above the rue de Calais. It's 1916 and they were living in Paris." He paused, reaching out to touch the photograph of the richly coloured painting. "So luscious. Those textures."

Elspeth's eye moved to the commentary on the painting. "I see that they compare it to Dutch paintings. Why?"

Matthew cocked his head, to look at the painting from a different angle. "Light, I suppose. There's that wonderful light coming in the window, isn't there? The Dutch liked to capture light like that in their paintings. And there's a window – we're in a room looking out of a window. That's another Dutch thing."

"Vermeer?"

Matthew touched her hand gently; an unexpected gesture. "Yes. Vermeer. Remember the *Woman in Blue Reading a Letter* – that light flooding in from the window. That's why those paintings are so arresting. They just make you stop. Like that. Just stop."

"And?"

He moved the book away. "And you think, that's just so beautiful. It's something to do with taking a moment and capturing it and distilling all the beauty it contains."

She sat back in her chair. She would tell him now. "Matthew . . ."

But he was not listening. Reaching into the drawer of his desk, he took out the Sotheby's catalogue. "There's something else I want to show you," he said as he began to leaf through the glossy pages.

"What's that?"

He turned the catalogue over to show her the cover. "A sale of Impressionist and Postimpressionist paintings in London. See?"

She read the inscription on the cover. "Day sale," she said.

"That means it's not as important as an evening sale," Matthew explained. "The day sales are when they sell the middle-ranking stuff. You won't find any Rembrandts or Matisses being sold during the day. It's the evening for that sort of thing – greater theatrical possibilities."

She tried again. "Matthew, I went . . ."

"But look at this," Matthew went on. "It's somewhere here. Lot number . . . sixty-two. Yes, here it is. Look at this." He passed her the catalogue. "Isn't it lovely?"

Elspeth sighed. There was no point in trying to tell him now, she thought. And there would be time – there would be plenty of time. She could tell him this evening, back at the flat. It might be better to do it there, anyway, as it would give him the time to react – in whatever way he was going to react. She turned her attention to the catalogue. *A woman on a sofa in the small drawing room. 1922.*

The painting was undeniably beautiful. "I see what you mean," she said. "But . . . but look at the estimate."

Matthew seemed unconcerned. "Eighty thousand. High enough to be in an evening sale."

"But it says eighty to a hundred thousand pounds."

Matthew shrugged. "Nobody else may be interested. I could get it under the bottom end of the estimate. Maybe seventy-five, something like that."

"Seventy-five thousand pounds?"

His tone remained casual. "And I suppose I need to remember the auction house's commission. They add twenty-five per cent to that."

Elspeth gasped. "So that means it could cost a hundred thousand anyway – even if you get it at the bottom of the estimate."

Matthew made an insouciant gesture. "That's what Vuillard costs. He's a very great artist, you know. You don't get great artists for peanuts."

"But what are you going to do with it – if you get it? Who's going to buy it?"

"I'll sell it to a client."

She pressed home her objection. "Who? Which client?"

Matthew frowned. "I'll find one. I'll put it in the window. Somebody will walk past who likes Vuillard."

Elspeth stared at him. "Yes, probably a lot of people who like Vuillard will walk past, but how many of them will have a hundred thousand pounds – more, in fact, because you'll have to add something to make a profit. A hundred and twenty thousand pounds?"

"There are a lot of wealthy people in Edinburgh," said Matthew. "Somebody will buy it."

Elspeth closed her eyes. This was all going wrong. She had not come to the gallery to get into an argument with Matthew about whether or not he could sell Postimpressionist paintings. He could not, she thought, but that was not the point.

She had wanted to tell him about the triplets, which was, after all, the most important news that they, as a couple, had ever received. And he had started to talk about Vuillard and auction prices and clients who she thought really did not exist at all.

She felt Matthew's hand on her arm. "Elspeth?" he asked. "Are you all right?"

She opened her eyes. She felt her tears returning. "I'm having triplets," she said.

Matthew remained quite still. His eyes opened wider, she thought, and one corner of his mouth moved downwards. But otherwise it was as if he had suddenly frozen. Then suddenly his eyes turned upwards, and his eyelids closed.

He fell forwards, taking with him the catalogue. Elspeth let out an involuntary scream. She reached forwards, but he had slipped past her and hit the floor. There was a bumping sound, like the knocking of wood on wood.

"Matthew!"

He did not move. The catalogue was underneath his head, the picture of the Vuillard painting directly beneath his jaw, the paper crumpled.

## 36. *Fear a' Bhata*

Since the departure of Miss Harmony, Bertie had had two new teachers. The loss of Miss Harmony had been keenly felt by the children, no more so than by Bertie, who had completely sympathised with her when, driven to distraction by Olive, the teacher had momentarily lapsed and pinched Olive's ear. That, he thought, was something that anybody having contact with Olive could be forgiven for doing, and it seemed to him very unjust that she should leave simply on account of that. He had been pleased, though, when she had married Matthew and all the children had been invited to the wedding. Olive had been included in this invitation, which struck Bertie as an exceedingly and unnecessarily generous thing to do. It offended him that Olive had expressed

no regrets over the incident – in which he felt she was entirely to blame – and indeed had made a number of exaggerated claims as to what had happened.

"I liked Miss Harmony," Olive was heard to say. "It's just a pity that she tried to tear my ear off."

"But she didn't," protested Bertie. "It was just a little pinch, Olive. I saw her."

"It's a pity she didn't tear it off," Tofu interjected. "You deserve it, you little cow."

"I forgive you for those crude words," said Olive. "I forgive you, Tofu, but I'm afraid that God won't. He's going to really sort you out when you die. Just you wait."

Bertie sighed. He was used to this sparring between Olive and Tofu, but he wished that it would not happen. Miss Harmony was gone, and he believed she was happy enough in her new life. There was no point, he thought, in raking over old coals, and of course they had their new teacher to get used to now that the temporary stand-in had been replaced.

Miss Harmony's replacement was one Miss Maclaren Hope, like all the staff at the school a well-trained and committed teacher. She came from the Isle of Skye, by way of Aberdeen University, and had about her that gentleness and slight dreaminess that is often associated with the Hebrides, both Outer and Inner. She was fluent in Gaelic and played the clarsach, which enchanted the children and even managed to put a thoughtful expression on Tofu's face. She was keen on singing, too, and soon had the entire class singing Gaelic songs such as "Fear a' Bhata" and "Braigh Loch Iall." Even Tofu sang, sitting quite still – which was unusual for him – staring up at Miss Maclaren Hope as she led them through the lovely, liquid sounds of the Gaelic.

"'Fear a' Bhata'," she explained, "is a song sung by somebody who is thinking of her friend, who is a boatman. Will he come to see her? Will she see his boat approaching over the water, or will she close the door with a sigh, realising that she will have to wait until the following day before she sees his boat?"

"Couldn't he phone her?" asked Olive.

Miss Maclaren Hope smiled. "This song was written before people had mobile phones, Olive. Or even ordinary phones, for that matter. So no, he couldn't phone her and tell her whether he was coming to see her or not. She would have to wait, down by the seashore, where the kelp is strewn by the tides. She would have to wait, with the soft evening breeze from the outer islands, gentle upon her brow." She paused. "That is why she is singing this lovely song, you see."

One of the innovations introduced by Miss Maclaren Hope was a weekly show-and-tell session. This involved one of the members of the class bringing in an object of some sort – a photograph, a book, an ornament, or a picture – and discussing it with the others. It had been a great success. Hiawatha had brought in a crystal radio set that his father had built as a boy, and this had enabled the class to look up crystal radios and discuss how radio waves worked. Pansy had brought in a book on flower arranging, which her mother used for the class on that subject that she ran in the local church hall. When it came to Tofu's turn, he had brought in the wheel of a vintage motorcycle that his father had been restoring, which he had stopped doing.

"Tofu's dad's too weak to do anything anymore," Olive whispered to Bertie. "He's a vegan, you see."

Bertie looked anxiously at Tofu, who fortunately had not heard.

"It's true," Olive continued sotto voce. "Have you seen him when he comes to collect Tofu at the school gate? The only reason why Tofu's still alive is that he steals so many sandwiches at school. Otherwise he'd be just like his dad. Just about dead."

"My mummy says that Tofu's dad is fine," pointed out Bertie. "She said he's very healthy."

Olive looked pityingly at Bertie. "You shouldn't believe what adults say, Bertie. I'm surprised that you don't know that already. Most adults lie. It's a well-known fact."

This conversation had been cut short by Miss Maclaren Hope. "This is very interesting, Tofu. Old motorcycles are intricate pieces of machinery and this wheel shows us just how beautifully they were made. It's very heavy, though, so do be careful when you roll it about. And what does this tell us, boys and girls?"

"You need two of them," said Hiawatha. "One's no good."

"Indeed," said Miss Maclaren Hope. "That is undoubtedly true. Motorcycles have two wheels and cars have . . . How many wheels do cars have, boys and girls?"

So the session continued. And now it was Bertie's turn, and he was having difficulty in thinking of what he could bring to show-and-tell. Tofu's wheel had been a great success, as had the crystal radio. Bertie's problem was that he felt that there was nothing of interest in his house. There were no machines and the books, which mostly belonged to his mother, were mainly by Melanie Klein. Bertie did not want to bring any of those in. Nor did he feel that he could bring in his contraband *Scouting for Boys* by Baden-Powell. That book was too precious, and he feared that it might be confiscated on the grounds that it advocated the carrying of knives. So what was there left to bring?

Then it occurred to him. Ulysses. He could bring his baby brother. Why not? There was lot that could be said about Ulysses.

## 37. *Political Crisis*

Untoward incidents are often the result of a series of misunderstandings. In this case, the first misunderstanding arose out of a remark that Bertie dropped into a conversation with his mother while he was accompanying her along Cumberland Street on a walk to Stockbridge. Would it be possible, he asked, for him to take Ulysses to school one day to show him to everybody there? Irene, who was conducting a conversation on her mobile phone at the time – she was talking to the organiser of Bertie's yoga classes – only listened to Bertie with half an ear, if that, and replied that of course it would be all right. Ulysses always travelled with her on the 23 bus when she went to collect Bertie in the afternoon, and she assumed that Bertie had in mind her arriving slightly early and taking the baby in to be introduced.

Bertie had not meant that. He had envisaged taking Ulysses in by himself. His brother could then be looked after in the classroom until it was time to go home. This would give him a feeling for the Steiner School, he thought, and would provide more than enough for Bertie to talk about in the show-and-tell.

He then asked: "May I take him in myself, Mummy?"

And Irene, who was now not listening at all, replied: "Of course, Bertie, of course."

It was in this way that the whole unfortunate series of events was set on course. There was no real fault on either side: Bertie thought that he had been given permission to take Ulysses to school, and Irene thought that she had merely promised that she would one day take him for a brief visit to the classroom. And there the misunderstanding might have remained, had it not been for a further bit of confusion, this time involving Stuart.

On most mornings it was Irene who went with Bertie on the 23 bus. Every couple of weeks, though, Stuart would arrange to go to work later and would accompany Bertie on the bus, thus allowing Irene the luxury of a long lie-in. Ulysses was a sound sleeper – in the mornings – and so it was not uncommon on such days for Irene to be able to lie in bed until well after ten. And this is what she thought would happen on the morning in question.

Stuart was first out of bed. "I'll take you to school today," he said to Bertie when he went into his son's bedroom to waken him. He had then gone back to the kitchen, and it was there that he received an urgent call from his immediate superior in the government office in which he worked as a senior statistician. An embarrassing report had just been published in the morning papers revealing that slightly under 19 per cent of Scottish children were illiterate when they left primary school at the age of twelve. This was particularly embarrassing in a country that made much of its educational tradition.

Stuart was used to awkward statistics, and he knew how uncomfortable politicians felt about them. On rare occasions there was nothing that could be done, and the statistics had to be left as they were, but usually it was possible to find some other contrary statistic that made things look better from the political point of view.

Thus, although it might well be true that 19 per cent of twelve-year-olds could not read, the shock involved in this brute fact could be mitigated, perhaps, by discovering a statistic that revealed that they had far fewer dental fillings than was the case, say, thirty years ago, before the age of fluoridation. This statistic could then be fed to the press to gain immediate time. Later, a further statistic, to the effect that the ability of the age group in question to use a computer, had improved considerably. The fact that most twelve-year-olds used computers exclusively to play shoot-'em-up games might not even be raised at all, and, if it was, public attention may well have shifted anyway.

"You'd better get down here this instant," said Stuart's boss. "The journalists are braying like dogs, and the Heid Bummer is wanting some good figures pronto, if not prontissimo." This was the way senior civil servants spoke; the Heid Bummer, also known affectionately as the High Heid Yin, was the First Minister of Scotland, a popular politician known for his nimble footwork. If he was distressed to find that almost one-fifth of Scottish children were illiterate, then his distress would be taken very seriously by the civil servants who surrounded him. What they really needed to find, of course, was a statistic that revealed that in England even more than one-fifth of twelve-year-olds could not read; that would take the heat off and provide considerable political satisfaction. But this did not appear to be the case: twelve-year-olds in England, it appeared, all had their noses buried in Joyce, Beckett, and Gerard Manley Hopkins.

"The government's sunk," said Stuart's boss. "Our only hope is that the general population will be too illiterate to read this report anyway. But get here right now, Stuart, and see what you can do."

It was in the face of this call that Stuart quite forgot that he was due to take Bertie into school. So when Bertie went into the kitchen, there was no sign of his father. His mother, he knew, was asleep, and he did not want to wake her up. Irene valued her long lie-ins, and Bertie felt that it would not be helpful to disturb her. So he made his own breakfast, put the dirty plate in the dishwasher, and wrote a note to be left on the kitchen table.

Dear Mummy,
Daddy has gone to the office. I think he has forgotten that he
was going to take me to school. So I'll go by myself – I promise

you I won't cross the road except with the green man. I'll take
Ulysses too as it's my turn for show-and-tell and Miss Maclaren
Hope will be really pleased to see him. She can sing him a
Gaelic lullaby if he gets tired and starts to girn.

Lots of love, Bertie

## 38. *Show-and-Tell*

Ulysses was delighted to wake up and find Bertie looking over the
edge of his cot. He cooed with delight as his brother lifted him out
of bed and set him carefully on the changing table. Bertie was quite
familiar with the routine, as he had observed and helped with every
step; so Ulysses was soon dry and comfortable and Bertie began to
rummage in the cupboard for suitable clothes for him. He quickly
dismissed the small dungarees that his mother favoured, and found,
to his great delight, a completely unused baby's sailor suit at the
back of a drawer. This had been a present to Ulysses from Stuart's
cousin in Troon, but had been consigned to oblivion by Irene, who
had remarked that she thought there were quite enough uniforms
in this world without babies being dressed in sailor suits.

With Ulysses in his sailor suit, Bertie sponged his face, combed
his few wisps of hair, and carried him to his pushchair. He would
give him something to eat in the bus, he thought – a piece of cake,
perhaps, and the yellow plastic cup from which he liked to drink
milk. But for now everything was ready, and all he had to do was
slip out of the flat without waking his mother.

Ulysses continued to beam, especially when he realised that
Irene did not appear to be coming. That caused him to chuckle
with pleasure and to clap his little hands together.

"Shh, Ulysses," said Bertie. "Mummy loves her lie-ins. We
mustn't wake her."

Getting Ulysses down the stairs in the pushchair was not easy, and there was a dreadful moment when Bertie thought that he would lose control, but that passed, and soon they were out on Scotland Street, walking confidently up to Drummond Place. At the top of the street they turned right and made their way in the direction of Dundas Street and the 23 bus. Bertie felt extremely adult and responsible as he pushed his brother along, and if one or two heads turned in surprise at the sight of a small boy in evident charge of an even smaller one, his manifest self-assurance made them conclude that all was well.

Once they had boarded the bus, the magnitude of the adventure on which he had embarked came home to Bertie. Not only was this the first time he had been on a bus by himself, which was in itself a major milestone, but also it was the first time that he had been in sole charge of Ulysses.

"I hope that you're going to be good," whispered Bertie, as he balanced Ulysses on his knee. "And you mustn't be sick, understand?"

Ulysses seemed to grasp the gravity of the request, as he stared solemnly at his older brother and began to nod his head in apparent agreement.

"Good," said Bertie. "Good boy."

The bus journey was uneventful. Ulysses, entirely content with Bertie's company, gurgled appreciatively each time the bus turned a corner, but regurgitated nothing. And when they came to the stop at which Bertie normally alighted, Bertie managed to carry both Ulysses and his pushchair with no difficulty at all. From there, the walk along Merchiston Crescent and Spylaw Road was simplicity itself, and in no time at all they reached the school.

Miss Maclaren Hope was out of the classroom when Bertie entered with Ulysses.

"What have you got there, Bertie?" asked Olive suspiciously.

"Have you brought a doll? Boys shouldn't play with dolls, you know."

"It's my little brother," said Bertie. "He's called Ulysses."

"Good!" shouted Pansy. "A real live baby. Can I have a go with him, Bertie?"

Olive was quick to take command of the situation. "No," she said peremptorily. "I'll take him. Give him here, Bertie."

Bertie handed Ulysses over gently. "Keep him the right way up, please," he said. "He doesn't like going upside down."

"I know how to hold a baby," snapped Olive. "I've held hundreds of babies. They really like me."

"That's because they can't see very far," said Tofu, who had appeared from the back and was peering at Ulysses.

Olive ignored this taunt, and busied herself with tickling Ulysses under the chin. "I like his sailor suit," she said. "And his nose is really cute, Bertie. You should be proud of his nose."

"I am," said Bertie.

"I'm a bit worried about what Miss Maclaren Hope is going to say," went on Olive. "I think that we should hide him in case she says that he's not allowed."

"Yes, hide him," agreed Pansy. "Then we can take him out at playtime."

"He's not a toy," said Bertie mildly. "It might be better to . . ."

"No, Pansy's right," said Olive. "We should make a little bed for him in the cupboard."

Bertie tried to point out that Ulysses might not like being put in a cupboard, but was quickly overruled by the girls, who had now taken complete control of their young visitor.

The cupboard had been opened and several jerseys laid down to form a makeshift bed when Miss Maclaren Hope came back into the room. In the silence that followed, Bertie looked at Olive, who quickly handed Ulysses back to him.

"I've brought my little brother in for show-and-tell," he

explained. "He won't be any trouble, Miss Hope. He's very nice."

"What a sweet little boy," said the astonished teacher. "But . . ."

"He looks like my last psychotherapist," said Bertie. "Especially his ears."

"Well, that's very interesting, Bertie, but where's your mummy? Is she here as well?"

Bertie explained that his mother was having a lie-in. And so Daddy was somewhere in the school? No, he was not; he had to go into the office. And so . . . "I think that we'd better make a phone call," said Miss Maclaren Hope. "And if you don't mind, Bertie, I'll hold little Ulysses for the time being."

Bertie and Miss Maclaren Hope left the room and made their way to the office. "Mummy said I could bring him," explained Bertie. "I asked her."

Miss Maclaren Hope pursed her lips. "Well, be that as it may, Bertie, I think though that Ulysses is just a tiny bit young to come to school. So we'll just give Mummy a quick ring and see if she could come up and get him. Don't you think that's best?"

Bertie did not. But he realised that this was not the point. It was such a pity for Ulysses, he thought: he was enjoying himself so much and now this. And when his mother arrived, he knew exactly what Ulysses would do: he would be sick. He would have to warn Miss Maclaren Hope about this, but it was difficult to know how to put it – it so often was.

## 39. *Which World Am I Living In?*

On the morning on which Bertie took Ulysses to school, Angus Lordie followed his normal routine of an early walk with Cyril round the Drummond Place Gardens, followed by a breakfast of coffee accompanied by two croissants. Living on his own, he felt no inhibitions about reading at table, alternating between a book, which he read on Mondays, Wednesdays, and Fridays, and a newspaper or magazine on the other four days of the week. The newspaper was invariably *The Scotsman*, where he turned first to Duncan Macmillan's art column – if it was a Macmillan day – or to Allan Massie, both of which writers he was in complete agreement with on all subjects. If it was a day for a magazine, then it would be the art review in *The Burlington Magazine*, where, in view of his impending trip to Italy, he was currently taking a particular interest in articles on Italian subjects. Thus a review of "Altarpieces and their Viewers in the Churches of Rome from Caravaggio to Guido Reni" was read over a croissant and strawberry jam; and coffee, black and strong, was the perfect accompaniment to an article on newly discovered miniatures by Pacino di Bonaguida.

After breakfast, Angus Lordie went through to his studio, followed by Cyril, who usually padded after him if he moved rooms, settling himself in an accustomed spot and watching his master for any signs of dog-related activity: the fetching of a lead would be a signal for immediate enthusiastic barking; the fetching of a dog bowl would bring an immediate wagging of the tail and the protrusion, over canine canines, of a ready-to-serve tongue. But while Angus was painting, Cyril knew that as little distraction as possible was wanted; this reminded Angus of the rule in the Savile Club in London where, on the members' breakfast table, is displayed a sign saying *Conversation not preferred*. He had enjoyed an absurd exchange with Domenica on the subject.

"Such wording is so polite," he remarked. "Yet it's unambiguous: there is no prohibition of conversation, but to initiate it would be to go against the wishes of the committee, and that should, in civic society, be enough to inhibit."

"Oh yes," said Domenica. "But one can't have polite requests in all situations. What about parking regulations? Do you think that people would obey polite signs that simply requested them not to park?"

Angus thought about this for a moment. "They might do so in Edinburgh, don't you think? Can't you just imagine it? We wouldn't have signs saying *No Parking*, or *Parking Prohibited*; our signs would confine themselves to saying *Parking not Preferred*. And should a driver ignore such a sign, then a traffic warden would place a small ticket on his or her windscreen. This would read: *This is rather inconsiderate of you. Please don't park here, if you don't mind awfully. Thank you.*"

Domenica stared at him. "Which world are you living in, Angus?"

Angus looked rueful. "Not this one, I suppose. But don't you think that there's a point in having some idea of a better world? Don't most people have something like that?"

Domenica admitted that some did – Utopian socialists, for instance, who believed in the perfectibility of man if only we could establish economic justice and the conditions that went with that. "But they are so few these days," she said. "Most people now believe that the world is hopelessly flawed and that at the most we can tidy it up around the edges."

"And religious people?" asked Angus. "Don't most religions

have an idea that the world can be made better – if only people would see the world from their point of view, which of course not everybody does?"

"They do, I suppose," said Domenica. "And that swells the numbers of those who believe that we might have a better future. But . . ."

*Which world am I living in?* The question haunted Angus. He was an artist and he believed that he had a vocation. He had to create – that is what he wanted to do, and he believed that the need he felt to do this was as important to him as food and drink. He could not envisage life without the ability to pick up a brush and put paint to canvas; it was not something he did because he earned his living in this way, or because it kept boredom at bay; he did it because that was the reason why he got out of bed each morning. He lived to paint.

And yet, he wondered what good this powerful urge had done either him or the world in general. Artists, like anybody else, had a social purpose, which was . . . what? To increase the amount of beauty in the world? If this was what artists were for, then he was, in a sense, a mere decorator. Or did the creation of beauty have a purpose beyond the deed of its creation? Beauty and truth were linked, he had always assumed, and to create beauty was to state a truth. And if one stated a truth, one was revealing that truth to others and that, surely, was worth doing for itself.

As an artist he was committed to beauty, and yet what contribution to an understanding of beauty had he made? He thought of his portrait painting. When he painted a portrait he tried to capture something about the essence of the sitter. The perception of that essence might have an uplifting effect on the person who gazed upon the painting, but that, he thought, was rare, and was possibly restricted to portraits of beautiful sitters. It did not apply, he thought, to his unfinished portrait of Ramsey Dunbarton, the retired solicitor who had been so inordinately proud of playing the part of the Duke of Plaza-Toro in *The Gondoliers* at the Churchhill Theatre. His portrait of Ramsey, not completed because of the death of the sitter – in Angus's studio – added nothing to human understanding. All that it said was that there was once a man who looked like this, who was painted by this particular artist. It was of no greater interest, Angus told himself, than an entry in an old telephone directory. Such entries say there was once a person called this who lived at this address and who could be reached at this number.

I must do something permanent, he thought. And then he thought of Italy, and of all that it meant for our sense of beauty. I shall paint something of great significance there, he thought.

He shivered. Something was upon him – filling him with a sense of power and possibility. A great painting, he thought. At last.

## 40. *A Moment on Queen Street*

Angus painted for two hours before pausing. The canvas on which he was working was an undemanding one – a group portrait commissioned by a bank of its board of directors. He had chosen to portray the directors in both standing and sitting poses, casually placed around a boardroom, with one even looking out of the window and caught only in profile. The commission had preceded the disaster that struck the bank, a few months before the howling winds of financial crisis had stripped away the clothing of centuries and exposed alarmingly shaky foundations. Angus had finished the sittings when this began, and had awaited instructions from the bank as to what to do. Several of the directors had gone: was he to paint out their faces in the way of official artists of the old Soviet Union, where discredited members of the Politburo found themselves over-painted with vases of flowers? No such instruction came from the bank, which, having agreed to pay his fee, felt obliged to honour the contract.

"Perhaps I could paint one or two of them looking regretful," Angus suggested to the bank official who had made all the arrangements. "Would that do? It would be recording a particular moment in banking history, and might therefore be of greater interest in the future. What do you think?"

This had been greeted with silence. Then the official said, "I'm not sure if all of them are regretful. Some of them, certainly, but not everyone at that level seems to have donned sackcloth and ashes."

Angus thought about this. There had been general calls for punishment and retribution, with eager *tricoteuses* taking up their station outside corporate headquarters, but this had left him feeling vaguely uncomfortable. There had been greedy bankers, but almost everybody else had been greedy too. Did those who rejoiced in the high returns on their savings stop to think that they were part of the problem, that they were rentiers? Did those who ran up high credit card bills stop to think that they were part of the mountain of debt that the reckless economic party was building up? Many first stones had been cast, he thought.

"Or a *paysage moralisé*?" asked Angus. "There's a window in the picture. There could be a *paysage moralisé* outside."

The official cleared his throat. "You must forgive me – that's not a banking term."

"The landscape does the work," explained Angus. "One paints an allegorical landscape to make a point about life. A barren valley. High mountains presenting an obstacle to the traveller. Burning haystacks."

"How interesting. But somehow . . ."

"No, I understand. Nothing disturbing."

So now he stood before his easel, adding the final touches to a picture that he suspected would never be fully displayed. It was an act of piety on the part of the bank, recording the board in happier times, but its destiny would be to hang – if it were to hang at all – in some back room or corridor, away from the bright offices in which the real business of the bank was conducted. The prospect of his work being relegated in this way filled him with despair and made him all the more determined to do something that mattered. This brought his thoughts back to Italy. Italy was the solution, at least for artists. If there was any country that was the spiritual home of artists, then it was Italy, which had been succouring the artistic soul for centuries. Italy would recharge him, would provide him with the inspiration for a new phase in his work.

He put down his brush, not even bothering to wipe it or dip it in spirit; he would do that later. He looked at his watch. He could go to Big Lou's for coffee, but somehow he wanted something fresh, something different. A walk perhaps and then . . . Yes, Italy . . . He had no clothes that would be suitable for Italy. Domenica and Antonia would be bedecked in large straw hats, no doubt, and cool blouses, whereas he had his Harris tweed and his moleskin trousers (with their paint stains) which nobody could wear in Italy.

"Cyril," he said. "We're going shopping."

Cyril understood only one word of that: his name. But there was no mistaking Angus's body language, and all dogs are expert interpreters of body language. Leaping to his feet, Cyril gave two enthusiastic barks to indicate readiness. The lead was fetched and the two made their way downstairs.

It was a walk of some fifteen minutes to the premises of Stewart Christie & Co. in Queen Street. Inside the shop, an assistant greeted Angus and had a kind word for Cyril. Then he listened to Angus's request: a tropical jacket – linen, preferably – and a lightweight pair of trousers. Perhaps a few shirts, too, and a Panama hat.

Cyril watched as the garments were brought to Angus for approval. He showed no interest in the jacket and the trousers, but the Panama hat engaged his attention, possibly for its evident chewability.

Angus cast an eye about the shop as his purchases were being wrapped. He noticed a tray of large, coloured handkerchiefs; one, a spotted red bandanna, stood out from the rest. He looked down at Cyril, who was gazing up at him with dark, liquid eyes. How would Cyril look, he wondered, with a red bandanna around his neck? He made his decision.

Outside, Angus and Cyril began to walk back along Queen Street. The day, which had been slightly overcast to begin with, had cleared. Now the sky of high summer was empty – so empty that blue had been attenuated into a shade so pale that it was almost white. The trees in Queen Street were heavy with leaf; green luxuriance as counterpoint to the grey-and-honey tones of the buildings.

Cyril trotted beside Angus, an undoubted spring in his step, the red bandanna contrasting nicely with the dark of his coat. He feels enhanced, thought Angus; and so too might all of us be enhanced – by a touch of red, by a fine day, by being alive in this splendid city, this heart-entrancing place.

## 41. *Psychotherapeutic Matters*

Most of us, if pressed, are made uneasy by change. We recognise its importance in our lives and there are occasions when we persuade ourselves that it is for the best – which, of course, it often is – but at heart we are concerned that, if change comes, it will bring with it regret.

This is particularly so when it comes to those who look after us. Doctors and dentists retire or move, much as the rest of us do. This is usually much regretted by those who are their patients, who then have to get used to a new face and a new approach to the aches and afflictions to which flesh and bone is heir. And the same must be said of the disappearance of plumbers, who understand the idiosyncrasies of our U-bends and lesser drains; of mechanics, who remember our suspension as if it were their own; of postmen, who are familiar with the shed where we like our parcels to be left, or with quite the right angle at which to press our sporadically functioning doorbells.

The worst of all such changes, though, is a change of psychotherapist. The problem with this is that the narrative is interrupted; for months, perhaps years, the patient has discussed himself or herself with the psychotherapist. Now, quite suddenly, it seems that this discussion has been abandoned by one side. For the patient it must be like telling a long joke only to find, some time before the punchline, that the audience has changed and does not know what went before. Why were these three men in the balloon, may we ask? Would you mind going back to the beginning?

In psychoanalysis, the full-blown, long-drawn-out, daily unburdening that can take years, or decades, to complete, the change of an analyst can be a disaster. Indeed, such is the dependence that may develop between analyst and analysand that many psychoanalysts simply cannot find it in themselves to retire, and continue to sit and listen to their patients until the very end, either for the patient or the analyst. Freudian lore is full of stories of analysts who have died of sheer old age in their psychoanalytical chair; or patients who have similarly succumbed while on the couch. The narrative falters and stops; the word-association suddenly becomes one-sided, with words hanging in the air unanswered.

This dependence, though officially discouraged in psychoanalytical circles, can be quite touching. In both Vichy and occupied France, psychoanalysis hardly flourished. There were, however, a few elderly analysts who were, on liberation, accused of collaboration. These had little alternative but to move to Morocco, where they established themselves in Casablanca. Their patients moved too. And when these elderly psychoanalysts died, their patients arranged, in due course, to be buried alongside them. Thus did the relationship continue beyond the grave, as if the analyst lay interred for all eternity, patiently listening to all the unresolved issues emanating from the next-door plot.

Six is not an easy age at which to change one's psychotherapist, and indeed Irene was concerned that the experience would be so traumatic for Bertie that therapeutic support would be required for the consequences. This, of course, was not the case, as Bertie, who was an entirely normal little boy, had no need of psychotherapy in the first place. But she was loath to accept that, and when Dr. Hugo Fairbairn, author of *Shattered to Pieces: Ego Dissolution in a Three-Year-Old Tyrant*, went off to Aberdeen, she was concerned that his successor, Dr. St. Clair, would be able to pick up the strands of the complex therapeutic process to which Bertie had been introduced.

For Dr. Fairbairn, the offer of a chair from the University of Aberdeen had come at an opportune time. The chair in Aberdeen was prestigious, and it would give him the opportunity to write a book that he had recently been planning, *The Psychopathology of the Over-Intrusive Mother, or Mater Dentata*. But there was more to it than that, and had his own decision been subjected to the scrutiny that he gave to decisions made by his patients, it would have been apparent that Dr. Fairbairn was running away from Edinburgh because of what he had himself termed his rucksack of guilt.

This guilt came from the fact that he had, many years ago, slapped a particularly trying young patient, Wee Fraser, after Wee Fraser had, in a quite unprovoked manner, suddenly bitten him.

Many years later, with Wee Fraser now fifteen or thereabouts, Dr. Fairbairn had met him on a bus to Burdiehouse; Wee Fraser, dimly remembering the psychotherapist, but not to the extent of knowing who he was or how their paths had previously crossed, had, as a precautionary measure, head-butted him. Whereupon Dr. Fairbairn had struck the boy, possibly dislocating his jaw, and run away. This, in guilt terms, had piled Pelion upon Ossa, or, in Scottish terms, Ben Nevis upon Ben Macdui. What could one do, in such circumstances, but flee? And in what direction to flee but north?

The choice of north was highly significant. Those who flee south flee to an imagined territory of forgiveness; they flee to Mother; to a place where whatever they did is no longer important; Mother forgives, she always has and always will.

Spain, Portugal, Italy – those countries where the Marian visions appear so unexpectedly in grottoes or olive groves – these are places to which those overburdened in the Protestant north go for solace or forgetfulness, to get away from the stern judgement of the north. Dr. Fairbairn went north because he wished to appease reason.

He was replaced by Dr. St. Clair, who therefore became Bertie's psychotherapist. He came without preconceptions and would have discharged his young patient more or less immediately, had there not been that unfortunate misunderstanding about wolves. This had made him decide to continue with treatment, and Bertie, as ever, acquiesced. What could he do?

One cannot divorce one's mother, especially when one is only six. All one can do, really, is wait until one turns eighteen, that milestone at which adulthood and independence begin. But between six and eighteen is a gulf of years wider than an ocean, or a desert, or any of those features which, at the age of six, seem endless, seem infinite.

## 42. Life and Chance

Dr. St. Clair was younger than Dr. Fairbairn. At thirty-two, a good twelve years separated them, but that was not by any means all. Dr. St. Clair was Australian, of Scottish ancestry, while Dr. Fairbairn, who had been born in Selkirk, had never lived outside Scotland, apart from during a brief period – just over a year – when he had been a registrar at the Tavistock Clinic in London. But the differences did not stop there: Dr. Fairbairn was inclined to accept the diktat of Vienna – he was deeply immersed in Freudian interpretations – whereas his successor, being the product of an eclectic training, was open to a wide range of explanations of human behaviour and, of course, misbehaviour. His approach was more philosophically inclined than Dr. Fairbairn's, stressing the role of thought and choice above that of emotional states and the dark promptings of the id. Indeed, had a coin once tossed on a particular summer evening in Melbourne fallen one way rather than the other, he would have studied for a degree in philosophy rather than one in psychology, and his whole life would have been different. That, of course, is a sobering thought, and it stayed with him; if the broad shape of a life can be determined by such a chance, then what claims can there be for freedom, for self-determination? We are putty, surely, in the hands of the gods, foolish to think that we are in control of the lives we lead.

And it does not stop there. It is salutary to remember how many of the features of our lives are not only not our own creation, but the result of events that took place even before we were born, sometimes several generations ago. And this applies not only at an individual level, but at a collective one too: what we are depends, to an extent, on where we are. That one is born in Aberdeen, or Chicago, or Gdansk – or wherever it is – dictates one's culture and, to some extent, moulds one's outlook on life. That is hardly a novel observation, but still bears reflection upon.

For a long time being Scottish brought, for many, a particular view of the world: a resilience in the face of difficulty, a certain intellectual seriousness, a belief in individual responsibility and individual salvation – concomitants all of the Scottish Reformation. But had John Knox been more in touch with his feminine side, it might have been different; iconoclasm might have been less pronounced – and less artistically destructive – and rather than the nineteenth-century cliché of the Scottish ship's engineer, one might have had the cliché of the Scottish interior decorator. It did not happen, of course . . .

That is all to do with the social self – the bit that is determined by the fact of being a member of a group rather than being solitary; when it comes to the family, how much more vivid is the impression that one's fate is formed by the actions of others. Each one of us is a palimpsest on which our parents have written, and beneath their writing is the writing of their parents. Thus is family pathology transmitted, and although behavioural geneticists may argue amongst themselves how genes determine behaviour, the rest of us have no difficulty in seeing familiar traits being passed on from parent to child to grandchild.

This explains, but may not comfort. A child unhappy today because his father is incapable of showing him affection may not know that his father was similarly deprived by his own father, and, even if he did, would be unlikely to be consoled by such knowledge. To be doing no more than to repeat the past is rarely viewed as an excuse, least of all in the eyes of children.

And even if complete freedom of will is illusory, there are still crucial decisions we make that we might not have made and that reverberate down the years. In the case of Dr. St. Clair, such a decision had been made by his grandfather, who, reaching for one book in the library, had inadvertently taken another and found himself accidentally immersed in an account of life on a farm in Victoria in the late nineteenth century. That St. Clair was a final-year medical student at the time, the son of a bank manager from Dumfries, and on impulse had decided to write off for information on medical careers in Australia. It was a cold, raw day in February, a month when anybody might be tempted to seek warmth and sunlight elsewhere; that undoubtedly affected his decision. Had it been a fine spring day, then the prospect of working in Aberdeen, which would otherwise have happened, might not have been so unattractive; but it was not, and the letter was written. Information came back, together with an invitation to apply for a post, and that letter determined the shape of several lives, including that of his grandson, Bertie's psychotherapist.

That pattern, of course, had been repeated thousands and thousands of times during the twentieth century, when Scotland was bled of its people, as it had been bled before, when the Highlands had been cleared. The doctor had been fortunate; he came from a background that was economically secure; for most, the experience was a far chancier one: discarded by an industrial system that had prospered on their labour, they went with very little, scarred in body and soul by the hardships of the factories and foundries of Motherwell, of Glasgow, of the Clyde. He met these men on the boat, as they made the long journey south; men who felt privileged because they were heading for a place that people described as the lucky country after their own had treated them so badly.

Again, pure chance intervened. The ship's doctor, who sat at the same table in the dining room, said to him: "You don't have to take the job they've offered you, you know. I can fix you up with something far better up in Queensland. That's the place to go."

He should have said that he would think about it, but he did not. It was hot, and the journey seemed interminable. He accepted the offer, largely because he wanted to do something – anything – to break the tedium of the voyage. By this decision, taken so lightly, he dictated the course of his life, the life of his son, and that of his grandson. It was this decision that meant eventually that it was a Dr. St. Clair, rather than anybody else, who became Bertie's psychotherapist, and therefore came into fateful contact with Bertie's mother, Irene.

## 43. *A Scotsman, His Life and Marriage*

Dr. St. Clair's practice in Brisbane flourished. People felt reassured by the quietly spoken Scottish doctor, with his habit of nodding sympathetically as people described their symptoms. He prospered and, although he never forgot that he was a Scot, he never returned to Scotland. There were plans to do so, of course, particularly after his marriage; his new wife, who had never been out of Australia, liked to hear him talk about Dumfries and about Edinburgh, too, which he told her was more beautiful than Venice and Paris put together. "I'll show you," he said. "We'll walk through Princes Street Gardens together and have coffee in the Brown

Derby. And we'll go shopping in Forsyth's, and Jenners, too, and motor out to Gleneagles. And, oh, you'll love it, my dear, and you'll bless the day that you agreed to marry a Scotsman, for all his faults . . ."

"Which are none to speak of," she said. "Or none that I notice, darling."

He got as far as arranging long leave from his practice, and enquiring with a shipping agent for a passage home, but the war intervened. Doctors were needed, and the two partners with whom he ran the practice had seven children between them. "It's me," he said to his wife. "I'll have to go."

Her father had been at Gallipoli, and had told her about it on one of the rare occasions when he spoke of the subject. At the end of his narrative, which was interrupted at several points by sobbing, he took her hand. "Never again," he said. "Never. Never. Whatever happens elsewhere, Australia must never get caught up in all that."

So when her husband said that he felt that he should volunteer, she begged him not to. "There are other doctors," she said. "Plenty of them."

"There aren't," he said.

"Well, just wait a while. See what happens."

"I can't. I couldn't look at myself in the mirror if I didn't go."

She was silent. I'm going to lose him, she thought.

He was posted to Malaya as the medical officer of an Australian infantry unit. He was used to the heat of Brisbane, but his overwhelming impression was of unrelenting humidity and unrelieved boredom. The men were healthy, and apart from treating malaria and the occasional surgical emergency in which he assisted the other medical officer in his unit, a surgeon, he did not have much to do. The surgeon was an Irishman who had settled in Darwin. He was good company and had a fund of improbable stories, but he drank. On many occasions he was barely sober enough to stand in the operating theatre and Dr. St. Clair was obliged to take over, receiving more or less intelligible instructions from the surgeon swaying behind him. "There's a thing in the middle there," the surgeon said. "The name escapes me at the moment, so it does, but I wouldn't cut that bit if I were you. Frightful amount of blood swirling around down there. So just take out that wee thingy over there and Bob's your uncle. My God, I wish I could remember my anatomy a bit better. We had a wonderful chap in Dublin who taught us everything we knew about the subject. Great fellow, so he was. Professor Mac-something-or-other. Bit of a Scotsman, like yourself. Had a moustache and a glass eye. Or a glass moustache, was it? Anyway, we put a leg in his car one day just to give him a wee fright and he took not a blind bit of notice. Pretended not to care, or so we thought, until one of the fellows pointed out that the leg was on the passenger seat and since that was the side that he had his glass eye he probably didn't see it! We had to bring it back to the dissecting room. Terrifically amusing business. Those were the days, so they were. Whole world's different nowadays. Lots of old women running the show. Careful! Not there – a bit further down, near the what's it called? That's better. Cut that bit off. I wish I had my glasses."

At least the boredom ended when the Japanese invaded. Pushed south into Singapore, he was kept busy dealing with the flood of casualties from the fighting on the peninsula. And then suddenly it was over. He had been billeted in a bungalow belonging to a harbour official and had been catching up on sleep after a twenty-hour stint of duty when his host told him it was all over. "There are a few boats getting out," he said. "I can get you on one of them if you hurry."

"I have to get back to the casualty station."

"It's in enemy hands. You can't. You've got five minutes."

He had gone, and found himself on a sampan with an Australian general and a handful of staff officers. The general, who had handed over his command before leaving his men to their captors, sat on the deck of the boat and looked moodily towards the shore. He watched him. What should a general do in such circumstances, he wondered. Should he stay and join his men as a prisoner of war, or should he escape, if he can, and live to fight another day? He wanted to speak to the general, but he seemed sunk in his thoughts, and Dr. St. Clair left him to himself.

Later, when the party split up, Dr. St. Clair fell into Japanese hands and was taken to Changi. He resumed his role as a medical officer, coping with what primitive supplies they had, surviving forced marches and the horrors of the labour camps. He became more of a nurse than a doctor, tending to men dying of dysentery and starvation, making representations when he could to the guards. He learned about cruelty; about the ease with which one person may kill another, by a nod of the head, by a tiny movement of the lips; he learned about all the workings of inhumanity. And then, as suddenly as he had been captured, he found himself free. He wondered how the Japanese would respond to defeat: would they fall upon those very swords they had used to decapitate their prisoners? He looked into the face of his erstwhile captors, and saw nothing. They were like puppets, he thought; puppets whose strings had been cut from above.

He returned to Brisbane. None of his clothes would fit him now. You sent a man off to war, he thought, and you got a skeleton back.

She said, "Let's not talk about it. Let's forget that all this happened."

He looked at her. He could not speak, even had he wanted to. He wept. She held him, remembering how her father had wept over Gallipoli.

She became pregnant and they had a son. This was Dr. St. Clair's father.

## 44. A Move to Moray Place

"We can't stay here," Matthew announced. "I like India Street – it's one of the nicest streets in the New Town – but how can we stay here? How?"

Elspeth cast an eye down on her stomach, now rather larger, she imagined, than it would otherwise have been. The thought of three babies within her – three! – made her feel slightly light-headed. I'm going to be vast, she thought; really vast. I'll require scaffolding. "I don't see what you mean. What's wrong with India Street?"

Matthew shook his head. "It's not India Street itself," he said. "In fact it's nothing to do with India Street. It's to do with us – all six, no, five of us. You can't have three children in this flat – you just can't."

Elspeth looked around. "But it's a really large flat," she said. "Lots of people – virtually everyone – makes do with much less space. We're lucky."

"Of course we're lucky. I know that. But how are you going to get three babies up the stair? Impossible."

Elspeth thought about this. "No . . ."

"Well, there you are," said Matthew. "We're going to have to move."

She saw that he was right. But where could they move? Was Matthew planning a move into suburbia – to the braes of Corstorphine, to the glades of Colinton, to the Braids? This was all territory with which she was unfamiliar, her idea of it being long avenues of well-set bungalows with neat little gardens behind carefully manicured hedges. Such places were undoubtedly comfortable, but she wondered whether anything happened there. Matthew, she thought, might be unhappy in such circumstances; he was more urban than suburban, and it was difficult to imagine him wheeling the triple pushchair off to Blackford Pond to visit the ducks. And yet, that's what people did; they went off into the suburbs and were never seen again.

"All right," she said. "I suppose we're going to have to get somewhere more suitable. But where? Corstorphine?"

Matthew shook his head. "No, I don't think so. Corstorphine is fine for . . ." He paused, uncertain how to complete the sentence. What was Corstorphine fine for? He was not sure. It was not far from the zoo, of course, and he had heard that at night one might hear the lions roaring. He was not sure how he would react to that. It might make one think one was in the Serengeti, or it might make one reflect on the whole question of keeping such great, proud beasts in northern captivity.

"So, where then?"

Matthew looked up at the ceiling. "Well, what do we need? Somewhere on the ground floor. Somewhere with a garden where we can play with the baby . . . babies. Somewhere within reach of the gallery so I don't have to sit in a bus all morning. Somewhere . . . comfortable."

Elspeth thought for a moment. She had seen a large *For Sale* notice recently and remembered thinking that the place that it was advertising might be rather attractive. But where was it? It took a few moments to recall, but then it came to her and she smiled with pleasure at the recollection.

"Just round the corner," she said.

"Ann Street?" Matthew asked.

"No, not Ann Street. They have a committee, you know, to decide whether you can live there."

Matthew shook his head. "I don't think that's true. I know people who live in Ann Street, and they're not like that. They're very welcoming – within reason, of course." He paused. "They do have a list, though, of people who should not be allowed to live there. It's quite a long list, actually. Apparently there are seventeen names on it."

"I'd love to know who's on it," said Elspeth, smiling.

"Wouldn't we all," agreed Matthew. "I've heard about one or two people who are said to be on it. I thought it was a bit unfair. I knew one of them, by the way."

"Oh? Who?"

Matthew told her, and then gave her the details. Elspeth listened with an increasingly incredulous expression. "Really?" she said.

"Yes."

"Well, you can see their point of view," she said.

"But anyway, Ann Street is not on my list. So we need to look elsewhere."

Suddenly she remembered. "Moray Place!" she exclaimed. "That was where it was."

"Where what was?"

"The FOR SALE sign that I saw. I was trying to remember where it was. It was Moray Place – on the northern side – you know, the bit that looks down over the Water of Leith and those gardens. That side."

Matthew looked doubtful. "That's not going far. In fact, it's just round the corner. I thought that we might make a slightly bigger move than that."

"But why move far away just for the sake of it? We're not trying to get away from anything, are we?"

Matthew shook his head. "Of course not. I just imagined that a move would take us a little further afield than that."

"You could still walk to work," Elspeth pointed out. "And there are those wonderful gardens."

"True . . . true. But then there are . . ."

Elspeth looked at him quizzically. "You mean the nudists?"

"Yes. You do know, don't you, that half the committee of the Scottish Federation of Nudists lives there? Or so I'm told."

Elspeth nodded. It was an open secret, although one would not have thought that of one of the very grandest addresses in

Edinburgh. And yet one could see the attraction of Moray Place, with its gardens that were well protected from snell winds from the north.

"I don't think it really matters," she said. "Nudists are generally fine. I had an aunt who was a nudist. Nobody talked about it, of course – they just said that Aunt Dot was off on one of her little holidays again. As children we had no idea – and couldn't understand why we were never shown her holiday photos. 'Not quite suitable for those of tender years,' she said."

Of course, that answer merely served to whet the appetite, and she and her brother had, while staying with their aunt, crept into the room where she kept her photograph albums and taken the relevant volume off the shelf.

"No!" exclaimed her brother, as they opened the album. "Look at that!"

Elspeth glanced at the photographs. "That's the airline's fault," she said knowingly. "They must have lost their suitcases for them, with all their clothes. It happens all the time, especially with . . ." And here, with all the innocence – and perspicacity – of youth, she named an airline.

## 45. *In Moray Place*

The decision to move, like many such decisions of great personal importance, was made quickly. Within ten minutes of Matthew's mentioning the unsuitability of India Street for triplets – or of top flats in India Street for that purpose – he and Elspeth found themselves firmly committed to what in Scotland is called a flit. Scots words are usually very descriptive and apt for their purpose – "dreich" describes moist, foggy days perfectly; to be "trauchled" is to be exactly as the verb suggests; and "fantoosh" is virtually onomatopoeic in its capture of flashiness – but "flit" is surely misleading. Few people flit in the carefree way that the word implies; most flits are traumatic, trauchling experiences that test the psychological and material resources of the flitters. So even if the decision to flit was quickly and painlessly taken by Matthew and Elspeth, the actual flit would surely be much more demanding.

The proximity of Moray Place, though, made the first stages of the process simplicity itself. On the very day on which Matthew raised the subject, he and Elspeth made an appointment with McKay Norwell, the selling solicitors, to view the flat in question. "It's a very attractive flat," the solicitor said over the telephone. "We have several notes of interest."

Matthew's heart sank at this news. The system of blind-bidding for property in Scotland was attractive to a seller, who might hope that what was effectively a process of auction would drive the price up, but was a nightmare for the purchaser, who would never know how much to bid. It all depended on how badly somebody wanted the property: a flat in a popular part of town might have ten people chasing after it – possibly even more – and those with the deepest pockets would have the best chance of getting it. Matthew had heard of a flat that had been on the market for offers over four hundred thousand pounds going for five hundred thousand. And then there were the heartbreaking stories of people who had missed a house they yearned to possess by ten pounds. Of course there was always somebody who was happy with the outcome, and the couple who bid ten pounds more might have loved it ten pounds more, but there were usually those who were bitterly disappointed.

"We mustn't raise our hopes," Matthew warned, as he and Elspeth made their way to the appointment to view. "There'll be other people looking at it. We may not get it, you know."

"Of course," said Elspeth.

"And we may not want it anyway," said Matthew. "It may be awful."

Again Elspeth said, "Of course." But she was already mentally moving into the flat, wondering whether the curtains from India Street would fit the windows at Moray Place.

They arrived outside the building. The front door, painted black and with a brass numeral attached above the letterbox, gave directly on to the pavement.

"You'd only have to get the pushchairs up over these two steps," said Matthew. "That won't be hard."

Elspeth nodded. She was looking at the high, elegant windows on either side of the front door. They would definitely need new curtains.

Matthew rang the bell and the door was answered by the solicitor's assistant, a young woman, who led them into the hall. There was a brochure, setting out the floor plan and the details of each room. "Here are the particulars," said the young woman, handing them folders. "Please wander around – and let me know if there's anything that needs explaining."

The young woman went off to read a magazine in the kitchen, while Matthew and Elspeth made their way along the corridor that led to the garden end of the flat.

" 'Particulars,' " whispered Matthew. "It's a great word, isn't it? Such a lovely, old-fashioned ring to it. Just right for solicitors. Like the word 'corporation.' Please send me particulars of your corporation."

"Corporation?"

"Tummy," explained Matthew. "If somebody has a large stomach, it's called a corporation in polite conversation. In Edinburgh. As in 'He has a substantial corporation.' "

Elspeth glanced down at her stomach. "I have an increasingly large corporation," she muttered. "And it's going to get even larger."

Matthew touched her arm lightly. "My darling! You'll go back to normal size – after the baby . . . babies."

"I hope so."

"You will. Of course you will. People who have triplets don't look massive forever. That's not the way it works."

They reached the end of the corridor. Somewhere, a clock was ticking loudly – a sound that served to emphasise the overall silence of the flat.

"It's so quiet," said Matthew, peering into the room ahead of them. "Apart from that clock."

They entered the drawing room, a large room that stretched out to a set of wall-high windows overlooking a terrace. For a few moments they stood quite still. Then Matthew turned to Elspeth and looked at her enquiringly. "Do you see yourself here?" he asked.

She walked into the middle of the room. "It's very elegant. Our stuff . . ."

He reassured her. "Our stuff will be all right," he said. "And if it isn't, we can get some new stuff – or some new old stuff. There's that place down in Leith that sells all that Georgian furniture. We could go there."

Elspeth moved to the windows. The garden outside, which was surrounded by a high wall, had been carefully tended. It sloped down sharply, and at the end, beyond the top of the wall, the view was of the tops of the trees in Lord Moray's Pleasure Garden beyond.

She gazed at the trees for a few moments, noticing how the wind was making them sway slightly. They were like the surface of a green sea, she thought; a green sea of gently moving leaves.

She turned to Matthew, who was standing at the other end of the room, peering at a painting on the wall.

"What is it?" she said.

Her voice sounded small in the large room. She repeated her question, unsure that he had heard it.

His reply was half mumbled. "Fergusson," he said. "A picture of a woman reading. His sister, I think. He painted his sister reading – I've seen another one just like this somewhere."

Her eyes were drawn to the garden again. There was a small lead statue placed close to the wall on one side. Half of the child's face was in shadow; the other in the sun. It was a small child, a girl, with skirts that reached almost to the feet. It was very skilful, she thought, to make lead seem so light, so flowing. She thought that she might draw Matthew's attention to this and say . . .

She fell – not to the floor, but half-way across a chair, so that her head did not hit the ground. As she fell, she saw for a moment that face of the child. The sun had disappeared behind a cloud and the light that had played on the statue was no longer there.

## 46. *What We Really Are*

After Angus Lordie had made his purchases at Stewart Christie in Queen Street, he decided to walk directly to Domenica's flat in Scotland Street. He had intended to visit his friend the day before, but had been distracted from his purpose by a series of telephone calls and minor disturbances. His electricity meter had to be read; there was a parcel delivery for his neighbour, who was out at the time; there was a surveyor who wanted to get access to the shared roof space because the flat next door was for sale and his ladder was not long enough; and so on. By the time all of this had been dealt with, his morning, he felt, was ruined, and it was too late to visit Domenica, who would have left for Valvona & Crolla by then. She went every day, it seemed, often for small purchases – a handful of mushrooms, a few slices of salami, a single serving of pasta.

"You could do a big shopping trip once a week," Angus had once pointed out to her.

"Please mind your own business, Angus," she had replied. And when he had looked injured by this abrupt response she had relented and explained. "Shopping is a small, quotidian transaction. We need these to anchor our lives."

He had looked at her blankly, and she had continued. "The day needs to be punctuated, you see. The hours of the Church, for instance – lauds, terce, sext, and all the rest – are a way of breaking up the day, a way of making landmarks in our lives."

He had smiled. "You're talking like an anthropologist."

"I am an anthropologist, Angus." She paused. "Or I was."

He looked thoughtful. "Surely one doesn't stop being an anthropologist – just because one isn't doing anthropology. Would I stop being an artist if I stopped painting? I'm not sure about that."

"That's interesting," said Domenica. "Does a doctor stop being a doctor when he or she stops practising? I don't think so. He could resume practice."

Angus looked up at the ceiling. Talking to Domenica sometimes required one to think really hard – rather harder than he was accustomed to thinking. She was like a sudoku, in a way – not that he should make that comparison openly. He pulled his thoughts together. "But a politician doesn't remain a politician once he's out of politics, does he? Or a plumber?"

"The politician – no. The plumber, yes, because it's a skill. Rather like the doctor. That's the difference, perhaps. If the description of what you are is based on a skill, then that's what you remain."

A further thought occurred to Angus. "What if you want to stop being something and people say, 'No, you can't stop being that,' because once you're it, you're it for life? What then?"

Domenica rose to make coffee. "Give me an example."

Angus shrugged. "Oh, membership of a religious faith, for example. Some groups say you can't get out. If you're in, then you're in and that's it."

"Apostasy," said Domenica. "Yes, that's difficult. It depends on whether you accept the group's view. I wouldn't – in most cases."

"If I joined the Mafia," said Angus, "would I be a mafioso forever? Or would I stop being one if I resigned?"

"I don't think you can resign," said Domenica. She paused, and smiled at Angus indulgently. "But I wouldn't call you a mafioso for the rest of your life. I would call you a reformed mafioso."

"But the label would always be there?" asked Angus. "It wouldn't ever go away?"

It took Domenica some time to answer this. And when she did answer, she was brief. "No, it wouldn't go away," she said.

Angus raised an eyebrow. "So one can never change? Not completely?"

That, she accepted, seemed hard. Could we never become something different from what we started off as? People did change – they clearly did, and she knew many examples of people whom she knew who had changed completely. Angus himself had changed, she thought. He was far less . . . how would one put it? Difficult? And even Cyril . . . She stopped. That was the example for which she had been searching.

"Cyril," she said. "Take him as an example. Whatever moral effort Cyril made – no matter how hard he tried – he would still be a dog, wouldn't he? It's the same with us. There are some things about us that are fundamental to our identity – things we can't change. That bit always remains."

"But that fundamental bit is very small, don't you think?" asked Angus. "I can't stop being a man, can I? But I can become a very different sort of man."

"Yes," said Domenica. "You could. Of course, some men do

stop being men, don't they? If one undergoes sex reassignment and takes on a female identity – surgery, the lot – then you stop being a man."

She looked at Angus. It was difficult, if not impossible, to imagine him as a woman. It was difficult, in fact, to imagine any of the men of her acquaintance as women. And yet some men did want to become women and tried so hard, and some women wanted to be men and made a similar effort. It was not easy to empathise, but one had to. Imagine waking up every morning and feeling that there was something fundamentally wrong with the way things were; it would be insupportable. And yet, did ordinary human empathy require people in general to believe things that simply were not true? Some aspirations were unrealistic. The middle-aged may wish to be seen as young, but did that mean that people should treat them as youthful simply because that was what they wanted? Did courtesy and consideration for the feelings of others go that far?

"But do you ever stop being a man?" asked Angus. "Or are you a woman on the outside and a man inside?"

"Some would say those are merely social labels," said Domenica.

"And Cyril might say that being a dog is merely a social label," Angus retorted.

Cyril did not say that, of course. He was listening to this conversation, but there had only been one word so far that he had recognised – which was Cyril. He was not sure what that word meant – it was different from walk, which he understood very well. The word Cyril meant, in his mind, that something was going to happen. It was a verb. He had no idea that it was him, that he was an object.

He waited for some further sign, but none came. So he lowered his head and went to sleep. Before he dropped off, pictures came to him, and scents too. He saw a field, and a path. He saw a ball in the air, describing an arc across the sky.

He smelled something rich and exciting; rabbits, perhaps. He saw a face peering at him. He saw water at the edge of sand. He heard verbs.

## 47. *The Symbolism of Birds*

The conversation that Angus had with Domenica over personal identity was just one of the many exchanges they had on such topics. He did not have such conversations with anybody else – not with Matthew, with whom he spoke about day-to-day things, although they did discuss art from time to time; nor did he have them with Big Lou, to whom and with whom he tended to listen, rather than engage in conversation. Domenica was different; she made him think.

And of how many of one's friends could one say that, he wondered. The answer, when he came up with it, was very few. There were his friends in the Scottish Arts Club, with whom Angus had lunch from time to time; all of them were good conversationalists, but for the most part the talk was lighthearted. They talked about other artists, about shows, about who had said what to whom, and about what was going on at the National Gallery of Scotland; a broad enough agenda, of course, but not the same as the agenda he pursued with Domenica. Why, he asked himself, was that? The question came to his mind as he climbed up the stairs that morning to Domenica's flat. And the answer, which came on the second landing, outside the door of that awful Pollock woman, the one whose ankle Cyril had so embarrassingly nipped, was revelatory. He had those conversations with Domenica because she, uniquely amongst his friends, understood him. It was as simple as that.

He stopped, and looked down at Cyril. Something was worrying the dog, as the hairs on the back of his neck were bristling. Was there a cat about? It was the reaction commonly produced by taunting feline presence, only this time rather more pronounced.

"Anything wrong, Cyril, old chap?"

Cyril now growled – a low, throaty utterance.

"My goodness," said Angus, reaching down to reassure the dog. "Traces of feline? Quite understandable, of course."

But it was not that – not that at all. As Angus bent down to pat Cyril, the door on the landing opened and Irene looked out. For a moment her expression registered confusion – what was this man doing on the landing? – followed quickly by recognition and understanding.

"Oh, it's just you," she said.

Angus inclined his head politely. "Indeed it is."

"And that dog of yours," said Irene, looking at Cyril with a mixture of distaste and disapproval.

"Cyril," said Angus. "My dog."

Cyril stared at Irene and gave another low growl.

"He's a most unfriendly creature," said Irene.

Angus ignored the comment. "And how is your little boy?" he asked. "Bertie, isn't it?"

"He's fine," said Irene. "And we have another one now. Ulysses."

Angus suppressed a smile. "Such a nice name," he said. And thought – but did not say – *for a Greek*.

Irene nodded absentmindedly in response to the compliment. There was something else on her mind. "You're an artist, aren't you, Mr. Lordie?"

Angus inclined his head again. "A humble limner," he said.

"And somebody told me that you paint portraits."

"I do indeed. I paint other subjects, of course, but I suppose one or two people know me as a portrait painter. Not exactly Henry Raeburn, of course, but a portrait painter nonetheless."

Irene wrinkled her nose. "Raeburn was so predictably bourgeois," she said. "All those pictures of the propertied classes, all congratulating themselves."

Angus was silent.

"I'm really of the John Berger school myself," she went on. "I look behind the sitter and see the possessions. Those portraits are all about power and ownership."

Cyril growled very softly.

"But not all portraits are like that," Irene conceded. "I'm sure that yours aren't. I'm sure that you have abundant psychological insight."

"I would hope to get a bit of that," mumbled Angus. Really, this woman! What they said about her was absolutely correct. She's insufferable – quite insufferable.

Irene now emerged fully from the doorway. "You wouldn't care to paint Bertie, would you?" she said. "I've read about this big portrait competition. The BP Award, I believe it's called. In fact, I went to see some of the portraits when they came on tour. Some of them were very good."

"I'm glad you approved," said Angus. "Portraiture is rather unfairly neglected, I think . . ."

Irene interrupted him. "Bertie would make a very interesting subject," she said. "He's a remarkable little boy."

"I'm sure he is," said Angus. He saw Bertie from time to time in Drummond Place – a rather lonely little boy, he thought, who had once told him that he would like to have a dog. That's right. And then he had said something about his mother not allowing him to have animals for some reason or another.

"Yes," said Irene. "Bertie perhaps against a suitable background . . ."

"I usually do studio portraits," said Angus.

"There's that wonderful portrait of Seamus Heaney," Irene enthused. "Do you know the one? It has Heaney against a background of a laurel bush, with birds on the branches of the bush. We could have Bertie . . ."

"I know the portrait you're talking about," said Angus. "It's in Belfast, I think. The Ulster Museum. Of course birds are used as a symbol for poets, aren't they? Sometimes unconsciously, of course. The Westwater portrait of Hugh MacDiarmid has seabirds flying around in the background." He looked at his watch. "You must forgive me. I'm expected at Domenica Macdonald's upstairs."

Irene cast a dismissive look upwards. "I'm sure you'll find her in. I fear she doesn't get out a great deal." She laughed. "But do remember about painting Bertie. Should you wish to, we'd be delighted."

Angus nodded. "Thank you."

He completed the climb up the stairs and rang Domenica's doorbell.

"I met your downstairs neighbour," he said. Domenica sighed. "She suggested that I paint Bertie's portrait," Angus went on.

"There's no end to her ambition for that poor child," said Domenica. "But let's not dwell upon such matters. We have so much to plan for the Italian trip."

"Good," said Angus. "I've just been to buy a few clothes. I can't wait."

"Very soon now," said Domenica. "I've been to the bank and picked up some euros. Such a pity about the lire. I would have had hundreds of thousands of them. And such a colourful currency."

"The world is very grey now," said Angus.

"And Antonia showed me a photograph of the villa . . ." She broke off.

"And?"

"I can't believe her cheek. I really can't."

"Why?"

"She pointed out that the villa is very small, and actually only has two bedrooms."

"Oh . . ."

"Yes. And would you believe it, but . . . but she's put you in with her in one of the rooms – separate beds, she hastened to point out – while I've got the other room to myself."

Angus gasped. "Me? Sharing with her?"

"Yes," said Domenica.

"But that's outrageous," said Angus. "If anybody has to share, then it should be the two of you . . . Sorry, but that's only appropriate . . . I'm not old-fashioned, of course . . ."

"Of course not."

"And Cyril?"

"Outside."

## 48. *The Breaking of the Heart*

"I suppose she's trying to be modern," suggested Angus. "It's like those awful mixed-sex wards in hospitals. The theory was that it was old-fashioned to put men in one ward and women in another."

"People hated it," said Domenica. "I remember going to visit somebody who was utterly miserable. She was in a ward with ten men, and she was the only woman. It was a nightmare."

"Antonia might have liked that," said Angus.

Domenica laughed. "Perhaps. But I'm not sure that she is simply trying to be modern. I think that . . ." She paused. Angus was looking away, and she could sense his embarrassment. "Well, I'm sorry to have to say this, but she's ruthless, that woman. She wants a man and she doesn't care who it is. It all shows how desperate she is."

Angus thought about this. Was Domenica implying he was the bottom of the barrel and only a desperate woman would show any interest in him? That was hardly flattering. With his new outfit from Stewart Christie in Queen Street, and Cyril with his red bandanna, they might look quite the thing – in the right light.

Domenica herself had realised the tactlessness of her remark, and was thinking of ways to repair the damage. Angus was more sensitive than people thought, as men often are, and she would not like him to think that she believed that no reasonable woman would consider him attractive.

"I mean that she's generally desperate," she said. "On all matters – desperate across the board."

Angus shrugged. It's all very well having one new outfit, he thought, but I can't wear that all the time. Should I go back to Stewart Christie and get some more clothes?

"Yes," said Domenica. "Her desperation is quite extraordinary. There is nothing to which she will not stoop. Remember the blue Spode teacup? Remember that business?"

Angus frowned. "But I thought that you found your teacup in here – after we had gone in next door to pinch it back."

Domenica waved a hand airily. "Well, another one did indeed turn up. But I'm not sure that it was the same as the one that went missing. I still think it's likely that the one I saw in Antonia's flat was mine. After all, she had no other blue Spode – not a scrap. And you don't have single teacups – you usually have a set."

"Well, whatever that was all about, we shall have to watch Antonia very carefully."

Domenica thought this good advice. "And you, Angus, are just going to have to refuse to share a room with her. Be direct. Tell her to her face."

Angus shifted uncomfortably in his chair. "There must be a more tactful way of dealing with her. Perhaps we could write to one of those social advice columns and ask how to deal with a situation like this."

"Those columns are certainly useful," she said. "I suspect that they would advise you to come up with some reason for wanting to sleep alone. Perhaps you could say that you're a terrible snorer and nobody could possibly sleep in the same room as you. They're very good with answers like that, those columns."

"I could tell her I was a somnambulist," said Angus brightly. "I could say that I pose some – not a great deal, but some – danger to those around me when I'm asleep."

Domenica thought this a very good idea. "And perhaps you could pretend to sleepwalk while we're in the villa. That would confirm what you said."

"Cyril suffers from somnambulism," said Angus. "Not very often, but from time to time."

"Are you sure?"

"Yes. He gets up out of his bed and wags his tail. Then he walks off to the cupboard where I keep his lead and he sits outside it.

"I've seen him do this several times. I just gently lead him back to his basket and he lies down again. The vet says that it's nothing to worry about."

Domenica glanced at Cyril, who looked back at her and smiled, his gold tooth flashing in a ray of sun. "Somnambulism raises some very interesting issues," she said. "I read somewhere about an experiment which some sleep researchers had conducted in Montreal. They had a woman who suffered from nocturnal somnambulistic snacking."

"What?"

"She sleepwalked at night and raided the refrigerator. She was putting on an awful lot of weight as a result. But she had another problem – she had a phobia for snakes – ophidiophobia, I believe it's called. So they told her to drape a large rubber snake over the fridge before she went to bed at night."

"And that worked? No more nocturnal snacking?"

"Yes, that worked. But – and this is the interesting part. She forgot to put the snake in position one night, and when she went downstairs the next morning, she had a Mother Hubbard moment – no food. All snacked."

"Oh."

"Indeed. This shows that while she was asleep she was, at some level, aware of the fact that she had forgotten to put the snake in place. The inhibition against going to the fridge was therefore not operating. So this suggests that . . ."

Angus waited. He was interested to find out just what the implications of this were.

Domenica looked thoughtful. "It means," she began, "that we can still be expected to behave ourselves when we are asleep."

"Surely not," said Angus. "If I say something terrible in my sleep, I would hope not to be held accountable. I don't think . . ."

"But it shows what you really want to say," interrupted Domenica. "It's rather like drunkenness. Nice people are nice when they're drunk – nasty people are nasty." She paused. "Auden said something similar about the weather, if I remember correctly. He said that nice weather is what nasty people are nasty about and the nice take pleasure in observing. Something like that."

Angus rose to his feet and crossed to the window. "I never tire of your view," he said. "Never."

"It's a great consolation," said Domenica. A consolation for . . . for . . . Well, it was a consolation for everything, really.

"And look at that sky," said Angus. "We're so fortunate, aren't we? To live in a country where the sky changes virtually every moment; where its colours, its attenuated blues, its whites, its purples, break the heart, and then break it again, afresh, every single day."

## 49. *Chinoiserie*

When he saw Elspeth collapse, for a moment Matthew was unable to do anything, experiencing, for the first time in his life, a complete paralysis of disbelief and indecision. Then, once the initial shock had passed, he leapt forward, knocking over a small mahogany table. The noise of the toppling table, which had supported a small glass bowl, now smashed, was drowned by Matthew's cry of anguish.

The solicitor's assistant was in the kitchen, where she was absorbed in a copy of *Scottish Interiors*. The feature she was reading was an article on a house in a Fife fishing village that had been restored by a Dundee architect and his wife. Everything was white, as far as she could make out, and minimalist. She held the page away from her to test the perspective. No, definitely too many sharp corners and hard surfaces. Could minimalism not be a bit softer?

Then she heard Matthew. She looked up. It was not the first time that she had heard people exclaim – and very occasionally swear – when looking round a house. These exclamations were often the result of disappointment with the décor – or, on occasion, vociferous disapproval. Then there were arguments, when one member of a couple liked the layout of a house and another did not. That led to tension and, again very occasionally, open arguments. But this was different: something had clearly happened. They've broken something, she thought. People will insist on picking things up and then they break them. And then we have to go back to the owner and explain what has happened. Never they, be it noted – we.

She put aside *Scottish Interiors* and made her way into the drawing room. There she saw Matthew bending over Elspeth, who appeared to be half draped over one of the chairs. For a moment she thought that he had knocked her down – that the scream had come from her, not him, and that a disagreement over architecture had taken a rather serious turn. But then Matthew turned to her and shouted that she should call an ambulance.

The assistant took out her mobile phone and dialled the emergency number. A voice answered quickly and took the address. "Stay where you are. Somebody will be with you very soon."

Then Elspeth sat up. Matthew looked at her for a moment in complete astonishment, as if she, a female Lazarus perhaps, was defying death itself.

"I think I slipped," said Elspeth. "Sorry."

"You didn't slip," said Matthew. "You collapsed. Oh, my darling, are you all right?"

"Of course I'm all right," said Elspeth, struggling to get to her feet.

"You should sit down," said the assistant. "I'll make some tea and then the ambulance will arrive."

Elspeth laughed. "I don't need an ambulance. I slipped, that's all."

"You didn't," said Matthew. "You collapsed. Your eyes were closed. You were unconscious."

"I don't think so," said Elspeth. "If I had been unconscious, then I wouldn't remember what happened. I slipped, on that rug."

"Then should I call the ambulance people and cancel?" asked the assistant.

"No," said Matthew. "We must get Elspeth to hospital as soon as possible."

Elspeth reached out and placed a hand on Matthew's arm – a calming gesture. "Come on, Matthew, let's not overdramatise the situation. Maybe I did faint. People faint during pregnancy."

Matthew frowned. "Only if something's wrong."

The solicitor's assistant shook her head. "No, I think your wife's right. I know somebody who fainted quite a few times when she was expecting her first baby. I saw her do it several times. And the doctor explained that it was all to do with inadequate blood supply."

"Yes," said Elspeth. "I'm expecting triplets, you see."

The solicitor's assistant gasped. "Poor you . . . I mean, congratulations."

Elspeth thanked her. "It's exciting," she said. "For both of us."

"Triplets," said the assistant. "That's probably why you fainted. Anyway, I'm going to phone the ambulance people and call them off. All right?"

"I suppose so," said Matthew. "Although I do wish you'd go and be checked up on. People shouldn't faint just like that."

The assistant went back into the kitchen to make the call, leaving Matthew and Elspeth in the drawing room.

"I'd like to look at the rest of the flat," said Elspeth. "I really like this place, you know. That lovely garden. This room. Everything, so far."

Matthew took her arm solicitously. "You should hold on to me," he said.

"Oh, Matthew! Don't be ridiculous. I'm unlikely to faint again. I'm fine."

He looked doubtful, but relinquished his grip. "Please be careful."

"I shall." She smiled at him. He cared so much for her, and if that meant that he fussed a bit, then that was better than the opposite, an indifferent husband. Would it last forever, she wondered; would he be like this when they were middle-aged, and beyond? She imagined that it would; Matthew was not fickle in any way, she had noticed that.

They heard the solicitor's assistant on the telephone. "No, she's absolutely fine. It was just a faint. About thirty seconds, I think. Yes, I'll tell them they should go the health centre. Thank you."

"I don't need to see the doctor," said Elspeth. "You don't go to the doctor every time you faint. Victorian and Edwardian women fainted regularly – every day, didn't they?"

"I don't know," said Matthew. "I don't see why they should have done that."

"Because it was considered ladylike," said Elspeth. "If you fainted a lot, it showed that you were a person of refined temper-

ament. The world was just all too much, and so you fainted. You fainted if you saw something unpleasant."

"Like Aunt Ada," said Matthew. "Remember? Ada Doom in *Cold Comfort Farm*. She saw something nasty in the woodshed and never recovered."

Elspeth smiled. "I always wondered what it was."

"Best not to ask," said Matthew. He opened a cupboard on the landing. "Nothing nasty inside," he said.

They went into the first of the bedrooms.

"So restful," said Elspeth. "Look at that lovely wallpaper, Matthew. Chinoiserie."

Matthew looked at the wall behind the bed. The wallpaper was of a pale-green shade; the design, which was Chinese in style, depicted delicately rendered birds perching on twigs and branches; a tiny bird, one of those birds so small that they would disappear within the clenched fist, balanced upon a wisp of grass.

"This is where we'll sleep," whispered Elspeth.

He looked at her. She was smiling at him gently, with that smile that made him so proud to be the one she had chosen to be her husband, to be the father of her baby . . . babies.

## 50. *Matthew Is Decisive*

Matthew continued to press Elspeth to visit the doctor, but she was adamant. "I just don't need to go," she said. "My blood pressure was checked two days ago and they said it was more or less what they would expect. I'm fine, Matthew – I really am. You can't wrap me in cotton wool."

That came across as criticism rather than imprecation – which was not her intention. "I'm sorry, my darling," she said quickly. "I very much appreciate your concern – I really do, but you mustn't worry too much about me. I'm quite strong, you know."

He put his arm around her shoulder. They were walking back around Moray Place after having viewed the flat and, had they been watched from a window above – and they were – they would have seemed to all intents and purpose as the young couple in love – he with his arm about her shoulder, in perfect step with each other; such tenderness.

"Look," said the watcher to her companion. "Look down there. That young couple we've seen in India Street. He has that gallery, I think. She's got a lovely, gentle face. Rather like a Madonna."

"So touching," said the companion. "Do you think they've been looking at that flat? The one for sale?"

"I'm not sure that a young couple could afford that," said the watcher.

"We can hope."

"Yes, we can hope."

"Perhaps they might even join the Federation."

"That might be nice. We could pop a leaflet through their door once they move in."

"Yes, that's a really good idea."

Unaware of the eyes upon them, Matthew and Elspeth turned the corner into Darnaway Street. "Well?" said Matthew. "What do you think?"

"I like it," said Elspeth. "There's something special about it. It's so quiet. Did you notice that? Not a whisper of traffic."

"I heard the trees moving in the wind," said Matthew. "That's all."

Elspeth looked at him enquiringly. "Did you find out about the price? I've left my copy of the brochure back there. I suppose we could get another copy from that nice woman who showed us round."

But Matthew had seen the price. "It's not cheap," he said. "But then it's Moray Place."

Elspeth hardly dared ask. She had bought her flat in Sciennes at what seemed to her to be an exorbitant price, but it would be nothing when compared with the price of these flats in the Georgian New Town.

"We can afford it," said Matthew. "We'd get a good price for our flat. People like India Street."

"You're holding back," said Elspeth, in mock accusation. "I can take it, you know."

"All right," said Matthew. "They're asking for offers over eight hundred and fifty thousand pounds."

Elspeth stopped walking. "Eight hundred and fifty thousand pounds?" she repeated slowly.

Matthew confirmed the figure with a nod. "So that means we'll have to pay quite a bit more than that if we want to get it. You heard what the lawyer at McKay Norwell said. She said they had several notes of interest. That means there's going to be competition."

"Maybe we shouldn't bother," said Elspeth. "I'm not sure if I want to get into a bidding war."

Matthew, who still had a protective arm about her, gave her a squeeze. "But you loved it," he said. "I could tell. You really felt at home, didn't you?"

He knew; he had seen her expression. Yes, she did want it; she wanted it badly; but eight hundred and fifty thousand pounds? For a flat? With eight hundred and fifty thousand pounds one could buy a small farm in Ayrshire; or a slightly down-at-heel chateau in a less fashionable part of France; or . . . there were so many things one could do with eight hundred and fifty thousand pounds.

"How much do you think we'd get for India Street?" she asked.

Matthew thought for a moment. "I saw an advertisement for a flat like ours in Northumberland Street," he said. "And Northumberland Street is a little bit less desirable than India Street. Five hundred and twenty thousand."

Elspeth, being a teacher – even one who had been obliged to resign – at least could do mental arithmetic. "A three hundred and thirty thousand pound shortfall," she said. It seemed such a discouragingly large sum; surely Matthew would see that.

But all he said was: "Yes. That's about it."

"Well, we can't afford that," she said. "So we need to find somewhere else."

Matthew shook his head. "No, we don't. I can get hold of that. Have you forgotten . . ."

He did not complete his question. He felt embarrassed about his situation, even with Elspeth.

"Have you got that much?" she asked.

Matthew was taken aback. Had he never told her? Perhaps not.

"Elspeth," he whispered. "I'm not short of cash."

She looked away. "I didn't suppose you might be. But that's a very large sum."

"But we can easily afford it," said Matthew. "If you want it." He paused. "And as far as I'm concerned, I'd really love to live there."

"Then let's go for it," said Elspeth.

"All right," said Matthew. "I'll phone our lawyers the moment we get back to the flat."

Our lawyers: it was not a phrase that Elspeth had ever had occasion to use. It sounded immensely grand to be able to say our lawyers, but it seemed entirely natural for Matthew.

"I didn't know that we had lawyers," said Elspeth.

"Well, we do. And I'm going to phone them and ask them to put in an immediate offer."

They had now reached India Street and were beginning to make their way down it to their doorway. After Moray Place, India Street seemed rather modest, and yet it was comfortable and on a human scale. Did they really want to move somewhere more formal? Elspeth was not sure. And yet, the thought of all those steps, even now, in early pregnancy, was beginning to daunt her.

"How much will we offer?" Elspeth asked.

"I'll see what the solicitor says. But it's likely to be nine hundred and fifty. Nine hundred and sixty, maybe."

She said nothing. That was almost a million pounds, and when stamp duty and lawyers' fees and all the rest were added, it probably would end up being at least that much. Is this what she wanted? To be living in what the popular press would describe as "a million-pound flat"? Is that what she wanted, when there were so many people who made do with such small and cramped space; people for whom a million pounds was an impossible, distant dream? Did she want to be part of that world, the world of elegant Georgian interiors and the quiet ticking of clocks? Had she made a mistake in marrying Matthew, and was she now simply confirming that mistake by going along with something that seemed to be so alien, so far away from all that she had ever been, as to be about somebody else, some other Elspeth Harmony who had nothing to do with the real Elspeth Harmony – whoever that was?

## 51. A Letter of Comfort

As soon as they reached their flat in India Street, Matthew went into the room he used as a study and looked up the telephone number of Turcan Connell, the lawyers who looked after his affairs. They had bought the gallery for him; they had advised him – rather perspicaciously and effectively – on the disposition of the funds that his father had so generously, and unexpectedly, showered upon him. They were a comforting presence in his life, rather like a godfather or a trusted uncle, who would stand between him and a world that contained so many potential snares and disasters.

The partner with whom he dealt listened to what he had to say about India Street. She had not heard about the triplets. "Congratulations," she said. "You must create a trust."

Matthew thanked her. "And move," he said.

"Ah."

Matthew explained about the flat in Moray Place. She approved. "That side in particular has wonderful views. And it has a garden?"

"It does," said Matthew.

"You'll need to get it surveyed."

Matthew was silent for a moment. "I want to buy it," he said. "There's going to be stiff competition. I want to put in one of those quick offers."

The lawyer frowned. Matthew could hear the frown. "A timed offer?"

"Yes. They're asking for offers over eight hundred and fifty thousand. I thought that if we put in nine hundred and fifty they might take it straight away."

The lawyer cleared her throat. "Well, they might, but they might want to give the other people a chance – the ones who have noted an interest." She hesitated. "And although we can make it subject to survey, I would advise rather strongly against going in with an offer when you haven't checked up on some pretty basic things."

Matthew tried to sound firm. "I want it," he said. "Elspeth loves it. I want to get it for her."

The lawyer understood. "I have to advise you of the dangers," she said. "But ultimately it's your decision. Are you sure?"

He was sure.

"Then I'll phone their solicitors and have a word with them. Who is it?"

"McKay Norwell. They're in Rutland Square. I spoke to their property person, Lesley Kerr, I think it was."

"I know her," said the lawyer. "And they're a good firm. I'll have a word."

Matthew put down the phone and went into the kitchen, where Elspeth was boiling an egg. "I suddenly felt hungry," she said. "I know it's odd to be sitting down eating a boiled egg on impulse, but . . ." She shrugged.

"You can have a boiled egg whenever you want," said Matthew. "You can have anything – anything."

She looked at him fondly. Dear Matthew – he was so generous. And yet she did not want anything. She wanted only those things that she deserved, and she was not sure that she deserved all this attention, all this solicitude. She was not sure that she deserved a flat in Moray Place just because she had walked past it and decided that she might like to live there. Would it be different, she wondered, if Matthew had actually earned all this money? Would her feelings of guilt be any different then? Or should she not feel guilty about good fortune – whatever its source? Was it a peculiar Scottish trait to feel guilty about what you had in this life; was this all down to the Reformation and to the stern doctrines of individual effort and merit that had sprung from all that? Such an effect did exist – she was sure of it; she had had an uncle who had felt like that. Anything good, anything positive, was seen by him as a dubious privilege that would be paid for dearly; even a fine day – in Scotland a rare gift of those most fickle local weather gods – would be paid for by cold and damp later on. The bill for a warm spring was a miserable, rain-sodden summer; the bill for happiness was subsequent anxiety about the loss of exactly that happiness – it was a bleak system of double-entry book-keeping, but one that had a firm root in the Scottish psyche. And was that what she was like, she asked herself.

The egg boiled, and Elspeth sat down to eat it. Matthew sat at the table opposite her. He was jumpy – she could tell that. And this nervousness increased until the telephone rang and he shot up from his chair to answer it.

It was his lawyer. "I've spoken to Lesley Kerr," she said. "And she's drawn my attention – quite properly – to an issue with that place. She's worried that the sellers have done something to the flat."

"But of course they have," said Matthew. "They've decorated it really well. And the kitchen was beautifully done up. That Clive Christian person – really very swish."

"Not that," said the lawyer. "She said that they had removed a wall."

Matthew was silent.

"Are you still there?" asked the lawyer.

"Yes. But people remove walls, don't they?"

"They do. But you have to remember something: Moray Place is listed. It's an important piece of architecture and you have to get permission to do anything to a listed building. The people who owned that flat didn't. They just took a wall out."

"Oh. But why are they telling us this?"

"Because it'll come up in the transaction. Her clients know that they must reveal it. She says quite rightly that everybody needs to be aware of the problem."

Matthew thought for a moment. "So which wall are we talking about?" he asked.

"One in the middle," said the lawyer. "Apparently."

Matthew sighed. Across the room he saw Elspeth looking at him. He loved her so much. He wanted her to have that flat. He wanted them to be in that bedroom with the Chinese-themed wallpaper. He could see her in the garden, sitting near that lead statue of the young girl with the skirts.

"Look," he said. "I really want to go ahead with this. Please put in that offer. We can deal with bureaucratic difficulties later on."

"I'm not at all sure that removing a wall from a listed building is a mere bureaucratic difficulty," said the lawyer. "And I don't think you'd get a letter of comfort from the council for this sort of thing."

"A letter of comfort?"

"It's a letter that says that even if something has been done, it's all right and you can go ahead. But I don't think that you can get them for infringements of listed building requirements."

A letter of comfort, thought Matthew. What a marvellous term! And wouldn't we all like to get letters of comfort from time to time? Even one letter of comfort a year would be enough. *My dear*, such a letter would say. *Don't worry! Everything will work out for the best.*

## 52. *The Meaning of Always*

"Don't you think I should use this time to practise my saxophone?" suggested Bertie. "Or even my Italian, Mummy? I could go to Valvona & Crolla with you and translate the labels on the cans and packets."

"No, I don't," said Irene, taking Bertie by the hand and beginning the walk up Dundas Street to psychotherapy. "Your saxophone playing is coming along really well. Grade Seven already, Bertie, and you're only six!"

"When will I be seven?" asked Bertie. "I've been six for ages."

Irene laughed. "Being seven is a state of mind, Bertie. You'll be seven on your next birthday, but you can be seven inside, you know, any time."

Bertie frowned. He was used to his mother making elliptical comments which, for the most part, it was safe to ignore; this one, however, related to birthdays – an important subject for a child, and one about which there should be no ambiguity.

"How can you be seven inside?" he asked. "Am I seven inside?" It was clutching at straws, of course; to be seven inside would be no substitute, he thought, for being seven on the outside.

Irene did not answer for a few moments. She was preoccupied with thoughts of Bertie's new psychotherapist, Dr. St. Clair. She realised that she did not know much about him – other than the fact that he was Australian – and she wanted to find out more. There was something about him that intrigued her; some of the same quality that she had seen in Dr. Hugo Fairbairn. Why, she wondered, were these people so interesting? Did psychotherapy as a career attract a certain type of man, who might then appeal to a certain type of woman? If it did, then what type of woman was she? Intelligent, I suppose, thought Irene; women who have no time for those matters which occupy so many women still in a state of false consciousness – cooking, friendship, romance, clothes. What a shameful list, she thought; how limiting; and how fortunate was she, Irene, not to be in a state of false consciousness, unlike other women.

The attractiveness of psychotherapists, she decided, lay in their ability to interest themselves in what other people were thinking. It was quite simple, really: for most of us the topic of greatest interest in this world is undoubtedly ourselves. That is where the real fascination of the world lies – what happens to us, and what we think about it, is infinitely interesting, even if it is of surprisingly little moment for others. Psychotherapists understood this, and made it their concern to find out what we were thinking. In this respect, they showed that quality which marks out the sympathetic from the unsympathetic, and of course that was attractive – of course it was. I myself am *simpatica*, thought Irene, that is obvious enough, but we are surrounded – surrounded – by those who are not.

"What were you saying, Bertie? Mummy was busy thinking."

"I asked how you could be seven inside," said Bertie.

"Oh, yes. Well that's subjective age, Bertie. It depends on how you feel and think inside you. So you may be twenty, but not feel twenty. Sometimes there are such people. People who don't grow up, for example."

"Like Peter Pan?" asked Bertie.

Irene shook her head. "Peter Pan? Oh no, Bertie. Peter Pan was a projection of J. M. Barrie's fantasy, Bertie. He was a wish fulfilment. Peter Pan would have loved to grow up, but he wasn't allowed to by Barrie. And that's because Barrie wanted to regress to that age himself. That's where he was stuck."

Bertie looked concerned. "Can you get stuck, Mummy?"

"Yes, you can, Bertie. Lots of people are stuck."

"Even in Edinburgh?" asked Bertie.

"Even in Edinburgh, Bertie. Edinburgh is full of people who are stuck. Most of them don't realise it, of course, but they're stuck all right."

"Are you stuck, Mummy?"

Irene laughed. "Certainly not, Bertie. I assure you – I am far from being stuck!"

"And Ulysses? And Daddy? Are they stuck?"

Again Irene laughed, but less spontaneously, perhaps. "Ulysses is currently at the oral stage, Bertie. You may have noticed that he sucks everything he can find. He wants to eat everything up, you see. That's perfectly normal. As long as he moves on, which I am sure he will. And as for Daddy, of course . . ." She faltered. Stuart was clearly stuck, but she did not feel that she could explain that to Bertie.

Poor Stuart, she thought. Stuck in that dreadful office in the Scottish Government. Stuck with all those other statisticians conjuring up figures for ministers who were themselves stuck. It hardly bore thinking about.

"Is Daddy stuck?" persisted Bertie.

"No, of course not. Daddy is entirely . . . You mustn't worry about Daddy, Bertie. Daddy is fine . . . in his own way."

Bertie looked relieved. "But I still think it might be better to do something else," he said. "What about Italian? There's always Valvona & Crolla . . ."

"We aren't going there just now, Bertie. And there are better ways of practising your Italian than reading the labels of packets of pasta and tins of goodness knows what. No, Bertie, we have an appointment with Dr. St. Clair, and we must keep it. That's all there is to it."

Bertie looked down at the pavement, making sure that he did not tread on any of the lines. Tofu had said that somebody had been lost in Edinburgh only the week before because he trod on the lines. The police were looking into it, he said, but they had been able to come up with nothing. All they found, said Tofu, was his shoes.

Bertie did not believe this entirely, as Tofu was known to be a terrible liar. But there were many things that one did not really believe that one did not want to disbelieve, just in case they might be true – which they clearly were not, of course. There was stepping on lines for one thing, and then there was Santa Claus. He did not exist – obviously – but if one stopped believing in him – if one professed disbelief – then there was a risk, surely, that one might get no presents.

He sighed. They were now at Dr. St. Clair's door, and Irene was poised, ready to press the doorbell.

"Mummy," he said. "Wouldn't it be funny if you had another baby and . . ."

Irene looked down at him with amusement. "Mummy is not going to do that, Bertie! Two boys are quite enough."

"No, what I was going to say was: wouldn't it be funny if you had another baby and he looked like Dr. St. Clair – just like Ulysses looks like Dr. Fairbairn?"

Irene bent down. "Bertie," she hissed. "What did Mummy tell you? Never, ever say things like that. They are very, very rude, Bertie!"

"But you always said I should say what I'm thinking," protested Bertie. "You did."

"Always doesn't mean always, Bertie – you should know that. Always means generally. And sometimes it means never. Just remember that."

## 53. *An Offer Is Made*

After he put down the telephone on the conversation with his lawyer, Matthew went into the kitchen, where he found Elspeth sitting at the table, a cup of tea in front of her.

"I've done it," said Matthew.

"Put in the offer?"

Matthew nodded, and sat down. He felt slightly light-headed; Elspeth had already fainted that day and he wondered whether he would be next. If he did, he could imagine people thinking that this was a striking case of sympathetic reaction in pregnancy, as where a father-to-be shares psychosomatically in the discomfort of the expectant mother. There were plenty of men, he gathered, who felt stomach pains and put on weight during the pregnancy of their wives and partners. This was different, though; this was the light-headedness that comes from having spent close on one million pounds. And even if he had not actually spent it, then he had as good as done so. Was he bound by what he had done, he asked himself. He tried to remember what the lawyer had said – something about the whole thing needing to be formally concluded in writing. If that were so, then he could still get out of it – not that he would want to; Matthew was a man of his word and thought to do that would be like accepting an invitation to lunch subject to the proviso that if a better invitation came along then one would take that in preference.

"How much did you offer?"

"We," corrected Matthew. "My money is your money, remember. What did I say: with my worldly goods I thee endow."

They had been married in the Church of Scotland, but the minister had agreed to the use of parts of the liturgy of the Scottish Book of Common Prayer, which Matthew liked for its richness of language. "Computers can marry one another according to the modern wording," he had said. "But not me. I want 'Dearly beloved we are gathered here together' . . . and words like that."

Elspeth looked at him. "Our money then," she said. "How much did we offer of our money?"

"Nine hundred and seventy-five thousand," said Matthew. "I discussed it with the solicitor. She looked up some recent transactions and said that this should be an attractive figure, even if another flat in Moray Place went for one million three hundred thousand pounds recently. But that was bigger, having both the ground floor and the drawing-room floor."

Elspeth was silent. For a moment it occurred to Matthew that she might faint again. What happened if they both fainted at the same time? Who would be left to revive whom?

"Nine hundred . . ." she began weakly, and then trailed off.

Matthew tried to sound businesslike. "Yes. If you put in one of these timed offers, then you really have to take their socks off."

"Knock their socks off," corrected Elspeth. "You don't take somebody else's socks off – you knock them off."

Matthew frowned. "But how? How can you knock socks off? You have to peel socks."

Elspeth did not think it really mattered. "Metaphors don't always mean what they say," she said. "That's the point of metaphors."

"Well, we put in the offer and . . ." Matthew looked at his watch. "And we should know quite soon."

Elspeth winced. "When do we have to pay?"

"When we get entry," said Matthew. "I think that this should be soon enough – there's nobody living in the flat at the moment. All we have to do is to move our stuff out."

"And sell this place," said Elspeth.

"I know somebody in Rettie's," said Matthew. "They'll do it."

"And what if we have to pay for Moray Place before we sell India Street?" asked Elspeth. "Will we need a bridging loan of a million pounds?"

"I can do that," said Matthew. "Remember, my father gave me over four million pounds."

"But isn't that in shares?" asked Elspeth. "This would have to be cash."

Matthew shrugged. "Don't worry," he said.

Twenty minutes later the telephone rang. As he picked it up, Matthew felt his heart beating more quickly. He closed his eyes. Had he done the right thing?

"I'm happy to report success," said the solicitor. "Moray Place is yours. They accepted immediately. In fact . . ." She hesitated momentarily. "They said that the client was delighted to sell it to you and accepted your offer. They noted that you accepted and understood the listed building consent issue. I said that you did, as you instructed me. So you are now the proud owner – or al-most – of a flat in Moray Place. Congratulations."

Matthew swallowed hard. "I'm very pleased," he said. But he did not sound very convincing.

"Entry will be in two weeks' time," went on the lawyer. "They insisted on that, I'm afraid."

"Of course," said Matthew weakly. "That will give us time to get things organised at this end."

"I hope that you're very happy in your new home," said the lawyer.

"We shall be," said Matthew.

He rang off and went back to the kitchen to give Elspeth the news. He found her with her head in her hands, in tears.

"Darling! Darling, darling! Why . . . Why are you crying? It's good news. It's ours."

This did not bring the desired reaction, but only seemed to increase her tearfulness.

"Please don't cry," pleaded Matthew, placing an arm around Elspeth's shoulder. She nestled her head against him. He felt her tears, warm against his cheek. The tears of another person, he thought; another's tears.

"I didn't mean to cry," she sobbed. "I didn't. It's just that everything is suddenly so complicated. I thought that getting married would be simple – that I would feel just the same, but married, if you see what I mean."

Matthew did not. He stroked her hair gently.

"And then," Elspeth went on, "it all seemed so strange. The babies. The house. The million pounds. Everything."

"Don't you want to move?" asked Matthew. "Don't you want to live in Moray Place?"

He had not expected her answer. "No," she said. "I want to stay here. I want to stay here with you. I want it just to be us. Just the two of us. That's what I want."

Matthew tried to comfort her. Just the two of us. But they were no longer just two – they were five. Did this mean that she did not want her triplets? Is that what she meant?

"Not just the two of us," he whispered. "Five."

Elspeth caught her breath, and then sobbed all the more. Matthew did not know what to say, or what to do. He remembered what his father had once said. It had been at a Watsonian rugby match, and Matthew's father had turned to his son and said, à propos of nothing, "Matthew – remember one thing. Women see things differently from the way men see them. You remember that."

## 54. *The Therapeutic Hour*

Dr. St. Clair opened the door to Irene and Bertie. He smiled. "Ah yes," he said. "Mrs. Pollock and young Bertie. It's that time already, is it? I was reading something and didn't notice what time it was."

"Bertie and I were just talking about subjective time," said Irene. "Weren't we, Bertie?"

Bertie nodded. He did not want to be here, and he did not want to start discussing subjective time all over again with Dr. St. Clair.

They went into the waiting room.

"Bertie, you just sit there like a good boy for a minute or two while I have a wee talk with Dr. St. Clair," said Irene.

Bertie sat down obediently.

"You can read those magazines," went on Irene. "Bertie is a great reader, Dr. St. Clair. He was reading when he was three."

"Good heavens," said Dr. St. Clair. "That's early."

Bertie buried himself in an old copy of *Scottish Field*. He wished that his mother would not discuss him in front of other people, but she always did.

"Yes," said Irene. "He read quite voraciously – fairly advanced things too – if you can call Stevenson advanced, which I do not. He read *Kidnapped* when he was four. And he had read all of Roald Dahl by the time he was five. All of it. Not that I approve of Dahl, who is, I think, very misguided on a number of points, but it was quite an achievement on Bertie's part."

"I've always liked Roald Dahl," said Dr. St. Clair. "There's a certain anarchic tendency there."

"Yes," said Irene. "And patriarchal too. Do you think that he was one of those authors who punished women?"

Dr. St. Clair looked puzzled. "Punished them?"

"Yes," said Irene. "Look at Flaubert. Madame Bovary was punished – and punished very convincingly. And what about poor Anna Karenina? She was punished, wasn't she?"

"Perhaps," said Dr. St. Clair. He looked at his watch. "But time is marching on and maybe . . ."

Irene interrupted him. "I'd just like a few words with you first, if you don't mind." She moved decisively towards the door of Dr. St. Clair's consulting room and he followed her, glancing back at Bertie as he did so. The door closed behind them.

"Is everything all right?" asked Dr. St. Clair, gesturing for Irene to sit down. "He seems cheerful enough."

"On the surface," said Irene. "But I'm not sure if all is well underneath. He took my other child – little Ulysses – off to school the other day. Abducted him."

Dr. St. Clair frowned. "Abducted?"

"Yes. He removed him from the flat while I was having a lie-in and my husband – rather thoughtlessly, it must be said – had gone off to work. Bertie took it upon himself to remove Ulysses and take him to school. The first thing I heard of it was when I received a frantic call from the school."

"Unconscious hostility towards a sibling," said Dr. St. Clair. "It's common enough."

"Exactly," said Irene.

"He might grow out of it, of course. Sometimes these things are resolved naturally and the children end up being the firmest of friends."

"And sometimes they don't."

Dr. St. Clair conceded that Irene was right; sometimes the hostilities of the nurseries lasted well into adult life. He had seen that in cousins of his who did not talk to one another, even at family funerals.

"I had a professor in Melbourne who wrote about that," he mused. "A rather wonderful book, actually, *Siblings But Not Siblings*. I always thought that a rather good title."

"Very good," said Irene. "Tell me: did you do all your training in Melbourne?"

"My bachelor's degree in psychology," said Dr. St. Clair. "And my PhD as well. Then I went to Sydney for a rotation of hospital attachments. Clinical psychology departments."

"And your PhD," probed Irene. "What was the topic?"

"Attachment theory," said Dr. St. Clair.

"Fascinating," said Irene. She had noticed Dr. St. Clair's boots; they were ankle-length, in brown leather, like the boots she had seen in pictures of Australian stockmen.

"Did you come from a farm?" she asked. He seemed taken

aback by the question, and she sought to reassure him. "I just wondered," she said.

"My father was an accountant in a stock agency up in Queensland," said Dr. St. Clair. "So it was a farming background in a way. But I wanted to get away. I wanted to get to Melbourne, Sydney – anywhere."

"We all do," said Irene encouragingly.

"Yes. I went off to university. My father wanted me to study commerce, and that's what I applied for. But when I got to university I discovered that I couldn't stand the BCom curriculum and I decided to transfer to philosophy or psychology. I actually tossed a coin – would you believe it? It landed on tails, which was psychology."

"How symbolic," said Irene. "Heads for philosophy – for the mental – and tails for the psychological."

Dr. St. Clair nodded. "Yes, I see what you mean. Anyway, so I did the degree in psychology and my parents only found out about it when they came for the graduation. My father said, 'Look, son, they've put your name in the wrong column! They've got you down for some fancy degree in psychology. Better make sure they give you a pukka BCom certificate!' That's when I told him."

"And how did he take it?"

Dr. St. Clair sat back in his chair. "He was a bit nonplussed. He asked me why on earth I wanted to do something like that when a degree in commerce could have got me started with one of the larger companies. I explained that I was interested in human nature and that human nature was infinitely more exciting than business. He said nothing after that, and I think he eventually accepted my choice. I never wanted to kill my father, you know."

Irene tilted her head slightly. "Not even subconsciously?"

"Who knows what we think subconsciously?" said Dr. St. Clair. "That's why it's called the subconscious."

Irene laughed. "Of course. So what happened then?"

"I enrolled for the PhD. I did not have much money, and so I stayed as a sort of lodger I suppose with a widow called Phyllis who lived in a Melbourne suburb. She came from a family that had interests in a chemicals factory, and the house was quite comfortable. I was quite happy there."

"She was your mother," said Irene.

Dr. St. Clair smiled. "Perhaps."

"Go on."

"Well, she looked after me very well. She always had something cooked for me when I came back in the evening – things I liked – tapioca pudding, ox-tail stew – but not in that order, of course! After dinner we fed the scraps to the two dachshunds that Phyllis had. They were called Eugene and Riley."

He paused. He was enjoying himself, talking about his life back in Melbourne.

"Do carry on," said Irene. "Eugene and Riley. Do tell me about them."

## 55. *Men Can Cry*

"They were rather odd little dogs," said Dr. St. Clair, looking up at the ceiling. "They were both long-haired dachshunds, which I rather prefer to the smooth variety – you know, the ones that look to all intents and purposes like a frankfurter. They were intelligent little dogs, and very loyal once they had accepted you as a friend. And I wanted a loyal friend, I think."

"Oh?" said Irene. "Why do you say that?" His comment sounded like a complaint, she thought – the complaint of one who had suffered, perhaps, from disloyalty in friends.

He hesitated before replying, and she had to urge him on. "Tell me," she said. "I'll understand."

Dr. St. Clair looked out of the window. It was such a long distance away, such a long distance; a different world. And it was a long time ago, too, when he was twelve and had been sent to the Anglican school in Toowoomba. "It was a boarding school," he said. "We lived in Toowoomba and so I was able to go as a day boy – most of the others were boarders. They were the sons of pastoralists. Some of the stations they came from were the size of Scotland, you know – or almost. Vast places. "I was fairly unhappy there. The boarders knew one another well and so the day boys were the outsiders. You know how cruel boys can be – children in general. Girls are as bad, I suppose."

"Some girls," said Irene. "Not all."

Dr. St. Clair nodded. "Well, you had to look after yourself. And you needed friends for that. And anyway, at that age friendship is terribly important for all sorts of reasons. You yearn for a friend, a good friend, a loyal friend. David and Jonathan, so to speak.

"There was a boy in my year called Gavin. His father had one hundred and twenty thousand acres up on the Tablelands. He told me that he had shot a crocodile when he was ten. 'I wasn't meant to,' he said. 'But I did. It got too close to us. I had to. Dad said, "Get that croc, Gav. Quick, before he gets us."'"

Irene said nothing. She was watching Dr. St. Clair. This is a very fascinating man, she thought.

"So, he shot a crocodile."

"Yes. But he was not like most of the others. He seemed . . . well, kinder than them. He used to do my mathematics homework for me sometimes, when I found it a bit difficult. We used to take it to a place behind the cricket grounds, where there was a stand of eucalyptus trees. When the wind came up, the sound that these trees made was like that of the sea breaking on the shore. You know that sound. Boys went there to smoke – we didn't care, did we? We were immortal. Cigarettes killed other people, not us.

"We became blood brothers. We each made a cut in our palms

and then pressed our hands together so that the blood would mingle. Then we shook hands again and swore that we would be loyal to one another for the rest of our lives. 'You ever need help,' said Gavin, 'come to me.' And I said, 'Same here.'

"Two years later, Gavin said to me, 'Get out of my sight, St. Clair. I hate you.' Just like that. I went home that day and my mother found me sitting in my bedroom looking at the ceiling. She said, 'Something upset you? What is it?' And I said nothing, because children don't tell their parents about what is wrong; they deny grief and all the cruelties that they inflict on one another. So once she had gone out of the room, I remember just sitting there crying – crying in private – for the end of my friendship. I thought I would never find another friend like him. Never.

"But I was really telling you about those two dachshunds, wasn't I? I got sidetracked onto loyalty. Yes, they were loyal little dogs, even if they were a bit snappy from time to time. They had back problems, you see, because of being so long. Eugene had the worst twinges, I think. He was very low-slung and sometimes his stomach would touch the ground as he walked along. And if somebody patted him too vigorously his back would hurt and he could nip them. Not badly – just a small nip.

"When I lodged at Phyllis's place, the dogs became quite fond of me. They used to follow me around, and if there was a storm they would come into my room and hide under the bed. They were frightened of thunder, I think – Riley in particular. He used to whimper if there was any thunder or lightning about.

"They used to love going out into the garden and digging up the flowerbeds. They were looking for something, I suppose, but I never found out what it was. Ancient bones, perhaps? Dachshund songlines? Who knows? We're all looking for something, of course, even if we don't know what it is. And most of us don't know, do we?

"I left Phyllis's place after I finished my PhD. A few years later, when I was working in Sydney, I had a Christmas card from her. Eugene died, she wrote. Poor dear, his back gave out eventually. Riley sends his love. He still remembers you. That's what she wrote. And you know what? I cried. Not just for Eugene, or for Riley, who must have missed Eugene, but for everything. For the end of friendship, for loss, for the great spaces that exist between us, for the loneliness that is a condition of even this most crowded world. I cried for everything. I'm not ashamed to say it. Most men won't admit it – but I will. I don't care. And Gavin? I never saw him again, except once when I was in Sydney. I saw him on television. He had invented a new form of padlock and had won a prize for his invention. I saw him on the news, getting the prize. They showed a close-up of his padlock."

He stopped; Irene sat quite still.

## 56. *From Scotland with Love*

Of course the long conversation that Irene enjoyed with Dr. St. Clair took most of Bertie's therapeutic hour. In fact, by the time that Dr. St. Clair had finished his reminiscences – having been encouraged by Irene at regular intervals – there was not much more than five minutes left for his real patient. This suited Bertie, who much preferred to sit in the waiting room than to field the often impenetrable questions which his psychotherapists, both Dr. Fairbairn and Dr. St. Clair, threw at him. Of the two, Bertie had a slight preference for Dr. St. Clair, who appeared less disturbed, he thought, than Dr. Fairbairn, but it certainly suited him very well if his mother diverted the psychotherapist's attention for virtually the whole hour.

"Well, Bertie," said Irene as they left the consulting rooms and began to walk back along Queen Street, "that wasn't a very long session for you, I'm afraid. Mummy needed to talk to Dr. St. Clair about one or two little matters."

"That's quite all right, Mummy," said Bertie cheerfully. "I don't mind sharing Dr. St. Clair. You can take as long as you like, you know."

Irene smiled, and bent down to give her son's cheek a playful pinch. "That's very kind, darlingissimo," she said. "But next week you must have the lion's share. Mummy doesn't need help."

Bertie looked at his mother doubtfully. He thought that she probably did need help, but he was a polite little boy and did not like to say that.

"And you had a good read of *Scottish Field*?" asked Irene.

"Yes," said Bertie. "I read an article about Mr. Darnley."

"Mr. Darnley?"

Bertie explained. The article had been fascinating, and he had read it three times, as he often did with things that really interested him. "Mr. Darnley married Mary, Queen of Scots, you see. He was a tall man with very long legs . . ."

"Oh, that Darnley," said Irene. "Henry Darnley. Soi-disant king of Scotland. Yes, I see."

"And they blew him up," went on Bertie. "When he was walking along Chambers Street, near where the museum is. They blew him right up and he died."

"I don't think it was Chambers Street in those days," said Irene.

"Edinburgh was terribly small then, Bertie. That would have been fields with cows and other bucolic creatures. Even Scotland Street was just a hillside, you know."

Bertie absorbed this. "It was very sad," he said. "Do you think he came to bits when they blew him up, Mummy?"

Irene smiled. "He undoubtedly would have felt somewhat disjointed," she replied. "But you must remember, Bertie, that they were all pretty shocking people in those days. Scotland was full of warring factions. That's what they were like."

"And is it any different now?" asked Bertie.

Irene thought for a moment. "One might be tempted to say that not much has changed," she said. "But that's a large subject, Bertie."

"I felt very sorry for Mr. Darnley," said Bertie. "He was much taller than most people in those days and they were all plotting against him. There was a man called Bothwell."

"Yes, indeed," said Irene. "And I suspect that he might have had something to do with Darnley's unfortunate end. But then Darnley was rather wicked too, Bertie. You must remember that. Mary had a secretary called Rizzio who was stabbed to death by some of these noble hooligans. Darnley was pretty clearly implicated in that."

Bertie listened carefully. He was trying to picture Darnley, and he decided that he was probably a little bit like Tofu. In fact, the more he thought about it, the closer the similarity seemed. And as for Mary, Queen of Scots, she must have been rather like Olive in many ways – and Olive should perhaps take note of the fate that befell Mary, just as Tofu should perhaps contemplate what happened to Darnley.

They continued their walk. Bertie suggested that rather than turn down into Dundas Street they should continue to Valvona & Crolla with a view to buying some Panforte di Siena, but Irene vetoed this. "Daddy is looking after Ulysses, Bertie," she said, "and he has to get into the office."

Stuart, who was busy writing a report, was able to work at home from time to time, and this enabled Irene to attend various meetings of groups with which she was involved. There was the Melanie Klein Reading Group, which met every three weeks; there was the New Town Community Council, to which Irene had been elected unopposed; and there was her charitable enthusiasm, Assistance for Romania, which specialised in the collection of second-hand clothing and items of furniture which were then sent out to Romania in large containers. It was this cause that she suddenly remembered as they turned off Dundas Street and began to walk along Great King Street.

"My goodness, Bertie," Irene said. "I quite forgot! Today's the day that we're sending the containers off to Romania. They're bringing them to Scotland Street playground and sending them from there. The Lord Provost is coming."

"Can we go?" asked Bertie.

"Of course we can go," said Irene, looking at her watch. "Not only that – we must go. I'm on the committee, you see, and they expect me to be there."

"And Ulysses?"

"Yes. We'll go back to the Scotland Street and let Daddy get into the office. Ulysses will come with you and me. I'm sure that they'll have a piper to play at the send-off. He'll love that."

They increased their pace. There was now no conversation; Bertie remained lost in thought over Darnley and his difficulties, and Irene was thinking of the Romanian containers. There were three being sent off that morning: one that was entirely full of clothing – and rather good clothing at that; one that was full of kitchen tables and chairs; and one that had large quantities of household essentials – chemical cleaners and dishcloths and things of that nature. These would all be distributed in areas of need in Romania, including to a number of hospitals and orphanages. It made her feel warm just to think of it – to imagine the Romanians opening the containers and delightedly trying on Scottish tweed coats and the like, uttering cries of enthusiasm in Romanian as they did so. How grateful they must feel, she thought; and how they must appreciate the large legends on the side of the containers: *From Scotland to Romania, with love.*

They reached the flat. Stuart was anxious to get to the office, and said barely more than a few words.

"Daddy's head is full of figures this morning," said Irene, jokingly, as she put Ulysses into his pushchair.

Ulysses looked up at his mother, and was sick.

## 57. *Bonnie Irene's Noo Awa*

Once Ulysses was cleaned and dressed in fresh clothes, the three of them made their way down the stair and out into Scotland Street.

"It's a pity that Ulysses is sick so often," said Bertie. "He's quite a nice little baby when he's not actually vomiting."

"His little stomach is finding its way in the world," said Irene breezily. "He'll grow out of it, without doubt."

"Mind you, Mummy," Bertie went on, "I've noticed that he only seems to be sick when he sees your face. Have you noticed that?"

Irene pursed her lips. "Nonsense, Bertie! That's quite untrue."

Bertie frowned. He was a completely truthful child and he would never think of making anything up – unlike people like Tofu, and Olive, and Hiawatha for that matter. And Pansy.

"But it is true, Mummy," he persisted. "Ulysses is never sick when I pick him up. Or Daddy. He's never been sick – not even once – when Daddy is with him."

Irene ignored this. "Now look, Bertie, this is no time to discuss such matters. We are going to watch a very important occasion. So let's concentrate on that rather than on speculating about Ulysses's entirely random regurgitation. *Basta, Bertissimo!*"

Bertie looked down the hill. At the end of Scotland Street, the old marshalling yard, now partly waste ground and partly a children's playground, was filling up with people. Three large container lorries were lined up, bright balloons tied to protuberant rearview mirrors.

"Are they going all the way to Romania, Mummy?" he asked.

"They are indeed, Bertie," Irene said proudly.

Bertie asked how long that would take.

"About three days, Bertie. They go by ferry to Belgium and then drive all the way across western Europe to Romania. Can you tell me the countries they'll cross?"

"Belgium, Germany, Austria, Hungary, and then Romania," rattled off Bertie.

Irene thought for a moment. "Yes," she said, hesitantly. "That sounds about right. They are very hardy men, those drivers. They sleep in little beds in the backs of their cabs, you know, Bertie."

They negotiated their way down the steps to the yard. One or two other members of the committee greeted Irene, who shook hands with one of the drivers. A piper who was standing nearby was given a signal, and started to tune his drones. Soon the familiar skirl, so spine-tingling, so stirring in its effect, filled the air. And at that point, a large official car drew up and a tall, rather dignified man stepped out.

"That's the Lord Provost," Irene whispered to Bertie.

The Lord Provost shook hands with several people and was shown the containers before he made a short speech wishing the convoy a safe and uneventful journey. There was applause and the piper, who fortunately had stopped for the speech, resumed playing.

"I shall just go and take a look at the containers," said Irene. "You stay here with Ulysses, Bertie. I won't be a minute."

Bertie stood beside Ulysses's pushchair and watched the people in the crowd milling about the open rear doors of the containers, inspecting the contents stacked within. "They're going to be very pleased at the other end, Ulysses," Bertie said.

Ulysses gurgled his agreement.

Engines started and there were cries from several members of the crowd. "Bon voyage!" shouted somebody. And another shouted, "Good luck!" The piper, on cue, struck up with that most poignant of farewells, "Will Ye No Come Back Again?"

Slowly the container lorries moved off. Bertie waved, and continued to wave until they had turned onto the road and disappeared from sight. Then he looked around for his mother. The crowd was thinning out now, and Bertie began to feel a bit anxious. His mother had said that she would only be a minute or so, and that was already about ten minutes ago.

He waited patiently with Ulysses. Now there was virtually nobody there – just a few teenagers who were standing gossiping and giggling by the fence. Bertie was not sure what to do. His mother must have gone home. Perhaps she had forgotten she had them with her; or perhaps she needed to go to the bathroom urgently and had rushed back to the flat.

He made his decision. There was no point in staying any longer, he thought. The best thing for him to do would be to return to the flat and see if she was there. If she was not, then he could wait outside the door until she came back from wherever it was that she had gone. Yes, that would be what Mr. Baden-Powell would have advised in such a situation.

He started on his way, and within a few minutes he was outside the door of the flat. Trying the door, he found that it was locked, and there was no reply when he rang the bell. Ulysses watched him with interest.

"Well, Ulysses," said Bertie. "We're just going to have to wait here until Mummy comes back. Sorry about that."

He sat down, and that is where he was when Domenica came up the stairs about forty minutes later and came upon him.

"Hello, Bertie," she said. "Are you locked out?"

"I don't know where my mummy is," said Bertie, his voice wavering. "I thought that she would come back, but she hasn't."

As Bertie told her what had happened, Domenica listened wide-eyed. That woman, she thought, is very peculiar, sure enough, but this takes the shortbread – hands down.

"I think that you had better come up to my flat," she said. "Then I can look after you until Mummy comes home." Then she added. "And I might just phone the police too."

Bertie looked alarmed. "The police? Why?"

Domenica wondered how to put it tactfully. "Well, Bertie, it sounds as if your mummy might have . . . lost her way. The police could help find her."

Bertie swallowed hard. Like all young children, he blamed himself for misfortune, and now he was in no doubt at all that this disappearance of his mother was somehow his fault. It was he who had wished that she would stop talking so much, or at least stop talking about the things that she tended to talk about; it was he who wished for more time by himself; it was he who wished that he was eighteen and free to move to Glasgow, or Paris. All of this evidence was now amassed against him, indicting him for this disaster. He had wished his mother gone, and now she was. Be careful of what you wish for, Bertie Pollock! They were the very words that Olive had used a few days earlier, when she had seen Bertie looking thoughtful. Well, they were wise words, unexpectedly prescient, as wise words sometimes prove to be.

Bertie drew a deep breath. It was all his fault.

He began to cry.

Oh, poor wee boy, thought Domenica, as she bent down to comfort him. Poor, poor wee boy.

## 58. Painful Questions

Over the next few days, the police made several visits to Scotland Street, and the neighbourhood, now abuzz with speculation, became accustomed to the sight of white police cars parked in the street. Throughout the vicinity, posters appeared on the railings bearing the legend *Have you seen this woman?* Underneath was a photograph of Irene, followed by a brief invitation to any member of the public who had spotted her after her recent disappearance at the foot of Scotland Street to contact the Gayfield Square Police Station without delay.

Stuart, on compassionate leave from the Department of Statistics, underwent several searching interviews with police officers, while Bertie and Ulysses were looked after by a woman police constable in the room next door.

"I'm sorry that we have to ask this question, sir," explained the senior police officer who had taken over the case, "but is it possible that your wife was perhaps seeing somebody?"

Stuart looked blank. "Seeing somebody?"

"You know, sir, having an affair?"

Stuart opened his mouth to say something; but he could not speak.

The police officer was sympathetic. "As I said, we don't like to pry into these private matters, sir, but it's often the case that missing persons have been seeing somebody else and have simply gone off with that person. We had a case recently – and I won't mention any names, of course – where this woman went missing and her husband had no idea that she was carrying on with a man in Dundee. She just went off with him, without a word of warning. It was a total surprise."

"My wife . . ." Stuart began, but then stopped himself. He had been intending to say, "My wife is not that kind of person" – but he suddenly asked himself whether he really could say this, and he felt that he could not. He had remembered Hugo Fairbairn and the remark that Bertie had made about the relationship between Irene and the psychotherapist. "She really likes him, you know, Daddy," Bertie had said. "I think he's her best friend actually. When Dr. Fairbairn is sent to Carstairs, I'm sure that Mummy will visit him there." Stuart had smiled, and dismissed it as one of Bertie's amusing little remarks, but then there had been that rather disquieting comment that Bertie had made about the appearance of Ulysses. Again, he had not paid much attention, but now the issue was being raised and it all came back.

Noticing his hesitation, the police officer gave a gentle nudge. "You can talk to us in complete confidence, you know. Nothing you say will go beyond these walls."

Stuart nodded. He felt miserable; it was disloyal, surely, even to make the suggestion. "It's possible she may have," he said at last.

The police officer looked away tactfully. "I see. And do you think that this affair is still going on?"

Stuart bit his lip. "He went up to Aberdeen. Of course, I can't be sure whether there was anything going on."

"Nobody can be sure about such matters, sir," said the police officer. "People can be very discreet. Understandably." He paused. "Was everything all right at home?"

Stuart shrugged. "I think so. My wife is not necessarily an easy person. She's a bit . . . a bit opinionated. She has strong views."

It was clear that this interested the police officer. "Strong views on what?"

"On everything, I suppose."

The policeman nodded. "But you hadn't had a recent row? Nothing that could have made her go off suddenly – without any warning?"

Stuart shook his head. "No. Nothing like that."

The policeman cleared his throat. "There's one other thing,

sir. I'm sorry to have to bring this up, but you might know that we have a note in our files about contact between you and a certain Glasgow underworld figure. Could this have any bearing on your wife's disappearance, do you think?"

Stuart gasped in astonishment. "Underworld figure?" he stuttered.

"One Aloysius O'Connor," said the policeman. "More generally known as Lard O'Connor. Now deceased."

"But I hardly knew him," Stuart protested. "I left my car outside his house by mistake. That's all."

"And yet you were observed visiting the Burrell Collection with him," said the police officer quietly. "Does one go to a gallery with a complete stranger? And you were accompanied on this little cultural outing by one Gerald Sean Flaherty, known to our colleagues in the Strathclyde Police as the Sage of Maryhill, not a man widely believed to be interested in the arts. Yet you all went to this gallery together."

Stuart looked dazed. "I really didn't know these people," he said. "And anyway, I don't see what this has to do with my wife's disappearance."

"It very likely has nothing to do with it at all," said the officer. "But I'm sure you'll understand why we have to look into all possible explanations." He paused. "And I'm afraid, sir, that I am very concerned over this case. You see, women do not normally leave their children – their husbands, yes, but not their children. So this makes me very concerned about your wife's welfare."

Stuart looked down at his hands. Of course it had occurred to him that Irene had met some terrible fate, but this was the first time that anybody in officialdom had been prepared to acknowledge that.

The officer spoke gently. "So you'll understand why I must ask this question: did she have any enemies?"

"Lots." Stuart had not intended to answer in this way, but the response came spontaneously. "She didn't deserve them, of course, but sometimes she was a bit outspoken. People are rarely ready for that."

The policeman nodded. "Anybody in particular?"

Stuart thought; it was difficult to list the arguments that Irene had had with various people. "No," he said. "It was mostly over smallish things – small ideological things."

"Is there anybody who would stand to gain from her disappearance?"

Again Stuart answered quickly, without thinking. "I would."

The policeman looked at him. There was something troubling about his gaze; it was a look of scepticism, Stuart decided. That was understandable enough; he must have to deal with all sorts of meretricious behaviour.

"Could you tell me where you were at the time that she went missing?" The voice was low, almost as if inviting a confidence.

"I was at work . . . and I've got twelve people to prove it."

The officer raised a hand in a calming gesture. "That's fine. I have to exclude you – that's all."

"Well, I resent the implication."

"I'm sorry about that. But I had to ask. And, look, I know how you must feel. And I wish I could allay your fears, but frankly I'm very worried that something very unfortunate indeed has happened to your wife. I'm so sorry. I really am."

## 59. *Regret on Corstorphine Road*

Domenica missed much of the drama surrounding Irene's disappearance. This was because Irene disappeared on a Friday and it was on the Saturday that she, Antonia, and Angus left Edinburgh for Italy, accompanied, of course, by Cyril.

"I feel a bit guilty leaving at such a time as this," she remarked in the taxi.

"I can't say I do," said Antonia. "It makes absolutely no difference whether or not we, as neighbours, are there. What can we do?"

Domenica looked at her reproachfully. "We could offer support."

"I did that," said Antonia. "As no doubt you did too. But beyond that, I really can't see what we can do. Stuart seems to be coping remarkably well."

Angus shook his head sympathetically. "Poor man. I can just imagine how he feels."

All three were silent; all knew the extent to which Stuart was dominated by his wife.

It was Domenica who spoke first. "I can't say that I ever struck up a rapport with her," she said.

"Nor can I," said Antonia quickly.

"Cyril bit her once," observed Angus. "He couldn't stand her, I'm afraid. Remember that, Cyril?"

They all looked down at the dog, who returned their stares with a friendly look, the sun glinting off his gold tooth. Then he winked at Antonia.

"No doubt she'll turn up," said Domenica. "She was probably depressed, or something like that, and decided to kick off the shackles and go away for a while. People do that in that state of mind."

"That must be it," said Angus.

Antonia was less sanguine. "Or she was abducted," she said. "You'd be surprised at the figures. An extraordinary number of people are actually abducted and kept somewhere against their will."

"What are the figures?" asked Angus. The taxi had now reached Murrayfield and was driving past a row of solid suburban villas; talk of abduction against such a background seemed to him to be inherently improbable; but then, he reminded himself, many crimes, even the most horrendous ones, took place in circumstances of banality.

"Oh, I can't recall them exactly," said Antonia. "Surprisingly high, though. Mostly women, I'm afraid, being abducted by men." She looked accusingly at Angus, as if he were in some way complicit in the crime.

"I doubt if any man would dare abduct Irene," said Angus.

Domenica looked displeased. "I don't think that we should talk lightly about this," she said. "A neighbour is missing, after all."

Angus looked shame-faced. "We couldn't really have cancelled," he said. "The tickets were bought, the villa made ready, everything . . ."

"No, you're quite right," said Domenica. "Life has to go on. So I suggest that we try to put it out of our minds for the time being and hope that when we return Irene will be safely restored to Scotland Street and all will be well."

The taxi sped on. Angus looked out of the window, his eyes drawn to the sky above the rooftops of Corstorphine. The sky, he thought, is like the sea; now that we have mastered it, it links us to the most remote of places. He had often thought that of the sea when he found himself on the shore – marvelling at the idea that it was all one body of water; that there was no interruption, nothing more solid than water standing between him and the farthest limits of distant continents. That made him believe that the seas do not separate us, but link us; and so too did the sky, now that we could slip into long tubes of metal and hurtle our way through the air to remote places of our choosing. So India was not a world away, but only seven hours, and Italy was virtually next door – three hours, if that; the time that one might take for a walk in the Pentlands.

He closed his eyes, feeling the morning sun warm upon his face.

And it was the same sun that would greet him when they stepped off the plane in Pisa, he thought, although there, somehow, it would seem so much more reliable, so much friendlier. The Scottish sun was so easily distracted from its task, so quick to think of excuses not to shine, so reticent in conferring its favours.

He opened his eyes to see Antonia watching him. She was smiling. "I do hope that you find inspiration in Italy, Angus," she said.

He returned her smile. "I am sure I shall. It's so many years since I was there. Just after art college, in fact. I went there for two months on one of the travelling scholarships they gave in those days. I don't know if they still do. Probably not."

"We are very ungenerous now."

"Yes," said Angus. "Just think: I was allowed, on public funding, to go to Italy and to soak in everything that it had to offer. They were paying me just to look."

"And to feel," said Domenica. "To experience."

Angus nodded. "Exactly. And of course I felt that I had the whole world at my feet. When I went into the Uffizi and wandered round its galleries I felt that there was no reason why I should not in due course create paintings that were just as good as these, just as magnificent. I really did. I felt such confidence."

Domenica touched the sleeve of his jacket. "Your work is very good."

"Hardly."

She laid a hand on his arm. "Of course it is."

"Yes," said Antonia. "She's right. We all love your painting."

Angus lowered his eyes. "I went there to look, but I didn't go to learn. That was my mistake. I should have tried to learn technique. I should have apprenticed myself to somebody. But I did none of those things. I had picnics in olive groves, I sat in cafés in Florence and Siena, I was like one of those silly characters from E. M. Forster's novels. I wasted the opportunity."

"But we all waste opportunities," said Domenica. "Every single one of us. Every young person does it. It's because we think we have so much time, and then, when we realise that our time is finite, it's too late." She paused. "That's just the way it is, Angus."

He sighed. "Yes, I suppose you're right."

Cyril moved against his leg, resting his head on his master's foot.

"Of course there is such a thing as the second chance," went on Domenica. "We may waste our first trip to Italy, but that doesn't mean that we need waste our second."

## 60. The Comfort of Friends

"I feel really sorry for you, Bertie," said Olive. "I heard what happened, and I felt really sad. I want you to know that." Bertie, feeling somewhat disinclined to play, was standing at the edge of the playground at school; Olive, accompanied by Pansy, had come over to him, and now both girls were staring at Bertie, trying to ascertain whether or not he had been crying.

"You mustn't hold tears in," said Olive. "It's better, you know, if you let yourself cry. We won't laugh at you, will we, Pansy?"

Pansy shook her head. "Poor Bertie. You must feel awful. And just think – you were the last one to see her alive. That must make you feel really dreadful."

"Yes," said Olive. "That's really bad." She paused. "I don't suppose there's any news yet, is there?"

"I don't think so," said Bertie. "The police are looking for her. Maybe she just got lost."

Olive looked at him with pity. "I don't think so, Bertie, do you? You don't get lost at the end of your street, do you? No, I don't think she's lost."

"She's probably kidnapped," suggested Pansy.

Olive considered this possibility. "Maybe," she said. "People do get kidnapped, even if they don't have all that much money. Maybe they mistook her for some rich person and are holding her in a cellar somewhere."

"Or an old castle," said Pansy.

"Could be," said Olive. "Somewhere like Tantallon – you know that old castle near North Berwick? We went for a picnic there once and I thought that it would be a really good place for kidnappers to hold people. Do you know if the police have looked in Tantallon yet, Bertie?"

Bertie shook his head. "They've put notices up in Scotland Street," he said. "They have pictures of my mummy on them."

Olive looked disapproving. "I don't think that's a very good idea, Bertie. That could annoy the kidnappers. They don't like people going to the police."

"No, they don't," said Pansy. "That's probably made it a whole lot worse."

Olive agreed. "I wonder if they've sent a ransom demand yet, Bertie? Have you had a letter yet?"

"I don't think so," answered Bertie. "My dad hasn't said anything about it."

Pansy remembered something. "Sometimes they cut off the

person's ear, Bertie. Then they put it in an envelope and send it to their house. That shows that they've got the person."

"That's correct," said Olive. "I've heard about that. That happens quite a lot in Italy. But now we're all in the European Union."

"They may have sent your mummy's ear already," said Pansy. "Maybe your Dad just thought it was junk mail and threw it away."

"That's quite possible," said Olive. "We never open our junk mail. We just throw it away. It never crosses our mind that there could be somebody's ear in the envelope."

"Usually it's just from Chinese restaurants," said Pansy. "They send takeaway lists, but most people just throw them away without reading them."

Bertie said nothing. He wished that Olive and Pansy would leave him alone; he did not want to talk to them, nor to anybody. He only wanted to be by himself.

"You will let us know if we can help," Olive now said. "I think that your dad will find it very difficult to look after Ulysses by himself. You know how useless men are with babies."

"Very useless," said Pansy. "Boys too."

"So maybe the best thing would be for Ulysses to be adopted," Olive went on. "There are plenty of people looking for babies to adopt. Even ugly ones like Ulysses."

"He's not all that ugly," said Bertie mildly.

"Oh, but he is, Bertie," said Olive. "My mummy saw him with your mummy in George Street one day. She said that she had a terrible shock."

"That's not to say that he's not a really nice little baby," said Pansy comfortingly. "And people who really want a baby maybe won't even notice his face."

Olive now moved the discussion on from Ulysses. "Where was your mummy when you last saw her?" she said.

Bertie explained about the containers of clothing and household essentials that were being sent off to Romania, and Olive nodded gravely. "I've heard all about that," she said. "It's a really kind thing to do – even if it's useless."

"I don't think it's useless," said Bertie. "I'm sure that they're really pleased to get them."

"No they aren't," said Olive, peremptorily. "I've heard that the Romanians are really fed up getting all this useless old Scottish clothing when they've got their own jeans to wear. I've heard that the moment those lorries turn back, the Romanians chuck all the stuff in the bin. That's what I've heard."

Bertie was on the point of refuting this when their attention was suddenly distracted. A door at the side of the school building opened, and they saw their teacher, Miss Maclaren Hope, come out into the playground. She looked about her, and then, seeing Bertie, she gave an excited wave.

Bertie, wondering what he had done wrong, began to walk over towards the teacher. She, however, was coming to him, and had broken into a run. "Bertie!" she shouted. "Bertie – I've got some wonderful news for you!"

Bertie stood stock still.

"Your mummy is safe and sound!" panted Miss Maclaren Hope. "Safe! Quite safe! And she should be back later today. Your daddy will come and collect you."

Bertie felt an overpowering sense of relief. "Back?" he stuttered. "She's back?"

"Yes," gushed Miss Maclaren Hope. "And do you know what happened, Bertie? She got stuck in one of those big containers. They closed the door by mistake while she was inside. Can you believe it? Poor Mummy! And they didn't hear her banging on the side until they had got right the way to Hungary! And then the silly Hungarian police arrested her and didn't understand what she was saying. But fortunately everything was sorted out and she's almost back in Edinburgh."

Olive, who had now sidled up, patted Bertie on the back. "That's such good news, Bertie," she said. Then, looking at the teacher, she went on, "We were comforting him, Miss Maclaren Hope. Pansy and I were comforting him."

"That's very kind of you," said the teacher. "It's at times like this that one needs one's friends, don't you agree, Bertie?"

Bertie nodded.

"So I think we should all go inside now," said Miss Maclaren Hope. "And we can all make nice Welcome Home cards for Bertie's mother. Agreed?"

## 61. *Big Lou on Art and Fashion*

"So," said Big Lou, as she directed a jet of steam through the milk for Matthew's mid-morning coffee. "So – Moray Place it is, then. Going up in the world, I see."

Matthew laughed. "India Street to Moray Place is not going up in the world at all," he said. "Sideways, perhaps. But not going up."

Big Lou, of course, had no time for the games of Edinburgh society. She lived in Canonmills, at the bottom of the hill, and would be very unlikely to move, she thought, upwards, downwards, or even sideways. She knew her neighbours, and liked them. Everybody on her stair was helpful, fulfilling their duties on the cleaning rota, and there were never any noisy parties. In fact, there were never any quiet parties either, but that suited Big Lou, and all the other neighbours, very well.

"I'm really happy with the flat," said Matthew. "And there's a garden, Lou. A really nice garden. You should come and see it."

"What are you going to grow?" asked Lou. "Tatties?"

Matthew shook his head. "They don't go in for tatties in Moray Place," he said solemnly. "Flowers, I suppose. And some bushes, perhaps we'll plant some . . ." He trailed off; he had never gardened.

"Aye?" said Big Lou. "Some what?"

"Some ground cover," said Matthew quickly. He had seen the expression somewhere and it had stuck. Ground cover was definitely the thing.

"Was it expensive?" asked Big Lou. "Fifty thousand?"

Matthew stared at her in disbelief.

"More than that?" asked Big Lou. "Sixty?"

"A bit more, Lou," he said, adding, "Quite a bit more."

Big Lou handed him his coffee. "It's nonsense," she said. "This town's becoming far too expensive for its own good. For fifty thousand you could get a really good place in Arbroath."

"I doubt it," said Matthew. "Not today."

Big Lou shrugged. "Maybe I'm a bit out of date."

Matthew raised an eyebrow. "You could be. Just a bit."

Big Lou changed the subject. "That's Angus away," she said. "Dog and all."

"I envy him going to Italy," said Matthew. "It's the spiritual home of all us artists."

Big Lou looked at him. "You're not an artist."

"Or those concerned with buying and selling art," added Matthew sheepishly.

Big Lou was not convinced. "To be an artist you have to be able to paint or make sculpture or do something like that."

"No you don't," said Matthew. "Not anymore. The artists who do well these days are precisely those who can't paint. And as for sculpture, that's very old-fashioned, Lou. Installations are the thing now." Matthew looked around the room. "Take your coffee machine, for example. That has two prices: the price you pay for it if you buy it in a kitchen equipment shop, and the price you'd get for it if you put it on a plinth in a gallery and labelled it *Age of Steam* or *Chrome III*."

"Oh yes?"

Matthew nodded. "Yes."

"So if I put it in your gallery I'd get a large price?"

"No," said Matthew. "Not you. It would have to be put in by somebody who had been recognised by the cognoscenti as conferring artistic validity to the object. That would mean that you would have to be chosen by the people who create the market. If they chose you – if some big collector said Big Lou is eminently collectable – then that would confer that status upon you. You'd be anointed, so to speak. Thereafter anything you presented as art would be ipso facto art."

Matthew drew breath. "And another thing. It couldn't be my gallery because I can't confer validity. It would have to be one of the galleries that are accepted as being the sort of place where coffee makers – or anything, for that matter – can be sold as art. I'm not in that line of apostolic succession, so to speak."

Big Lou was thinking. "The Dutch tulip affair," she said. "I was reading a funny wee book about social hysteria – about how folk get things into their heads and go mad for a while. There was something about witchcraft."

CHROME III

"Moral panics," prompted Matthew.

"Yes. That sort of thing. Didn't the Dutch go mad about tulips back in the – when was it – 1600s? Didn't they pay terrific prices for tulip bulbs? And these bulbs got more and more expensive and people fought to have the rarest ones they could get hold of. Sheer stupidity."

"Yes," said Matthew. "And then suddenly somebody said, 'Hold on, it's just tulip bulbs, and tulip bulbs aren't really worth the price of a house.'"

"And everything collapsed. Yes. Do you think that people in the art business know about the tulip disaster?"

Matthew smiled. "I suspect that they know only too well. But the problem is, they can't do anything but keep up the entire pretence and carry on buying these banal conceits because if they didn't their collections would be worthless. Who would want to buy a shark in a tank of formaldehyde? Especially if the shark started to decay and fall to bits? You have to pretend that it's still important, still worth keeping, because if you didn't you'd lose millions of pounds."

A silence ensued as the two of them contemplated the creation of value in the valueless.

"Pat," said Matthew suddenly, looking at his watch.

Big Lou frowned. "I haven't seen her for an awful long time."

"Well, you're about to see her," said Matthew. "She's coming in this morning. About now."

"Why?"

"I'm taking her on in the gallery again," explained Matthew. "I've got my move coming up and I need to help Elspeth get everything ready. So I'll need two helpers, rather than one."

Big Lou absorbed this information. She liked Pat, and she was pleased that she would be seeing her again. She was worried, though, that Pat would not approve of Matthew's new assistant, Kirsty. Certainly, Big Lou had not taken to her, even if she could not put her finger on the exact reason. Too glamorous? Possibly. But there was something more to it than that. Big Lou did not trust Kirsty – that was it; trust – a concept so hard to define and yet, in its absence, so unmistakable.

"It won't work," she said to Matthew.

"Why?"

Big Lou shrugged. It would not be easy to explain it to Matthew, because he was a man and men often did not understand these nuances. No point in trying, she decided, but at least he might understand folk wisdom. "We used to say in Arbroath," she pronounced, "that you can't have two women in the same kitchen."

## 62. *Unwelcome Thoughts*

It was as Matthew was crossing the road on his way back from Big Lou's that he saw Pat walking down the hill towards him. From the safety of the pavement he stood and waved. She waved back before quickening her pace.

"I'm sorry I'm late," she said as she reached him. "It took longer than I thought."

Matthew smiled. "You don't have to apologise. I was talking to Big Lou and I suddenly remembered that I'd arranged to meet you."

They had not shaken hands, nor embraced, as long-lost friends might do. Between them there was that strange half-intimacy of former lovers, a feeling that can so easily become awkwardness, but which, in their case, had not. It was fondness, really; that fondness that comes, in Rupert Brooke's words, from having done one's best and worst and parted. Now, in the moments after a rather stiff beginning, Pat suddenly leaned forward and gave

Matthew a kiss on his cheek. He moved, though, surprised, and she ended up kissing him on the lips. He reached out and put a hand upon her shoulder; she did the same.

And then he recoiled; a social kiss, as meaningless and often less warm than a shaking of the hands, had become something else. He had felt within him, around where he imagined his heart to be, although it could have been anywhere within his chest, a physical sensation that signalled desire.

She looked concerned. "What is it?"

He did not meet her gaze, but looked away; the 23 bus, lumbering down the hill, passed within yards, and he saw for a moment his reflection in the windows, fluid, as on water.

"What?"

She reached out to touch him. "Is something wrong?"

He shook his head. The social self reasserted itself; he was married again; there was nothing between him and Pat; they were in the street, in broad daylight, about to have what amounted to no more than a discussion between employer and part-time employee.

"I've got a lot on my mind," he said. "Let's get back to the gallery."

They began to walk. "I'm sorry I've been out of touch," said Pat. "I've been working rather hard. And I've moved, you know. I'm in Warrender Park Terrace. A flat right up at the top."

He could see it. "One of those big flats?"

"Yes. I've got a round room, because it's under the tower."

He smiled at her. And then, unbidden, there came into his mind an image of Pat in her room looking out towards the crown spire of St. Giles' and to the Castle, like a ship, its ramparts protection against waves that were the clouds, and he saw her at her window and then as she walked, unclothed, across the room. It was a vision sent by Eros, who does not ask our permission for his whisperings.

He almost stumbled.

"Careful," she said. And then, seeing his expression and noting the sudden high colour, she asked, "Are you sure you're all right, Matthew?"

He sought to reassure her, but even as he did so, the vision returned and took his hand, and . . .

"Oh," he muttered.

"Matthew?"

He forced himself to think of something else, a trick mastered by every schoolboy troubled by wandering thoughts in mathematics lessons. In his case he had always thought of the Forth Bridge, and of its painting; a subject sufficiently devoid of emotional significance to distract one from the temptation of fantasy.

"What are you thinking of?" asked Pat.

The question, posed in innocence, could hardly be ignored. For a moment he was tempted to tell her, to say that he was picturing her in her flat in Warrender Park Terrace, but he could not do that, and so, without thinking, he answered, "The Forth Bridge."

She frowned. "Odd. Why are you thinking of the Forth Bridge?"

"I sometimes do," he said lamely. "The old bridge, that is. The railway bridge."

"Matthew, are you sure you're all right?"

They were nearing the gallery, but she had stopped and laid a hand gently on his arm. She looked at him searchingly, and he realised then why he had always been so attracted to her: her eyes. And then he thought: how ridiculous that one can feel for a person on such slender, inconsequential grounds.

"I've been under a lot of strain," he said. "Elspeth is having triplets."

Pat gasped. "Three?"

"Yes."

"It must have been . . ."

"A shock," he supplied. "Yes, it was. But we've adjusted to it. And we've got a move on top of it. We're going to Moray Place."

"Moray Place?" She was silent for a few moments, remembering the invitation that she had received to the nudist picnic there.

"Yes, it's a really nice flat. With its own garden."

The discussion of Moray Place had brought him back from the territory that had so surprised and appalled him. He was back to being Matthew, the husband of Elspeth, and father of triplets. The moment of danger, it seemed, had passed.

"But let's not talk about all that," he said. "I'm really pleased that you can work for me again."

They had reached the gallery and were standing in front of the glass door at the front. Pat looked in, through the door, and saw, at the back, the figure of Kirsty, who was bending down, looking in one of the print drawers. "Matthew?" Pat began hesitantly.

"Yes?"

"That's her, is it? The other girl working here?"

Matthew glanced into the gallery. "Yes, that's Kirsty."

Pat suddenly drew Matthew away. "I'm not going in," she said.

"Why? What's wrong?"

"I know her," said Pat. "I know that girl."

"So?"

"I can't work with her. I just can't." She paused. "And you can't either."

"What do you mean I can't work with her? I've been working with her for the last two months."

Pat shook her head. "Matthew, listen to me. Do you know who she is? Clearly not. Kirsty is a big figure in a group called Woman's Revenge."

He savoured the name of the organisation: Woman's Revenge. It spoke to its purpose, he decided; it was not an organisation that really needed a mission statement to clarify anything.

"They punish men," whispered Pat. "They're dangerous."

"Then I'm going to have to get rid of her," he said. "Where's the problem?"

"That's the one thing you can't do," said Pat. "Remember? Woman's Revenge."

### 63. *Italy at Last*

"Here we are," said Angus, looking out of the window at the squat, unexceptional buildings that made up Pisa airport. "And you'd think that their control tower would lean – but it doesn't. How disappointing!"

Domenica, seated next to him, glanced past his shoulder. "How amusing!" she said. "The Leaning Control Tower of Pisa."

Antonia, who was occupying the third seat in the row, had not heard Angus's remark. "Did Angus say something witty?" she asked. There was an air of anxiety about her question, as if she feared that she was somehow excluded by what had gone before. She had tried to sit next to Angus on the journey, but Domenica had pointed out that while Angus occupied Seat 6A, her own boarding pass very clearly said 6B, and Antonia's, she assumed, said 6C.

"That's notional," said Antonia. "We have seats 6A to 6C at our disposal – that's all the letters mean."

Domenica was not to be so easily overruled. "No," she said, shaking her head. "When an airline gives you a seat number, then that is where they want you to sit. They don't say, 'Please sit some-where around here,' they say, 'You are to sit in this exact seat.' It is quite clear – unambiguously so, if I may venture an opinion."

Antonia had listened to this thin-lipped. "I don't think . . ." she began.

"Moreover," Domenica continued, "if people were to change seats off their own bat, then the weighting arrangements in the plane could be disturbed. Airlines put people in certain places in order to balance the aircraft. I was told that once by a pilot of my acquaintance. He explained it quite clearly. They do not want people to shift about – therein lie the seeds of anarchy."

This discussion, which had taken place while they were at Edinburgh airport, waiting to board the waiting plane, was polite, but revealed the fault lines which lay perilously close to the surface of the entire outing. Domenica knew that Antonia had her eye on Angus, and was aware, too, of her neighbour's deter-mination somehow to snare the artist on this Italian trip. But resolute and calculating as this intention might be, so, too, was Domenica determined that Angus should not be enticed by this woman; if anybody were to take on Angus, then it would be she who would do the taking on, and that, she had decided, was what she now should do. And in the pursuit of this objective, it was clear that at the very start of the trip she should sit next to him; this would give her a vital head start on Antonia, who would have to address any remarks she wished to make to Angus either through or across her.

This position had proved to be highly advantageous. Thus, when Antonia had, by way of conversation, asked Angus whether he could see the Alps through his window, she herself had been able to provide an answer. "No, I don't think he can," she said. "Particularly since we are still currently above the Netherlands."

And then, later into the trip, when Antonia had tried to ask, above the background hum of the aircraft's engines, whether Angus had enjoyed the limp, damp sandwich which the airline had so kindly distributed to its passengers, Domenica had again been able to deal with the situation in an entirely satisfactory manner. Angus had been aware of the fact that Antonia was saying something to him, but had not been able to make out what it was.

"I believe Antonia said something," he said. "What was it?"

"It was nothing important," said Domenica.

And now, as they taxied on the runway at Pisa airport and Antonia asked about Angus's witticism, Domenica was again able to fob her off. "He made a remark about the control tower," she said. "That's all."

Antonia's irritation showed clearly. "Well, what did he say?"

"Nothing much," said Domenica. "Oh, look over there – no, I suppose you can't see from where you're sitting – but there's a set of steps waiting for us. How thoughtful of the dear airport."

"They would hardly expect us to jump down from the door," said Antonia, in a surly tone.

Angus turned to Domenica. "Did Antonia say something?" he asked.

"Nothing much."

They deplaned, as the language of aviation so neologistically puts it, and were then bussed to the terminal, where they were debussed. There then followed a brief and entirely wordless encounter with the Italian border authorities, who glanced at their passports in a pitying way before waving them through.

"It's so sad," said Domenica, "that the land of Dante and Michelangelo should be guarded by such men. Even if they have such ornate uniforms."

Angus smiled. "All Italian officials have splendid uniforms," he said. "I remember reading about the formation of an Italian railway company in the nineteenth century. They spent much of their time and start-up capital on designing elaborate uniforms for their officials."

"They have a proper sense of theatre," said Domenica.

Antonia disagreed. "Running a railway has nothing to do with theatre. It is all about engineering."

"At which these people excel," said Angus. "Engineering, opera, great art – is there nothing they cannot do?"

"They are very talented people," said Domenica. "And I do hope that their talents run to transporting suitcases from A to B without losing them."

"And transporting dogs too," said Angus.

"Of course," said Domenica. She had forgotten Cyril was with them and had made the trip in considerably less comfortable circumstances, somewhere in the hold.

They need not have worried. By the time they found themselves in the baggage reclaiming area, they saw that Cyril was already there. He too had been deplaned and was sitting patiently in his travel crate with its barred front and its special water dispenser. He knew immediately that Angus was in the room and barked loudly to attract his master's attention.

"Cyril!" shouted Angus. "Cyril! *Siamo arrivati!*"

They made their way quickly to join him. Cyril attempted to lick Angus's hands through the bars, his tail thumping wildly against the sides of his portable prison. Bending down, Angus released the catch on the front of the cage, and Cyril bounded out. There then followed an orgy of licking and emotional canine howling as dog and master were properly reunited. For Cyril the last few hours had been an ordeal; a time of roaring noise and strange, unsettling movement. But now that was all over and Angus had been restored to him; the discomfort and confusion could be forgotten – it simply did not happen.

Then Cyril suddenly stopped in his tracks. He turned his head and lifted his nose, pointing it in the direction of the carousel on which the suitcases were now beginning to appear. One piece of luggage, in particular, attracted his attention, making the moist end of his nose twitch uncontrollably.

## 64. *Services to the Republic*

Angus was the first to notice Cyril's odd behaviour. "I think Cyril's picked something up," he said to Domenica and Antonia. "Look, his nose only twitches like that when he's got a whiff of something very interesting."

They all looked at Cyril, who was now standing quite still, the fur of his coat bristling as he sniffed into the air.

"One of the suitcases," said Domenica. "Do you think that he's seen yours, Angus? Have you got anything of his in it?"

Angus shook his head. "No, Cyril travels pretty light. In fact, he's come with nothing."

Cyril now began to growl.

"What is it, old chap?" Angus asked. "Picked up something?"

Cyril's answer was now to bound across the room towards the luggage carousel. Extracting a lead from his pocket, Angus called him back sharply, but Cyril paid no attention. He was now at the carousel, trotting around after a rather battered red backpack. He uttered a bark, and then, seeing that nobody was reacting, another one, louder this time. This second bark was sufficient to attract the attention of a sergeant of the Carabinieri, who was standing idly at the side of the room, talking to a man in a grey business suit. The officer, along with the man in the suit, now sauntered over towards Cyril.

"I'm sorry about my dog," said Angus, who had walked across the room to join them. "I'll get him under control in a moment."

The man in the suit turned to Angus and smiled. "Your dog is interested in that red pack," he said, in well-enunciated English. "Is it your own luggage?"

"No," said Angus.

The man looked interested. "He has smelled something, would you not say?"

"Yes, I would say that," said Angus.

The man in the suit now said something in rapid Italian to the Carabinieri sergeant, who nodded and then stepped forward to retrieve the red backpack. As he did this, Angus, who happened to be looking in the right direction, saw a young man watching from a corner of the hall. It was clear from his expression that he was thoroughly dismayed and, as the officer retrieved the pack, he began to move towards the door.

"Excuse me," said Angus, tugging the sleeve of the man in the suit. "That young man over there . . ."

The man looked round, saw what was happening, and gave a sharp instruction to the Carabinieri officer. The officer, dropping the backpack, reacted quickly. Drawing a pistol from the white leather pouch attached to his gleaming Sam Browne belt, he shouted out at the young man, who froze where he was.

Domenica and Antonia watched it all unfurl. The young man, seeing the approach of the Carabinieri officer, dived for the door, but was not quick enough, and the door was locked anyway. There was further shouting and a certain amount of confusion amongst the passengers, who saw the gun being drawn and immediately assumed that a terrorist had chosen this moment to detonate the bomb that would immediately add them all to the morbid statistics of the unending and seemingly unendable conflict. But there was no explosion, and no shot either. The young man simply folded up, and was quickly dragged away by several other Carabinieri officers, who had suddenly materialised in the baggage hall.

Over the confusing hour that followed, Angus and his companions were given an insight into the extraordinarily quick and efficient operations of the Italian security forces. They were all led into a room at the back. "You are only witnesses," explained the man in the suit. "You are not suspects. Please do not think that we suspect you of anything . . ." He paused, and looked at each of them in turn. "That is, unless you have anything to hide."

"We have nothing at all to hide," said Angus, who had emerged as spokesman for all three of them. "We are simply here on holiday."

"Of course," said the man. "And we have much to thank you for." He signalled to a colleague, who left the room briefly and returned with a large white package.

"You can guess what this is," said the man.

Angus raised an eyebrow. "Drugs? Cocaine?"

"Exactly," said the man. "It was in that backpack. Not very expertly concealed, but had it not been for your dog, well, I doubt if we would have found it." He looked down at Cyril, who was sitting at Angus's feet. "Such a dog is truly remarkable. Do you know that in Italy we have special orders for people who do good service to the state?"

"One can become a *cavaliere*," ventured Angus. "Or is it a *commendatore*?" He knew that his friend Richard Demarco had been awarded something of that sort for services to art.

"There are various grades of the order," explained the man in the grey suit. "To become a Cavaliere di Gran Croce decorato di Grande Cordone is a very great achievement. Below that, there are five lesser grades of the order, culminating in the simple Cavaliere Ordine, of whom we have many thousands. That is not to say that it is any disgrace in being a *cavaliere* fifth class. For many of us, that would be an achievement indeed."

Angus nodded; becoming a *cavaliere* fifth class, he imagined, would be rather like getting the MBE.

"These awards, of course, are not available for animals," continued the man. "However, the Italian state holds in high regard acts of animal heroism of which, if I may say so, this remarkable act of your excellent dog here is a prime example."

Angus glanced at Cyril, who looked up at him with the look of one who does not quite know what is going on.

"I cannot guarantee it, of course," said the man. "But suffice it to say that my department will be submitting the name of your dog to the Council of Ministers, with a strong recommendation – and I do mean strong – that he be made a *cane-cavaliere*. That is the order which is awarded principally to dogs who have provided good service to the republic. It is given, for example, to sniffer dogs who have saved lives in earthquakes or avalanches – that sort of thing."

"And my dog . . ."

The man raised a finger. "Indeed. Your dog."

Angus was at a loss as to what to say. Cyril had been in Italy precisely fifteen minutes before rendering a service to the Italian state and ensuring himself a recommendation for an award. It was, he thought, a good omen for the trip ahead. To arrive in a foreign country and be immediately recommended for decoration by the state was, he thought, a very promising beginning.

## 65. *The Impact of Italy*

This auspicious beginning to the trip put Angus in a particularly good mood for the journey from Pisa to the villa. Their hired car,

a Fiat Venti Cavalli, was big enough for the entire party and all their luggage, but only if Cyril sat on Angus's lap. This he was happy to do, sticking his head out of the window and sniffing with intense interest at the passing Italian air. The smells, of course, were quite different from those attendant on a comparable Scottish journey, and none of the human passengers had even the faintest inkling of how exciting was the olfactory tapestry that Cyril now enjoyed. The world as it reveals itself to the canine nose is far richer than we can possibly imagine, and includes not only that which is there – which is interesting enough – but also that which was there before; so, while the human eye may see signs of the impact of man – farm walls, grain towers, well-worked farms – the dog picks up so much more: historic scents that have been layered upon the landscape and have not gone away. We, then, may look at a Tuscan field and see furrows, stones, dry white earth; this would be thin fare for the dog, who will know that those furrows were ploughed by oxen, that birds had pecked at the seeds sown by the farmer whose boots in turn left behind them a story quite of their own, of tramping upon a cellar floor, of walking amongst olive trees, and of so much else. All this Cyril now picked up and relished, quivering with excitement at the intellectual challenge of interpreting and classifying this bewildering array of scents.

Domenica was at the wheel. Nothing had been said about this; she had merely announced that she had arranged the car. Angus did not own a car and, although he possessed a licence, had more or less forgotten how to drive; Antonia, by contrast, would have driven had Domenica not been – in her view – so controlling.

"I'll be very happy to share the driving with you," she said as they left the suburbs of Pisa behind them. "Just let me know when you want a break."

"How kind," said Domenica. "But, alas, I appear to be the only driver listed on the car rental contract. How very unfortunate."

Antonia said nothing, but in her mind she filed this away as yet another example of Domenica's taking over. There had already been several incidents in the plane, when she had monopolised Angus and barely given her a look-in; that was bad enough, but if this were to be the pattern of the trip, then she would have to be dealt with. Angus was not here for the sole delectation of Domenica, thought Antonia, even if it was true that the older woman had met him first. The fact that one has met a person first does not confer any greater right to that person's company; that would be absurd. Perhaps Domenica needed to be reminded that she, Antonia, was an artist – in that she was a writer – just as Angus was, and that this meant that there was a bond between the two of them to which Domenica, as a non-artist, could not hope to aspire.

"I feel so . . . so exhilarated," she said. "Just to be here in Tuscany." She gestured to the countryside outside the car. "What artistic soul could be anything but quickened in such a place? Don't you agree, Angus? As an artist?"

Angus smiled. "Indeed," he said. "This is landscape to which one can hardly be indifferent."

Antonia now continued. "I suppose that even those of us who

are not artists," and here she looked pointedly at Domenica, "must feel something too. Not as intensely, perhaps."

Domenica kept her eyes fixed on the road. "We have a long family association with this part of Italy," she said evenly. "My parents, in fact, met in Florence. My father, you see, was instrumental in setting up the British Library there. He was with the British Council for many years. They had many friends here. And I came for the holidays – quite often, in fact. My very first boyfriend was Italian, you know. I was sixteen and there was this delightful boy whose father was the Conte di something or other, and we played tennis . . ."

"Such a dull game," interjected Antonia. She did not want to hear about this Italian boy and his father, the conte; a typical story, she felt, of upper-middle-class pretension. And what was this about visiting as a child? She thought that Domenica had lived in India when she was young, not Italy. Was she making the whole thing up?

"Tennis?" said Angus. "Tennis dull? Surely not. I'll play tennis with you, if you like, Domenica. I'm a bit rusty, but I used to play quite a lot. Do we have a tennis court at the villa, I wonder?"

"I don't think so," said Domenica. "But had we had one, then we could certainly have played."

Antonia smiled grimly. Really, Domenica was the end. If we had a tennis court then we should have played! Domenica was not unlike that Jane Austen character who announced that if she had learned to play the piano then she would undoubtedly have been rather good at it. Well, if this was the way Domenica wanted it to be, then she would not flinch from the prospect. If there was to be a direct battle for the attentions of Angus, then she, Antonia, had an advantage that no amount of clever verbal play on Domenica's part would be able to deal with: she was younger than her. That brute fact gave her an inestimable advantage: she was younger, and any man was bound to be more interested in a younger woman – that was how men were. They might pretend it to be otherwise, but such claims would ultimately always be shown to be hollow; Angus would be no exception.

They continued with their drive until at last they saw the small hill town of Sant' Angelo in Colle rise up from the plains. They were still some distance away when they saw it, and it was faded and attenuated in hazy outline, almost unreal, like a backdrop painted by an artist whose palette runs only to gentle shades of blue.

"That's where we're going," said Domenica. "See? Over there."

Antonia and Angus were silent. The sight of such beauty can make us quiet with fear; fear that it might not be real, fear that it might be taken from us, as is everything that we love, which is only on loan to us.

## 66. *Pacta Sunt Servanda*

The return of Irene proved to be a low-key affair. On the day of her repatriation, Stuart took Bertie to school on the 23 bus and assured him that his mother would be there to collect him at the end of the school day. And indeed she was – as Bertie made his way to the school gate he saw Irene talking in an animated way to a small knot of raptly attentive parents, describing to them, he imagined, her remarkable ordeal.

"There's your mother, Bertie," said Olive as they approached the gate. "Nobody thought they'd see her again, but she's back. My dad says it's a great pity."

Bertie frowned. "What's a great pity?"

"That your mum was taken away in a container," said Olive. "Or I think that was what he meant. Of course he might have meant that it's a pity she's come back. I've got no way of telling. But that's what he said."

They returned to the flat on the bus.

"I was worried about you, Mummy," said Bertie.

"Of course you were," said Irene. "But we must put these little things behind us. I am, if anything, strengthened by the experience, Bertie. To be taken to Hungary in a container is but a small thing, Bertie. And I hear from Daddy that you were extremely brave about it all. As was Ulysses, I gather."

Bertie said nothing. He did not think it would help to tell his mother how cheerful Ulysses had been during her absence; how he had refrained from being sick and how his appetite had improved. Life, he realised, would return to normal, which it did almost immediately. Yet not everything was unchanged by Irene's unfortunate experience; while Irene was away, Bertie had been comforted by his father, who had promised him that as soon as the crisis was over and Irene was restored, he would take his son fishing in the Pentlands. It was a long overdue promise, and Bertie was not going to forget it quickly. A few days after Irene's return, Bertie raised the topic with Stuart, reminding him of his undertaking.

"You promised," he said. "And you have to keep your promises, you know. *Pacta sunt servanda*, Daddy."

Stuart looked at Bertie in unconcealed astonishment. "Where did you get that from, Bertie?"

"It's Latin," he said. "It means that you should keep your promises. I read it somewhere."

"Well, of course I shall."

Bertie pressed home. "When?"

Stuart thought. He was still on compassionate leave, and in his view Bertie was entitled to a few days' leave too. "Tomorrow," he said.

Bertie's eyes widened. "But tomorrow's a school day, Daddy. I have to . . ."

Stuart smiled. "That's perfectly all right, Bertie. You can have the day off."

Bertie's jaw dropped. "Just like that?"

"Yes," said Stuart. "Just like that. You've had a very difficult time, with Mummy being away."

Bertie looked thoughtful. Yes, it had been difficult in that he had felt anxious and concerned, but in other respects . . . He did not like to admit it, of course, but it had been, in some respects, glorious. No yoga. No Italian. No psychotherapy.

"So," Stuart continued, "we'll go fishing in one of those lochs in the Pentlands."

"But won't I get into trouble?" asked Bertie.

"No. Not at all. I'm your father, Bertie, and I take the view that you are quite sufficiently educationally advanced to take the occasional day off school. After all, there you were quoting Latin expressions to me – *pacta sunt* something or other – what exactly was it, Bertie?"

"*Pacta sunt servanda*," said Bertie. "I read all about it, Daddy. It's a principle of international law. It means that you must keep your word." He thought of Tofu. Tofu needed to have this rule explained to him. And Olive too. And Hiawatha, who had recently promised Bertie to give him a packet of crisps in exchange for a peanut-butter sandwich and had then reneged on the agreement on the grounds that he had been crossing his fingers at the time.

Stuart nodded.

"What is international law, Daddy?" asked Bertie.

Stuart raised an eyebrow. "It is, I believe, the system of rules that countries have to obey."

Bertie thought of this. "And do they?" he asked.

"When it suits them," said Stuart. "Otherwise no. Otherwise they say that the rules are all a bit vague."

"I see," said Bertie. He was now thinking about fishing. "Where will we go?"

"We'll try one of those lochs up there," said Stuart, pointing vaguely in the direction of the Pentlands. "I can borrow a couple of rods from somebody round the corner. I know a man who's got all the necessary stuff, Bertie."

Bertie moved from foot to foot with excitement and pleasure. "And can we have sandwiches, Daddy?"

"Yes," said Stuart. "We'll take sandwiches. And I'll buy some crisps from that garage opposite the ski slope. They have lots of crisps there, Bertie."

Bertie closed his eyes in sheer pleasure at the thought. And when he opened them, there was his mother, who had been in the kitchen when this conversation with his father had begun.

"What's all this, Stuart?" Irene asked. "What's this about crisps?"

Stuart swallowed hard. Bertie noticed this, and looked away.

"Bertie and I . . ." Stuart faltered. Bertie felt his heart miss a beat within him.

Irene kept her eyes on Stuart. "Yes?"

"We're going fishing, Mummy," Bertie blurted out. "We're going fishing in one of those lochs in the Pentlands. Daddy's going to get some crisps so that we can eat them while we're . . ." Now he, too, faltered. But he plucked up his courage. "Tomorrow."

"Tomorrow?" said Irene. "But tomorrow's a school day, Stuart. Bertie can't . . ."

Stuart closed his eyes. "Decision taken!" he said firmly. "No school for Bertie tomorrow. Fishing. All decided!"

Bertie looked at his father in sheer admiration. Then he looked at his mother. Her eyes were narrowed.

"Stuart," she said quietly. "A little word with you in the kitchen, if you don't mind."

Bertie held his breath.

"No need," said Stuart breezily. "It's all settled. I've told Bertie it's all fixed up. End of story."

"Yes," said Bertie. "*Pacta sunt servanda*, Mummy."

Two against one, thought Bertie. Two against one. No, three, if you counted Ulysses.

## 67. An Outing Begins

They drove out of town in the Pollocks' old Volvo, the same Volvo that had been so often mislaid and that on one occasion had even been left in Glasgow by mistake. Or not quite the same, perhaps: a Volvo had been left in Glasgow and one had been returned to Edinburgh at the instance of the late Lard O'Connor (RIP), but while the car that Stuart had thoughtlessly left in Glasgow had five gears, the vehicle that had been returned to Edinburgh had only four. Stuart had felt uneasy about this, but had left the matter where it lay; a gear either way made no real difference in this life, he felt; most people got by with four, and only the self-indulgent or indeed the unashamedly selfish would insist on five. Bertie, however, remarked on the difference; this was not really their car, he thought, but again expedience triumphed and he made no further mention of his suspicions.

Now, sitting beside his father, strapped into the passenger seat, he watched the well-set Edinburgh landscape go past. As they reached Holy Corner, he pointed to the Episcopal church where the First Morningside Cub Scout Troop met weekly under the watchful eye of their Akela, Mrs. Rosemary Gold.

"That's cub headquarters," he said to his father. "We have so much fun."

"I'm sure you do, Bertie," said Stuart. "I had fun when I was in the scouts." He paused. "A long time ago now."

Bertie looked at his father with admiration. "You were a scout, Daddy?"

"Yes," said Stuart. "I was, as it happens."

"And did you go camping with the other boys and girls?" asked Bertie. He wanted his father to answer yes; he wanted his father to have had camping experience, as it meant that it was possible – just possible – that he might take him camping one day. Just the two of them.

Stuart shook his head. "I went camping, but it was just boys," he said. "Not boys and girls in those days, Bertie."

Bertie turned in his seat and stared at his father with wide, solemn eyes. "You mean . . . you mean that there were no girls?"

Stuart nodded. "The scouts were for boys, Bertie. Girls had brownies and guides. That was the way things were."

Bertie was silent for a few moments. In those days, then, Olive would not have been allowed to be a cub; she would have had to go to brownies. He closed his eyes and imagined cub scouts without Olive; it would be wonderful, he thought.

"Why did they start letting girls join cub scouts?" he asked. "Especially since boys aren't allowed to join the brownies?"

Stuart looked thoughtful. No boy in his right mind would want to be a brownie, he thought, but he could not say that, not these days. "Perhaps they thought that it would be better for boys to have girls in the cub scouts, Bertie."

"It isn't," said Bertie quickly.

Stuart smiled. "Come now, Bertie. Girls just like to have fun, same as boys."

"Are you sure, Daddy?" said Bertie, thinking of Olive and Pansy. "I think there are some girls who want to stop boys having fun."

Stuart swallowed; he could name one, and fairly close to home too. "Oh, I don't know, Bertie. Maybe you'll look at things differently when you're a bit older."

"When I'm seven?" asked Bertie.

"Well, possibly."

Bertie tried to imagine what the world would look like when he was seven, but his mind wandered. They were now going past the Braid Hills Hotel and the Pentlands were beginning to rise up on the horizon. He saw the ski slope at Hillend and the brooding summit behind it; he saw the line of green hills marching off to the west. In a few minutes they would be out of the city and in a hinterland of small glens and hidden lochs; in a few minutes, although he could hardly believe it, they would be catching fish.

They stopped, as Stuart had promised, at the petrol station at Hillend. While Stuart filled the tank, Bertie was allowed to wander about the shop, looking at the chocolates, sweets, and racks of potato crisps that tempted the visitor. He chose two packets – one ready salted and one flavoured with tomato sauce. "A good choice, Bertie," said Stuart, as he came in to pay for the petrol. "And how about some chocolate?"

Nobody had ever said that to Bertie before. How about some chocolate? It was not a complex phrase, but its power, its sheer, overwhelming sense of gift and possibility filled Bertie with awe. Well might more of us say these words to others, and more frequently – how healing would that prove to be. "Look, we've had our differences, but how about some chocolate?" Or: "I'm so sorry: how about some chocolate?" Or simply: "Great to see you! How about some chocolate?"

"Chocolate?" said Bertie. "Chocolate, as well as crisps?"

Stuart smiled. "Why not?"

Bertie looked at the trays of chocolate bars laid out so temptingly; thus might the siren voices tempt the sailor; thus might Faust falter and conclude the bargain. He hesitated, and then made his choice – a bar of gold-wrapped Crunchie with peppermint-flavoured air holes.

"And?" said Stuart, looking down at his son's choice, reading the label of the tempting confection. "Peppermint-flavoured air holes? An interesting concept."

Bertie looked up at his father. "And what, Daddy?"

"You can't just buy one," said Stuart. "Pick another two, Bertie. We've got a long day's fishing ahead of us."

Bertie stared at the array of chocolate bars. Some of them he had heard of – discussed by the children at school. Olive, in particular, was an authority on the subject. "I've tasted them all," she announced, with an air that implicitly challenged anybody who might doubt her. "It's a pity you've never tried them, Bertie."

"It's not Bertie's fault he's not allowed chocolate," said Tofu. "It's his mother. She's a cow, isn't she, Bertie?"

Bertie said nothing; Olive glared at Tofu. "I doubt if you know what I'm talking about, Tofu," she said. "You get soya chocolate at home, I suppose. Soya chocolate! Hah!"

Pansy, who had joined the discussion, laughed. "Poor Tofu," she said.

Tofu fixed his gaze on Olive. "You stink," he said.

It had not been an edifying discussion, and Bertie put it out of his mind as he reached out and picked two further chocolate bars, more or less at random. Then, following his father, he made his way to the cash desk.

Once back in the car, he laid the chocolate and crisps out on his lap and stared at them. They were real. This was really happening. He was going fishing with his father, and the sun had burst out from behind a bank of cloud, now dispelled, filling the sky, touching all Scotland, and all its hills, it seemed, with gold.

## 68. The Need for Evidence

Matthew spent little more than an hour in the gallery that morning. It had not been easy: he had been completely taken aback by Pat's disinclination to enter the door once she had glimpsed Kirsty through the window.

"But you hardly know her," he protested. "You said so yourself."

Pat peered through the glass: she could just make out the figure of Kirsty in the back room. "She's bad news, Matthew. She really is."

Matthew sighed. "You can't just say things like that. What do you mean, 'She's bad news'?"

"Just that," said Pat. "Some people are . . . bad news. One can't necessarily say much more than that." As she spoke, she thought of Bruce. He was bad news; very bad news, really. But if you had to describe exactly why he was bad news, it would be difficult: somehow one would not get just the right flavour of the numerous ways in which Bruce failed the good news test. It was the same with Kirsty – and yet she was not sure how to explain all this to Matthew.

"She has a reputation," she said.

Matthew looked at her in astonishment. "But everybody has a reputation. A reputation can be quite neutral, or even good. You have to have evidence, anyway."

Pat looked away. Matthew was not making it any easier for her. What could she tell him? That Kirsty had been responsible for not just one young man abandoning his degree course, but two? That she was said to have been responsible for the most disastrous skiing trip in the history of the university ski society? That she had stolen the boyfriend of a girl in Pat's year, and had dumped him after a mere three weeks? These were only some of the charges outstanding against Kirsty, but she wondered how she could provide the evidence that Matthew appeared to need.

Pat had surrendered, and they had gone into the gallery, where

Matthew had witnessed their meeting. Nothing had happened; they had been polite to one another, and indeed Kirsty had seemed quite pleased to see Pat. Then they had discussed a rota and how they would split the hours between them. That, too, had been quite amicable.

"You see?" whispered Matthew to Pat, when Kirsty went to fetch something from the back room. "What's the problem? She's fine – she really is."

"Just you wait," Pat whispered back. "I'm not making it up, Matthew. I'm not, you know."

Shortly before twelve, Matthew had left the gallery in the charge of the two girls. He was meeting Elspeth for lunch, he explained, and then he was going to Moray Place to see the surveyor whom they had commissioned to survey the new flat. "I probably won't be back," he said. "So could one of you lock up at five?"

Kirsty agreed to do this. "Pat and I will be fine," she said. "Won't we, Pat?"

Pat had nodded, but Matthew had noticed the look of reservation, a glance in his direction. He chose to ignore it. Women were odd about these things, he told himself. Half the time it's unspoken jealousy – Kirsty was a rival; that must have been it. It was all reducible to competition between members of the same sex; competition for the scarce resource – men. That was what Matthew thought.

He left the gallery and made his way to Glass and Thompson's café at the intersection with Heriot Row. As he went down the couple of steps to the front door, he saw that Elspeth was already there, sitting at one of the tables opposite the service counter, reading a magazine. Matthew appeared at her table and put his hand over a page of the magazine. "Boo," he said.

Elspeth smiled. "I was reading my horoscope."

"Rubbish," he said, sitting down. "Pure fiction."

She shrugged. "Plenty of people believe in them."

Matthew pointed out that people believed in all sorts of ridiculous things. "There are few limits to human gullibility," he said. "Flying saucers and so on. Angels. Horoscopes. It's all wishful thinking."

"Angels?" asked Elspeth. "You don't believe in angels?"

He was unsure as to whether she was joking. "No," he said. "I only believe in things I can see." He paused. "Has there ever been a confirmed sighting of an angel? Has anybody ever photographed one?"

Elspeth thought about this. "So you only believe in things that you can photograph?"

He hesitated. But it was true, he thought: we should only believe in that which we can either see for ourselves – with senses that we can trust because we experience them directly – or in things that can be proved to be perceptible to others. That was where photography came in. If something could be seen, then it could be photographed. And if there were no photographs, then that meant that either nobody had ever had a camera ready at the right time, or the thing in question did not exist. There were no photographs of angels. None.

"Yes," said Matthew. "That's what I believe. If something exists, then it should be possible to photograph it."

"Such as love," said Elspeth.

Matthew frowned. "What's love got to do with it?"

"Does love exist?"

Matthew laughed. "Of course it does. I love you, don't I?"

"But you can't photograph it," said Elspeth simply. "You can't, can you?"

Matthew smiled. "That's different. Love is an emotional state."

"Is it?" asked Elspeth. "Is that all it is?"

Matthew looked at the menu. "I wonder what their mozzarella is like?" he asked. Then he pointed to the magazine. "What does your horoscope say, anyway?"

Elspeth looked down at the page. She thought that she had won that little debate, but Matthew obviously did not want to pursue it. So she read from her horoscope. "The stars say," she began. "The stars say this: 'You will receive advice from a well-intentioned person. Do not disregard it. You will also meet an old friend who needs your help and understanding. Do not turn him or her away.'"

Matthew nodded in mock seriousness. "Very wise," he said. "And what about me? Will I meet an angel, perhaps?"

Elspeth ignored the jibe. "Your stars," she said, looking down the page. "Here you are. 'You will be given a warning. The person who gives you this warning will have your interests at heart. Do not ignore what he has to say to you. Lucky colour: yellow. Lucky number: 3.141.'"

"Pie?" said Matthew, looking back at the menu.

## 69. *On Subsidence*

Matthew looked at his watch. "We have to hurry," he said. "The surveyor will be there in fifteen minutes."

Elspeth sighed. "Do I have to come too?" she asked. She suddenly felt heavy, as happened quite frequently now. And she was hungry too, although she had just finished a plate of mozzarella and tomato salad, with no fewer than five small pieces of bread. Again this was something that seemed to happen rather regularly now – a meal would no sooner be finished than she would feel incipient pangs of hunger. It was the triplets, of course, and if they were demanding at this stage of the pregnancy, then she could imagine what they would be like when nine months was almost over. And after that? She had already experienced a disturbing dream in which she found herself in the kitchen surrounded by piles of cans of baby food – hundreds of them, some open and disgorging porridge-like substances. She had awoken hungrier than ever.

Matthew reached forward and laid his hand on her forearm. "Of course not, my darling. You don't have to bother about surveyors. I'll go."

She smiled at him fondly. Dear, considerate Matthew. "But you will ask him about the kitchen, won't you? Ask him about changing the position of the sink."

Matthew shook his head. "That's not what surveyors do, my darling. That's what architects are for. That chap I played squash with – Alex Philip – I'll ask him. He's an architect – and a pretty good one." He paused. "Surveyors look at terribly dull things. Rot. Subsidence. That sort of thing."

Elspeth looked concerned. "Subsidence?"

It was a word to strike terror into any Edinburgh heart. The subsidence of parts of the New Town meant that building societies might be reluctant to advance money on certain streets, with the result that prices could be depressed.

"There's no subsidence in Moray Place," said Matthew calmly. "Moray Place is rock solid. It's the east end of the New Town that has the problem."

"One of the lecturers at Moray House lived in Gayfield Square," said Elspeth. "He invited all his students round for a drinks party once. He showed us how if you put an orange on the floor at one end of his living room it would roll to the other end under its own steam."

Matthew nodded. "Yes," he said. "I knew people who ended up living on one side of their flat because everything rolled in that direction. It was very strange – half of each room was very cluttered and half was very empty."

She looked at him; there were times when she was uncertain whether to take him seriously; times when he made absurd suggestions – flights of fancy – and would then wait for her to tumble to the conceit. He had once told her that in Japan precedence at road intersections was based on age, with older drivers giving way to younger ones, and she had for a few moments believed him. But now?

"I don't believe you."

"No?"

"No."

He looked disappointed. "It could happen," he said. "And such people would have heels of different heights on their shoes – so that they could walk about their flats without listing to one side. And then . . ."

She interrupted him. "The surveyor."

"Yes, of course." He rose from the table and leaned forwards to kiss her on the cheek. "I'll be back in an hour or so, maybe less. This is going to be a formality. He'll whizz in and out – shine his torch round a bit, maybe – and that'll be it."

He made his way along Heriot Row towards Moray Place. Arriving outside the flat – now with its SOLD notice very satisfactorily displayed – he tried the front door, to discover that it was still locked; the surveyor was not there. The flat was not yet his, in the sense that he had not yet been granted what his solicitor

had described as entry and actual occupation, and so he did not have the key – that would have been entrusted to the surveyor for the survey, to be returned afterwards to the selling agents.

He looked up at the sky. When you owned property, you owned it from the ground all the way up to the sky – or so he assumed – which meant that he owned, or would soon own, that bit of sky directly above his new garden. This also meant that the clouds that crossed that little patch of land were, for a moment, his; as was the rain that fell on that same bit of ground. And if a bird should land on one of his shrubs, it was, for a few moments, his bird. He smiled. That, surely, was not true. We did not own these wild creatures – not really; nor did we own the land, whatever the law might say about that. Some lines of a poem came back to him, and he struggled to remember who had written them – Norman MacCaig? Yes, it was him, he thought. He had asked who owned a glen – the tycoon who possessed it, or he, who was possessed by it. Matthew knew the answer.

He was lost in these thoughts when the surveyor arrived. He heard a vehicle drawing to a halt and the engine being turned off. He looked round.

Bruce emerged from the car.

"Oh . . ." It took Matthew a moment to remember. Bruce was a surveyor – of course he was. And he specialised in domestic property – he had told him that once in the Cumberland Bar. But . . . Bruce, of all people, was hardly a figure to inspire confidence.

"Hah!" said Bruce. "Surprised you, didn't I? When I got the call from the lawyers I recognised the name. I wondered if there could be two people of the same name in this town, but then I thought: only one with the readies to buy this sort of place! How are you doing?"

"Not badly," said Matthew. "We're moving from India Street and . . ."

"Yeah, yeah," said Bruce, extracting a set of keys from his jacket pocket. "Let's go and take a look. Bit gloomy, isn't it? I can't stand these big New Town places. Give me the creeps. Still, somebody likes living in them."

"It's rather nice, actually," said Matthew. "And the garden . . ."

"Yeah," said Bruce. "Cool."

The back of Matthew's neck felt warm. It was none of Bruce's business; he was here to look at structural issues, at rot and damp and matters of that sort. He was not here to make aesthetic judgements.

"Let's go in," said Bruce. "Let's go in and see what's wrong."

## 70. *Supporting Walls*

They stood in the hall.

"Dark," said Bruce. "I can't stand these dark entrance halls. It's like entering a cave, isn't it?"

Matthew said nothing. The hall was on the dark side, but no darker than many. And the flat was on the ground floor, which was always darker than the drawing-room floor and the floors above. What did Bruce expect? Mediterranean light?

"Gloomeee!" said Bruce, extracting his torch from his pocket. "I suppose it'll be all right, though, if you carry a torch with you most of the time."

Before Matthew could utter any refutation, Bruce had moved across the hall and was poking about in the corridor. "You know, it's not usual to have the client with you as you do your survey," he remarked. "It could influence you. You don't want to see the place through the client's eyes – you want to see it through your own."

"I could wait in the garden," said Matthew.

Bruce reassured him. "No, don't go. I quite like having somebody with me. You never know when the floor's going to collapse. Especially in buildings like this . . ." He stamped lightly on the floorboards. "Only joking, of course. Ha ha, et cetera. Did you hear about that surveyor who looked up the chimney of some house in Perthshire and got stuck? Terrible story. Nobody knew he was doing the survey and he could have died. But somebody came in and heard him and they got him out. Poor chap. Too fat, I suppose. I go to the gym. You go the gym, Matthew?"

Matthew thought of his New Year resolution. "I try to. But you know how . . ."

"Didn't think that you were the gym-going type," continued Bruce. "No disrespect. It's just that some people look like Mr. Universe – others don't. You know how it is?"

Not having seen Bruce for some time, Matthew had forgotten what it was in the other man's manner that was so objectionable; now he remembered. It was his utter self-confidence, his breezy insouciance, his tactlessness, his lack of attention to anything that anybody said to him. And there were probably other failings, too, that would reveal themselves as one got to know Bruce better.

"Anyway," said Bruce. "Let's take a look at this place. What did you pay for it, Matthew?"

Matthew was about to tell him, but Bruce was not listening.

"I notice that you didn't ask for a valuation," Bruce went on. "So I won't give you anything in writing. But I can give you a verbal valuation if you like. It won't cost you anything extra. You want it?"

Matthew was uncertain. Bruce, however, continued. "In its current condition – which is not brilliant, I'd say – about seven hundred thousand tops. Maybe a tiny bit more in a good market. What did you pay, Matthew? Six fifty?"

Matthew said nothing. Bruce looked at him, waiting for an answer that did not come.

"You didn't pay eight, did you?"

Matthew turned away. "It's private," he said.

Bruce shrugged. "Oh, well. Let's go through here . . . Hold on, hold on."

Matthew watched as Bruce looked up at the ceiling.

"Odd space," said Bruce. "Usually you find . . ."

"I think they did some alterations," said Matthew. "The lawyer said something about not having had permission. I thought that it wouldn't matter too much as we weren't planning to sell it again in the short term."

Bruce frowned. "Hold on . . . Look, you see up there? There? Yes. That's where a wall used to join the roof. That's what they took away. And it went all the way to where that Chinese thingy is – that cabinet."

Bruce pointed to the far side of the room where a large Chinese display cabinet reached all the way up from floor to ceiling.

"Yes," said Matthew.

Bruce turned to look at him. He lowered his voice. "That wall, Matthew, was a supporting wall. You see – look up there. You see that bulge in the ceiling? That's your proof."

"A supporting wall?"

"Yes," said Bruce. "And you know what a supporting wall does?

It supports. And you know what happens when you take away a supporting wall? You have no support."

"But if that were the case," said Matthew, "then wouldn't the ceiling have come down?"

Bruce nodded. "It should have. But you see that cabinet over there? That, I think, is holding up the ceiling. Move that and the whole thing comes down."

Matthew stared at Bruce in horror.

"And here's something else," said Bruce. "If the ceiling comes down, then that could bring down the ceiling above it, and so on – all the way to the top flat and the roof. And if that happened, then the flats next door could lose vital support and come down as well. So the whole of Moray Place could fall over like a house of cards."

"Oh," said Matthew.

"So the fact of the matter," Bruce said, relishing his newly found Jeremiah role, "the fact of the matter is that all of Moray Place is probably being supported by one Chinese cabinet. Quite a thought, that!"

"So what do we do?" asked Matthew.

Bruce smiled. "Don't move the Chinese cabinet."

Matthew moved past Bruce and out into the garden. He felt empty. Was it too late to change his mind? He thought it was. Of course they could get a structural engineer and have some remedial work done – that was the obvious thing to do – but what would Elspeth think of him if she discovered that the flat on which he had just spent an inordinate amount of money was not only worth much less than the sum he had paid, but was also on the verge of collapsing?

He walked to the end of the garden. There was a small stone bench against the wall there and he sat down on it. Somewhere in one of the nearby trees, a bird burst into song; and then there was a child's voice and a woman saying something to the child.

Did the neighbours know, he wondered, of the deadly peril they were in? Should he warn them and should they evacuate the whole of Moray Place while his missing supporting wall was replaced? He had no doubt but that it was his duty to do that, but it would not be easy.

He closed his eyes. His life, which only a few months ago had seemed uncomplicated, now seemed to be beset with problems and dangers.

## 71. *Arrival at the Villa*

They had received very clear instructions as to how to reach the villa. These were now read out by Angus as Domenica drove and Antonia stared dreamily out of the car window.

"According to this, we come to a milestone that says twenty miles to Montalcino," said Angus, consulting the piece of paper given to him earlier by Antonia. "Then, after a further ten miles, we start looking for an unmarked road to the left."

"Kilometres," said Antonia.

Angus studied the handwritten instructions. "No, miles. Look, they've written miles."

He handed the piece of paper to Antonia, who looked at it cursorily and then shook her head. "Yes, it appears to be miles, but that must be a mistake. The Italians don't do miles."

Domenica joined in. "But the person who wrote these instructions – your friend – is not Italian. She obviously thinks in miles and realised that we would be doing the same."

Antonia shook her head again. "But what about the milestone? That's not going to be in miles, is it? Why would the Italians put miles on a marker? It must be kilometres."

Angus sought a compromise. "Let's just look for something

that says twenty. It doesn't matter if it's twenty miles or kilometres or even leagues. Then, when we've gone ten kilometres we look for a road. If there is no road, we do an additional . . . however many kilometres would make it up to ten miles."

"The wisdom of Solomon," announced Domenica. "And there, if I'm not mistaken, is the stone."

They passed the white marker and ten kilometres later they came to the road. This led sharply down, and then levelled off to follow the ridge of a line of gentle, rolling hills. The sides of the hills were covered here and there with rows of vines, lines of dark green that made it seem that the land had been touched by a giant comb. At the edge of the vineyards was scrub bush – a tangle of trees and shrubs, punctuated at points by signs of human attention: a small grove of olive trees, a parade of towering cypresses planted along a track that might once have been an avenue on some grand, now vanished, latifundium.

Domenica drove slowly; the road was unpaved and the tyres were throwing up barrages of tiny stones that sounded sharp against the side of the car. After a short while, the land suddenly opened up on one side and they realised that they were travelling on a small escarpment.

"Look over there," said Angus. "Oh . . ."

Domenica slowed the car.

"That will be Sant' Angelo in Colle," said Antonia. "I've seen pictures of it."

"Such beauty," said Angus. "Can it be real?"

It was, although it gave every appearance of being a dream. Domenica applied the brakes and the three of them stared for a moment at the sight of the small town, seemingly suspended in blue air like a delicate, shimmering mirage. Cyril, for whom any sight was perfectly possible, attended not to any of that, but to the smells which were now assailing his nostrils – smells that were unfamiliar to him but urgently begged for investigation. Sticking his nose out of the open window, he drew in his breath, and then gave a bark of eager anticipation.

"He wants us to get there," said Angus.

They continued their drive. They were close to the villa, which according to the instructions lay only a short way from the farmyard that they could now see coming up on their left. The farmer's wife, they were told, had the key and would open the villa for them.

She was waiting for them, having spotted the car coming. Domenica addressed her in Italian, which brought a warm gush of welcoming words. Antonia witnessed this sour-faced.

"She didn't say she spoke Italian," she muttered to Angus. "She has such talents."

"It will be very useful," said Angus. "My own Italian is rather weak. I get by, but not very well."

"So everybody seems to speak it," said Antonia resentfully. "I suppose even Cyril."

Angus smiled. "What about you?"

"I speak German," said Antonia. She was not to be upstaged by Domenica; she would not allow it. "And French. And a bit of Spanish."

"But not Italian?" said Angus.

There was no time for further discussion, as the farmer's wife had extracted a key from the pocket of her apron and was gesturing for them to follow her. They left the car where it was – the villa was reached by a small track that would not admit a vehicle. It was not far away, separated from the farmyard by little more than a straggle of olive trees. The farmer's wife explained that she had already stocked the kitchen with some basic supplies – a salami, some bread, pasta. They could get more from Montalcino itself, which was only a twenty-minute walk away on the other side. They could drive, of course, as had some Scozzesi who had stayed in the villa last month were unable to cope with walking in the heat.

They came to the villa, which was a smallish, square building of stone topped with a roof of red tiles. There were wide eaves, and shade, and the doors and windows looked invitingly dark and cool in the harsh light of noon. They went inside and were shown round, the farmer's wife opening shutters as they went from room to room.

"We shall sleep in this room," said Domenica, as they went into the larger bedroom. "Which bed would you like, Antonia?"

Antonia made her choice, sulkily.

"And that, I believe, will be your room, Angus," Domenica continued, pointing down the corridor. "You have the better view, but then, you are an artist, and that is your right."

Angus fetched their luggage while Domenica and Antonia investigated the kitchen and received instructions in the operation of the hot water system. Now installed, they sat on the small veranda and looked out over the hills. The air was loud with the screech of cicadas, the sky so high and empty that it was barely blue, more a washed-out, exhausted white.

"I read a poem once," said Angus, breaking the silence. "It was about angels in Italy. How they are seen flying across a sky exactly like this. Flying on great white wings."

"It's such a pity that angels don't exist," said Domenica. "This would be such a perfect setting for them."

## 72. *Mistah Kurtz, He Dead*

Over the next few days, Domenica, Antonia, and Angus settled into a routine at the villa. The Italian summer heat was less fierce than usual, and it was possible to walk about in comfort throughout the day, with the possible exception of a couple of hours around noon, when the sun was directly overhead and such shade as the trees afforded was sparse and pinched. That did not matter a great deal to the party; outings into Montalcino took place after breakfast, which was a leisurely meal taken under the vine-covered pergola at the side of the house. From the breakfast table, they watched Signora Ochilupo, the farmer's wife, as she hung out laundry in the farmyard below or carried hay from the barn to the stalls of the three white oxen that pulled the farm's antiquated cart. There was little sign of the farmer himself, although occasionally they spotted him pruning vines or scratching at the surface of the soil with a large and unwieldy hoe.

"Timeless agriculture," said Domenica. "Not producing very much, I fear. But doing what their parents and grandparents and great-grandparents did. In the same place too."

"Which we have lost," said Angus. "We have lost that sense of connection with the past, haven't we?" He looked into his coffee cup as he spoke. He had not started to paint yet, but the germ of a painting had planted itself in his mind. He would paint a rural scene in which the sense of continuity and linkage would be explored.

Signora Ochilupo insisted on accompanying them on their first expedition into the village. Not all the shopkeepers were to be trusted, she explained, and prices could be inflated for foreigners. If she went with them, they would be charged the same prices as the locals. She could advise them, too, she said, on the best cheese and salamis.

Domenica assumed responsibility for the cooking. Nothing was said about this, and neither Angus nor Antonia argued with it. Angus was in charge of wine, and bought several bottles of the Ochilupo wine as well as some rather more reliable-looking Rosso di Montalcino and, at considerable expense, a couple of bottles of Brunello. A supply of bones was obtained for Cyril, who had settled more or less immediately into his new existence and had found a good spot under an old olive tree where he could lie and watch the oxen and the few straggly sheep which grazed in the olive grove. He accompanied Angus into the village, too, and had made the acquaintance of several Italian dogs, who had accepted him after only the briefest period of suspicion and distrust.

Angus began to paint; Antonia busied herself with her historical novel set amongst the early Scottish saints of Galloway, and Domenica read. Each had his or her spot in which to pursue these interests, and if there had been tension at the beginning of the trip, there was none now.

"I could stay here forever," said Domenica. "Doing just this – which is largely nothing."

"I know what you mean," said Angus. "I could too."

"We mustn't vegetate," said Antonia. "Florence beckons."

"I suppose so," said Angus. "The Uffizi. And the Brancacci Chapel at Santa Maria del Carmine. Could I put in a special plea for a visit to the Brancacci Chapel? I want to see the frescoes."

"Anything is possible," said Domenica, adding, "now that we are in Italy."

"There is a fresco by Masaccio," Angus went on. "St. Peter baptising the neophytes. And there are the most extraordinary hills in the background – rather like anthills."

"We shall certainly see those then," said Antonia.

"And Cyril," said Angus. "Cyril would love to see pictures of St. Francis for whom, as a dog, he must have a special affection. There is a lovely one of the saint with birds perching on his arms. I think it's in the Chiesa di San Francesco."

"If he's allowed in," said Antonia.

"I cannot imagine that animals would be barred from a church dedicated to their patron saint," said Domenica. "But one never knows."

"Of course dogs have their own patron saint," Angus pointed out. "St. Hubert of Liege is one, as is St. Rocco. I'm a bit hazy on

St. Hubert, but St. Rocco I know a little about. He went into the forest to die of the plague but was befriended by a dog who brought him food it had stolen from its master's table. He is often depicted with a dog at his feet – the dog bearing some food in its mouth."

Domenica laughed. "I find the whole idea of patronage so colourful," she said. "I'm afraid that I don't know if there is a patron saint of anthropologists. One would have thought that an occupation as hazardous as anthropology can sometimes be should have the protection of a saint or two, but there we are. We must struggle on bravely."

"If there is none, then it's a curious omission," agreed Angus. "Bearing in mind that there are patron saints for some very obscure occupations. Did you know that there is one for greeting-card manufacturers? St. Valentine of Rome, quite appropriately."

Antonia got up and went off to her room. "I must write," she said. "All this talk of saints has reminded me of my own Scottish saints. I must return to them."

Once she had gone, Angus turned to Domenica. Lowering his voice, he said, "Have you noticed anything odd about Antonia?"

"Where does one begin?" she whispered.

"No, seriously. When I came out here this morning she was standing over there looking out towards Sant' Angelo. I said good morning to her but she appeared not to hear me. So I went up to her and stood beside her and do you know what? Her eyes were closed, and she was shivering. Like this. Shivering all over."

"Perhaps she was cold," said Domenica.

Angus shook his head. "No, it wasn't that. When she realised I was there she opened her eyes and said to me that she had been transported. Then she started to mutter. She said, 'The beauty! The beauty! The beauty!'"

Domenica frowned. "Like Mr. Kurtz in *Heart of Darkness*? Doesn't he say, 'The horror! The horror!'?"

Angus nodded. "Mistah Kurtz, he dead – to quote T. S. Eliot, and Conrad, of course."

Domenica was silent. Then she said, "We must be watchful."

"Yes, we must," said Angus.

## 73. *The Possibilities of Florence*

The trip to Florence took place the following day. Leaving early, to allow for errors of navigation, they drove slowly along the dirt road that followed the ridge of hills before reaching the outskirts of Montalcino. From there, the way led down, following a winding route that took them through vineyards and oak forests to a wide plain below. There was little traffic on the road at that hour – an occasional lorry, struggling up from Siena with a load of supplies for the hill villages; a few private cars carrying sleepy villagers to work in some bigger town; a tractor with its spraying arm swinging drunkenly across both lanes of the road.

The morning sun was gentle, the sky quite empty of cloud. Angus, sitting in the front passenger seat, looked out over the fields on either side. There was a railway line and what looked like a scarecrow, but which revealed itself to be a man, as the figure suddenly straightened up and walked away purposively. I could paint that, he thought: a field with a man who looks like a scarecrow but is not. He smiled at the thought. Perhaps what seems to be a statue might move too; perhaps David might suddenly get down from his pedestal in the Piazza della Signoria and go for a cup of coffee with Neptune descended from his fountain. Anything could happen in Italy, he thought; the impossible was possible, and thank heavens for that – that there should be this beautiful country where art made everything feasible.

Domenica, although concentrating on the road, allowed herself a quick glance in the driver's mirror at Antonia, seated directly behind her. Her neighbour, she noted, was dressed in a rather peculiar white frock, suitable for a hot day, perhaps, but somewhat theatrical in its effect. But that was not what interested her; it was the expression that caught her eye. Antonia was staring out of the window with what could only be described as a glazed look.

Domenica spoke breezily. "Everybody all right?"

Angus smiled. "Of course. I was just thinking about what lay ahead of us. The art. I feel like . . . a boy about to enter the sweetie shop."

Domenica nodded. "And you, Antonia? Everything all right?"

There was no answer. Domenica looked anxiously in the mirror and Angus half turned in his seat.

"All right?" asked Angus.

Antonia came to. "What?"

"Are you all right?" asked Angus. "You looked a bit . . . distracted."

"The beauty!" muttered Antonia.

Angus exchanged a quick glance with Domenica.

It seemed that Antonia thought that further explanation was required. "It's so intensely beautiful," she said quietly. "The landscape – look at it. Those cypresses over there – such melancholy trees – they make me want to weep; they really do. And did you see that tiny shrine as we came down the hill? A little shrine to the Virgin, with a minute bunch of flowers laid on the ledge before it. Where would one see that in Scotland?"

"Not in a great number of places," admitted Angus. "But then we are a Protestant country. Or were."

"Oh, it's nothing to do with religion," said Antonia. "It's to do with beauty. It's to do with the fact that there are people here who beautify their public space – even their roadsides. And what do we do? We destroy our landscapes, render them ugly with great pylons, with giant metal windmills."

Angus agreed. "Yes, you're right. We're insensitive to beauty – for the most part. But that's why we've been coming to Italy for years. We come to get in touch with beauty. To have our souls restored."

Domenica listened to this exchange. There was nothing wrong with Antonia, she decided. She was affected by the change in surroundings, but so was she, and so was Angus. It would be odd if they had come to Italy and felt exactly the same as they felt in Scotland. What would be the point of travel if one felt exactly the same once one reached one's destination?

They continued the journey. As they approached Florence the traffic became more intense, even though they had avoided the main highways and followed, as far as possible, quieter back roads. At last they reached a place where, in a small piazza on the edge of an industrial area, they were able to leave the car. A taxi then took them on the final leg of the journey into the centre of the city.

"The Ponte Vecchio," Antonia suddenly screamed. "Look!"

The taxi driver swerved, alarmed by the sudden shouting.

"You must excuse my friend here," said Domenica in Italian. "She is Scottish, you see. Scottish people are prone to sudden outbursts."

The taxi driver nodded. "That is well known," he said. "Normally it is connected with football, I believe."

"Not in this case," said Domenica. "Architecture."

"What did you say?" asked Antonia.

"Nothing important," answered Domenica. "But look over there – we can ask him to drop us there. The Uffizi is just round the corner, I think."

They alighted from the taxi and made their way to the point where a queue was forming outside the ticket office of the Uffizi.

"We must prepare for a long wait," said Domenica. "Angus, I suggest that you take Antonia to a café and get a coffee. I shall keep our place in the queue and then I can nip off for coffee when you return."

Angus and Antonia walked off. Domenica, standing in the line of people that already snaked out of the sheltering loggia, looked at her fellow art lovers. She amused herself for a while speculating on the nationality of those about her. There was an American couple, neatly turned out but laden with equipment: water bottles, umbrellas, waterproof ponchos, folding stools, and so on. They would be comfortable, thought Domenica; which was what she had always felt lay at the heart of the American dream – comfort. And there was nothing wrong with that; after all, a civilisation that sought discomfort would be peculiar indeed.

And in front of that American couple was a small group of Germans, each immersed in a guidebook. Seriousness of purpose, thought Domenica, and again she thought that there was nothing wrong with that; Europe needed German gravitas.

Behind them, a gaggle of Italian teenagers, preening themselves, fiddling with mobile phones, texting each other although they were only a few yards apart; the need to be part of a group, she thought; to be reassured. Which was how we all felt at sixteen; and still did, of course, but in a rather different way.

## 74. In Proper Boots

Back in Scotland, Stuart and Bertie swept along the Biggar Road as it skirted the slopes of the Pentlands. "Do you think there are any fish in the loch, Daddy?" Bertie asked.

"Certainly, Bertie," said Stuart. "Trout. Large trout."

"Perhaps we'll catch them then," said Bertie.

"I think that's highly likely," said Stuart. "Especially if you . . ." And here he lowered his voice. "Especially if you use a worm, Bertie."

"But I thought we had to use flies," said Bertie.

"Not if you're under seven, Bertie. You can use worms if you're under seven. And I got hold of some. Big, fat, juicy worms. Trout can't resist them, Bertie."

They were now approaching the turn-off to the Flotterstone Inn, and Stuart slowed the car down. "Flotterstone," he said. "This is where we park the car and start to walk."

They parked under a tree a couple of hundred yards from the inn. Stuart extracted the rods and the fishing bag from the back, and they both set off, Bertie holding on to his father's free hand, his chest out, his head held high. As they made their way up the reservoir road, the crows flew up in strident protest from the bordering fields.

They saw sheep, and a small herd of cows that gazed ruminatively at them as they passed. They saw the wind send a flurry of teased-out cirrostratus across the otherwise empty blue sky, moving high over the summit of Turnhouse Hill and on towards Scald Law farther to the west. Stuart stood still for a moment, watching the movement of the cloud, and thought of how it looked just like those pictures of clouds streaming past the high ridges of Everest; and thought, too, of how those high things drew people to them, lowly, earth-bound creatures that we were.

"Would you like to climb up there one day, Bertie?" he asked, pointing up at the line of hills. "It's not difficult, you know. We could hike up there quite easily and then go all the way on to Nine Mile Burn."

"In proper boots?" asked Bertie.

Stuart smiled. "Yes, I could get you some proper boots. They make them in your size, Bertie." He realised, though, as he made the promise, that he did not know what size of shoe his son took. Bertie was his son and he did not know that, and he felt a sudden, sharp tug of shame.

"Thank you, Daddy," said Bertie. "That would be very nice."

They walked on in silence. They had reached the point now where the ground rose up to meet the wall of Glencorse Reservoir. Bertie was tiring, Stuart thought, and he offered to give him a ride on his shoulders. But Bertie declined, thanking his father politely. He could walk faster, he explained, and they were almost there, were they not?

"You're a sport, Bertie," said Stuart.

Bertie savoured the compliment. He was not sure what a sport was. If it was somebody who was good at sport, then it was kind of his father to say it, but he did not think that it was really true. He had not had the chance to play sports – not real sports, like rugby – and he was not sure whether he would be any good. The school, though, had recently broken with its tradition and formed a rugby team. Bertie now told his father about this.

"We have a Steiner's rugby team now, Daddy," he said.

"Ah," said Stuart. "That's interesting, Bertie."

"Yes," said Bertie. "I'm not in it. You have to be twelve. They played Watson's the other day."

"Indeed?" said Stuart. "And who won, Bertie?"

"Watson's," said Bertie. "It was 84–0 at the end. Actually, they stopped it early for some reason."

Stuart suppressed a smile. "Bad luck, Bertie. But I'm sure that they'll do better next time." He paused. "What do you think went wrong, Bertie?"

Bertie thought for a moment. "I think it's because our team was told that they should share the ball, Daddy. So they did. They shared."

Stuart looked at Bertie in astonishment. "That's not the way that rugby's normally played, Bertie. If you share the ball in rugby then . . . well, it doesn't work, Bertie."

"But we have to share, don't we, Daddy?"

"Not in rugby, Bertie. You're meant to try and get the ball away from other people."

"But isn't that selfish, Daddy?"

"I'm afraid it is, Bertie. But some of these games are a bit selfish. It's in the rules, so to speak."

"So we lost because we shared the ball," said Bertie, reflectively. "And maybe also because they were mostly girls in our team."

Stuart bit his lip. "I see," he said. "Oh well, Bertie. There we are. At least everybody had fun. That's the important thing."

Now they had reached the reservoir – a long, L-shaped loch that stretched back into the fold of a glen. There was a small island not far from the shore – an island covered with pines on the edge of which various water birds were poised. On a small stony beach beside the road, three green-painted rowing boats had been drawn up; it was one of these that Stuart had hired for the afternoon.

Soon they were out in the middle of the loch. Stuart shipped the oars and picked up the rods. He had a fly on the end of his line, but at the end of Bertie's he now fixed a float and a hook. Then, reaching into the pocket of his Barbour jacket, he took out a small plastic bag. Several large, succulent worms twisted about in a handful of damp soil. One of these was threaded onto the hook and the rod was passed to Bertie.

"There you are, Bertie," said Stuart. "Tight lines!"

Bertie tossed the float and line into the water. The hook,

weighted by its worm, sank down into the peaty water below, down into brown depths. Then, almost immediately, the float bobbed up and down before sinking sharply beneath the surface of the water. Bertie saw what was happening, and shouted out in excitement. Then he began to reel in, just as his father had taught him before they left Scotland Street.

Up through the water came a large trout; a flash of silver; a dart of light; the fulfilment of a small boy's dream. Soon it was on the surface, or just beneath it, and its tail twisted and hit the water with a splash. Bertie jerked the rod up, bringing the fish up into the air.

"Careful," shouted Stuart as Bertie lowered the rod again. But it was too late; the sudden movement relieved the line of its strain and the fish was off the hook.

"I really caught it, Daddy," he said, his voice faltering. "I really caught a fish, didn't I?"

Stuart put an arm round his son. "Yes, you caught it, Bertie."

"It was big, wasn't it, Daddy?"

Stuart nodded. He saw the tears in Bertie's eyes and his heart went out to him. You poor little boy, he thought. You poor little boy.

They continued to fish. Bertie was bitterly disappointed by the loss of the trout, even though Stuart did his best to comfort him. Fishermen lost fish, he explained – one was not a proper fisherman unless one lost a fish. And they would have released the fish back into the water anyway, and so it did not make much difference, did it? Bertie thought about this. He would have liked to have at least touched it, but yes, he supposed that he would only have had it for a minute or so more had he landed it properly.

They rowed out into the middle of the loch. Stuart showed Bertie how to cast a fly and gave him his rod to try it out. Bertie was not very good at first, but after a while he became a little bit better. Then he returned to using a worm, but although there were what seemed to be nibbles, these could equally well have been the action of the wind on the water, causing the float to bob suspiciously.

They had started fishing late, and they did not break for lunch until well after three. Stuart beached the boat on the far side of the loch and he and Bertie pulled it up onto the shore. Then they sat down on the heather and while Stuart ate a sandwich, Bertie tackled his packets of crisps and several chocolate bars. It was heaven for him – pure heaven – to be sitting with his father, eating this wonderful, forbidden food, having almost caught a fish, and not having to think about psychotherapy, yoga, or Italian lessons.

"Couldn't we live out here?" asked Bertie, as he opened his second chocolate bar. "We could buy a tent and pitch it over there by those gorse bushes. We could catch fish for our tea. It would be jolly nice, Daddy."

Stuart smiled indulgently. "A good idea, Bertie, but not all that practical, I'm afraid. I don't think Mummy would like living in a tent."

Bertie had not envisaged her being invited, but was too polite to say so. "Perhaps Mummy might be more comfortable in Scotland Street," he said. "We could go and visit her from time to time. And Ulysses. We could visit him too."

Stuart said nothing. He lay back on the heather, his hands under the back of his head, staring up at the sky.

"It would be such fun, Daddy," said Bertie. "Just you and me."

"Mmm," said Stuart. "Maybe. But I don't think we could leave Mummy all on her own – or all on her own except for Ulysses. It wouldn't be very kind, would it?"

"No," said Bertie. "Maybe not. But it's nice to think about it. As a sort of wish."

Stuart steered the conversation into safer waters. "If I could give you three wishes, Bertie," he said, "what would they be?"

Bertie thought. "For lots of chocolate," he said. "Lots of chocolate – enough for me and all my friends for at least ten years."

"Very nice," said Stuart. "And the second wish?"

"For Olive to go and live in Glasgow," said Bertie. "And, if I can have this as part of the second wish, for Tofu to stop spitting at people and telling fibs."

"I see," said Stuart. "And the third?"

"To be seven," said Bertie quietly.

Stuart said nothing for a few moments. Then he broke the silence. "Seven, Bertie? But you will be seven in due course. You don't have to waste a wish on things that are going to happen anyway."

"But I want it to happen now," said Bertie. "If I wait, it seems that I'll never be seven. It always seems a very long way away."

Stuart reflected on this. "It can't be long now," he said. "You'll be seven in November."

"But that's ages away," said Bertie. "I want to be seven now, Daddy. That's why I wished for it."

Stuart tried another tack. "Do you think things will be different when you're seven?" he asked.

"Yes," said Bertie. "People will treat me with . . ."

"Yes, Bertie?"

"With more respect," said Bertie in a rush. "They won't push me around quite so much."

"Are you pushed around at the moment, Bertie?"

Bertie did not hesitate. "Yes," he said.

"By . . ." Stuart was about to say "By whom?" but he stopped himself in time. "Oh well, Bertie. Seven will come along, sure enough. Let's carry on fishing. You never know your luck. And the fish don't know that you're only six."

They pushed the boat back out and started fishing again. Stuart caught a trout this time and immediately handed the rod to Bertie. "You land it, Bertie. This can be your fish."

Bertie began to reel in, but the line soon slackened off and he gave the rod back to his father. "Got away," he said. "Again."

At five o'clock, Stuart decided that it was time to stop. He rowed the boat back to the point from which they had set off. Then, once the boat was safely secured, they set off back towards the car park at Flotterstone.

"I think I know a short cut," said Stuart, pointing to a path that led off to their right. "Let's go this way, Bertie."

They branched off, Stuart taking the lead as they followed the rough path that made its way sharply down a bank. At the bottom the path traversed a burn by means of a small wooden footbridge. They used this to cross, and then followed the path as it turned this way and that through a thicket of gnarled Scots pines.

"Are you sure about this path?" asked Bertie.

"Of course," said Stuart. "It's a really good short cut. You'll see, Bertie."

The continued on their way. The weather had changed, now, and an unseasonal haar rolled in from the sea. This cast a mantle of white over everything, reducing visibility so that they could see very little beyond the next tree.

"I think we might be lost," said Bertie. "Do you know where we are, Daddy?"

"Have faith in your father, Bertie," said Stuart. "Any moment now we'll find ourselves at Flotterstone."

But they did not. They now found themselves gaining ground, and the path seemed to be changing direction.

"Shouldn't we turn back?" asked Bertie. "Wouldn't that be safer?"

"You should never turn back, Bertie," said Stuart. "What did Harry Lauder say? Keep right on to the end of the road. That's what he said, Bertie."

"But Mr. Lauder was probably on the right road in the first place," said Bertie. "It's all right to keep right on to the end of the road if you're on the right road. Otherwise, it isn't."

## 76. A Real Boy's Room

Notwithstanding his son's qualification of the otherwise sound advice of the late Harry Lauder, Stuart insisted that he and Bertie continue along the path they were on. They were now gaining height – another reason, thought Bertie, why they should turn back; this path, he felt, was leading them farther into an unknown part of the Pentlands from which they might well not extricate themselves before darkness. And the light, as it was, was already fading, what with the haar, which had blotted out all sight of the sun, and the hour of day.

"Is there a mountain rescue team in the Pentlands?" asked Bertie.

"Mountain rescue, Bertie? No, I doubt very much if there are any of those people around here. This isn't the Cairngorms, you know. You find them up in the Cairngorms or places like Glencoe, not the Pentlands."

Bertie absorbed this information in silence. It did not help his state of mind to think that there was no chance of rescue from what was becoming an increasingly worrying situation. Presumably people lost their way in the Pentlands, and presumably there were people who slipped and sprained their ankle and could not make their way home on their own. Who looked after them? He wondered whether it was the First Morningside Cub Scout Pack. It would certainly give them something to do if they were to be put in charge of the Pentlands, although it would be very dispiriting to be rescued by Olive, he thought. Or Ranald Braveheart Macpherson, for that matter; that would be far worse, as Ranald's legs looked so thin and spindly and would hardly inspire the victim of a mountaineering accident with any confidence.

The haar was now becoming very thick indeed.

"What if the path goes over the edge of a cliff, Daddy?" asked Bertie, his voice seeming to echo in the swirling mist.

"Highly unlikely, Bertie," said Stuart. "Paths don't go over cliffs; they follow the contours of the hill. That's what we're doing right now, and any moment now we shall find ourselves on the A702. Then we shall simply walk back to Flotterstone, retrieve our car, and travel home to Edinburgh. Have courage, Bertie."

Bertie swallowed. Having gained height, they were now losing it again, but the vegetation around them had changed. Heather had given way to pasture, and there was a drystone dyke looming up through the white porridge of the haar.

"We'll follow this dyke," said Stuart. "Dykes always go somewhere, Bertie – that's a tip for you to remember. I shouldn't be surprised if this dyke doesn't lead to a farm somewhere. And farms always have tracks that take you to public roads. So we'll be fine – you mark my words."

They walked on. The haar was lifting slightly now, and ghostly trees began to make themselves visible. And then, as they surmounted a small knowe, they saw lights in the middle distance. A few yards later and the lights were shown to be coming from a farmhouse, to the rear of which was a small cluster of trees and a steading.

"There you are, Bertie," said Stuart. "Right on cue: a farmhouse. We can ask directions there – not that I think we're really lost."

They approached the farmhouse, a comfortable-looking building with white harling and blue-painted doors and window frames. Stuart went up to the front door and knocked loudly. Inside the porch a light was switched on and there was the sound of an inner door being opened. A woman appeared, dusting her hands on a white apron tied around her waist.

"Sorry to disturb you," said Stuart. "But I think that we're a bit lost. We're trying to get to Flotterstone."

The woman smiled. "Well, you're very lost, if you ask me. Flotterstone is way over that way – behind the hill."

"Ah," said Stuart. "I see."

The woman looked past Stuart. "And there's your wee boy. My, he looks a bit bedraggled. I think you should come away in and I'll make you a cup of tea."

Stuart thanked her, and he and Bertie went inside, removing their boots and leaving them in the front porch alongside a collection of well-used farming footwear.

"I have a son about your age," said the woman to Bertie. "He's called Andy. We call him Wee Andy because his father's called Andy too. What's your name?"

"Bertie. I'm Bertie Pollock."

"Now that's a fine name," said the woman. "I know some Pollocks. They farm over at Muckle Buggie. You're not related to them, are you?"

Stuart shook his head. "We're Scotland Street," he said.

"I'm sure that's very nice," said the woman. "Muckle Buggie is a sheep farm over near Symington. They've been there for a long time. Always Pollocks."

"Ah," said Stuart.

They went through to the kitchen. There, seated at the table, drawing on a piece of paper, was a boy of about Bertie's size. The boy stood up when the visitors came in and smiled broadly.

"Andy, this is . . ."

"Stuart, and my son, Bertie."

The boy nodded to Bertie, and gave him an encouraging smile. Bertie smiled back.

"Andy," said the woman, "while I put the kettle on, you take Bertie up to your room and show him your things."

Andy walked round the table and indicated to Bertie that he should follow him out of the kitchen. Bertie did so, and the boy led him along a narrow corridor to a staircase at the end.

"My room's in the attic," he said. "Nobody goes up there, just me and my brither, who's in the room beside me. He's twelve. He goes to Merchiston. That's a school in Edinburgh – just for boys."

Bertie nodded. "I've heard of it." Olive couldn't go there, he thought.

"I'm going there next year," said the boy. "I'm going to get my brither's old uniform. And his rugby boots. You play rugby, Bertie?"

Bertie swallowed hard. "Not yet."

"I think you'll be good at it," said Andy.

Bertie beamed with pleasure. It was such a kind thing for anybody to say. He liked this boy.

They went into Andy's room and Bertie drew in his breath. There, on the wall above Andy's bed, was a stag's head, the antlers reaching out almost into the centre of the room – or so it seemed.

"That fella comes from Morvern," said Andy. "My Uncle Jimmy got him. He says he'll take me stalking when I'm bigger. When I'm eight, he says."

Bertie looked around the room. There was a display case with a stuffed grouse, a small woodwork bench, and a large box of Meccano.

"Would you like to see my penknives?" asked Andy.

Bertie's eye widened. Penknives, in the plural. He nodded wordlessly.

## 77. *Bertie's Dream*

"This penknife," said Andy proudly, "is specially set up for catching mushrooms."

"I don't think you catch mushrooms," said Bertie. "You find them."

"That's true," said Andy. "Same difference, though. You see this bit here? That's the brush for brushing the dirt off the mushroom once you've caught . . . found it. And this blade here is for cutting the mushroom in half. See?"

Bertie took the proffered penknife and examined it. "It's made in Italy," he said, pointing to the inscription. "See? It says Italia."

Andy nodded. "You speak Italian?" he asked.

"A bit," said Bertie.

"You must be jolly clever, Bertie," said Andy. "I only speak English."

Bertie acknowledged the compliment. "Thank you," he said. "Italian is very easy. I could teach you, if you like."

"That's a good idea," said Andy. "I could learn Italian and we could make a fort."

He extracted another penknife from the drawer beside his bed. "And this one here is a really good Swiss Army penknife," he said. "The Swiss Army is famous for only fighting with penknives. They don't use guns, you know."

"I've heard that," said Bertie.

"And here's another Swiss Army penknife," Andy continued. "It's a bit smaller, but it's still really useful. This blade here is for cutting bits of wood. And you see here? That's a set of scissors." He paused. "Would you like it, Bertie? You can have it, if you like. I've got that bigger one – you can have this one."

Bertie's heart gave a leap. "Are you sure?"

"Yes. I want you to have it. You're my friend, you see. So I want you to have it."

Bertie took the knife from Andy. "Thank you," he said. "You're my best friend now, you know. My very best friend."

Andy nodded. "Same here."

They shook hands. It was a solemn gesture, cementing the new friendship, and it seemed to Bertie then that his entire life had changed. He slipped the penknife into his pocket, relishing the smooth feel of its casing and its solid, reassuring weight. He was about to say something more, to thank Andy again for the gift, when they heard Andy's mother calling from down below.

"That's my mum," said Andy. "She's calling us."

They went downstairs. The farmer's wife had laid two cups on the kitchen table, alongside a plate of scones. Two glasses stood beside the cups and at their side was a large bottle of orange-coloured liquid.

"Oh, good," said Andy. "Irn-Bru, Bertie."

Bertie was puzzled. "Iron what?"

Andy looked at him in astonishment. "Don't you know what Irn-Bru is?"

Bertie shook his head. "We don't have things like that," he said.

"Irn-Bru is really good for you," said Andy, reaching for the bottle. "I'll pour you a glass. You'll see."

Bertie looked at his father. Stuart smiled. "Try it, Bertie. I think you'll like it."

Andy poured a glass of the fizzy orange liquid and passed it to Bertie. "It's made of girders, Bertie. It makes you really strong."

Bertie took a sip, swallowing tentatively and then gulping the drink down. He had never tasted anything like this before, and he loved it. Andy filled his glass again. "You can burp if you like, Bertie. You're allowed to burp when you drink Irn-Bru."

Bertie burped.

"That's good," said Andy, finishing his glass, and then burping too.

A few minutes later, Andy's father came in. He shook hands with Stuart and listened to the account of their walk through the haar. "I'll run you back in the Land Rover," he said. "After our tea."

Andy looked at his father. "Couldn't Bertie stay the night?" he asked. "He could go home tomorrow."

"It's up to Bertie's dad," said the farmer. "It's all right with us."

Bertie looked anxiously at Stuart, willing him to agree.

"Well," said Stuart. "I don't see why not."

They all drove in the Land Rover to take Stuart back to the car park at Flotterstone. Then they returned to the farm and the two boys were given a large meal of sandwiches, spaghetti bolognese, custard, ice cream, and Irn-Bru. The meal was eaten in quiet contentment; Bertie sat and looked at his new friend, who smiled back at him. Then they were given half an hour of play before bedtime.

"Do you have psychotherapy?" Bertie asked Andy.

Andy shook his head. "We mostly have cattle," he said.

Bertie nodded. "Yoga? Do you have to do yoga?"

Andy thought for a moment. "I like strawberry-flavoured best."

When the time came for bed, Bertie was lent a spare pair of his friend's pyjamas and given the top bunk of Andy's bunk bed. With the light switched off, the two boys continued to talk in the dark. There was so much to say: Andy told Bertie about a ghost who lived in the steading and had been a pirate before he was shot by a cannonball. Bertie told Andy about the fish that he had almost caught that afternoon, and how it was great and silver and powerful. Andy then told Bertie about how his brother had fallen out of a tree and broken his arm. Bertie told Andy about the time he had seen a car reverse into a lamppost.

Bertie's happiness was complete. He had been vouchsafed a glimpse of what life might be; a life of freedom, of adventure, of penknives, of Irn-Bru. It all seemed too good to be true, and in his heart he knew that it was not true. The next day he would return to Scotland Street and the spell would be broken. There would be more psychotherapy, more yoga, more Italian *conversazione* with his mother.

He closed his eyes, drifting off to sleep. He dreamed that he was walking along a path in the Pentlands, with a friend beside him, a warm presence; and that warm presence was a boy called Andy. And Andy reached out and gave him a penknife, and he thanked him, and they both started to run – it was so easy, so easy, as it is easy to run in a dream – and before them was a glen with waterfalls and caves, and a loch, blue and silver, on which a pirate ship was under sail. And there was sunlight, and glasses of Irn-Bru in which that sunlight was caught, liquid, golden, forgiving.

## 78. An Incident in a Café

While Domenica joined the queue for admission to the Uffizi Gallery, Angus accompanied Antonia in the search for a suitable café in which to have a cup of coffee and, if possible, a light breakfast. They had not eaten before they left the villa, and both now felt growing pangs of hunger.

"I know it's not what one normally has for breakfast," said Angus, "but I could do with a slice of pizza. Thin. Very tomatoey. And perhaps just a hint of anchovy on the top. That, and lashings of coffee."

"Entirely understandable," said Antonia. "What is being on holiday but allowing yourself to do that which you do not do at home? I shall join you in a pizza. Oh my, this place is so beautiful. Look at that. Just look at it. An entirely ordinary street, but so beautiful. So very beautiful."

Angus glanced at her. "Yes," he said. "Italy is like that. The most humble corners are . . . how shall we put it? Rich in aesthetic possibilities."

"And the men and women!" Antonia continued. "Look at them. So handsome. We are surrounded by people who could have walked out of a Renaissance painting, don't you think? Botticelli could have placed them in one of his paintings – he really could."

Angus looked again at Antonia. It was understandable to be struck by the glories of Italy – animate and inanimate – but she was rather labouring the point, he felt. But that was what Italy did, he thought; and that was why people had come to Italy for hundreds of years – since the invention of the notion of the journey of the spirit – they had come here for precisely this. Antonia was merely articulating what people must feel.

They did not have far to walk before they found a small café that looked suitable. It was in a largely residential side street, tucked between a carpenter's studio, in the window of which a couple of freshly made, ornate coffins were stacked, and a laundry. A rather dirty plate-glass window revealed an interior shelved high on either side, the shelves stacked with biscuits, bottles of wine and olive oil, packets of coloured pasta. At the far end was a counter behind which a high pizza oven could be seen.

They went in and joined the small knot of people at the counter. The proprietor, wearing a dirty vest and a white chef's cap, was engaged in loud conversation with some of his customers as he manipulated a large flat tray out of the oven. On this was a massive square of sizzling pizza, a square yard or more in extent, which he then proceeded to cut into manageable squares with a set of gardening shears. These squares were tipped onto pieces of greaseproof paper and handed out to the customers, including Angus and Antonia, together with a small glass of raw, red wine.

"Perfect," said Angus, as he started upon the pizza.

"Oh, I could die and go to heaven," said Antonia. "And look, he's making coffee. We can have coffee after we have had this wine. Oh, this is so perfect, Angus. I could faint with excitement, I really could."

Angus frowned. "Not really, I hope."

Antonia sighed. "I'm overcome, Angus. I'm quite overcome."

He tried to sound matter-of-fact. Really, Antonia was gushing rather a lot. "It is fun, isn't it?" he said. "I think Domenica should come here when we get back to the queue."

They finished the pizza and wine and signalled to the man in the vest for coffee.

"I have never seen the Uffizi," said Antonia as they waited. "You know, I have been dreaming about it. Last night, for instance, I found myself there. It was a great revelation, and I am convinced that when I go in today I shall feel as if I have already visited it."

"Oh yes?"

"Yes. And do you know, I am sure that I shall cry. I have been reading a book called *Pictures and Tears*. It's all about how people can burst into tears when they are confronted with great art. They cry. Have you ever cried on seeing a painting, Angus?"

Angus shook his head. "I don't think so. I've been stirred, of course, but I don't think I've cried."

"That is because we live in a time when artists have eschewed tears. Art today is a matter of intellect. Artists want us to engage intellectually with what they have to say. They do not want us to feel a sudden surge of emotion. How different it was . . ." Antonia looked about her, and gestured in such a way as to embrace not only the café but all Florence. "How different it was in Renaissance times. The artists who walked on these very pavements wanted us to be uplifted, to experience intense emotion in our encounter with beauty. That's what they wanted. Lippi, Ghirlandaio, Botticelli – they wanted us to cry, Angus."

Angus shifted from foot to foot. He wished that Domenica had been there; she would have been able to deal with this sort of thing from her neighbour. Was Antonia turning peculiar? Was this a normal reaction to Italy – to go on and on about beauty and art and crying? Was she drunk? Some people had very little tolerance for alcohol, and it was possible that even this small glass could have had this effect on Antonia. He looked at his watch.

"We mustn't keep Domenica waiting," he said. "They could be opening the doors shortly."

Antonia gasped. "Opening the doors?"

"Yes. The Uffizi should open soon."

She closed her eyes. "And we shall be inside too. Just think."

Angus sighed. "Really, Antonia," he said, a note of irritation creeping into his voice. "You're making a bit of a meal of it. It's just a gallery. A very important one, of course, but just a gallery. You wouldn't go on like this if you were paying a visit to the National Gallery on the Mound, would you? I'm sure you wouldn't."

Her reaction to this mild rebuke took him completely by surprise. "Oh, Angus," she shrieked. "Don't you realise? Don't you understand what is about to happen? We are about to come face to face with the *fons et origo* of Beauty itself, laid out before us, and you talk as if it were an entirely quotidian outing to . . . to Bathgate!"

Angus looked about him. "Please, Antonia, please don't shout. People are looking at us."

"As well they might," Antonia retorted loudly. "They are looking and thinking: what a complete philistine that man is! What an insensitive brute! That's what they're thinking, Angus Lordie!"

## 79. *Unbearable Beauty*

"Listen," whispered Angus as he drew Domenica aside. "Antonia is behaving very, very strangely."

It was as much information as he could give without alerting their companion to the fact that she was being discussed. Domenica, though, was quick to sense that something was wrong, and nodded to Angus to confirm that she understood.

"I don't think I'll go off for coffee," she announced. "I believe that the doors will be thrown open very shortly and this queue will begin to move."

"The doors will be opened," muttered Antonia. "Opened to beauty."

Domenica and Angus exchanged glances.

"Now we must agree what we are to do once we get in," said

Domenica in a matter-of-fact tone. "I suggest that we split up and agree to meet somewhere in, say, three hours' time. That will give us each an opportunity to linger in front of our favourite works of art without holding others up."

Angus looked nervously at Antonia. "A good idea. Is that all right with you, Antonia?"

Antonia smiled. "It is indeed. I shall . . ." She paused. "I shall make my way to the *Birth of Venus* and absorb that. Then I shall . . . Oh, there is so much that I plan to do."

The queue started to move. Under cover of the excited chatter that accompanied that, Angus was able to whisper again to Domenica. "She's clearly heading for some sort of crisis. She really is. Her eyes – take a look at her eyes. Her pupils are dilated. Do you think she's taking something?"

Domenica cast a glance at Antonia, who was standing a short distance behind them, studying a guidebook that she had extracted from the pocket of her coat.

"She could be. It would explain this rather manic muttering about beauty. We shall just have to watch her. I propose to follow her at a discreet distance once we're in and see what she gets up to."

"I'll do the same," said Angus. "I don't want you to follow her by yourself." He paused. "Do you think she's dangerous?"

Domenica raised an eyebrow. "I've always taken the view that she constitutes a danger to men, but no, I don't think that she's likely to be violent. Still, you never know. Do you have a whistle on you?"

Angus did not.

"A whistle can be useful in an emergency," said Domenica. "But so few people seem to carry one these days."

They reached the admission booth and Domenica purchased tickets. Antonia stood behind Angus; he noticed that her knuckles were white from the clenching and unclenching of her fists.

They went in. "Now," said Domenica, "we shall all meet here in exactly three hours. Then we shall go for a late lunch over which we shall be able to discuss the treats that we're about to see."

"Good," said Angus. "Quattrocento here I come!"

"*Che bellezza!*" muttered Antonia, wandering off towards the first of the galleries. "Oh, *che bellezza!*"

Domenica and Angus held back under the pretence of consulting a guidebook. Then, after a minute or two, Domenica indicated that they should discreetly make their way towards the gallery to which Antonia had been heading.

It was Angus who heard the commotion first. Grabbing Domenica by the arm, he gestured towards the source of the noise, just inside the gallery.

"Quick," he said. "Follow me."

The two ran in the direction of the shouting that was now plainly emanating from within. When they reached the doorway to the gallery, their worst fears were confirmed. There was Antonia, prone on the floor, shouting and writhing, while about her stood a circle of concerned security guards. Another man in uniform

was running from the opposite end of the gallery, accompanied
by several young women.

Angus strode forwards, followed by Domenica.

"Please stand back," said one of the security men in Italian.
"There is nothing to see."

Angus spoke quickly. "We are the friends of this unfortunate
lady," he said.

The security men let them approach. One of them was crouching down beside Antonia, trying to reassure her.

"Antonia," said Angus. "Antonia, what's wrong?"

"*Che bellezza*," muttered Antonia, looking at Angus without
any real sign of recognition. "*Che bellezza insopportabile!*"

The man who had come from the other end of the gallery now
spoke into a handheld radio before turning to address Angus. "This
lady is not at all well," he said in perfect English. "I regret that she
may be suffering from Stendhal Syndrome. It is quite common, and
so I have ordered a stretcher. We shall take her to the psychiatric
clinic at Santa Maria Nuova. They are very experienced."

Angus turned to Domenica. "Stendhal Syndrome," he said. "We
should have seen it coming. My goodness, we were blind."

Domenica looked puzzled. "Stendhal Syndrome?"

"It's a form of hysterical reaction that afflicts some people when
they come face to face with great art," said Angus. "Stendhal
suffered from it when he came to Italy. It's rather like Jerusalem
Syndrome, which affects people who go there and get carried
away by religious ecstasy."

The stretcher-bearers now arrived and quickly rolled Antonia
onto their stretcher. Then they carried her away at a fast trot.

"There will be an ambulance at the side door," said the official.
"I do regret this somewhat inauspicious start to your visit to the
Uffizi. Please accept our sympathy. I assume that you will wish to
call at the *ospedale psichiatrico* where your poor friend is being
taken."

He gave them the address, which Angus wrote down on the back of his guide to the Uffizi.

"Most unfortunate," said Angus, as they made their way out of the gallery. "I wish I'd put two and two together earlier."

"You mustn't reproach yourself," said Domenica. "How were you to know? One doesn't expect an Edinburgh person to behave in quite so Mediterranean a fashion."

Angus shook his head. "You've got it quite wrong, Domenica. The whole point about Stendhal Syndrome is that it affects people from the north. We are the ones who come here and are overcome by the beauty. No Italian would think twice about it."

"Well, it's still very regrettable," said Domenica. "Poor Antonia. It can hardly be very pleasant to go on holiday and be put away in a psychiatric hospital – even if one deserves it, and even if it's the best place for one to be." She paused. "Should we go and buy her some fruit? Or is it tactless to give fruit in such circumstances?"

"I'm sure that it would be appreciated," said Angus. And then he said, "I wonder how long she'll be in."

"Several weeks, I should imagine," said Domenica. "Which leaves just you and me at the villa, Angus."

## 80. Antonia's Condition Explained

Domenica and Angus arrived at the Santa Maria Nuova Hospital three hours after Antonia had been taken away in her ambulance, its siren echoing through the narrow Florentine streets. The delay was deliberate and was not indicative of a lack of concern on their part; there was no point, Domenica suggested, in arriving contemporaneously with the patient: the doctors would need to make their admission examination and it would not help them to have anxious friends tugging at their clinical sleeves. So they continued with their visit to the Uffizi, taking in if not everything they had hoped to see, then at least some portion of it.

At the hospital they were ushered into a small, sparsely furnished waiting room outside the office of the clinical director. A secretary attended to them, offering them a glass of water and a small plate of biscotti while they waited.

"Such courteous people," said Domenica as the secretary left the room. "Can you imagine the National Health Service offering anybody biscotti?"

"Alas, I cannot," said Angus, helping himself to one of the small, brittle biscuits. He examined the biscuit carefully, as if looking for something. "This reminds me of Proust's madeleine cake. Perhaps that's why they keep them in a psychiatric institution – to promote Proustian reflections that might, in turn, aid diagnosis."

"Highly unlikely," said Domenica.

Their conversation was interrupted by the sound of footsteps outside, followed by the entry into the room of a tall man in a white coat.

"Please excuse my tardiness," said the doctor. "I am Professor Sergio Novelletto. I am sorry to have kept you waiting."

They both stood up to shake the doctor's hand. As Domenica took his hand, he drew hers up to his lips and kissed it in an elaborate display of formal manners. Then he invited them to sit.

"I have been at the bedside of your poor friend," he said, looking by turns at Angus and Domenica. "It is a classic case of a crisis brought on by excessive exposure to art and to . . ." he looked out of the window at the Florentine skyline, "and to these antique and beautiful stones. We call this condition Stendhal Syndrome, as you may be aware. Indeed it is here in this very institution that the pioneering work on this condition was done.

My distinguished colleague, Professor Graziella Magherini, had the honour of naming this condition. She is the author of the standard work on the subject, *La Sindrome di Stendhal: Il malessere del viaggiatore di fronte alla grandezza dell'arte*. So we are well placed to treat the crises that this unfortunate condition brings about."

"We have heard of it," said Angus.

The professor inclined his head gravely. Domenica noted the immaculately groomed head of grey hair. "I am sure that you have," he said. "So many travellers have been overwhelmed by art in this city. Goethe, John Ruskin, Henry James – there are many illustrious names of those for whom this condition has been only too real – and now to this list we add the name of your dear Scottish friend, la Signora Antonia Collie. What a great pity!"

"Will she be all right?" asked Domenica.

"Oh, I have no doubt of that," said the professor. "The duration of the crisis varies, of course, but it is usually the case that the more educated, sophisticated independent traveller recovers rather more slowly, I'm afraid to say. Perhaps such people have more sensitive souls than those who arrive in organised tours – I am not sure. Perhaps we shall never know."

The professor paused for a moment before continuing. "I gather from my secretary that you are all from Edinburgh."

"That is true," said Domenica. She was about to add that Antonia came from Fife originally and that she might therefore have a less sensitive soul – and might therefore recover more quickly – but she decided not to raise this possibility.

"That interests me," said the professor. "I have visited Edinburgh on a number of occasions. My great friend Henry Walton was professor of psychiatry there, of course, and I have been privileged to see his considerable collection of Chinese ceramics. But there is something more: I have been told by my Edinburgh colleagues that they encounter a very similar condition in Edinburgh, the Edinburgh Syndrome, which manifests itself in a very similar crisis to that encountered in Stendhal Syndrome cases: shortness of breath, palpitations of the heart, disorders of colour perception, and so on. In the case of the Edinburgh variant, this principally occurs amongst visitors who see rather too many Fringe shows in rapid succession, followed by a visit to your renowned military tattoo. It is at that point, later in the evening, when the massed pipe bands march onto the Castle Esplanade, that those who are at risk develop Edinburgh Syndrome and have to be removed to the Royal Edinburgh Hospital."

Domenica and Angus listened to the professor with rapt attention.

"Remarkable!" said Domenica. "I was quite unaware of this." She paused. "But tell me, *chiarissimo professore*, how long will our dear friend have to remain in your care?"

The professor thought for a moment. "I believe that the best thing to do will be to keep her here for a couple of days while we stabilise her and observe her. Then we shall move to the care of a very fine community of nuns in the countryside, the Convent of the Tiny Sisters. They are very solicitous of patients such as these, and she will be well cared for. She should spend three weeks with the sisters before she is fit enough to travel." He looked enquiringly at Domenica. "Will that be all right?"

Domenica nodded her approval. "You are very kind."

"It is nothing," said the professor. "I only regret the disturbance that this must cause to your own holiday plans."

"That is but as nothing," said Domenica quickly. "We shall rise above it, shall we not, Angus?"

"Completely," said Angus.

They chatted with the professor for a few minutes more. He asked them where they were staying, and told them that he knew the area well. He had a friend who had a villa nearby and he would be happy to write a letter of introduction to this person and suggest that Domenica and Angus be invited for dinner.

"He keeps a very good kitchen," said the professor. "And a fine cellar too. His grandfather was one of the principal producers of Brunello di Montalcino, and some of the bottles in his cellar go back to the early 1930s."

"He is a fortunate man," said Angus.

"Indeed," said the professor. "But we are all fortunate in one way or another. The task for most of us is to identify in what way that is, would you not agree?"

## 81. A Terrible Mistake

It was a curious coincidence of the sort that, although quite explicable in terms of statistical likelihood, nonetheless leaves us surprised, or at least vaguely unsettled. By such a coincidence, on the very day that Antonia Collie experienced her intense bout of Stendhal Syndrome and collapsed on the floor of the Uffizi Gallery, Matthew felt disinclined to get out of his bed in India Street and found himself burying his head under the pillows when Elspeth brought him an early morning cup of tea.

He had not slept well. His dreams had been vivid and vaguely disturbing; not nightmares in the conventional sense, but nevertheless characterised by a feeling of foreboding, by a sense that something vaguely unpleasant was about to happen. And while the light of dawn, and, a fortiori, a cup of tea will normally put such dreams into perspective, this did not happen today. On the contrary, when Matthew awoke it seemed to him that reality, if anything, was slightly worse than the uneasy world of his dreams.

There were several things worrying Matthew. First, there was the gallery, where he felt that he had got himself into an impos-

sible situation with his new assistant, Kirsty – she of the extraordinarily tight jeans. Even if he had not spoken to her about it, he was not satisfied with her work; he felt that she discouraged, rather than encouraged, customers by what Angus Lordie had described as her "rather overpowering presence." This was, of course, a polite way of saying that she was a flirt, and this meant that when couples came into the gallery to look round, inevitably the wife would cut short the visit in order to get the husband away. Yet although he was convinced that she was not suited to the job, Pat had also warned him that it would be impossible to get rid of her because of her membership of some obscure and frightening organisation dedicated to the intimidation of men.

That was one issue. The other was the question of the flat that he had purchased in Moray Place and into which he and Elspeth would shortly be moving. Bruce's report on this flat had been discouraging in the extreme. Not only did he suggest that Matthew had grossly overpaid for the new property, but he also claimed that the unauthorised removal of an internal wall by the previous owner had left the ceiling being effectively supported by nothing but a large Chinese cabinet. Matthew had not mentioned this to Elspeth, with the result that the knowledge had become even more burdensome to him. What if Elspeth decided to move the Chinese cabinet, as well she might? Would that bring down the ceiling and, on the domino principle, the neighbouring flat and then all of Moray Place? Surely not; and yet he could not bring himself to confess to her that he had made a foolish mistake.

Elspeth noticed the pillow over his head. "Matthew?"

There was a muffled sound from the bed.

"Matthew, what's wrong? Are you not feeling well?"

From underneath the pillow, Matthew let out a groan. "Yes," he said. "I mean, no. Or not quite. Oh, Elspeth . . ."

He flung the pillow aside and stared up at his wife. There were tears in his eyes.

"Oh, Matthew!" She bent down and embraced him where he lay. "My darling Matthew! You're crying. My darling, what is it?"

He told her, sobbing as he spoke, feeling the burden of his secrecy ebb away as the truth was laid bare. "I've made a terrible mistake with Moray Place," he said. "they took a supporting wall away and the whole thing's being held up by a Chinese cabinet. And the gallery; that girl, Kirsty – Pat says that I can't get rid of her because she'll do something terrible to me and I saw her looking at a Vuillard in a catalogue and I think that she's going to buy it behind my back and then we'll have to pay because she'll have bought it on the gallery's behalf and what if the money . . . and she's got these really tight jeans which she wears deliberately and makes women drag their husbands away without looking at the paintings and Big Lou says . . ."

"Hush. Hush. My darling, this is all nonsense. Just nonsense."

"It's not," wailed Matthew. "Bruce said that if we moved that cabinet then all of Moray Place will fall down and Pat said . . ."

Elspeth put her hand against his brow, just as she had done as a teacher when one of the six-year-olds had become hysterical.

"Calm down," she said. "Just calm down. You're under strain because of the move. That's normal. Everybody finds a move stressful. I'll sort out this Chinese cabinet business."

Matthew was suddenly alarmed. "Don't touch it!" he said. "If you move it, then the ceiling . . ."

"I'll sort it out," said Elspeth. "Don't worry. Nothing's going to fall down. And as for Kirsty, I'll sort her out too. She's a student – she'll get another job easily enough, and it's not as if it's her livelihood. I'll get rid of her today."

She brooked no argument. "You stay in bed," she said, rising to her feet. "You get some more sleep – you obviously didn't sleep very well last night. I shall go along to sort things out in Dundas Street. Then I'll get a decent surveyor along to Moray Place and we'll sort out this cabinet nonsense. Leave it to me."

Matthew did not argue, and by the time that Elspeth left the flat after breakfast, he had fallen into a dreamless, untormented sleep. Elspeth looked in on him before she left; he appeared so vulnerable, she thought, so innocent, as men do in sleep. The strongest, the most masculine of men, she thought, can look like a baby when his head is on the pillow and his eyes are closed. It reminded her of human vulnerability; here we are with all our human pretensions, with our mastery of the world about us, with our clever machines and our elaborate conceits, and we are no more than children who must, like the smallest of creatures, surrender to sleep and the powerlessness of oblivion.

## 82. *Shocking Developments*

Quietly closing the door on Matthew, Elspeth went about the task of sorting out the two problems troubling her overstressed husband. Several telephone calls later, an arrangement was made to meet a surveyor in Moray Place at noon that day. That achieved, she then telephoned the gallery and suggested that she meet Pat and Kirsty at Big Lou's at 10:30 a.m. Kirsty, who took the call, was doubtful at first, but agreed to the suggestion when Elspeth made it clear that Matthew had authorised the meeting and would expect her to be there. This was not strictly speaking true; Matthew did not even know of the meeting, but Elspeth interpreted his earlier assent to her sorting things out as clearly covering a meeting at Big Lou's.

Elspeth was there first, and Big Lou was already bringing her coffee to the table when Pat and Kirsty arrived. Elspeth noticed Big Lou's glance at Kirsty's tight jeans and knew immediately that she had an ally. Good, she thought; Big Lou understands.

"Well," Elspeth began, as the two young women sat down in front of her. "Let's waste no more time. As you are aware, the economy of this country is in a parlous state." She paused, watching the effect of her words. There was a frown from Kirsty; Pat, although attentive, gave nothing away. "So unfortunately one of you has to go. And it's you, Kirsty. Sorry about that, but there we are. You'll be paid up to the end of next week, but you can have your remaining time off. Sorry about this."

For a moment Kirsty said nothing. Then, without any warning, she leaned across the table, and pulled Elspeth's hair. Elspeth, taken aback, screamed, and Pat, after a few seconds of shock, turned in her seat and seized Kirsty's long blonde hair, giving it a sufficiently sharp tug to elicit a howl of protest from the other girl.

Big Lou, witnessing this from behind her counter, lost no time in making her way round the side and rushing over to join the affray. She seized Kirsty's hair on the other side – that is, on the opposite side of the head to that engaged by Pat – and tugged hard. There were further howls and a low hissing sound that came from one of them, although it was not immediately apparent from whom.

Big Lou was, of course, the most powerful of the three, and

she soon succeeded in lifting Kirsty from her seat, by her hair. She then changed her grip, seizing her by the right arm and half pushing, half dragging her to the door. In the course of this short journey, the tight jeans split, a jagged San Andreas fault opening across the over-taut denim.

"Oot," said Big Lou, bundling her out. "Nae ripped jeans in here."

Pat now lent Elspeth a comb so that she could tidy her ruffled hair. They were all shocked by what had occurred, but it did not take long for the conversation to return to normal. This was not before Big Lou had confessed that she had always had her reservations about Kirsty and that her departure was by no means premature. Pat agreed with this, and complimented Elspeth on her prompt and decisive action.

They spent the next hour in pleasant conversation about books. Big Lou had been reading William Dalrymple's *Nine Lives*, a book about the various forms of spirituality to be encountered in India. "I'm reading about the Jains at the moment," she told them. "Do you realise that they wear masks when they ride bicycles so that they don't destroy insects by swallowing them? And do you realise that they watch their footfall very closely to avoid crushing any living creature?"

"It must be difficult," said Pat. "I suppose I crushed a lot of things walking down from Marchmont this morning."

"The world is full of suffering and death," said Elspeth.

After this conversation, Elspeth made her way over to Moray Place. The new surveyor was waiting for her, and they went into the flat together.

"Very nice place this," said the surveyor. "One has to pay for these flats, though."

"How much?" asked Elspeth.

"Over a million," said the surveyor. "Or thereabouts – in this market. Very nice. Nice feel to it."

"Matthew was told that a supporting wall had been removed," said Elspeth. "Bruce Anderson said that the ceiling is being held up by that Chinese cabinet over there."

The surveyor burst out laughing. "Him? He said that? What absolute nonsense. Here, I'll show you."

And with that he strode across the room and gave the Chinese cabinet a good push. It moved several inches, and when he pushed it again, it moved some more.

"See? Absolute nonsense. And that's a strengthened beam in there – I'm pretty sure of it. You're quite all right."

"So Moray Place isn't going to fall down after all?" asked Elspeth.

"Fall down? Of course not. Moray Place is very sound structurally. These are beautifully built houses – strong as the Rock of Gibraltar – if the Rock of Gibraltar is still strong, that is."

"One used to use the Bank of England as a metaphor for strength," remarked Elspeth.

The surveyor laughed. "Used to," he said. "But that's another question altogether."

"So everything's fine?"

"Of course it is. This is a lovely flat in a very fine part of town. There's nothing wrong with Moray Place."

They left the flat shortly thereafter. "You can reassure your husband," said the surveyor. "Tell him that he's made a very wise purchase. I'm even a bit envious!"

Elspeth returned to India Street. Matthew had got out of bed but was still in his dressing gown. He looked at her half expectantly, half guiltily.

"I've just come back from Moray Place," she said. "You know what the surveyor said?"

Matthew put his hands to his head. "I don't want to hear it," he muttered. "I don't want to hear."

"Matthew, my darling! He said that it was a very wise purchase!

And he moved the Chinese cabinet. Nothing happened, Matthew, nothing!"

It took a moment or two for her words to sink in. When they did, he moved towards her, throwing his arms around her, showering her with kisses. It was a complete transformation; the self-doubting husband she had left that morning was nowhere to be seen; the gentle optimist she had married had returned.

"And?" he asked tentatively. "The gallery?"

She nodded. "Sorted out."

"Maturely?"

She hesitated. Was there much difference, she wondered, between the world of Olive and Tofu on the one hand and the adult world on the other? Not really.

"More or less," she said.

## 83. A Hinterland of Regret

Over the next few days, Domenica and Angus slipped naturally into a daily routine as peaceful and as soporific as the Tuscan countryside itself. Breakfast was taken on the patio at the front of the villa, gazing out over the gently rolling countryside to the little hill town of Sant' Angelo in Colle in the distance. Sitting over large cups of milky coffee, they discussed the day ahead with all the urgency and anxiety of those who knew that they had nothing to do – that is, with none of either. An outing might be suggested, but not necessarily acted upon – perhaps a run down to the abbey at Sant' Antimo or over to Monte Oliveto Maggiore to view the frescoes of Giovanni Bazzi, *Il Sodoma*. "Such an unfortunate nickname," said Domenica. "Like all nicknames, so unkind."

Angus did not think that true: there were affectionate nicknames, too, but he did not argue; not here in this setting, with the heat beginning to make the hills shimmer and the air fill with the orchestral shriek of insects.

"I'd also like to see his frescoes in Siena," he said. "In the Basilica of San Domenico, Domenica." He paused. "He depicts the life of St. Catherine of Siena. Such a tiresome saint, I'm afraid, with all her fasting and constant letter-writing. But she meant well, I suppose. She eventually gave up water – an ultimate sign of piety."

"And?" asked Domenica.

"That was the end," said Angus. "Giving up food is one thing, but water's another, I'm afraid. Her eating disorders made her seem very light, apparently. Her supporters saw her floating above the ground from time to time."

"Like St. Joseph of Cupertino," said Domenica. "Didn't he float?"

"No, he actually flew through the air. There's a distinction, you know. That's why he's the patron saint of air travellers."

Leisurely discussions about saints and their doings; talk of artists and their frescoes – all conducted against a backdrop of a landscape so entrancing as to be reminiscent of that which the great artists of the Renaissance had chosen for their paintings – filled the morning so effortlessly that the arrival of noon was always a surprise.

Antonia was not forgotten. There was a daily telephone call to check up on her progress. At first this call was made to Santa Maria Nuova in Florence, and then, after her transfer into the countryside, to the convent at which she was being looked after by the Tiny Sisters. For the first few days they spoke to a nun who reported on Antonia's condition, but after that the patient herself was allowed to come to the phone, and assured them that she was very comfortable and being well looked after by the sisters. "They are teaching me needlework," she said. "And I am joining in their devotions. The sisters are very welcoming." There was no mention of Giotto or Botticelli – a good sign, Domenica thought, in the circumstances.

And if Angus and Domenica found contentment in that place, so too did Cyril, perhaps to an even greater degree. For him the Italian countryside was an exquisite patchwork of possibility in which intriguing scents jostled one another for his attention. He had also made several new canine friends, a motley band of three high-spirited Italian dogs that had some connection with the nearby farm, although they did not appear to live there.

Their collars, inspected by Angus, for whom they had a particular affection, revealed their names: Claudio, Ernesto, and Cosimo, and there were traces of an inscribed address, too, but this had been worn away and was now unintelligible. The farmer's wife fed these dogs, but disclaimed ownership; they were, she explained, dogs who had always been there, descendants of a dog that had once belonged to a wiry shepherd who had ridden with great distinction in the Sienese Palio years before. That was all she knew.

Cyril met up with these dogs every day and went off with them on some mission, the details of which Angus was never able to ascertain. They returned at midday, their tongues hanging out for the heat, and enthusiastically drained the bowls of water he put out for them.

"It's strange," said Domenica from her deckchair in the shade. "It's very strange to think of Cyril having an independent existence. And yet he does, doesn't he? Didn't he have an affair once?"

"It was very brief," said Angus. "They only saw one another once. It was in Drummond Place Gardens."

"And yet she had puppies, didn't she? Six or seven, weren't there?"

Angus nodded. "Yes. And their owner landed me with them."

"What happened to them, Angus? You never told me."

Angus sighed. "I felt very bad about it," he said. "At least at first. I feared that I had made a terrible mistake giving them to a stranger whom I met walking through Drummond Place. Then I heard what had happened and I'm relieved to say the outcome was very satisfactory."

Domenica raised an eyebrow. "They found a good home? All of them?"

"Yes, as it happens, they did. They ended up in a small travelling circus in Ireland, would you believe? Finn MacNamara's Jumping Dogs was the name of the outfit. They were trained to jump through hoops and so on. Apparently they're very happy – dogs love performing. They're based in Cork, but go all over Ireland doing their tricks."

Domenica said that she thought this a very satisfactory ending. "As a child," she said, "I always wanted to join the circus. What child hasn't?"

"I wanted to go to sea," said Angus. "We used to go for holidays on Mull when I was a boy, and I loved watching the boats. I thought that there would be nothing more exciting than to be a stowaway. In fact, when I was eight, I tried to stow away on the MacBrayne ferry from Oban. My parents were watching me, of course, and saw me hiding in one of the deck lockers."

Domenica laughed. "Not a good choice of ship," she said. "You would just have gone backwards and forwards between Oban and Mull. Until you were eighteen perhaps."

"And now . . ." said Angus.

She waited for him to continue. What did he want to say? Those two words – *and now* – seemed to point to a whole hinterland of regret. And now it is too late. And now my dreams are but as dust. And now there is so little time left.

He said nothing further. She waited. A breeze, so gentle as to be almost undetectable, had blown up from the south, touching the branches of the olive trees, creating a ripple in the grey-green sea of leaves.

## 84. Icarus, Cyril, a Ducati

Nothing really happened – and then everything happened. Domenica would later find it difficult to reconstruct events: understandably, perhaps, so emotionally significant was that day, and so unexpected its central, crowning moment. Or was it really unexpected? Might she have detected in Angus's look, in the manner in which he seemed to be weighing every word he uttered, in the way that his hand was trembling as he handed her a cup of coffee, that he was on the verge of some moment of annunciation? Perhaps; and yet she did not, with the result that when Angus suddenly cleared his throat and addressed her, she was not ready for what was said.

"You know, Domenica, when you look at your life," he began, "by which I mean when I look at my life, I can hardly reflect upon it with complete satisfaction."

Domenica disagreed. "I don't know, Angus," she said reassuringly. "You've achieved something, surely. Your work is well regarded. You enjoy the privilege of being able to devote your time to painting – which is what you love, I believe. Many would consider you fortunate."

Angus shook his head. "No. That's kind, but no. I paint portraits of company directors and the like. That is all. I leave nothing of worth behind me – no great work, no painting that really adds to our artistic patrimony. I am, I'm afraid, something of a failure."

Domenica frowned at this. Angus was not given to self-pity – something that she had heard him railing against in others. Was Angus coming down with delayed Stendhal Syndrome? Who would be next? Cyril? Was there a veterinary equivalent of the unusual condition, a version that struck dogs who were suddenly confronted with a tantalising choice of exotic scents?

"Oh, I am aware of my relative good fortune," Angus said quickly. "And there is only one respect in which I might be more fortunate than I am already. And that is if you were prepared to . . ."

She looked at him politely. "Prepared to what?"

He was staring at the sky, as if inspiration were to be found in that quarter. Somewhere, over the hills, there was the drone of a tiny engine. Somebody is cutting wood with a buzz saw . . . The line from that poem about angels in Italy; so evocative. And then, over the brow of a hill, still a speck in the clouds, came a minute aircraft – a wing under which a man was suspended by rigging yet invisible.

"Icarus," muttered Angus.

Domenica looked up. "About suffering they were never wrong," she said quietly.

Angus had heard the line before; Domenica had quoted it to him on more than one occasion. "Yes," he said. "Auden is so right, isn't he? Icarus falling – the boy's white legs disappearing into the green sea – all unnoticed because the rest of the world has to get on with its business."

There was a silence. The tiny aircraft approached and was soon overhead. Icarus could be made out quite clearly, and he spotted them and waved. Cyril, looking up, barked, in greeting or warning – it was hard to tell.

Domenica returned her gaze to Angus. "You were saying: would I be prepared. Prepared to do what?"

He took a deep breath. "To marry me," he said quietly.

It was easier than he thought. Icarus did not fall from the sky; the ground did not open; the earth did not wobble on its trajectory.

If Domenica was taken aback, she did not show it. "How kind of you, Angus," she said. "What a sweet question."

He did not know how to interpret this. "I know I'm nothing much," he said. "And I have Cyril. And my clothes, I know, are a bit old-fashioned."

She looked at his trousers, at the frayed collar of his shirt, at the scuffed moccasins. A man's clothes were no impediment; look at what Elspeth had done for Matthew's wardrobe. His crushed-strawberry corduroy trousers, the distressed-oatmeal sweater, were either dealt with already, Domenica believed, or soon would be.

"Oh, Angus," she said. "You're perfect as you are. You. Your clothing. Even your dog. All perfect." She paused, noticing his astonishment. "And as for your question, the answer is: of course. I'd love to marry you."

He gave a cry, and reached out for her hands, gripping them tightly in his.

"I didn't think you'd say yes," he said. "I thought . . ."

"But of course I'd say yes," said Domenica. "We've been friends for years, haven't we? And we look on the world with much the same eyes, don't we?"

Angus nodded enthusiastically. "Yes, we do. Certainly we do." He paused. "Of course, there is the question of . . ." He looked over towards the place where Cyril was stretched out in the shade.

Domenica followed his gaze. "Cyril? I don't see an issue there, frankly. I've rather come to like him recently, as you may have noticed. And he'll be happy living in . . ."

A shadow crossed Angus's face. They had not begun to discuss that arrangement. His flat in Drummond Place was larger than Domenica's flat in Scotland Street, and he thought it would have made sense for them to establish their common home there. But now he remembered that Domenica had been born in Scotland Street, and might be reluctant to move.

"We can discuss all that later," he said. "There'll be plenty of time for details."

They sat for a moment, neither saying anything, both savouring this moment, which would, they knew, define the rest of their lives. And they were only nudged out of this state by the sound of a motorcycle making its way up the track to the villa.

Angus got up and went to greet their visitor.

"James!" he exclaimed, as the motorcyclist removed his helmet and laid it on the petrol tank of the dusty silver Ducati.

James Holloway raised a hand in greeting. "I heard you were here," he said. "And I just had to pop in. I've been in Siena, inspecting a painting. A possible portrait of James V has turned up – I looked at it yesterday. And now, duty done, I thought that I might take a few days to ride around these hills. And what do I find? Half of Edinburgh tucked away in various villas. Quite extraordinary."

Angus laughed. "Actually, we have some news," he said. "Very important news."

"Tell all!" said James.

## 85. *The Timetable of Happiness*

Rapidly abandoning his motorbike, James Holloway rushed to congratulate Domenica.

"The best of all possible news," he said, kissing her lightly on both cheeks. "Some might say long overdue, but good news often is, isn't it?"

Domenica smiled. "One mustn't rush these things." They both laughed.

"And now," James said. "We must celebrate. A party, I'd say? This evening? Here?"

Angus said that they would love to celebrate, but was the idea of holding a party not somewhat ambitious? "There'd just be three of us," he said. "You, me, and Domenica."

James raised a finger in contradiction. "There are actually plenty of your friends within hailing distance, more or less. Leave it to me."

By happy coincidence, Mary and Philip Contini were not far away, staying in a small village where they were sampling a particularly fine olive oil. They told James that not only would they be happy to come to the party, but, more than that, Mary would roll up her sleeves and do whatever she could with whatever supplies Domenica had in her kitchen. They would bring olive oil.

There were others who were equally obliging, with the result that when the guests started to arrive at six o'clock that evening, a miracle on the scale of that performed at Cana was in the making. Loaves and fishes had been found in abundance as Italy opened her store cupboards in a spontaneous display of generosity and good feeling. There was more than enough.

"We're very lucky," said Angus, as he stood beside Domenica and surveyed their group of friends.

"Look at everybody," said Domenica. "Who would have thought it? Alistair Moffat – I'm right in the middle of his wonderful history of Tuscany, and there he is. Will Lyons, here to cover a Chianti festival for the paper. Andrew and Susanna Kerr – off to some lecture on the Piccolomini library in Siena. Peter de Vink in a farmhouse just six miles away. The Cliffords – Tim about to find some long-lost masterpiece under a sofa in Montepulciano. Astonishing. Malcolm and Nicky Wood in Italy because she'll be singing at some concert in Florence. Amazing, Angus. Quite amazing."

Angus thought for a moment. "Poor Antonia!" he said. "She's missing all this."

Domenica did not reply immediately. She was not sure that Antonia would have enjoyed this occasion, as she had set her sights on Angus. But now that she was with the sisters in the convent things might be different – and there was some evidence for that. "Yes, of course," she said. "Such a pity. But I had the impression when I spoke to her last on the phone that she was thinking of . . . well, I felt that there was a hint of a vocation."

Angus smiled. "Would she make a very convincing nun?"

"Stranger things have happened. And for all we know, there may be a post–Stendhal Syndrome Syndrome. Who knows?"

"Not us," said Angus. He paused. "Edinburgh seems so far away, doesn't it. You know that I phoned Matthew earlier today? I told him the news. He said that he'd tell Big Lou. I'm sure that she'll be happy, although I do wish . . ." He left the sentence unfinished. He wished so much for Big Lou, and he was not sure that life would ever bring her what he wanted for her and what she deserved. There were people like that, he thought; people for whom one wanted only happiness because that is what they deserved, but who were destined to be denied it because the gods, and the world, were unfair. The queue for happiness was not well ordered, he thought; it stretched out and wound round corners, and sometimes, it seemed, the end was so hard to see.

Cyril was excited by the arrival of all the guests, whom he welcomed individually, licking their ankles, if exposed, nuzzling at hands lowered to pat him on the head. His own friends had arrived too – the three Italian dogs, Ernesto, Claudio, and Cosimo – and they joined Cyril in a search for scraps from the human repast – an abandoned piece of bread, a fragment of chicken, a twirl of tagliatelle.

As the evening wore on there were toasts. James made a short speech in which he referred to the positive omens that had accompanied this celebration of the engagement: an evening sky that was cloudless; a flight of birds that dipped and swung overhead, as if in aerial salute. All agreed with this view of things, and had the Italian Air Force aerobatic team swooped overhead, trailing smoke in the three colours of the flag, nobody would have been unduly surprised.

"You must say something," James whispered to Angus. "What about one of your poems?"

Angus stepped forward. He looked at his friends. He cleared his throat.

> *Dear friends,* he began, *there is no timetable*
> *For happiness; it moves, I think, according*
> *To rules of its own. When I was a boy*
> *I thought I'd be happy tomorrow,*
> *As a young man I thought it would be*
> *Next week; last month I thought*
> *It would be never. Today, I know*
> *It is now. Each of us, I suppose,*
> *Has at least one person who thinks*
> *That our manifest faults are worth ignoring;*
> *I have found mine, and am content.*
> *When we are far from home*
> *We think of home; I, who am happy today,*
> *Think of those in Scotland for whom*
> *Such happiness might seem elusive;*
> *May such powers as listen to what is said*
> *By people like me, in olive groves like this,*
> *Grant to those who want friendship a friend,*
> *Attend to the needs of those who have little,*
> *Hold the hand of those who are lonely,*
> *Allow Scotland, our place, our country,*
> *To sing in the language of her choosing*
> *That song she has always wanted to sing,*
> *Which is of brotherhood, which is of love.*

# THE 44 SCOTLAND STREET SERIES

**"Will make you feel as though you live in Edinburgh. . . .
Long live the folks on Scotland Street."**
—*The Times-Picayune* (New Orleans)

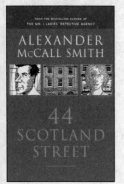

### 44 SCOTLAND STREET

All of Alexander McCall Smith's trademark warmth and wit come into play in this novel chronicling the lives of the residents of a converted Georgian town house in Edinburgh. Complete with colorful characters, love triangles, and even a mysterious art caper, this is an unforgettable portrait of Edinburgh society.

Volume 1
978-0-676-97724-0 (pbk)
978-0-307-37033-4 (e-book)

### ESPRESSO TALES

The eccentric residents of 44 Scotland Street are back. From the talented six-year-old Bertie, who is forced to arrive in pink overalls for his first day of class, to the self-absorbed Bruce, who contemplates a change of career in between admiring glances in the mirror, there is much in store as fall settles on Edinburgh.

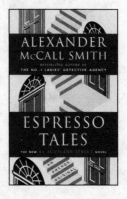

Volume 2
978-0-676-97819-3 (pbk)
978-0-307-37125-6 (e-book)

### LOVE OVER SCOTLAND

From conducting perilous anthropological studies of pirate households to being inadvertently left behind on a school trip to Paris, the wonderful misadventures of the residents of 44 Scotland Street will charm and delight.

Volume 3
978-0-676-97820-9 (pbk)
978-0-307-37123-2 (e-book)

## THE WORLD ACCORDING TO BERTIE

Pat is forced to deal with the reappearance of Bruce, which has her heart skipping—and not in the most pleasant way. Angus Lordie's dog, Cyril, has been taken away by the authorities, accused of being a serial biter, and Bertie, the beleaguered Italian-speaking prodigy and saxophonist, now has a little brother, Ulysses, who he hopes will distract his mother, Irene.

**Volume 4**
978-0-307-39708-9 (pbk)
978-0-307-37034-1 (e-book)

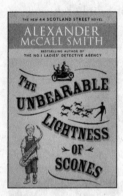

## THE UNBEARABLE LIGHTNESS OF SCONES

*The Unbearable Lightness of Scones* finds Bertie still troubled by his rather overbearing mother, Irene, but seeking his escape in the cub scouts. Matthew is rising to the challenge of married life, while Domenica epitomizes the loneliness of the long-distance intellectual, and Cyril succumbs to the kind of romantic temptation that no dog can resist, creating a small problem, or rather six of them, for his friend and owner, Angus Lordie.

**Volume 5**
978-0-307-39709-6 (pbk)
978-0-307-37306-9 (e-book)

## THE IMPORTANCE OF BEING SEVEN

Bertie is—finally!—about to turn seven. But one afternoon he mislays his meddling mother, Irene, and learns a valuable lesson. Angus and Domenica contemplate whether to give in to romance on holiday in Italy, and even usually down-to-earth Big Lou is overheard discussing cosmetic surgery.

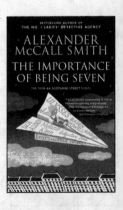

**Volume 6**
978-0-307-39962-5 (pbk)
978-0-307-39963-2 (e-book)

# THE CORDUROY MANSIONS SERIES

"A new cast of characters to love."
—*Entertainment Weekly*

**Corduroy Mansions**—Volume 1

978-0-307-39834-5 (pbk)
978-0-307-37525-4 (e-book)

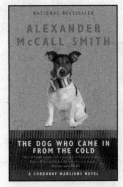

**The Dog Who Came in
from the Cold**—Volume 2

978-0-307-39964-9 (pbk)
978-0-307-39965-6 (e-book)

**A Conspiracy of Friends**
—Volume 3

978-0-307-36185-1 (hc)
978-0-307-36187-5 (e-book)

# THE ISABEL DALHOUSIE NOVELS

"The literary equivalent of herbal tea and a cozy fire. . . .
McCall Smith's Scotland [is] well worth future visits."
—*The New York Times*

**The Sunday Philosophy Club**
—Volume 1

978-0-676-97665-6 (pbk)
978-0-307-37040-2 (e-book)

**Friends, Lovers, Chocolate**
—Volume 2

978-0-676-97666-3 (pbk)
978-0-307-37041-9 (e-book)

**The Right Attitude to Rain**
—Volume 3

978-0-676-97667-0 (pbk)
978-0-307-37124-9 (e-book)

**The Careful Use of
Compliments**—Volume 4

978-0-676-97668-7 (pbk)
978-0-307-37171-3 (e-book)

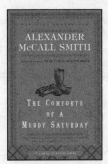

**The Comforts of a Muddy Saturday**—Volume 5

978-0-307-39700-3 (pbk)
978-0-307-36666-5 (e-book)

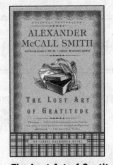

**The Lost Art of Gratitude**—Volume 6

978-0-307-39702-7 (pbk)
978-0-307-37305-2 (e-book)

**The Charming Quirks of Others**—Volume 7

978-0-307-39957-1 (pbk)
978-0-307-39958-8 (e-book)

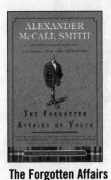

**The Forgotten Affairs of Youth**—Volume 7

978-0-307-39960-1 (pbk)
**Coming in October 2012**
978-0-307-39959-5 (hc)
978-0-307-39961-8 (e-book)

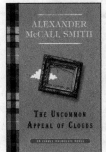

**The Uncommon Appeal of Clouds**

**Coming in October 2012**—Volume 9

978-0-307-36188-2 (hc)
978-0-307-36190-5 (e-book)

# THE PORTUGUESE IRREGULAR VERBS SERIES

**"Deftly rendered . . . [with] endearingly eccentric characters."**
—*Chicago Sun-Times*

Welcome to the insane and rarified world of Professor Dr Moritz-Maria von Igelfeld of the Institute of Romance Philology. Von Igelfeld is engaged in a never-ending quest to win the respect he feels certain he is due—a quest that has a way of going hilariously astray.

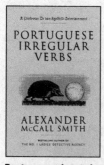

**Portuguese Irregular Verbs**

978-0-676-97679-3 (pbk)
978-0-307-37037-2 (e-book)

**The Finer Points of Sausage Dogs**

978-0-676-97680-9 (pbk)
978-0-307-37038-9 (e-book)

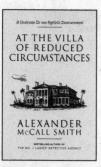

**At the Villa of Reduced Circumstances**

978-0-676-97681-6 (pbk)
978-0-307-37036-5 (e-book)

**Unusual Uses for Olive Oil**
**Coming in December 2012**

978-0-676-97955-8 (pbk)
978-0-307-37400-4 (e-book)

# THE NO. 1 LADIES' DETECTIVE AGENCY SERIES

Read them all....
## "There is no end to the pleasure."

*—The New York Times Book Review*

**The No. 1 Ladies' Detective Agency**—Volume 1

**The Great Cake Mystery**

For Children

**Tears of the Giraffe**—Volume 2

**Morality for Beautiful Girls**—Volume 3

**The Kalahari Typing School for Men**—Volume 4

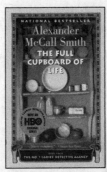

**The Full Cupboard of Life**—Volume 5

**Available in paperback, hardcover, and e-book editions.**

**In the Company of Cheerful Ladies** —Volume 6

**Blue Shoes and Happiness** —Volume 7

**The Good Husband of Zebra Drive** —Volume 8

**The Miracle at Speedy Motors**—Volume 9

**Tea Time for the Traditionally Built** —Volume

**The Double Comfort Safari Club** —Volume 11

**The Saturday Big Tent Wedding Party** —Volume 12

**The Limpopo Academy of Private Detection**—Volume

**Available in paperback, hardcover, and e-book editions.**

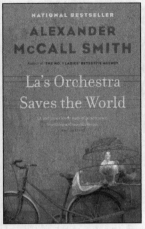